WIN SOME, LOSE SOME

USA TODAY BESTSELLING AUTHOR

Shay Savage

Dedication

For those whose lives have been touched by a child with autism.

Table of Contents

SHAY SAVAGE

Chapter 1—My Life is a Mess

"Oh shit, shit, shit."

The impact of the car behind me slamming into my bumper was brief but intense. Even after the shaking stopped, I could still feel the vibrations running through my body. Every muscle was tensed, and my brain was on overload.

A car accident. I've been in a car accident.

Bile crept up the back of my throat. My hands slid down the steering wheel slowly, leaving cold sweat from my palms on the faux leather wrapping. I closed my eyes and swallowed hard, wondering if there was any way I could possibly get through this without having a major panic attack.

Unlikely.

I had a hard enough time when something was slightly out of my normal routine. For that reason, my uncle had gone over possible crisis situations with me in the past, and a car accident was one of them. I just needed to remind myself what to do.

Make sure everyone is okay, and call 911 if someone is hurt.

Was I hurt? Was the person behind me hurt?

Taking mental note of my body, I realized I was physically fine—shaken up, but fine. I didn't know about the person or people behind me. I would have to get out of the car to figure that out. The problem was, I couldn't move.

Did the car still work? The engine hummed beneath the hood, and I figured the car was probably still drivable, so that answered that question. The impact hadn't been that hard. Since I didn't appear to be hurt, the person or people behind me might also be all right. Maybe there wasn't any damage to the car. Maybe I would survive this after all.

Squeezing my eyes shut, I reached over my lap and unbuckled my seatbelt. I wrapped my fingers around the door handle and focused on tensing my fingers enough to release the latch. I pushed the door open. My body remained tense as I slowly forced myself out of the car.

Make sure everyone is okay. Check for damage. You can do this.

"Dude, what the fuck?"

Startling at the sound, I glanced toward a blond guy with a ratty mullet pulled back into a ponytail. His lips were curled up into a snarl.

"Yellow doesn't mean stop, you idiot!" He crossed his arms and puffed out his chest.

The man's obvious aggravation at the situation should have sent me into a curled-up ball, but the absurdity of his claim grabbed my attention. For a moment, I forgot his belligerent manner and remembered the words in the driving manual I was given to study for my test.

"Illumination of the yellow or amber light denotes, if safe to do so, prepare to stop short of the intersection." My chin quivered and my eyes remained on the ground as I spoke the memorized words as if I were on autopilot. "I had time to stop. I can't afford to get a citation."

"Citation?" The blond guy threw his hands up into the air and leaned toward me. "You mean a ticket? You don't get a fucking ticket for *going*."

His words didn't make any sense at all. There was nothing in the law that said he couldn't be cited for such an offense. He could.

I studied thoroughly for the written portion of my driving test. If the light had been red, surely he would have thought running it was reason for a ticket. I continued to stare at the ground near his feet, trying to will myself to make eye contact, but I only managed to blink rapidly.

The guy tapped his foot as I looked over at the rear bumper of my car. The damage wasn't all that bad, but it was dented on one side, and now it was completely asymmetrical. In my chest, I could feel the panic rising again. I tried to swallow it down.

I needed to keep myself together. The man wasn't hurt. There was no one else in his car, and the damage was minimal.

I can do this.

"It's a good thing you didn't dent up my car," the man said as he stood right next to me. I could feel his glare on my tingling skin. From his stature and demeanor, I got the idea he was used to being taller than most guys, but we met nearly eye-to-eye. He had at least forty pounds on me, though, so the effect was similar.

"I'm sorry—" I started to say, but he interrupted me.

"I'd say you are!" His laugh was full of menace.

"I'm sorry," I repeated, "but you…"

I stopped. His demeanor and harsh stare were throwing me off. If I could just remember how I'd practiced scenarios like this one, I would be fine, but I couldn't focus enough to remember everything.

Insurance. I need to ask him for insurance information.

I took a deep breath and continued.

"If you could just give me the name of your insurance company—"

He took half a step forward and poked his finger into my chest—twice.

"Fuck. You."

I swallowed hard. I knew how to defend myself, but every martial art I had ever studied demanded strict adherence to the rule:

only use force if there is no other choice. I still had some choices left.

I made a sweeping gesture toward my bumper, cringing at the sight. I wanted to say something about how he had rear-ended me and was at fault, but I couldn't get the words out. I couldn't stop staring at the lopsided dent in the bumper. I wouldn't be able to drive it like this, not when I knew the bumper was back here, looking the way it did. I wouldn't be able to concentrate.

Would my insurance rates go up?

A fresh wave of panic smacked into my chest.

I was rarely angry at others. I usually reserved that type of emotion for self-loathing, but this guy was so obviously wrong. I pushed back another pending deluge of panic. I couldn't let that happen here at the edge of the street and in front of this Neanderthal . I took a couple of deep breaths, wishing I had enough money to go back to the therapist in town.

"Call the police," I whispered. I hadn't really meant to say it out loud, but I knew this was the next course of action if there was a dispute. I had a prepaid phone in my glove compartment for emergencies.

"Fuck that. You ain't calling nobody."

My skin crawled at his grammar. I needed to get back in my car and use the emergency phone, but my feet wouldn't move.

"Call police," I said again. My voice was monotone, and I was only dimly aware of what I was saying. I still couldn't move, and I tried to find something on the ground to draw my attention away from the situation. "Report the accident. Get insurance information."

I could feel the man's hot glare on my face, but I couldn't look at him. I was repeating "Call the police" over and over again. I couldn't make myself stop.

"Shut up!" The guy poked me in the chest once more. "Considering the piece of shit you're driving, I'd consider it a mercy killing. Here"—he shoved a little piece of paper at my chest, and I watched as it fluttered to the ground—"consider us even."

He laughed again as he turned around, got back into his car, and drove away.

I leaned down and picked up the bit of paper—I couldn't stand having litter in the street—and saw that it was one of those Powerball lottery tickets. I shook my head slowly as I stared at the paper without really seeing it. I always thought the lottery was a tax on people with poor math skills, and that fit the stereotype of the guy perfectly.

It didn't matter. I saw his license plate, and I would just let the insurance company deal with it. Having an uncle in the insurance business had definitely been a blessing over the past six months. He made sure the car and the house were covered so I wouldn't freak out. Travis was cool that way, like my dad.

Like my dad *was*.

I closed my eyes, took another couple of long breaths, and got back into the driver's seat. I tried to wipe my mind clear of the image of the bumper, but of course, it didn't work. I had to pull over twice to get myself back into driving condition before I completed the three-mile drive home.

Home.

The house was in a nice neighborhood, but there was nothing extravagant about it. Three bedrooms, two-and-a-half baths—a typical suburban place with a small yard and a mailbox with a cedar post. The property backed onto a large wooded area, which was good for hiding out alone. More than anything, it was…quiet.

I walked in and dropped my book bag on the little bench in the foyer before getting myself a glass of water. Mostly I ate stuff out of the freezer that I could heat up in the microwave. I hadn't cooked any fresh food for three days, and I tried to force myself to make some real food at least a couple of times a week.

All the recipes in my mother's old recipe box were designed to feed four people. All of them, I swear.

I put my glass in the spotless kitchen sink.

I took the glass out again, filled the sink with sudsy water, washed the cup, and then washed out the sink and dried it off until there were no water marks. By that point, I had completely lost my appetite, so I went into the den to do my homework.

Everything in the den was pretty much how my dad left it— papers, notes, and books all over the place. I couldn't stand messes, never could, but I couldn't bring myself to clean it up, either. Mom was more like me; she wouldn't even walk in here.

She *had* been.

Had been.

Past tense.

Passed on.

Passed away.

Deceased.

The words filled my mind, unbidden. I closed my eyes and hoped it would just stop, but of course, it didn't. My mind rarely went in the direction I commanded. I had to get up and leave the den. I stopped in the family room, but even the name of the room still set me off into panic attacks sometimes. All I could think about was how I had argued with Mom over the cooking show she liked to watch all the time. I had wanted to watch *Top Gear,* and the shows were always on at the same time.

I went back to the kitchen, thinking maybe I would cook something after all. I poked around in the cupboard filled with mostly packaged foods and ended up coming across a box of Thin Mints Mom had bought from a Girl Scout who lived down the street.

I lost it.

My dad had always said life was full of ups and downs.

"Son, you win some days; you lose others. That's just how it works."

Today was a lose day.

~oOo~

The next day, I walked through the large double doors of Talawanda High School in Oxford, Ohio.

Oxford was a small university town, divided into areas mostly devoted to the locals, the Miami University campus grounds, and Uptown Oxford, where everyone shopped and went out to eat. The shops mostly catered to the students, and most of the buildings even had student apartments on the second story, on top of the storefronts.   First-year students lived in campus housing, but upperclassmen lived in apartments and rented houses within a few blocks of Uptown.

Most of the kids in my class had at least one parent who worked for Miami University. My mother had taught math in the school of education. Growing up here was all right. I enjoyed summers the most when all of the students would leave Oxford to the townies, and I could find a parking space Uptown when I needed one.

I headed to my first class—AP Ecology. I'd managed to drive to school by repeating to myself over and over again: *I have an appointment with the body shop right after school lets out, and Travis is going to arrange for a loaner car until my bumper is fixed.*

A loaner.

Who knew what had been done in it?

I opened my locker and carefully placed the folders from my book bag into their proper places on the little metal shelf. The corresponding textbook was placed next to the folders in order of my class schedule, my meager lunch placed on the top shelf, and the empty backpack on the hook. Then I pulled out the ecology textbook and green folder to take to class.

I checked my watch and quickly headed to the classroom. I should get there with about ten seconds to spare. I couldn't stand being late, but I also didn't want to be there early. I walked inside Mr. Jones' lab and turned down the aisle toward my desk.

There was already someone in my seat.

He was a really big, wide-shouldered guy with a dark complexion. I hadn't seen him before, but he could have been one of the kids who transferred from Riley schools. I wasn't concerned about where he came from though. The problem was *he was in my seat*.

Maybe I should have been a few second earlier.

I stopped between desks—right between Aimee Schultz and Scott O'Malley—and just stared at the floor for a minute. I wasn't sure what I was supposed to do. That was the seat where I was supposed to be sitting. I had been in that seat all year, and it was spring. This was a two-semester course, so I had been in that same seat each and every school day for over a hundred days.

One hundred and twelve.

"Matthew, take a seat, please," Mr. Jones said from the front of the room. "It's time to start, and I've got a lot of material to cover before you break into groups."

Someone in my seat *and* group work. Double whammy.

I looked at the guy in the chair, then up at Mr. Jones. My pulse was beginning to pound in my temples, and I was having a hard time keeping my breathing in check. I kicked the toe of one foot with the heel of the other—trying to snap myself out of it—but it didn't work. I turned around and went up to the front of the class.

"Mr. Jones," I said, "there's someone in my seat."

"There aren't any assigned seats, Matthew," Mr. Jones said.

I stared at the papers on his desk. All of my teachers were supposed to know the ins and outs of my education plan, including some of my triggers such as unexpected change. Most of them were great about sticking to the plan, but Mr. Jones didn't seem to understand how much it could impact me.

"But…my seat…" I could barely hear my own voice.

"Devin just transferred here," Mr. Jones said. "There's an open seat behind Mayra."

Mayra.

Mayra Trevino.

I glanced over at the brunette with the long, wavy hair as she leaned forward with a smile on her face and chatted with Justin Lords. She had large brown eyes and full lips. She was trendy, popular, beautiful, and she was the co-captain of the girls' soccer team along with Aimee Schultz.

It could be worse. She was usually pretty nice to me. Justin, the American football king, was a whole other story. He'd given me a hard time since kindergarten. He was a classic bully, right down to the overbearing, overachieving father, who was also the football coach.

I closed my eyes for a moment and tried to get my bearings. My entire body was tense—poised for fight or flight. There was nothing to fight against, though, and flight would mean not graduating. I could have gotten my GED already if I wanted to go that route. I didn't want that. I wanted the diploma. I wanted to get into a good school so I could manage a decent career and be able to pay my sister's medical bills.

You can do this.

I tried grinding my teeth to see if that would help my feet move, but it didn't. I realized it was because my eyes were still closed, and I'd probably trip over my feet if I tried. I opened my eyes again and took a couple of shuffling steps to the other side of the room.

The other side.

Far from the door.

Shit, shit, shit.

With a shudder, I managed to sit down in the seat behind Mayra Trevino. She glanced back at me.

"Hey, Matthew!"

I crossed my arms on the desk and stared at the little hairs on my wrist. I took another long breath and closed my eyes, trying to imagine myself in my regular seat and that Mayra had just decided to sit in front of me. It didn't help much because if she were there, where would Joe sit? I shuddered a little.

"Hey," I managed to say quietly. Thankfully, Mr. Jones started his lecture then. What he had to say didn't help at all, though—group work.

Shit, shit, shit.

"Everyone will be divided into pairs, choose a potential risk to our biosphere Earth, explore the causes and potential implications of that risk, and then present your findings to the class."

Pairs. I relaxed a little. Joe and I had known each other since we were both pulled out of the regular classes in the third grade for our "superior cognitive abilities." He was the closest thing I had to a friend, and we always worked on projects like this together. When Mr. Jones had mentioned group work, I thought he meant a larger group. I didn't do well in those. I tried to keep my focus on the good news as opposed to the potential for public speaking, which just wasn't going to happen. Joe would do it for us.

"Justin and Ian, pair up. Joe and Devin, Aimee and Scott, Mayra and Matthew…"

"Wha-what?" I interrupted.

"You and Mayra will work on your project together," Mr. Jones confirmed. He smiled, and I wondered if he had brushed his teeth that morning.

"I work with Joe," I reminded him. Surely he just forgot.

"Joe's going to work with our new student," Mr. Jones said. "You will be working with Mayra."

My heart began to pound, and blood rushed to my ears, which also began to pound. I knew I wasn't going to be able to hold this one back, so I got up and ran out into the hallway.

I didn't look back. With sweat running from my hairline and onto my neck, I headed straight for the front door, trying to figure out where I could go to hide.

I couldn't sit in my car—not with the bumper the way it was—and there was no way I was going to hide out in either the bathroom or the locker room. One of the websites I ran was for a public health service, and I'd read the statistics. I wouldn't even walk into a public restroom without a hazmat suit.

I ended up just running laps around the football field.

Once I managed to calm down, I went to the office and tried to change out of AP Ecology and into anything else, anything that would give me the science credit I needed for graduation.

"I'm sorry, Matthew," the secretary told me, "but it's too late in the semester to switch."

"Is Mrs. Heath available?" Mrs. Heath was the special education consultant for the school. She worked in a lot of the schools around the county, and I met with her twice a year to go over my individual education plan.

"Mrs. Heath won't be on site until next Tuesday."

I wanted to bang my head against the wall, but giving myself a concussion certainly wasn't going to help. I couldn't just drop ecology for a study hall and graduate on time, and Mr. Jones was clear the project was going to be a major chunk of our semester grade, so I couldn't just opt out of the project. I was stuck. I would have to do it to keep my GPA up.

I heard the door open behind me and looked back over my shoulder to see none other than Mayra Trevino herself, followed by Aimee. Mayra reached over the counter and dropped a paper on the office desk before turning to me with a smile.

"I tried to wait for you to come back," she said quietly, "but Mr. Jones said we had to choose from a list today. I picked honey bees. I hope that's okay."

I just stared at her for a minute, watching the way her mouth moved while I tried to figure out just what the hell I was supposed to say back to her.

"Honey bees?" I finally managed to say.

"The depletion of honey bee populations could have a drastic impact on our ecosystems," she replied.

"Oh...um...I have work to do tonight," I finally said. "I can't work on it."

"Tomorrow, then?" she suggested. "We could work on it in the library or maybe at my place?"

Aimee shuffled her feet behind Mayra and tossed her long, brown hair over her shoulder. I wondered if she wanted to say something but was holding back. She had a soccer bag over her shoulder, and I figured they had already started practice for the spring season.

"Matthew," Mayra said again, "is the library okay?"

"Not the library," I said softly. That's where Coach Lords, Justin's father, worked as the librarian. He was as bad as Justin. He was worse, actually, because he had a position of authority within the school hierarchy. Every time he saw me, he badgered me to play football. They were always short on players, and if there weren't enough people signed up to play, the funding would be cut.

"Okay," she responded. "My place?"

"Your place?" I repeated, like a total idiot. Normally, I didn't make eye contact with people, but I couldn't stop looking at her eyes. I had never really looked at them before. Most people with brown eyes had speckles of a lighter color or a lot of variations in the hues, but hers were almost solid brown—like a chocolate bar.

"After school?"

"Okay." I could barely get the sound out because I had totally stopped breathing.

"Cool! Do you need directions?"

"No," I said. "I know where you live."

"Then I'll see you tomorrow!"

She turned to Aimee, and they both skipped out of the office while I tried to breathe again.

Different seat, different project partner, and soon a different car to drive—these were the kinds of things I couldn't have stack up on me all at once. Despite the run around the field, I was still too worked up to deal with any more surprises today. I quickly signed myself out of school and headed off to the body shop to get my car assessed.

"Sorry, kid," the guy at the body shop told me. "You have to be at least twenty-five to take out a rental car. It's policy."

"Oh," I said. "Sorry, I didn't know there was a rule."

"Don't worry about it," he said with a smile. "We'll get you back in your own car as soon as we can. I have to tell ya, though. We're pretty backed up."

And the stack of surprises grew higher.

I walked out of the shop door and moved around the corner of the building. There was a place to fill your car tires with air, and I sat on the curb, closed my eyes, and tried to get myself back together with little success.

Lose.

Chapter 2—Rainy Day Haircuts

Finally pulling myself up from the ground, I walked away from the shop and headed down the road. Of course, it started to rain about then—just a little sprinkle. The sprinkle quickly turned into a downpour, naturally, and I was sopping wet as I trudged down the sidewalk, staring at my feet as I went.

I stepped over every crack in the sidewalk, trying to pace my steps just right so I didn't have to walk awkwardly. As I came to intersections or driveways, I lifted my shoulders up a little higher until I got past. When I was a kid in the car, I would always lift my feet off the floor when we went past driveways—like I was jumping over them. The fixation on the act helped keep me calm and kept me from worrying about whether or not my clothes would be ruined by the rain.

I counted steps between drives. I counted red cars as they passed by me. I counted the number of breaths it took when I had to cross the street. As focused as I was, I didn't even hear my name at first.

"Matthew? Matthew, is that you?"

I looked up into the face of—once again—Mayra Trevino. She was in an older model, sky-blue Porsche, and she pulled over right beside me—facing the wrong way on the street.

"What are you doing in this rain?" she asked.

I could only shake my head at her.

"You want a ride home?"

"It's only another mile," I responded.

She sighed, looked a little exasperated, and pursed her lips together.

"Matthew, don't be ridiculous. You'll catch a cold or something."

"Viruses aren't caused by weather," I said.

"Let me give you a ride," she said more insistently.

"You're on the wrong side of the road."

"If I move, will you get in?"

I didn't know how to respond to that. It would make me feel better, that was for sure. Right now she was facing traffic, even if there wasn't anyone coming. It just didn't look right—not at all. Without waiting for me to respond, she backed up a little and repositioned the car at the curb on the other side of the road.

"Well, come on then!" she called out the window. "I'm getting wet here, too!"

"You don't have to do this!" I called back to her. About that time, the thunder started rolling in. Lightning burst across the sky, and the rain came down even harder.

"Get in the damn car, Matthew."

When she put it that way, I didn't really feel like I had a choice, so I looked both ways, lifted my shoulders, crossed the street, and went around to the passenger side. Standing in the rain was a little ridiculous, and I didn't want Mayra to end up all wet, so I got in the car.

I shivered, and Mayra turned up the heat in the Porsche.

"I'm getting the seat wet," I said quietly, and my heart began to pound.

Mayra laughed.

"I seriously doubt you could affect the resale value by getting the leather seat wet," she said. "Besides, this is a hand-me-down from my uncle. He found it at a car auction."

"I'm sorry," I said anyway.

"It's okay," she said. "Really. It will wipe right off."

I looked down at my hands in my lap and watched her out of the corner of my eye. It occurred to me that I had no idea what kind of a driver she was, and I inhaled sharply, feeling my breath catch in my throat. I wanted to close my eyes, but I had to keep them on her to make sure she didn't make any mistakes.

She was watching me closely, and her forehead was creased a little. She gave me a tight-lipped smile, then put the car into first and looked over her shoulder for other cars. She glanced at me once more and then pulled out slowly. She went the exact speed limit and kept her eyes on the road. Air filled my lungs again, and I felt myself relax a little.

"Where do you live?" Mayra asked softly. She didn't look over at me, and I was grateful she was concentrating on what she was doing.

"Acorn Circle," I told her. "At the end of Arrowhead."

"Oh, okay! That's over by Aimee's, right?"

"Yes," I said. "She lives six houses down and across the street."

Shit, shit, shit.

I became increasingly aware that I was in a vintage vehicle with the beautiful and popular Mayra Trevino, and I was about as ill-prepared to talk to her as I was to give her a gynecological exam.

In addition, I needed to learn when to shut the fuck up, even when I was only talking to myself. The images of Mayra getting a pap smear that suddenly filled my head nearly caused me to open the door and fling myself onto the pavement. My heart pounded in my chest, and my vision became blurry. I squeezed my thighs with my hands, trying to stop myself from shaking.

Don't do this…don't do this…not in front of her…please…

I was vaguely aware that the car had stopped, and Mayra was saying my name over and over. I squeezed my eyes shut, wishing I could do the same with my ears. My body jumped uncontrollably

19

when her hand touched my shoulder, and she said the only thing that could have caused me to answer her.

"Should I call 911?" Her voice was panicked.

"No!" I squeaked. "No…don't! I just need to get home."

"We're here," she said quietly.

I yanked at the door handle, which wouldn't budge the door. A strange sound came out of my throat when I yanked again and realized I was trapped. Before Mayra exited the car, I heard her tell me she would open the door, and she ran around to the other side. She opened the door, and I practically fell out on top of her.

Then I ran.

I ran straight for the front door, opened it, and slammed it behind me. I dropped down onto my ass just inside and leaned against it. I could hear her outside, yelling at me.

"Matthew! Matthew! Are you okay? Matthew, please open the door! I want to know you are all right!"

I ignored her. I closed my eyes, pulled into myself, and calculated pi.

"Matthew! Matthew, my dad is working from home today! I'll call him, and he'll break the door down!"

I wasn't falling for that. He would have no legal right to enter my house without the police and a search warrant. There was no just cause. She continued to call out pointless threats, and I went through the engine specifications of an Audi R8.

Finally, there was silence outside.

A moment later, there was knocking again.

"Matthew?" she called through the wooden door. "Matthew—I have your book bag."

Shit, shit, shit.

I'd left it in the car.

"You can't do your homework without it, so you're going to have to let me in."

Moaning, I grabbed at my hair and pulled. The minor pain helped me focus a little. There was no way I could get along for the night without the things in my book bag. My homework was there, if nothing else, and my lunchbox. How would I pack lunch for tomorrow if I didn't have my lunchbox? I forced a deep breath inside of me, stood up on shaky legs, and opened the door.

She smiled at me triumphantly, and I scowled back at her.

"Are you going to invite me in?" she asked.

"What if you're a vampire?" I replied and instantly wanted to smack myself on the back of the head for saying something so stupid.

"A vampire?"

"They, um…" I stammered. "They can't come inside your house unless you invite them."

"I promise I'm not a vampire."

"If you were, that's just what you would say."

We stared at each other for a moment, and I could see she wasn't going to back down. Besides, she hadn't relinquished my backpack, and it was still raining outside. I stepped off to the right, and she walked in past me.

She put the book bag on the floor as she walked in and looked around. I quickly grabbed it and put it on the bench where it was supposed to be before following Mayra into the family room.

"You're all wet, too," I said as I realized she was dripping on the carpet.

"Oh!" Mayra took a quick step back to the tile foyer. "Sorry about that. I can clean it up."

"It's okay," I said. It wasn't, but a wet floor wasn't a trigger point, so I wasn't going to get too upset about it. The carpet was old and easily cleaned. "I'll get you a towel."

I ran upstairs to the bathroom, taking out a large beach towel and examining it for a minute. It was blue and green with purple seashells on it and a little bit threadbare. I vaguely remembered my parents buying it when we were vacationing at Myrtle Beach.

I put it back, then tiptoed into the master bath to pull out one of the large, fluffy, cream-colored towels from under the sink there. It was soft and definitely classier than a beach towel.

Classy? A towel?

I shook my head and walked back downstairs.

"You live here alone, don't you?"

I squeezed my eyes shut for a second before handing her the towel. I tried to decide if I could handle her here, asking me a lot of questions. I wasn't sure why, but having her here really wasn't upsetting me too much. It was a little uncomfortable but nothing I couldn't handle.

"Yes," I said quietly. My mouth turned up in a half smile.

"You could have cool parties here," she exclaimed. "No parents!"

I froze, and the whole atmosphere of the room changed drastically.

"Oh shit, Matthew—I'm sorry!" she cried. "I wasn't…I just meant…shit, I wasn't thinking."

My body felt chilled, and I couldn't look up from the floor. I did manage to speak.

"It's okay," I said slowly. "I know they're dead."

She fiddled with the towel in her hands and shuffled her feet.

"I'm sorry," she said again.

I shrugged and just stood there, still looking at the floor. Some of the rainwater in my hair dribbled down the side of my face. I closed my eyes again.

"You're still soaked," Mayra said quietly.

She took a step toward me, and the next thing I knew, she was reaching up with the towel and rubbing it across my head.

She was so, so close to me—closer than any non-relative female had ever been—and she smelled so good. I inhaled slowly through my nose and tried to figure out the scent—something like peonies. For some reason, it seemed to relax me a little.

22

I opened my eyes and looked down at her. She had a slight smile on her face, and her gaze was fixed on her hands and the towel she was running over my head, which also felt wonderful. After a minute, she pulled the towel away from my mostly dried hair and tossed it over her shoulder. She looked at me for a moment, smiled a little more, and then reached up and ran her fingers through my hair. She pushed it back up off my forehead and then twisted it around her fingers.

"You need a haircut," she said.

"I know," I replied.

She fiddled with it some more.

"It doesn't stay where I put it," I said randomly, but it seemed to make her smile again.

When she smiled, her eyes lit up, too.

"I see that," she smirked. "Do you want me to cut it for you?"

I just stared at her, trying to comprehend what she was asking.

"I cut my dad's all the time," she said. "I'm good at it—I swear."

"You want to…cut my hair?"

"I will," she said, "if that's okay with you."

I couldn't seem to form any words to answer her, so I silently found a pair of hair-cutting shears and sat down on a chair in the kitchen.

Trying to stay still while Mayra was near me with a pair of scissors was not easy.

I knew I needed a haircut. I had planned on getting one at the end of the month, when I usually got paid for my website work. I just didn't have much extra money on hand. It was all budgeted exactly with the remainder going into the account for college. I kept whatever didn't round evenly for spending money.

The lady who usually cut my hair knew just how much to take off. I didn't like it if it was changed too much, and she had managed to figure out exactly how I wanted it cut after I freaked out on her once. Mayra didn't know, and even as I sat on the kitchen stool with the cream-colored towel around my shoulders, I felt myself start to hyperventilate.

"Not too much," I managed to gasp out as she came up behind me. "Please."

I felt her fingers moving through my hair right before a comb followed.

"Only a little," Mayra said as she leaned over to look in my face.

I kept my eyes away from hers, choosing to look down at the curve of her neck instead. She had very pale skin. There weren't many freckles or anything on it, either. I had a weird desire to touch it.

"I promise," she said. She touched me right underneath my chin and pushed against it until she turned my head to look back at her.

Looking people in the eye was never something that came easily to me. It always felt so…*confrontational*. Sometimes it was unavoidable, but I still tried to keep my eyes away from others whenever possible. It just wasn't comfortable.

There was still a smile on her face when our eyes met.

"Just a little," she said again. Her eyes were intense, and I flinched a bit. "Okay?"

"Just a little," I whispered back.

Sitting completely still, I closed my eyes and waited for her to be done. She pulled the hair away from my head in little bits. I would hear the snip of the scissors, and then she'd move to the next part. I tensed only a little at the sound when it came close to my ears. There was a strange feeling of unreality, like this was all just a dream, and I was still asleep, almost ready for the alarm to go off and wake me to get ready for school. I turned my head a little and looked at Mayra.

She was standing in the kitchen where my mother had cooked dinner. She was standing on the parquet flooring I had helped my dad install—making sure all the little wooden pieces were lined up just right. She was in the house where my grandparents had lived when I was born. It was just weird.

"All done!" Mayra announced. "Do you have a mirror?"

"Upstairs," I said.

"Do you want to go look?" She seemed nervous, and I wondered what she thought of being here with me, which made me realize something.

"No one has been in the kitchen since Mom died," I said, "except for my Uncle Travis."

Mayra took a half step back, and I heard her gasp. I stood from the stool and moved around her with my eyes on the ground. Once in the upstairs bathroom, I turned my eyes to the mirror over the sink. My hair was noticeably shorter. When I turned my head to the side and looked at it more closely, I determined it wasn't as short as the lady who usually cut it would have made it. Actually, it was better—less of a change but still a little shorter so I didn't have to worry about it getting too long. I was smiling when Mayra appeared in the mirror behind me.

"Is it okay?" she asked. "I didn't take much off."

"It's…just right." I looked at her eyes in the mirror and smiled back at her.

"Great!" she exclaimed. "Anytime you need a haircut, Matthew, just let me know."

"You'd do it again?" I asked. I could kind of wrap my head around her doing it this time. After all, she was here. I was here. And I needed a haircut. Could I consider the idea of Mayra Trevino actually coming here again with the intended purpose of shortening my hair? I couldn't fathom it.

"Of course," she said. "I like cutting hair."

I dropped my gaze from the mirror and thought about it, but I still couldn't see her coming back here and doing this again. Mayra moved up beside me, and I leaned forward on the sink, grasping the edge of it tightly. If I let go, I might run. She was *right next to me*.

"You don't really like things to change very much, do you?"

"No," I whispered.

"It's really okay, though?" she asked. "Your hair, I mean?"

"It's really okay."

"Can I ask you something else?"

"You just did," I reminded her. "That was a question. Did you mean it to be rhetorical?"

Shit, shit, shit.

I shut my eyes a second. I was pretty sure that wasn't an appropriate response. I remembered the school counselor's voice in my head.

"Focus and concentrate, Matthew. Try to think about the response before you say it. Is it appropriate for the situation? Does it fit the theme of the discussion?"

Mayra mashed her lips together, and I felt my shoulders tense up a bit.

"I was going to ask you if you didn't think something was okay, would you tell me it was?"

"Yes," I said truthfully. "At least, probably."

"Is your hair really all right?" she asked again. Her voice was full of concern and anxiety. "You can tell me if it isn't—I can change it a bit or at least know better next time."

"It's really okay," I told her. I watched my hands curl around the edge of the sink. My knuckles had gone white.

"I'm going to get going," Mayra said as she put her hand on my shoulder.

"I'm itchy," I said.

Mayra laughed.

"That would be from the hair I cut off, you know."

"I know. I need a shower."

"Well, I'm definitely going, then." Mayra snickered and headed back downstairs.

I watched Mayra walk through the front door, waving as she left. I shook my head to clear it and then took a quick shower. My head stayed in a bit of a fog for the rest of the afternoon. It wasn't a *bad* fog—just strange. I felt a little lighter or something. I cleaned up the hair on the kitchen floor and decided to do a load of laundry as well.

Dumping the dirty shirts and pants into a laundry basket, I took them downstairs to the washer. I checked everything that had a pocket, just in case I left something in one, which I almost never did. If something did get left in a pocket—like a tissue or something—and it ended up shredded and clinging to everything, I had to wash the clothes all over again.

I grabbed my jeans from yesterday and reached into each pocket in turn. Front right, back right, back left, front left. I didn't get past back right because there was some paper in there. I pulled out the lottery ticket that had been shoved at me as payment for my bumper.

I sighed. I was glad Travis didn't have any problems tracking the guy's license plate and all that. I took the ticket, folded it neatly in half, and put it on top of the dryer while I went through the rest of the clothes and started the machine. I picked up the ticket and went to the kitchen to find some dinner.

I tossed the ticket into the kitchen trash can and then started rooting through the freezer. I didn't really want another heat-and-eat dinner or something out of a box in the pantry. I was still a little bit chilled from the rain before, so I definitely wanted something warm.

Mayra Trevino was in my house.

She gave me a haircut.

I ran my hand through my hair and thought about how it felt when she was touching it. It was good. It felt good and weird. It felt weird now because it didn't take my fingers as long to get through it. It still wouldn't stay down—it was all over the place—but I was used to that.

I realized I was still smiling and decided to make shepherd's pie. I got out a bag of potatoes, peeled and cut them up, then put them to boil while I picked out a bag of frozen vegetables to go with it. I found some garlic bread, too, and decided that might round it out nicely.

When the potatoes were done, I placed everything in a casserole dish and stared at it. It was enough to feed an entirely family. A family I didn't have any more.

Not quite true.

I had my aunt and uncle. I tried not to rely on them too much, but sometimes it couldn't be helped. With the dish in the oven and the timer set for exactly thirty minutes, I pulled my cell phone out of my backpack.

"Travis, I need help."

I hated asking. I did it rarely, and when I did, I always felt like shit for it. He had already done so much for me, and I was asking for more. My fingers gripped the phone.

"What is it, Matthew?"

"They won't let me take out a rental car because I'm not old enough."

"*Shit, shit, shit*," Travis mumbled under his breath. "I didn't think about that, Matthew. I'm sorry. I'll come get you and take you home. You can use Bethany's car for a few days—she's still in Hong Kong."

"You don't need to get me," I said. "I got a ride home."

"Oh yeah? Did the body shop guy take you?"

"No."

There was a bit of a pause on the phone. Outside the window, two squirrels were running around the big pine tree. Their tails twitched as they chased each other in and out of the branches.

"Well, are you going to tell me who took you home? Focus, Matthew."

"Sorry," I mumbled. I guess it made sense that Travis wanted to know how I got back here. "Mayra Trevino took me home."

"Who's that?"

"A girl from my school." I thought about it and decided he was going to want more. "We're in ecology together. We have a project we're starting this week about bees. I'm supposed to go to her house tomorrow to work on it. It was raining, and she saw me on the road, and even though she parked on the wrong side, she moved, so I got a ride with her, and she cut my hair."

"Whoa!" Travis shouted into the phone. "Did I just hear you right? You have a girlfriend?"

"She is a girl," I said. The word he used—*girlfriend*—didn't quite hold meaning for me. "I'm not sure if we're friends or not."

"She cut your hair?"

"Yes. She said it needed it. I was going to wait until the end of the month."

"Does she work at a salon or something?"

"I didn't ask."

"Well, where did she cut your hair?" I could tell by the tone of Travis's voice that he was getting a little frustrated. I obviously wasn't giving him the information he wanted, but I didn't know what he wanted, so I wasn't sure how to fix it.

"In the kitchen."

"At the house?"

"Yes."

"*Your* house?"

"Yes."

Travis whistled into the phone.

"I think that counts as a friend, at the very least," he said. "Joe's not been over, has he?"

"No, we go to his house or Uptown to do stuff. He's never been here."

29

"Damn." Travis whispered again. "Well, I want to hear more when I get there, okay? I'll bring Beth's car over, and you can drive me back."

Travis arrived a few minutes later and ate most of my leftover shepherd's pie. He did less cooking than I did, and his wife, Bethany, traveled on business a lot. She worked for a textile company. He was also a really big guy and could pack it away. He was taller than me by a couple of inches and had curly hair. He and my dad looked a lot alike, both with dark hair and bright blue eyes. I looked like my mom.

"So tell me more about this girl," Travis said between mouthfuls.

"Mayra Trevino," I said. "Her eyes are brown."

He looked up from the plate and tilted his head to one side.

"That's all you got?"

"Oh, um…" I stammered. I didn't really know what to say about her. "I sat behind her today in ecology."

"I thought you sat by Joe."

"There was a new kid," I said quietly. I didn't want to think about it too much and bring the memory back. "He was in my seat."

"Did you take it okay?" Travis's tone was guarded.

"No."

"Shit—I'm sorry." Travis ran his hand through his hair. "I'll call the school again, okay?"

"I thought they wouldn't discuss me with you," I reminded him. "I'm eighteen, and there isn't any guardianship or anything."

"Well, they can listen even if they won't talk!" Travis said, raising his voice, which made me flinch. "I'll call that Jones guy myself. He obviously hasn't read your IEP or your 504 plan. He was supposed to talk to Mrs. Heath last semester. He shouldn't be putting you through that shit."

"Please don't," I said quietly.

"Why not?" Travis snapped back.

"Because," I said as I took a deep breath, "I'm already going to have to deal with the hit-and-run guy. I can't do both at once. It's too much."

With a huff of air through his nose, Travis conceded. He picked up his plate and fork and put them in the sink. I followed him and washed them both, put them away, and then I cleaned the sink. Travis knew if he washed them, I would just get them out and wash them again. We had an understanding.

"If your mom had passed a few weeks earlier, I would have become your guardian. I could go to that school and give Jones shit, then."

"Travis," I whispered. I felt my whole body seizing up on me.

"Sorry, kid." Travis looked at me and sighed. "It's just that...if I had more direct ties to you legally, I could do more for you."

"You do enough," I told him *again*. We'd had this same conversation twenty-four times. "I'm eighteen. Everything's in my name, and I'm okay."

"No, you aren't," he mumbled. "You need to go back into therapy. You had fewer attacks on that medication."

"I don't have any extra money for more prescriptions, and the therapy isn't covered," I reminded him. "Making up for what Medicaid won't pay for Megan's care is expensive enough. I can get back into it after I graduate. Once I'm at college, the financial aid stuff will kick in, and I'll be able to afford it."

"I told you I'd pay for it."

"And I told you I wasn't taking any more of your money. You can't spare it, and you're already helping with Megan."

"I still can't believe they didn't give *me* her guardianship. You shouldn't have to deal with all of this." He was whining, but it wasn't meant to be mean or anything. Travis fought to have both of us put under his care, but I proved to the courts that I was high-functioning enough to do it on my own.

31

"I should be her guardian," I said. "She's *my* sister."

"Your *older* sister," he emphasized.

"Only physically."

We stared at each other for a minute. We'd been at this impasse before.

"I'm doing all right, Travis," I told him. "I mean, I'm not really much more fucked up than I was before. I'm doing as well as can be expected for someone who lost two parents within three months, and it happened less than a year ago. All my other issues are just icing."

"Icing!" Travis snorted.

I ran my hand through my hair again, which reminded me of the haircut.

"You shouldn't be alone here," Travis said. He knew this argument was a lost cause, too.

"I'm not selling the house."

"You wouldn't have to."

"Travis," I growled.

"Fine, fine."

"I want to stay here," I said. I looked at him until he finally nodded. He knew this was a subject on which I would not budge. I wanted to be independent. I wanted my parents to know I could take care of myself *and* Megan without becoming a burden to Travis and Bethany. "The meds I take now work well enough. Megan's SSI covers her stuff, and the other supplemental income I get is enough to pay the bills. I'll take care of the issues at school, too."

"If you went to that other school in Cincinnati, the resources would be better. Bigger school, bigger budget, and more kids like you. They had that whole separate class for kids with Asperger's"

"I didn't want to change schools when I started high school, and I certainly don't want to change now. There are only three months left!"

"I know."

"I'm all right, Travis. Really. Even the social worker said so when she checked on me last week."

Travis sighed and nodded.

"If anything else happens in that class, I'm talking to Jones," he told me as he dropped the keys to Beth's Civic in my hand.

I drove him back to his place on the other side of town. We didn't talk much more. I wondered if the idea of talking to Mr. Jones might have put him off. I wondered if Mr. Jones taught when Travis went to school there. Travis was my dad's younger brother by twelve years, and it wasn't that long ago that he was a student at Talawanda High.

"Take care, kid," Travis said as he got out of the car. "I still want to hear more about this girl."

"Okay," I said. "Thanks."

As soon as the word was out of my mouth, I knew I had fucked up.

Mayra drove me home and saved me from the rain.

She brought me my book bag.

She gave me a haircut.

I hadn't said thank you.

Shit, shit, shit.

I couldn't let it go. I had to fix it.

Just when I thought the day was turning into a win, I blew it.

Lose—again.

Chapter 3—All the Reasons I'm a Disaster

The short, panting breaths coming out of my mouth were making me all dizzy and light-headed.

I sat in Bethany's car in the driveway of Mayra Trevino's house. I came here to thank her, but I couldn't get out of the damn car. Every time I tried, my insides felt like they were going to pop right through my skin and splatter over the cement.

I didn't understand myself at all. She had been in my house, and it hadn't caused any reaction like this. She'd been close to me, touched me, cut my hair. Why couldn't I walk up to her house and say thank you?

My hand grasped the handle of the car door, and I tried again. The result was the same. I dropped my elbows onto the steering wheel and put my face in my hands. I slowly shook my head back and forth while I growled and swore at myself.

Giving up on talking to her but still insisting on correcting my infraction, I turned the car back on and drove Uptown to the Hallmark store to look for a thank-you card. At least I could put it in her mailbox. I was pretty sure I could handle that. Thinking about it didn't seem to upset me.

None of the cards said "Thanks for the ride" or "Thanks for the haircut." I found some cards that just said "thank you" on them in gold script with the card all blank inside, so I bought one of those.

Then I sat in the car for thirty minutes trying to figure out what to say. I wrote a few words, then tore the card up and went back inside for another card. The cashier gave me a weird look, but I ignored her.

I did that two more times before I settled on something that I didn't think was too bad.

Dear Mayra,

Thank you for giving me a ride home and cutting my hair.

I'm sorry I forgot to say that before.

Sincerely,

Matthew Rohan

I took a deep breath and slid the little card into an envelope and sealed it. Then I flipped it over and wrote *Mayra* on the front. I looked at it for a bit and decided to add her last name—*Trevino*. I smiled as I drove back to her house and pulled up near the mailbox.

I realized I hadn't put her address on the front of the card, so I added that as well. Of course, since I hadn't planned to write that much on the card, it didn't all fit with the same-sized letters. At least I had the extra envelopes from the other cards I had messed up, so I ripped the card out of the first one and put it into a blank envelope. I wrote her name and address again.

Just before I put it in the mailbox, it occurred to me that the mail carrier just might think they were mailing a letter out, not receiving one, and could collect it and take it back to the post office. It didn't have a stamp or anything on it, so it could end up being lost completely. She would think I was insanely rude and might never speak to my again.

How would we get our project done?

I pulled the card back to my chest. Maybe if I wrote my return address on it, it would at least come back to me due to a lack of postage. How long would that take, though? Oxford mail wasn't known for being overly fast even when there is the correct postage on a letter.

I considered taking it up to her front door, but the thought immediately started my heart pounding. Just looking at the little, covered porch and thinking of myself walking up there and ringing the bell made my stomach clench and threaten to expel dinner.

Bethany would be really pissed if I threw up in her car.

That idea started a whole other attack. I dropped the card onto the passenger seat and got out of the car altogether. The air outside the car smelled fresh and clean, which helped calm me a bit. I leaned against the driver's side door and put my face back in my hands.

"Matthew?"

Shit, shit, shit.

I lowered my hands and saw Mayra Trevino standing at the curb near her mailbox.

"What are you doing here?"

I looked down to the street under my shoes and kicked at a tiny little rock there. There was another one a few feet away, so I kicked it, too. Then a third. I kept kicking rocks until there weren't any left in my reach and then started looking for more.

"Matthew? Are you okay?"

I didn't know how to respond. I wasn't okay, but focusing on the rocks had made the attack go away at least. I could breathe normally, and my heart wasn't pounding too much. I wasn't okay, though. I needed to give her that card, and I wasn't sure how to do that.

"Sometime you just have to do, son. Don't think. Just do."

Dad's voice in my head came at a pretty good time. I turned and opened the car door, leaned inside, and grabbed the card. If I gave it directly to her, at least it wouldn't get lost in the mail. I grasped the envelope in my hand, backed out of the car, and walked slowly over to where Mayra was standing. She was still calling my name as I raised my hand and gave her the card. I ran my hand through my shorter hair and cringed a bit as she reached out and took the card from me.

37

I couldn't stand to watch her read it, so I got back in the car and drove away.

It might not have seemed like much to anyone else, but I was reasonably pleased with myself.

Win.

~oOo~

School was particularly noisy the next day.

I tended to ignore most of the sounds around me as I walked through the halls, but I could tell people's voices were either just a little bit louder or maybe just more people were talking at once. Whatever it was, I didn't like it.

In ecology, the new kid was in my seat again even though I entered the classroom a good thirty seconds before the bell rang. I stopped at the front of the aisle, not walking the rest of the way to the seat. I knew if I said something to Mr. Jones, he would likely react the same way as before, and Travis would end up calling him. I really didn't want that to happen.

I wanted to take care of myself.

I stood there, looking at my feet.

"Hey, Matthew!" Mayra's voice sang out from the other side of the room.

Out of the corner of my eye, I could see Mayra stand up and walk over to me even though I didn't raise my head.

"Come on over and sit by me," she said. "We can talk about our project."

I jumped a little when she took my hand and started pulling me behind her. My feet didn't move—I think they were as confused as my head. I focused intensely on the feeling of her hand touching mine, and everything else in the room disappeared.

Mayra stopped and turned around.

"Will you sit behind me, Matthew?"

"Okay," I said softly, and my feet decided to go along.

I saw Justin Lords roll his eyes as Mayra led me to the seat behind her. She smacked him in the shoulder as she walked by.

"Hi, Matthew," Justin said in a weird, sing-song voice. "Are you having a wonderful day?"

I stiffened for a second, trying to figure out how I was supposed to respond. Justin never said anything remotely nice to me and usually ignored me altogether. Sometimes he'd shove me in the hall, but he never said anything polite.

I didn't believe he was being polite now.

"I had pancakes for breakfast," I said, then cringed. I wasn't sure if that was right, but I usually microwaved frozen pancakes in the morning when I was in a good mood.

Justin laughed.

"Fucking freak," he muttered.

"Shut up!" Mayra said through clenched teeth. "Go on and sit down. Jones is about to start class."

Mayra let go of my hand, and I sat in the seat behind her, just where I had the day before, and stared at the places on my skin that had been touching her. The seat was still way too far from the door, but every once in a while, Mayra would look back and smile at me, and I'd remember what it felt like to have her holding my hand.

"Did you hear about the lotto ticket?" Justin asked Mayra while Mr. Jones's back was turned.

"No, what lotto ticket?"

"The winning Powerball ticket—it was sold at the gas station in Millville. One hundred and twelve million."

"No shit!"

"That's what I said!" Justin beamed like cursing was something for which he should get an award.

"Who bought it?" Aimee asked as she leaned over her desk to listen closely.

"Whoever it was hasn't come forward yet," Justin replied.

"Wow!" Mayra whistled low.

"Watch for new Ferraris!" Justin laughed out loud.

"Justin, would you please pay attention?" Mr. Jones's comment snapped Justin out of his fantasy.

"Sorry."

After class, Mayra reminded me I was supposed to go to her house after school.

"See you about four o'clock, right? Do you need a ride?"

"No," I replied. "I have Bethany's car."

"Who's Bethany?" Mayra asked.

"My aunt."

"Oh, gotcha. Okay, I'll see you at four!" Mayra smiled and waved as she headed down the hallway. I just stood off to the side and watched her go. The bell rang, and I realized I was going to be late for my next class if I didn't move quickly.

After school, I drove to the Trevino house, sat in the driveway until three fifty-nine and then totally failed to get out of the car. Once the clock flipped to four o'clock, I knew there was no way I could go up to her door. I took a long, deep breath and drove back home.

Once I was back in my own house, I sat on the couch with my head in my hands.

I couldn't do this.

I couldn't work on a group project with Mayra Trevino.

There was just no way.

The doorbell rang, and I knew it was her long before she started pounding on the door and yelling at me to let her in. Remembering her tenacity from the day before, I relented and opened up.

"Matthew! Why didn't you come over?"

Taken aback by the abruptness of her question, I just stood there and stared down at her shoes—black Converse with bright yellow laces. I wondered why she picked laces that color since they obviously didn't come with the shoes.

"Matthew?" Mayra said. Her voice had gone soft. "Did you forget to come over?"

"No," I replied. "I was there."

"You were there?" she repeated. "Matthew, I waited for you, but you never came to the door."

"I couldn't."

"Why not?"

I glanced up at her face and then quickly looked away. I didn't know what to say to her, so I instinctively embraced the repetitive action of kicking the toe of my foot with my other heel.

"It's okay," Mayra said, "you can tell me."

She reached out and took my hand in hers. Her fingers coiled around mine. Her hands were really soft, and I wondered if she put lotion on them a lot. My mom's hands always got really dry in the winter, and she would put lotion on them every time she washed her hands.

"Matthew?"

"I just…couldn't," I whispered.

"Do you want to work on it here?"

"Okay."

I couldn't say no to her, so we set up the project stuff on the table in the dining room.

It was surprisingly easy to work with Mayra on the honey bees project.

In the past, I had only worked on projects with Joe. He was fine with other people for the most part though he tended to look down on them because they weren't as smart as he was. Everyone thought he was a snob. He *was* a snob. He didn't have a ton of friends either, but we had always worked well together.

Mayra was completely different from Joe. She was really passionate about everything we researched and often got excited when we would find some article on the internet that supported what she believed to be right. She also got really mad about some of it.

"I don't understand how something like this could just be overlooked!" she exclaimed again. "Doesn't everyone know all life is dependent on each other? People obviously just don't play enough dominoes anymore!"

She took a deep breath and let it out in a big whoosh. She looked over at me and smiled.

"Sorry," she said, "I get a little carried away."

I just shrugged.

"Should we think about the PowerPoint?" Mayra asked.

We hadn't talked about the actual presentation. I always focused on the written portion, which was almost done. I would just need to take my clunky old laptop into school to get the information printed. I could put it on a thumb drive, but I was afraid something would happen to the data if I walked too close to something magnetic.

We hadn't started the PowerPoint or even talked about it.

What if she wanted me to give the presentation? Joe knew better, but I hadn't worked with Mayra before. Maybe she would want to do every other slide, passing it back and forth between us. I'd seen some kids do it that way. My heart started pounding, and I squeezed my hands into fists beside the keyboard.

"Matthew," Mayra said. "You never stand up in front of the class. I know that. I'll give the oral part of the presentation."

I didn't realize I had been holding my breath, but it rushed out of me suddenly and forcefully. I was torn between wanting to thank her and wanting to be able to say that I could do it. I couldn't—I knew that—but I wished I could.

"Want to take a break?" Mayra asked.

"Okay."

"Got anything to drink?" Mayra asked with a smile.

"I have filtered water in a pitcher, Coke, and Sprite," I said, offering her a choice.

"I'd love a Coke!"

I smiled a little, too, and got up to get two cans of soda from the pantry and two glasses from the cabinet. I pulled out the ice cube tray from the freezer and carefully selected four cubes for each glass. I tilted the glass sideways to pour the soda. With four cubes, the twelve-ounce drinks fit into the glasses perfectly.

Carrying a Coke in each hand, I brought the glasses back into the dining room, which was attached to the living room and the kitchen. The whole floor made a circle you could walk around. Mayra had moved over to the couch, so I took our drinks and placed them neatly in the center of the coasters on the coffee table.

"Thanks!" Mayra said as she took a sip. "Mmm…it's so much better in a cup with ice. Justin always just has the cans in the fridge."

"You're welcome," I replied. I sat down on the other end of the couch. The comment about Justin had my head spinning a bit. I wondered if she usually worked on ecology projects with him and if she went to his house often. I tensed up again though I wasn't sure exactly why.

"Hey, Matthew?" Mayra said as she turned toward me. She moved closer to the center cushion and pulled one of her legs up underneath her. "Can I ask you something?"

"Okay."

"Something kind of personal?"

My fingers gripped my thighs. I tried to keep my breathing in check, but the number of possibilities of things she might ask me was too overwhelming. What did girls ask guys when they were together? I hoped she wouldn't ask me questions about soccer because I didn't know much about it at all. My dad had only been into the Cincinnati Reds, and the closest competitive sport Mom had gotten into was *Iron Chef*.

I jumped as her fingers moved slowly over mine. I dropped my gaze to her hand as she reached around and pulled my fingers away from my leg. She wrapped her hand around mine and then turned my hand over and laced our fingers together.

"Can I ask you?" she repeated.

"Okay." I kept staring at our fingers. They fit together really well. Thumb, thumb, finger, finger…

She took a deep breath, and her fingers moved up and down my fingers, stroking slowly. It was calming, and I pressed my shoulders against the couch cushions.

"What's wrong with you, Matthew?"

"Huh?" I sputtered. I was glad I didn't have a mouthful of Coke at the moment because it would have gone everywhere.

"I mean, I know you are…different. I heard people say you were…you know…retarded or something, but you're not. You're very smart—I can tell that. But you also aren't…aren't…"

"Normal," I whispered as I pulled my hand away. My heart was beating too fast. The couch seemed really, really small all of a sudden.

"Yeah, I guess."

I swallowed hard. I was frantically trying not to panic, but trying to *frantically* defeat panic really didn't work well. I closed my eyes, counted backwards, and tried to think of some way to respond to her that wouldn't make her immediately run for the hills.

"I'm sorry," Mayra said softly. "I shouldn't have asked."

I glanced at her eyes and quickly looked away again. The strange thing was I wanted to tell her. I wanted her to know, but I didn't want her to run away. I also needed to get the fuck out of that room immediately.

"I have to go." I pushed off the couch and tugged at my hair as I walked out of the family room and down the short flight of stairs to the lower level.

"Matthew—don't go! I'm sorry—really! I shouldn't have said anything. I just…just—"

I paused and glanced over my shoulder to see her standing at the top of the stairs.

"Give me a few minutes." I sounded like I was begging, but I didn't want her to leave—not yet. She nodded, and I ran off, flinging open the door to the basement and running down the stairs.

Once I got down into the cool, unfinished room, my breathing came easier. I closed my eyes and waited for my heart to calm down a bit, then reached down and pulled my shirt off over my head. I bent down and pulled off my shoes and my socks.

I walked slowly to the far side of the large, open room, picked up a pair of training gloves, and pulled them over my hands. I tightened the straps and lined up the Velcro perfectly around one wrist and then the other. I took one more deep breath and turned to the large heavy bag that took up most of that side of the basement.

I stepped onto the mat surrounding the bag and pulled my arms in front of myself to stretch out a bit. I clenched my hands into fists, stared straight at the center of the bag, and began to punch.

Right, left, right, left.

Left, left, right. Left, left, right.

Right, right, left. Right, right, left.

Equal number, each fist.

It didn't take more than the first few hits in the center of the bag before I was lost to the moment—no anxiety, no panic—nothing but me, the bag, and my fists.

Left, right, left, right.

Right, left, right, left.

My breathing was steady and each hit perfectly accurate. My feet carried me easily on the mat and around the bag.

Left, left, right. Left, left, right.

Right, right, left. Right, right, left.

Each impact traveled from my fists up through my arms and into my shoulders. My hips and chest tilted to receive each blow. My mind became empty and clear. I barely registered the slight movement near the door when Mayra entered. It didn't matter.

Right, left, right, left.

Left, right, left, right.

Kick left.

Kick right.

Roundhouse left.

Roundhouse right.

Butterfly.

I took a step back to the corner of the mat and tried to catch my breath. I knew she was still there, watching me silently, but it didn't matter. I didn't mind her being there. I leaned over and braced my gloves against my knees, exhaustion engulfing my limbs.

"I'll tell you," I finally replied when I found my voice again.

"You don't have to," she said.

"I know." I took a deep breath and righted myself again. "I want to."

Back in the living room, Mayra and I sat down on the couch with fresh glasses of soda.

"I don't know where to start." It was hard to admit that to her.

"Start with whatever you want to say," Mayra said.

I sat back against the cushion and took a long breath. I already knew the words I needed to say, which made talking about it easier.

I can do this.

"The first doctor said I had attention deficit disorder," I told her. "She said I couldn't focus on anything because of that. Dad said she was crazy—I was focused on everything at once. The next one said I had obsessive compulsive disorder."

I rubbed my hands on the thighs of my jeans and wriggled my toes around in the carpet. I was still hot from the boxing, and I hadn't put my shirt back on either.

"So, you're OCD?" Mayra asked. I realized I hadn't continued the story.

"Not…exactly," I replied. I glanced over and sighed before continuing. "Have you heard of autism?"

"Sure," Mayra said. "That's kids who can't talk to their parents, right? And they do the same thing over and over again?"

"Kind of," I replied. "There's a spectrum of autism. Some people have it a lot worse than others. The next doctor they took me to said I might have Asperger's Syndrome, which is a very mild form of autism. Actually, we're supposed to just say autism spectrum disorder now, but they still called it Asperger's when I was diagnosed. I started going to therapy then, but it didn't help much."

"So which one is it?" Mayra asked after some more silence.

"A little of all of it, I guess," I told her. "I have…"

I paused and mentally pushed down the panic in my chest again.

"…social *deficits*," I finally got out. "You may have noticed."

"You aren't like some of the other kids." Out of the corner of my eye, I could see Mayra shrug. "Sometimes it seems like it's hard for you to even be in the room with them. I thought it was because of your…"

"Because my parents died."

"Yeah."

"No, I was fucked up before then," I admitted. "It just got worse."

"Sorry," Mayra said. "I didn't mean to interrupt."

"I don't really fit Asperger's," I said, continuing. "People with Asperger's usually have one or two things that become fixation points. I have hundreds."

"Fixation points?"

"Once I start thinking about something, I can't stop," I said. "When I was up here before, all I could think about was hitting the bag. I had to go do it, or I'd drive myself nuts. But it's not always the bag. My sister is all about the clocks."

"Your sister?"

"Megan," I said. "On the autism spectrum, if I'm at one end, she is at the other. Megan has never said anything except the time."

"I don't understand," Mayra admitted.

"She knows what time it is *all the time*," I explained. "She will tell you it's eleven twenty-six a.m. She will tell you it is time to eat dinner, and she will tell you it is time to watch *iCarly*. She can also walk by and tell you how many clocks and watches are in the room and what kind they are. She doesn't talk about anything else at all. She's never even said hello to me or called me by my name."

Mayra sat with her hands in her lap and thought awhile.

"Where is she?" Mayra asked.

"In an autism institution in Cincinnati," I said. "When Mom got sick, she couldn't take care of Megan, and then when Mom was gone…well, I can just barely take care of myself. Most people who have some form of autism can't interact with others at all. I *can*, at least some of the time. It just has to be under certain circumstances."

"Like it's okay for me to be here, but you can't really come to my house, can you?"

"Not really," I whispered. I had no idea why I was speaking softly. I had no idea why I was speaking at all. I never told anybody about any of this outside of the therapist I quit seeing right after Mom died when the insurance wouldn't pay for any more sessions.

"Is it just because you haven't been to my house before?"

"I don't know what's inside," I said. My heart started pounding just thinking about it. "I don't know if there are dishes in the sink or if you have magazines on the coffee table or when your Dad might walk in or if he has a gun."

Mayra snickered a little.

"He never actually uses them outside of hunting and the practice range," Mayra told me. "He spends most of his time cleaning them."

"He still has guns."

"What's wrong with magazines on the table?"

"They might be out of order," I said. "They might be from different months, or magazines that don't go together might be touching each other."

Squeezing my eyes shut, I leaned over and put my face in my hands. I sounded ridiculous, and I knew it, but I couldn't help how I felt. I rubbed my fingers into my eyes and jumped when I felt Mayra's hand on my arm.

"Lots of people with autism don't like to be touched," I said.

"I'm sorry." Mayra pulled her hand away.

Shit, shit, shit.

I hadn't meant my words to be taken that way. We'd been talking about autism, and I was just stating a fact.

"I just meant…others don't like it."

"You don't mind?" Mayra asked.

"If…if I know it's coming," I said, clarifying. "I don't like to be surprised."

"Because that's not what you're expecting."

"Right," I said. I looked over to her, and Mayra was smiling just a little. I didn't know what made her smile, but there were a lot of times I didn't understand the behavior of others. I just wanted to get this over with. "So, they all finally decided I was just messed up in multiple ways."

"You seem to do pretty well."

I replayed her words in my head a few times, trying to decide if she was being sarcastic or not. I had a hard time picking up on sarcasm.

"I'm okay," I said softly. I took another long breath. "The doctor I had most recently said I had mild forms of Asperger's and ADD and had developed various obsessive-compulsive behaviors to combat those other characteristics."

"Does that really work?"

"Usually," I said. "As long as things are the way they are supposed to be, I'm fine. Here I'm fine. It's when I leave here that I run into things that are out of my control."

"Like Devin in your seat the other day," Mayra said with a nod, "and having to work with me on this project."

"Yes," I replied quietly. "So for me, it's all about finding ways to cope with what's in my head and finding ways to focus. To everyone else, the coping makes me look like an idiot."

"You aren't an idiot," Mayra said. "Aimee has ADD, too."

"She does?"

"Yeah. When she was little, she was on medication for it, but the meds made her cry all the time. Her mom got a bunch of books about different treatments, and now she has a really strict diet. That's why we play soccer. She's my best friend, and we started playing at the same time. As long as she gets enough exercise and eats right, she does okay without the drugs. I'm sure that doesn't work for everyone, but it does for her."

"I have to take the meds," I said. "Even if I work out, it's not enough."

"Aimee still gets a little scatterbrained," Mayra said with a smile. "I used to sit with her to make sure she got her homework done. She'd get distracted by anything and everything around her, but she's better about it now."

"Homework help." I stared at my hands and remembered Mom sitting with me and trying to get me to focus on math

49

problems. When I got distracted, she would turn the page around and make me do the problems upside down. It made the work more challenging, and I could focus better.

I felt her hand on my bare shoulder and I flinched a little, wondering if she'd been talking, and I had missed it.

"Is this okay?" Mayra asked.

I looked at her hand on my shoulder and thought about it being there and how it felt. I wasn't going into any kind of panic attack at least.

"I have panic attacks when things aren't the way I expect them to be," I said. "Those got a lot worse after Dad died."

"He was in the reserves or something, right?"

"National Guard," I said.

"There was an accident."

"Yes." My voice had dropped back to a whisper again. "They were up on the trails in the Appalachian Mountains, doing a training exercise. One of the hummers went off the road, and he was hit on the head by the tree it knocked down. Fluke accident."

"I'm sorry."

I shrugged. So many people said that during his funeral. I was never really sure what it was supposed to mean. The people who said it weren't responsible for the accident. Lots of them didn't even know Dad. They only knew Mom, or they were distant relatives or someone that I had never met before.

"Your mom?" Mayra whispered.

"Osteosarcoma." I felt a shudder run through me, and my skin went cold.

"Cancer, right?"

"Yes," I whispered. I gripped my legs with my fingers and tried to stop the shaking. I couldn't think straight—I couldn't even count. I tried to breathe deeply, but everything was coming out fast, and I was starting to get dizzy.

Mayra's hand was still on my shoulder.

"It's okay," she said. "You don't have to say any more."

"It was a month after Dad died," I said quickly. It was the only way I was going to get through it. Now that I'd started the tale, I had to get it all out. "She went in for something routine, and they said they saw a shadow on an x-ray. They thought she might have a slipped disc or something in her back. It was giving her a little pain, but it wasn't a disc—it was bone cancer. It had already spread. She asked them how long she would have if they did nothing—no treatment. My grandfather had cancer, too, and the treatments were worse than the sickness, Mom thought."

"What did they tell her?"

"If she did nothing, she would have eight weeks."

"Eight weeks?" Mayra gasped. I nodded.

"She started treatment right away—I wasn't even eighteen then. She thought if she did radiation and chemo and all that, she would at least live to see me graduate. She died six weeks later, twelve days after my eighteenth birthday. The cancer was in her blood, too."

I closed my eyes and tried to breathe normally again. My limbs felt icy and lethargic, and I wondered if I overdid it with the heavy bag. I did that sometimes. I would lose track of how long I had been down there. It wasn't just the physical feeling in my muscles though. My head felt numb and worn out, too.

"Matthew?"

I wondered how long I had been sitting there without saying anything or how long she'd been trying to get my attention.

"Yes?"

Mayra turned sideways and got up on her knees on the couch next to me. She started reaching toward me and leaning in at the same time.

"I just want to try something," she said. "Would that be all right?"

"Okay," I said. I wasn't so sure that it was, especially not when she reached out and ran her fingers through the hair on one side of my head. My hands started to shake a little, but then she ran her other fingers over the other side of my head, and it was okay again.

"I'm going to give you a hug," she said quietly as she leaned in more.

"Okay," I whispered back.

Mayra's hands moved down to my shoulders, and she was very, very close to me. I was suddenly quite aware of the fact that I was still not wearing a shirt or shoes or anything. I swallowed hard.

"Don't worry," Mayra murmured. She wrapped her arms around me and pulled my head to her shoulder. "You aren't alone."

As soon as my head touched her shoulder, my entire body gave out. I nearly fell against her as she held me tightly, and the burning sensation behind my eyes gave way to tears. I slowly wrapped my arms around her waist, inhaled her scent, and began to sob.

Letting go was an unexpected win.

Chapter 4—Ask Me No Questions

Though there was still plenty of natural light coming through the windows and lighting the room, I was groggy. I was also sore everywhere and keenly aware that I was lying in Mayra Trevino's arms. My body ached and my eyes burned. I was pretty sure I had bruised a couple of knuckles, but I couldn't remember the last time I felt so good.

At some point, Mayra and I had lain down on the couch and fallen asleep. I wasn't even exactly sure when or how long I had been crying earlier, but we were still lying together. Even before I opened my eyes, I could feel her arm around my shoulders and the other around my head, holding me against the spot on top of her arm and next to her neck. I had one arm beneath her body, around her shoulders, and the other was resting just underneath the tank-top she wore with my fingers splayed across the skin of her lower back.

I tilted my head to look up into her face, and I could see her eyes were still closed and her breathing steady. In the back of my head, I wondered why I wasn't panicking in the slightest. This was *new*. This was *different*. I always panicked at new and different. However, I was also surrounded by the most incredible scent. It was all warmth and comfort and security and serenity—and just *her*.

I tucked my head back into the crook of her neck and closed my eyes again.

In what felt like the next moment, I was startled awake.

"Holy shit, shit, shit!"

I opened my eyes. The light in the room was the soft, dim glow of dusk.

"Oh my God," Mayra mumbled under her breath.

I managed some incoherent sound before turning my head to look over my shoulder toward the sound that had originally startled me. Travis was standing in the open area between the foyer and the living room with his mouth hanging open and his eyes as big as Phobos and Deimos.

"Travis?" I was still really groggy. "What are you doing here?"

"I brought dinner," he said as he held up a paper bag from a Chinese restaurant a few blocks away.

"Oh no," Mayra said as she glanced around and noticed the low light in the room. "I need to go. Dad will be home soon, and I need to make dinner."

"Okay," I said. I still watched Travis. I couldn't understand why he was looking at me so strangely. Mayra was shifting around beside me on the couch.

"Matthew, you have to let go of me."

"Oh, yeah…sorry." I pulled my arms out from around her. She stood next to the couch, adjusted her jeans, and fixed her shirt. Her cheeks had gone really red, and she didn't seem to be acknowledging Travis at all.

"Matthew," Travis said after he managed to shake loose the weird look on his face, "introductions, maybe?"

Shit, shit, shit.

"Oh, yeah…sorry," I said again. "Mayra, this is my uncle—Travis Rohan. Travis, this is Mayra Trevino."

"Good to meet you, Mayra," Travis said with a toothy smile. "You must have been Matthew's savior when he needed a ride the other day."

"Yeah, it was raining really hard," she told him. Her face was getting redder by the second. "He was soaked."

"I bet he was." Travis pressed his lips together and raised his eyebrows. He snickered. "You probably were, too."

He was acting weird. I didn't get it.

"It was nice meeting you, too," Mayra said as she gathered up her things and placed them into her book bag. "Don't forget to bring your laptop tomorrow, Matthew!"

"I won't *forget*," I said with a furrowed brow. It was a pretty rare occasion for me to forget much of anything, certainly not something homework related.

Mayra laughed.

"No, I guess you won't!" She waved and headed out the door. "Bye!"

"Bye."

"Matthew Anthony Rohan!" Travis boomed as soon as the door was closed.

I half jumped out of my skin.

"What?"

"Did you fuck her?"

"Wha-wha-*what*?" I had to have heard him wrong.

"Did you have your dick inside of that hot chick who just waltzed out your front door?"

"N-n-no!" I stammered. "We just fell asleep!"

"With your shirt off and your hand up under hers?"

Everything clicked together. I was still, for all intents and purposes, half naked, and we had been lying all wrapped up in each other on the couch. My hand had been up her shirt though I really didn't recall when or how that happened.

"It wasn't like that," I whispered.

"Dammit, Matthew!" Travis bellowed. He dropped down heavily on the easy chair and stared hard at me. "Are you telling me you were alone in the house with that beautiful girl, and nothing at all happened?"

"Yes!" I swore to him, nodding my head quickly.

"You didn't even kiss?"

"No!"

Travis growled and stood up, grabbing the bag of Chinese carryout and heading into the kitchen. I followed, and he started pulling out little cardboard boxes of lo mein, Szechwan tofu, and rice. He slammed each one down on the table as he pulled it out of the bag, practically breaking open a little plastic packet of duck sauce.

"Travis, what's wrong?"

"Dammit!" he said, swearing once more. "Bethany's been gone for two weeks. How am I supposed to live vicariously if you aren't getting any either?"

He didn't really seem angry, but I couldn't understand what the hell he was talking about, so I grabbed an eggroll and dove in.

"So what were you doing, then?"

Travis was about as fixated on Mayra and me as I had ever been on counting cracks in the sidewalk.

"We fell asleep," I said again.

"What were you doing before then?"

I poked at my lo mein with the end of a chopstick. There were only a few left on the plate, and they were little pieces. If I poked them in the right directions, I could make letters. Ms and Ts were easy, but Bs were hard to make.

"Matthew!"

I jumped.

"What?"

He let out a long sigh.

"Why did Mayra come over?" he asked.

"We're doing an ecology project together."

Travis started coughing until rice came out of his nose. I narrowed my eyes at him as he finally stopped and looked at me, shaking his head.

"Let me guess," he said. "The effects of cuddling on the environment?"

"No," I said as I started cleaning up the empty containers and wiping down the table as Travis finished off the rest of the tofu, "honey bees."

"You really aren't helping here, dude," Travis said. He sounded really sad, and I didn't know why.

"What do you want me to tell you?" I asked.

"Tell me about Mayra."

"Okay." I finished putting everything in the trash and sat back down at the kitchen table. "She's in my ecology class, and Mr. Jones made me work with her."

"I got that much."

"Right." I ran my hand though my hair. "I was supposed to go to her house to work on the assignment, and I tried—I really did—but I couldn't knock on the door."

"So how did she get over here?"

"I guess she just came over when I didn't show up," I said. "I think she knew I had tried. I tried to go to her house once before."

"And she came over here to see you instead?" Travis asked for clarification, and I nodded. "And you're okay with her being here?"

"It's weird," I said. "I don't know why, but having her here doesn't bother me much at all."

"Uh huh." Travis chuckled. "So what's her story? She's one of the outsider kids in your class, too? She's really cute, but I know that doesn't always matter in those cliques and stuff. Is she smart? Maybe on the chess team or something?"

My brow furrowed as I tried to process what Travis was saying. Mayra was smart, but she wasn't those other things at all.

"She plays on the soccer team. She's a team captain."

"Oh yeah? Jock-girl, huh?" Travis's head bobbed up and down. "I guess that only counts when you're a cheerleader or something. Kids sure can be mean."

I shook my head.

"She's the captain of the team," I told him. "Or co-captain at least. Aimee Schultz is the other captain. Mayra was class president last year. She's really popular."

Travis flinched and narrowed his eyes.

"Really?"

"Yes."

"What's she doing with you, Matthew?"

It was my turn to flinch.

"I don't know."

Travis ran his hands though his hair. He stood from the kitchen chair and dragged me into the living room with him so we could sit more comfortably. He leaned forward with his elbows on his knees and looked at me. I stared at the coaster where Mayra's Coke class was still sitting. There were little beads of condensation coating the outside of it.

"Matthew," Travis said, "you and your sister are my only blood relatives. You know I love you and try to do just what your dad would have done for you. I think you are an awesome kid. You've done so much better than I ever would have dreamed after your mom was gone, too."

He leaned back and put his arms on the armrests as he tilted his head toward the ceiling. He rubbed his eyes.

"I don't know how to say this without sounding like an asshole."

"Say what?"

He sat back up and looked at me again.

"What does she want, Matthew?" Travis asked, his voice dropping a little. He sounded angry. "I love you like a son, but why would a girl like that be over here, wrapped up on a couch, alone with a boy like you?"

I stared at the droplets of water as they trickled down the side of the glass.

"She has to want something," he said, "and I just might have to find out what."

He stood up and started to pace around the room a little.

"If they're fucking with you for some reason, I'll fucking kill them."

"That's illegal," I reminded him.

"Well, I'll go tell on them!" he yelled. "I know most of their parents! She's Henry Trevino's daughter, isn't she?"

"Yes."

"Maybe I'll go talk to him."

I had an image of Travis walking up to Mayra's front porch—a place I couldn't even manage to approach—and talking to her dad, maybe even yelling at him. I wondered if Mr. Trevino would get mad and then tell Mayra she wasn't allowed to come and work on our project again.

"No!" I suddenly yelled. "Don't do that!"

"Why not?"

"She's not like that!" I said insistently.

"How do you know?" Travis said with a growl. "Matthew, you don't read people well. You know that. Remember the guy who came over and trimmed the trees last fall? He took you for two grand, and you couldn't afford that. He took advantage of you, dude. I don't want that to happen again."

"She's not like that," I repeated.

"Then why was she trying to make out with you on the couch?"

"She wasn't," I responded. "She was…was…just holding me."

"What the fuck does that mean?" Travis moaned, exasperated now.

"I told her everything," I said. "I told her about the doctors and how they don't know what I have. I told her about Dad and about Mom. I told her everything, and she held me, and I cried."

Silence.

Another bead of condensation worked its way to the bottom of the glass and onto the absorbent stone coaster.

"You told her about it all?" Travis finally asked quietly.

"Yes."

"You really cried?"

"Yes." My voice had dropped to a whisper again.

"Matthew—you haven't cried since they took Megan away. You didn't cry at the funerals or anything."

"I know."

Travis got up and walked over to the couch to sit beside me. He put one arm over the back of the couch and held the other one out.

"Come here," he said.

I leaned into him and he gave me a brief hug.

"Maybe I am an ass," he muttered as he let go. "And maybe I'm wrong. I worry about you, dude. I do."

"I know."

"You like her?" he asked.

"I don't know," I replied. I thought about it for a minute. "She smells good."

Travis chuckled.

"I bet," he said. "Are you going to have her over here again?"

"We still have some work on our project to do," I said, "so maybe. Probably."

"You gonna kiss her?" he asked as he wiggled his eyebrows.

I shook my head.

"You want to?"

"I don't know, Travis." I felt myself tensing up. "I don't know anything about any of that."

"I know Kyle gave you 'the talk' when you were younger," he said.

"'The talk'?"

"You know," Travis said with another raise of his eyebrows, "*that* talk."

"What talk?"

"Ugh!" Travis stood and took a few steps away before he turned around to look at me. "The sex talk!"

"Yes."

"I'd guess that talk was probably pretty...'mechanical' in nature."

"You can use machines?" I asked.

Travis began to laugh.

"Well...um...not what I meant," he said, "though yeah, you can."

A portion of the discussion between my father and me about sexual reproduction made a quick drive-by in my brain.

"I don't want to have a baby," I said.

"No, you don't, but there are all kinds of birth control and stuff out there. She could already be on The Pill."

I glanced up at my uncle for a long moment. My gaze danced around his eyes, and I could see he wasn't angry or upset any more. He seemed relieved, maybe, and I wondered if he thought I was going to actually have a girlfriend, like he mentioned before.

I wasn't so sure about that. He was talking about sex, and I hadn't even kissed her or anything. I was pretty sure you were supposed to do that first.

"Travis, I wouldn't have any idea what to do," I finally said. "I mean, not at all. I know what gets done but...nothing else."

"Well, dude," Travis said as he stood up from the couch, "I would sit here and tell you everything about it"—he chuckled again—"but if I did, I'd be here all night. You'd learn a lot, too. You would also freak out on me about every fourth word, so I'm not going to do it."

Travis grabbed his keys from the table near the door.

"But you know what?"

"What?"

61

"Google is damn handy." Travis continued to laugh softly as he went out the door.

Google.

Google what?

Dating?

Kissing?

Sex?

Is that what I wanted? To date Mayra? To kiss her? To…to…to…do *more*?

I hadn't the slightest idea.

I couldn't determine what I wanted, so I just locked up and went to bed.

~oOo~

The next day at school was about as strange a day as I could have ever imagined, stranger than rain when the sun was shining, stranger than the way peanut butter smells when it's wet, and stranger than vampires that sparkle. The worst part was first thing in the morning.

As soon as I walked into school, I heard my name being yelled from down the hall.

"Matthew! Matthew!"

Mayra came running down the hallway. There were some other kids with her, including Justin Lords, Aimee Schultz, and Carmen Klug. I slowed my steps a little as they approached, but I didn't stop my trek to my locker. That's what I did when I got to school—I went to my locker. My hands were shaking a little as I reached for the lock to work the combination.

"Mayra, what the fuck?" Justin grumbled under his breath as Mayra came up next to me.

"Hey, Matthew!" she said, ignoring Justin.

I squeezed my eyes shut for a second, then concentrated on the lock so I could align the numbers properly. It was difficult since my hands were shaking. I knew I hadn't responded to Mayra yet, but I couldn't decide how, especially with her other friends standing there. Should I just say "Hey" back to her? Should I say "Hey, Mayra"? Something else? Ask about the weather?

"Seriously, Mayra?" Carmen sneered. "He can't even say hello, for Christ's sake!"

My chest rose and fell with labored breaths as Carmen's words echoed through my head. She was right. Greetings were a strange concept for me. I didn't understand the point. No matter how many times I practiced, the whole activity was worse than going to the dentist and lying there with my mouth open. That was just when one person approached me, and now there were four of them, looming close.

"Shut up!" Mayra turned her head over her shoulder and hissed under her breath. She turned back toward me just as I managed to get the locker open.

I crouched down and started organizing the folders and the books from my book bag into the locker. Focusing on the items in the locker, I made sure everything was lined up precisely. I could hear them talking behind me in hushed voices, but I wasn't paying attention to the words until I felt Mayra's hand on my shoulder.

I startled, which elicited giggles from Carmen. Aimee elbowed her in the side, and Carmen called her a bitch. I glanced up to see Justin rolling his eyes and turning away dramatically from the row of lockers.

"Matthew, did you hear me?" Mayra asked.

I thought about it for a minute, but I couldn't come up with what she had said. The first bell rang, and I didn't have the right things for my period one class. My timing was all off.

"*Shit, shit, shit*," I muttered as I grabbed for the right things.

"Fucking freak." Justin snarled before he stomped off down the hallway. He continued to yell over his shoulder. "Just fucking forget it, Mayra! Find some other stray to take in!"

I couldn't catch my breath and started to hyperventilate a bit. I was feeling dizzy, and I couldn't decide if I should just grab my stuff and get to class or not. Maybe I should say something…ask Mayra to repeat her question, or maybe I should at least say hello.

Was it too late to say hello?

I had no idea.

"He's even panting like a dog," Carmen said, snickering.

Aimee glared at her and leaned close to her ear. Carmen's lip curled as she responded, and then she laughed out loud. Aimee gritted her teeth and continued to glare at Carmen.

I tried closing my eyes, but I could still hear the laughing behind me. I didn't think it was just Carmen anymore. I was pretty sure I heard someone start barking, too. Mayra was yelling at them to stop it, and the sheer amount of sounds around me—*about* me— was just too much.

I shut down.

Kneeling on the hard tile floor of the hallway in front of my locker, I slowly began to take everything out of it. One class at a time, I placed the correct textbook, associated folder, and spiral notebook next to each other. Once a set was in, I straightened them exactly, wishing I had a level with me and wondering if I could afford to get a small one at the hardware store to keep in my locker.

With all my attention on the contents of the locker, I blocked all sights and sounds coming from the hallway and the people around me.

I sat back a little on my heels and looked at what I had done. One of the folders had the edge of a paper sticking out the top, so I took everything out, fixed the paper, and started all over again. By the time I was done repeating the process for the third time, I looked up, and the school nurse was beside me with a cell phone held up to her ear.

"…completely non-responsive…yes, if you could, I think that would be for the best…"

She ended the call and looked down at me. I blinked a few times and saw Mayra Trevino over on the other side of the hallway with her back pressed up against the opposite row of lockers. She had her hand covering her mouth, and I wasn't sure, but I thought there might be tears in her eyes. Principal Monroe was there and a couple other faculty members too. There wasn't anyone else in the hallway, and I realized that first period must have already started.

I was late.

If someone was late to class, they always got a tardy slip. I'd never gotten a tardy slip before. Would it go on my record? Would it be seen on my college applications?

Shit, shit, shit.

I looked back down at the floor. I had no idea what I was supposed to do at this point. I didn't understand why there were people standing around me or why Mayra looked so upset. I wanted to get up and go ask her, but I didn't know what to say.

I felt a cold hand on my arm and I jumped, which caused me to bang the opposite shoulder against the locker door. As I rubbed against the sore spot, I glanced up to see Travis coming down the hallway.

"Hey, dude," he said as he walked toward me. He gave me half a smile and looked over to the principal and the nurse. "I got him—just give us some space, okay?"

I saw the others take a few steps backwards, but I mostly watched Principal Monroe as he walked up to Mayra and told her to go on to class.

"No!" she said. "I want to make sure he's all right!"

"Miss Trevino, Matthew's got his uncle here with him now. You move along."

"Not until I know he's all right!" She was insistent.

"It's okay." Travis walked over to them both. "I think Matthew wouldn't mind if she sticks around a minute. Might be better for him."

The principal gave Travis a weird look before shrugging and moving over to talk quietly with the nurse. Travis crouched down next to me.

"You with me, dude?"

"Yes," I said quietly.

"You want Mayra to stay?"

"No," I replied.

Travis looked surprised.

"Why not?"

"I don't know what to say to her."

"Why don't you start with hello? Then you could see where it goes from there."

"No."

"You sure?" he asked.

"No," I said again and then sighed. "I'm late for class."

"Not a problem, dude," Travis said. "You want to go there now?"

"I'll get a tardy slip."

"Nah, it's all good—I'll work it out." Travis's words were reassuring.

"You will?"

"Sure," Travis said with a smile. He wrapped his hand around my elbow and pulled me up. "You got the stuff for your first class?"

I reached down and pulled out the folder and the notebook before nodding.

"Maybe Mayra could walk with you," Travis suggested. "Then I can talk to Monroe about the tardy slip, and you can say hello."

I took a deep breath and tried to stop my hands from shaking. I had something that resembled a plan now, and that usually got me going when I was stuck. Travis was going to take care of the tardy slip, so that should be all right as well.

"Okay," I whispered.

Travis walked over to Mayra, and then they both came back next to me. At some point, the corner of my notebook had become slightly bent, which sucked. I'd have to write all the notes into a new one.

"Hey," Mayra said as she looked up at me through her eyelashes. They were definitely wet. "You have English first, right?"

"Yes."

Mayra walked beside me down the hall without speaking. We stopped when we got to the closed door of the classroom, and I knew I was forgetting something.

"Oh!" I exclaimed when I remembered what I was supposed to say. "Um, hello."

Mayra laughed quietly through her nose as she tilted her head up to look at me again. It was the first time I had noticed how short she was. She barely came up to my shoulder. She shook her head slowly, and when I looked back down to the ground, she reached out and placed her finger under my chin. She tilted my head back to look at her, and when I met her eyes, I could have sworn my stomach flipped over.

"Hello, Matthew," she said as she smiled at me. "Would you like to go to Houston Woods this weekend?"

I couldn't comprehend her question, so I just quickly ducked into the classroom. I needed distance and solitude to process what was going on inside my head, and I couldn't think about anything but the potential for a tardy slip.

Considering the start to the day, I didn't last long at school. About halfway through third period, there was a fire drill. It was just too much—too much *difference*. The school usually has fire drills after lunch, and third period is too early.

Travis had to come back to take me home. He didn't really say much on the way other than to tell me he wasn't going to argue about me taking the Valium he knew I still had in the bathroom upstairs. It had been prescribed for me after Mom died, but I had only taken it a couple of times. It always made me fall asleep when it wasn't time for sleep.

"You need the extra rest," Travis said. "Reset your system a little, okay? I'll stick around your house tonight until your normal bedtime."

I gave up. I didn't really mind him being there. He was in "no bullshit mode," and arguing with him was pointless. Once we were back at my house, Travis nuked a box of macaroni and cheese and then stared at me with his arms crossed over his chest until I swallowed the damn pill.

Today was one giant *lose*.

Chapter 5—What I Will Do for Cake

Groggy and disoriented, it took me a few minutes to even figure out I was on my couch, and it was the middle of the afternoon. It took a little longer to get my bearings because I could hear voices coming from the dining room.

"...hasn't been that bad for a while," Travis was saying. "The dude loves his routines, you know? You can't really get in the way of them and expect decent results."

"I didn't know..." It was Mayra's voice that responded to my uncle. "I just...I mean...I thought we kind of *connected* yesterday, right? No one ever asks him to go anywhere with us, and I thought I would ask him to go to Houston Woods this weekend. I didn't think..."

"I have to admit you gave me a bit of a shock," Travis said. "I suppose most uncles in my position would worry about walking in and finding their nephew on the couch with some chick. Honestly, I never dreamed it would happen."

I heard him laugh quietly.

"Don't get all embarrassed on me," he said. "You have to know what that looked like."

"We weren't—"

"I know," Travis said, interrupting her. "He told me. I'm also not an idiot, and I'm not a kid. I've seen enough of my wife's DVDs to know that he's a good-looking, well-built kid. I also know it would be damn easy to take advantage of him. If that happens, I'm not going to be particularly friendly."

Travis's tone had dropped low.

"So why don't you tell me just what the fuck is going on here?"

"What do you mean?"

"I mean your family has lived in this town as long as I can remember. I'm pretty sure you've been in Matthew's class since kindergarten. Why the interest now? And don't you even tell me you're not interested, because I'll call bullshit."

I squeezed my eyes shut, then blinked a couple of times. My eyes were all blurry and itchy, but I could still see the image of my uncle and Mayra sitting across from each other at the dining room table.

"What are you insinuating?" Mayra's voice sounded like a snarl. "That I want something from Matthew? What do you think I'm trying to do, steal his virtue or something?"

"You're gonna wake him up," Travis said in a deadpan tone.

I wanted to respond, but Valium always made my tongue feel weird. I couldn't manage to get any words out. Mayra dropped her voice down.

"You're implying that I'm out to get him."

"I have no idea what you're doing," Travis said. I could see his blurry shape lean forward with his elbows on the table. "But he's like a son to me, and I'm all he's got. Don't fucking mess with him. He can't take it, and between both parents and his sister being taken from him in the past year, he's been through enough."

"I wouldn't," Mayra said.

"So you tell me why"—Travis's voice dropped again and almost sounded like a growl—"after all the years you've been in the same class, why are you suddenly coming to his house to check on him?"

Mayra went silent for a minute, and then she finally let out a sigh before answering.

"I never paid any attention to him before," she said. "I remember trying to say hello to him when we were younger, but he never answered, so I stopped. When Jones said he had to sit next to me, he actually said 'hi' back when I greeted him. He'd never done that before. Of course, I heard about his parents—"

"It's a small town," Travis said.

"Yeah, exactly," Mayra said. "But I didn't even know he had a sister."

"She doesn't get out much."

"Yeah, he told me," Mayra replied. "I just started watching him a little then. I could tell certain things bothered him, but I wasn't sure exactly what or why. I was…curious at first."

"Curious? What, he's your science project now?"

"No!" Mayra said. "Not at all! I just…wanted to figure him out. We connected yesterday. I know we did."

"Connected to the point where he had to hit the bag," Travis said with a snort. "That's some connection."

"It was after that," she said.

"After you saw him naked."

"He wasn't naked!"

"Half, then." Travis let out a long sigh. "And what are you planning now?"

"I'm planning," Mayra said through clenched teeth, "to get our project finished and maybe see if we can't be friends or something. Are you going to be a total dick about it the whole time?"

"Maybe." Travis laughed. "I'm protective of him, so you better just get used to that."

"Fabulous." Mayra sneered back at him.

"And here's where I have to go against my instincts," Travis said, "because my instincts tell me to throw you the fuck out. There is no way in hell this shit is going to work even if you are sincere about it. Matthew's fucking awesome, and I love him, but he's about as high-maintenance as it gets. I just don't see some seventeen-year-old—"

"I'm eighteen," she said.

"Oh, yeah, that makes all the difference!" Travis stood up. "Now let me finish!"

He took a deep breath and ran his hands up and down his cheeks.

"I'm going against what makes sense," he said, "because this *feels* right. You really do seem to give a shit about him, and he's never talked to anyone else about his folks except his therapist and me. He doesn't even talk to my wife about that shit, and we've been married six years."

"Were you shitty to her when she first met Matthew?" Mayra snapped.

"Actually, yeah," Travis replied. He had been, too.

"Well, I guess it's good he has someone looking out for him," she said, "but you don't have to protect him from me."

"Is that so?"

"That's so."

I heard Travis huff out a short breath.

"Don't you hurt him," Travis said, "because if you do, I will hunt you down, Trevino. I was always taught not to hit a girl, so I'd probably have to resort to letting all the air out of your tires instead, but don't think that won't be as annoying as dog shit on your shoes after the fifteenth time."

"I won't," Mayra said as she shook her head back and forth. "I promise."

"Yeah, you will," Travis muttered, "but I don't think it will be intentional."

I moved myself into a sitting position and waited for the dizziness to pass.

"Hey there, sleeping beauty!" Travis called out. "You been listening?"

"Yes," I replied. "Leave her tires alone."

Travis laughed.

I couldn't just lie there anymore, so I pushed myself up and joined them at the table.

Very little was said as Travis ordered a pizza for us all, and we chowed down. Mayra and Travis kept looking at each other, but I wasn't in any condition to try to figure out what the looks meant. Even on a good day, I wasn't all that adept at reading body language.

"I'm heading out," Travis said as he finished dipping his crust in garlic butter, effectively finishing off the last of the pizza. "Bethany will be back tomorrow, and we'll have to figure out what to do with the car. We'll work it out, though. I can always drive her to work, and you can use hers until your car is fixed, all right?"

"Okay," I said.

"I can drive Matthew to school," Mayra said. She glanced over at me from behind her half-eaten piece of pizza. "I mean, if that would be okay with you. I don't mind, and it's not really out of the way."

I looked down at my empty plate and thought about that for a minute.

"You've been in my car before," Mayra said, reminding me.

"You went the speed limit," I recalled.

"Yes, I did," Mayra said with a tight lipped smile. "I would again, too."

I picked up my plate and went to wash it in the sink. When I grabbed for a dishtowel, Mayra was standing next to me and holding one up in her hand.

"I can dry, if you want."

Looking at the towel in her hand, I wondered if she could get all the water marks off the plate. Travis wasn't too bad at that, and

Mayra was pretty careful about such things. I could always wash and dry them again when she was gone.

"Okay," I said, and I handed her the plate.

"Dude," Travis called out from across the kitchen, "if you'll let her dry dishes, you gotta let her drive you."

He laughed, and I smiled a little. He had a point. Well, sort of. Driving and drying weren't the same thing, but they did have five letters in common. Maybe that would be close enough.

"What do you think?" Mayra asked. She sounded hopeful.

"Okay," I said quietly. "I still need to get Bethany's car from school since Travis drove me home this morning."

"How about I take you to school to get the car?" Mayra suggested. "It would be kind of a trial run for the next time."

A trial run sounded pretty good, really. It would be like going to school, but I wouldn't be worried about being late to class, so I agreed. Travis wiped the back of his hand across his face and grumbled about eating too much, and then he came over and leaned against the counter.

"I'm off," he said. "You all right if I go?"

"Yes."

"Okay," Travis said as he pushed away. He wiggled his eyebrows at Mayra. "You two be good!"

Mayra and I finished washing the plates and glasses after Travis left. She did a really good job of drying everything completely. I showed her which cabinets they went in and how the plates and glasses needed to line up with the pattern on the cabinet's lining paper. When we were done, I rode in Mayra's Porsche to pick up Bethany's car, and then she followed me back to my house so we could do some work on our project. We made some progress and then sat back down on the couch in the living room when we were done—Mayra on one side and me on the other.

"Matthew," she said, "I'm really sorry about this morning. I just didn't realize how you would react, and I'm going to punch

Carmen Klug myself if she ever says anything like that to you again. I didn't think they would do that."

I twisted my fingers around themselves and wondered how much more successful I would be at the act if all my fingers were the same length. That way, they could curl around my knuckles the same way on each finger and not be lopsided.

"Can I ask you something?" Mayra said.

"Yes," I replied.

"Do you remember what happened in the hallway?"

"I fixed the stuff in my locker."

"Anything else?"

"Not really," I admitted.

"Usually you remember things pretty well, though, don't you?"

"If I read something, I usually remember it. Also if I write something down—I think my fingers remember what I write."

I glanced over and smiled a lopsided grin at her.

"That's weird, huh?"

"No," she said, "it's not. I remember things better if I write them down, too. Then I read over it again, just to be sure."

"I do that."

"Well, then," Mayra said with a smile, "we have something in common, don't we?"

"I guess so."

Mayra scooted over a little closer to me.

"Is this okay?" she asked quietly when she was sitting right next to me.

I thought about it and decided it was, so I nodded.

"Can I ask you something else?"

"Okay."

"Sometimes things do change, right?" she said. "I mean, I know you don't like it—lots of people don't like change—but sometimes it has to, like driving a different car to school."

I nodded again.

"So how do you cope with that?"

"I think about it beforehand," I told her. "If I get upset just thinking about it, I usually don't do it, but if thinking about it is okay, I think about it some more. I imagine in my head what it would look like. Then when it happens, I'm not taken off guard as much."

"Hmm," Mayra murmured. She sat quietly for a minute before turning her body toward mine. "So, if you took some time before school starts to think about me coming up to you at your locker to say hello, would that be okay?"

I froze as I wandered through the scenario in my head. This morning was awful, but I had been blindsided. I thought about what it would look like to glance over my shoulder and see Mayra standing next to my locker with me. That led to wondering who else would be there in the hallway, looking at us.

"Would you have other people with you?" I asked.

"It would be better if it was just me, huh?"

"Yes," I whispered.

"Just me, then."

"Okay." I rubbed the tips of my fingers over my thighs, feeling the rough denim texture of my jeans. I went over various versions of Mayra coming up to me at school and saying hello. Sometimes she just said "Hey" or "Hi." In my mind, I echoed her back. It felt all right.

"Do you want to watch TV?" Mayra asked.

"Okay," I said.

"What do you like to watch?"

"*Top Gear*," I told her. "I like history shows, too. And *MythBusters*."

"I love *MythBusters*!" Mayra said with a smile.

We went to sit in the reclining loveseat in the family room where the TV was. I picked up the remote and flipped through the guide, but *MythBusters* wasn't on. We settled on *Big Bang Theory*.

"You're kind of like Sheldon, you know," Mayra said.

"Yeah, Bethany says that, too. She keeps telling me I should go to school for physics. I don't want to be like him though. He's mean to people."

"I think he's cute," she said, then tried to hold back a smile. Her cheeks turned pink, and I narrowed my eyes at her.

"What do you mean?"

"Just some of the things he does. He's so precise about everything. He thinks about things in a different way from everyone else."

"I guess so."

The show ended and the local news started up. Mayra's finger touched the edge of my hand.

"Thinking differently is okay, you know."

"I know," I said quietly. "Travis tells me that all the time."

"Aimee always felt different when we were younger," Mayra said. "She had a lot of trouble in class because she couldn't focus on what the teacher was saying. They thought she was learning disabled, but she wasn't. She just learns differently than other people."

"I get lost in my head," I said quietly.

"Aimee says that too." Mayra gripped my hand.

I glanced at her eyes for a second, and she smiled at me before I looked away again. Aimee was Mayra's best friend, the co-captain of the soccer team, and likely the valedictorian of our class. I hadn't considered that I might have something in common with her.

"Hey! They're still looking for the lotto winner," Mayra said as she nodded at the television. "The ticket was sold in Millville at the gas station next to the drive-through right on Highway 27, but no one has claimed it yet."

I didn't really have anything to add, so I just nodded. Mayra looked over at me, and her expression changed somewhat. She narrowed her eyes a little, and her brow got all creased up.

"You don't want to go to Houston Woods with a group of people, do you?"

"No," I said as I shook my head quickly.

Mayra's fingers grazed the edge of my hand again.

"I should probably go," she said. "It's getting late."

"Okay."

"Hey, give me your cell number," Mayra suddenly said. She grabbed an iPhone out of her pocket and unlocked the screen.

"I only have a prepaid phone for emergencies."

"Oh…um…well, let me write down my number, then."

I gave her a little pad of paper that sat next to the phone in the kitchen, and she wrote ten numbers right underneath her name on the paper.

"This way you can give me a call if your car gets done early or something," she said as she gathered up her school stuff and slung her book bag over her shoulder. "I'll see you tomorrow, okay?"

"Okay." A weird feeling came over me, and I didn't know what to make of it. My stomach felt like I had eaten too much or something.

"Matthew?"

"Yeah?"

"I really am sorry about this morning."

I looked down at my feet and wondered if I was supposed to say something. I had the feeling I was, but I wasn't sure what. Instead of replying, I just went through, in my head, various ways of accepting an apology.

The weird feeling in my gut got worse as I watched Mayra walk out the door and down the walkway to the drive. There was also a little tickle in the back of my head, which usually meant I was forgetting something. I walked all around the house—checking the doors and windows to make sure they were locked, verifying the stove was off, and seeing that all my homework and books were back in my book bag for tomorrow. I couldn't figure out anything I had missed, but the tickle was still there. It drove me nuts half the night. I went back and forth, wondering if I was forgetting something or if it was the Valium-induced nap.

I couldn't manage to sleep, so I got up and worked on my websites instead.

The day had started off pretty bad, but at the moment, I felt content.

Win.

~oOo~

Mayra picked me up and drove me to school the next day. I thought about it and thought about it beforehand, but I hadn't taken into consideration what other people were going to think of me getting out of her car in the morning. The entire parking lot was full of students and cars, and it seemed like they were all watching me as I climbed out of the blue Porsche.

Mayra came around the front and smiled at me. She didn't even seem to notice the way the other kids were looking at us as we walked into the school together. She talked the whole time, but I had no idea what she was saying.

I was just trying to keep myself breathing.

"I'll see you in ecology!" Mayra called out as she left me at my locker to join her friends. I didn't answer but spent a minute reorganizing my things and hanging up my book bag. After a few more breaths, I managed to get myself together enough to go to class.

Lunch was…weird.

I usually sat with Joe at lunch. When we were younger, Joe's friend Scott would join us, but now he sat with the other guys from the football team. These days, Joe and I sat alone at the end of one of the long tables. Mayra's friend, Aimee, always sat with Scott. I was pretty sure they were a couple now. Joe was usually sorting through his collection of Magic: The Gathering cards while snarfing down a few slices of pizza from the cafeteria, and I would eat the same thing I always made for lunch—peanut butter and strawberry jam, a mini bag of Doritos, carrot sticks, an apple, and a can of Coke.

I'd eaten the exact same lunch every day for as long as I could remember.

I had just dropped down onto the bench seat and opened up my lunch when Mayra came up beside me.

"Hey," she said quietly, "how's your day going?"

Joe stopped eating and looked up from his pizza. His gaze darted back and forth between Mayra and me. I froze with one of my hands halfway in my lunch bag.

"It's okay," Mayra said. She slowly reached out toward me, and her finger brushed lightly over the top of my hand. "I'm not staying or anything. I just wanted to let you know I have to leave early today. Dad has to take his car in for maintenance in Hamilton, and I need to drive him back. I won't be in ecology class and won't get home until later tonight. I talked to Travis, and he said your Aunt Bethany will pick you up when school is out. We'll work on the project some more tomorrow."

"No project tonight?" I said with a rush of breath. I didn't realize I had stopped breathing.

"No, I'm sorry," Mayra replied. "I didn't even know until about an hour ago."

"You talked to Travis?"

"Yeah, he gave me his cell number."

"Oh." I stared down at my sandwich. The edge of the crust was bent outward a little bit, and I wondered if the whole loaf was like that.

Mayra pulled her hand back and then leaned forward on the table. It put her lower than my head level, and she dropped even lower, turned her head sideways, and tried to look up into my face. I glanced at her but looked away again when she smiled.

"I'll be there tomorrow," she said. "Promise."

"Okay," I said. I started pulling the rest of lunch out of the bag.

"See you then," Mayra said as she stood back up and turned away.

I continued to arrange lunch. The sandwich, chips, and carrot sticks all went together, since I ate them all together. I would always eat one bite of each in a circle and try to make them come out even as I ate. I was pretty successful at it, too. I drank the Coke throughout, and the apple was always saved for last.

As I ate, I felt weird. That little tickling sensation was back again, and I didn't understand why. It occurred to me that I was a little disappointed that Mayra wouldn't be driving me home or coming to my house this afternoon. Why was that?

I was startled out of my thoughts by a loud bang caused by Justin Lords jumping up onto the bench seat of our cafeteria table and then sitting on the tabletop itself. I tried to ignore how *wrong* that was—sitting on the top of the table while feet rested on the seat—but I couldn't. His actions were so obviously wrong, no one would have to point it out to a high school senior.

"You aren't supposed to sit on the table," I said in a low whisper.

"Fuck you, you fucking freak." He practically snarled as he glared down at me. He placed his hands on either side of where my lunch was arranged on the table and leaned his face close into mine.

I wanted to back away, but I was frozen at the same time. His hands were so close to my lunch, it was nerve-wracking, and I couldn't focus on anything else. I was starting to get lightheaded and wondered if I was hyperventilating.

"I don't know what the fuck you are trying to do," Justin said, "but I was really close to getting Mayra back in time for prom until she got distracted by the little stray dog project named Mattie Rohan."

"Hey, Lords—leave him alone," Joe muttered. "He hasn't done anything."

"Did anyone ask you for an opinion, Joe-Joe?"

Joe didn't respond.

"So here's what going to happen, *stray*," Justin said as he leaned even closer to me. "You're going to stay the fuck away from Mayra, you hear me?"

"We have to work on the ecology project," I heard myself say in response.

"Finish it yourself!" he snapped. "I don't care what you have to do as long as you stay the fuck away from my girl."

That was when he reached his meaty hand over and flicked out his fingers. They came into contact with my apple, which then went flying off the table and onto the floor.

On the floor.

The floor.

Apples definitely shouldn't be on the floor, especially not the one I was going to eat for lunch.

Shit, shit, shit.

I couldn't eat that apple now. There was no way. I also had to have an apple with my lunch. I had an apple with my lunch every day. I didn't have any cash on me, so I couldn't buy another one, and I just had to have an apple.

I closed my eyes and started to count to one hundred by tens as fast as I could. I knew Justin was still talking, and I felt him smack my shoulder, but I didn't open my eyes. I just kept counting, switching the method every time I got to one hundred. I counted by twos, then threes, then prime numbers.

It wasn't helping.

Where was I going to get another apple?

Joe was saying something to Justin, but I couldn't make that out, either.

Could I just wash the one that was on the floor?

No.

Definitely not.

Combined with thoughts of the apple were thoughts of Mayra and thoughts of not working with her on the project anymore. She wouldn't come over to my house if we weren't working on the project. When my car was fixed, she wouldn't drive me to school anymore, which meant I would go back to only seeing her in our ecology class.

Sitting right by Justin Lords.

The thought of not being around her was almost as bad as the apple on the floor.

I couldn't even fathom it, so I opened my eyes and met Lords' gaze.

For the longest time we were just staring at each other. My entire body was tensed as if it were ready to spring, and there was definitely a part of me that wanted to haul back and punch him, but I wasn't wearing my gloves. Aside from not having my gloves on, Justin had this little dribble of slobber on his lower lip. It actually made a little bubble sitting there.

He was drooling.

I couldn't help myself; I laughed out loud—one single, explosive burst.

Justin reared back, and his eyes went wide as he moved back to the edge of the table and nearly lost his balance. That was even funnier, and I laughed again.

"What the fuck is your problem, freak?" he yelled, but I couldn't stop laughing long enough to respond.

Joe started snickering as well, though I don't know if he noticed the lip-spittle or not. Maybe he was just laughing at Justin nearly falling off the table. I told Justin sitting on the table like that wasn't right.

Justin shoved himself off the tabletop and stood back on the floor where he was supposed to be. He continued to cuss me out, but between Joe's laughter and my own, I couldn't really focus on his words. The little bit of spittle ended up on his chin as he backed away from the table.

"This ain't over, Rohan," he said. He pointed a finger at me and shook it. "Not by a long shot!"

He spun around on his heel and headed out of the cafeteria. I looked over at Joe, who was still snickering as he got up and retrieved my apple.

"I don't suppose you are going to eat this now, are you?" he asked.

"No," I replied.

Joe rubbed it on his shirt before taking a bite out of it.

"Gross," I mumbled as he walked away.

I watched Joe head over to the cafeteria line, buy another apple, and bring it over to set in front of me. I glanced up at him and gave him a half smile.

"Thanks."

"No problem," he said. "What the fuck is wrong with that idiot?"

I shrugged.

"So…are you dating Mayra Trevino now?"

"Um…" I didn't know what to say. "I don't think so."

Joe laughed again.

"You think maybe you should figure that out?"

I just shrugged again, and we finished the rest of lunch in silence.

~oOo~

"Your uncle is a big idiot," my Aunt Bethany said as soon as I got into the car. "Now tell me about the girl."

I looked down at the strap on my book bag. I wound my fingers around the strap, and then I wound the strap around my fingers. Beth didn't press; she just waited for me to answer.

"Her name is Mayra," I finally said as we pulled out of the school parking lot.

"I got that from Travis," Beth said. "I also got the idea he sent you off to the internet for info, which I told him was about as irresponsible as it could possibly be."

I didn't have anything to say about that though the conversation about using Google to research certain topics played back through my head.

"Did you?" Beth asked.

"Did I what?"

She let out a long, exaggerated sigh.

"Google sex," she said.

"No."

"Good." She sighed again. "That's the last thing you need."

Bethany turned into my subdivision and headed toward my street. She gripped the steering wheel kind of tightly, and I wondered what she was thinking about. She seemed agitated, and I wasn't sure if it was something I had said or done. When she pulled into my driveway, and I started to get out, she stopped me.

"Matthew, you know you can talk to me, right?" she asked.

I went back to staring at the strap of my book bag.

"You can," she said again. "You can ask me anything you want—about girls, relationships, sex—anything."

I could feel my body starting to rock back and forth in the seat. I tried to stop it, but that word—*sex*—kept going around and around inside my head. Bethany said something else, but I didn't catch what the words were. I felt her hand on my arm.

"Relax," she said quietly. "It's not something to be afraid of."

"I've never even kissed a girl," I said quickly. "I've never been even *close* to doing that. I don't think I could."

"Of course you could."

"No, I don't think so."

"What do you do before you try anything new?" she asked.

"Read about it," I replied. That was always my first step. "Then talk about it."

"I think this time it should be the other way around," Beth said. "Let's talk first, and then you can read more about it if you want."

"No."

"It won't hurt."

"It might."

"I'll make you dinner."

I glanced over at my aunt, whose cooking rivaled my mom's. She didn't do it often, either, and when she did, it was usually a special occasion like a holiday or someone's birthday. She made the best cakes in the world, too.

When Travis first met Bethany, neither Megan nor I would even acknowledge her. Megan didn't like her because she didn't wear a watch, and having someone new around the house set us both on edge. Megan would actually scream and cry when Beth came into the room. That all changed—for me, at least—the first time she took over my mom's kitchen and baked a cake.

My parents started using Bethany's cooking as a reward system for my therapy, which ended up being more successful than anything else my doctors and therapists had tried. My aunt and her cooking were a large part of the reason I was able to function in a mainstream school, and her cake had a lot do to with it. There wasn't much of anything I wouldn't do for a piece.

"Cake?" I whispered.

"Sure."

"Chocolate?"

"If you promise to try to stay calm while we talk," she said.

I thought about it for a while as we sat in the driveway in silence. The last time Beth had made a cake had been for New Year's, and it hadn't been a chocolate one. It was all white with sparkly fireworks in the frosting.

She knew my weakness, and with a sigh, I glanced over at Beth and nodded.

I couldn't say no to cake, so I guess we would be talking about sex.

Even though it made me feel like a nine-year-old, I sat at the kitchen table and licked the drippy chocolate batter off the beaters. It didn't even matter that I was still stuffed from dinner.

Beth was just finishing up so she could put the cake pan in the oven. I watched her smooth out the batter with a spatula, and the way her arm and the utensil moved together looked like a dance. She hummed while she worked, and I thought about my mom standing in the same spot, making dinner for me and Megan.

"You okay?" Bethany asked.

"Yes," I replied automatically. It was one of the few questions I had been *trained*, for lack of a better word, to respond to quickly. Mom worked with me forever after I cut myself on one of Dad's tools in the garage and just sat there bleeding while she waited for me to answer. Once she figured out I was hurt, she completely freaked out, and then she spent months making sure I would at least respond with a *yes* or *no* to those two simple words without having to think about it.

Beth opened up the preheated oven and slid the sheet cake inside while I finished licking the second beater. I groaned a little at the taste. It was just so good, I couldn't help myself. My aunt snickered and folded her arms across her chest.

"I wish your sister took to cake as well as you did," she said. The one thing you could always count on with Bethany was that she was going to say what she was thinking. Other people might hide their thoughts, but she never did.

"She never took to anything," I said, "unless you painted numbers around your face and attached clock hands to your nose."

She shook her head slowly.

"Come on," she said. "No stalling. Tell me more about Mayra."

I picked up the mixing bowl and beaters and took them to the sink. Beth sat at the table and watched as I washed everything. She didn't wash or dry right, and she knew I wasn't going to let her help. She didn't bother to ask anymore. What she lacked in dishwashing skills, she made up for in patience. Beth sat and waited without talking until I had finished the last of the measuring cups.

"I don't know what to say about her."

"Tell me what she looks like."

"She has brown hair and brown eyes," I said. "She's short."

"She's short or just compared to you?"

"She's short. She only comes about halfway up my chest."

"Hmm…" Beth hummed. "Go on."

"Her hands are small," I told her, "and I like the way her eyes look when she smiles."

"Is she pretty?"

"Yes," I replied without hesitation.

"Is she in your class?" Beth asked. "A senior, I mean?"

"Yes."

"She had a lot of boyfriends?"

I almost dropped the bowl I was putting away.

"I…I don't know," I finally said. "Some, I think."

"She's got the advantage," Beth said.

My hands started to shake.

"Stop it," she said with a warning in her voice. "You promised, and we've hardly even started. You still want that cake?"

"Yes."

"Then take a deep breath, get a drink, and join me in the living room."

I sat in the big, blue, overstuffed chair, and Beth sat on the matching couch. I pulled my knees up so I could wrap my arms around my legs—I felt safer that way—and waited for Bethany to continue.

"You like her?" my aunt asked.

I shrugged. I didn't know. I didn't even know what that meant, and I told her so.

"How do you feel when you are with her?"

I shrugged again, and Beth sighed dramatically.

"I'm going to take that cake home to Travis…"

"I don't know what to say!" I blurted out, a little concerned she would make good on her threat. "I feel…okay with her, I guess."

"Just okay?"

"Yes…no…I don't know!" I tightened my grip on my own legs.

"Deep breaths," she said, reminding me.

The smell of the baking cake was a good reminder, too. I could almost taste it already.

"She makes me feel…calm," I whispered.

"Calm is good," Beth said with a nod, and I agreed. "Travis said you talked to her about your mom and dad."

"A little," I admitted. "She asked."

"And you were okay talking to her about them? And Megan?"

I nodded.

"Is that how you ended up half-naked on the couch with her?"

"We weren't," I said. "I just…I was hitting the heavy bag, and I took my shirt off. We were on the couch, and we fell asleep."

"That's it?"

"Yes."

"Travis is an idiot," Beth said with a laugh. "He had me thinking you guys were about to get it on. Let's step back, okay?"

"Step back?"

"Have you been on a date with her?"

"No."

"Do you want to?"

"No."

"Why not?" Bethany sounded surprised.

"On a date, you go out to dinner and a movie," I said. "You're supposed to pay for the girl, and I don't have that budgeted."

"Is that all you got?" she said through pursed lips. "Nineteen-fifties dating references? You don't have to pay."

"I would want to."

"Would you?"

I thought about it for a minute.

"No," I said, revising my statement. "I guess not. I don't want to go out anywhere. I don't like being around that many people, and there are always a lot of people at the movies. Besides, the only places to eat in town are bars and that Mexican place. Either way, there will be students everywhere, and they're loud."

"Not overly romantic places," Beth agreed, "but there are better paces in Cincinnati."

"We would have to drive for over an hour," I told her.

"So?"

"What would we talk about?"

"What have you talked about before?"

"Our ecology project," I said, "but I don't think she'd want to talk about bees for a whole hour. You have to talk at dinner and on the way back, too."

"What else does she like?"

"Um…soccer, maybe?"

"Why do you say that?"

"She plays on the soccer team."

"So, maybe you could ask her about soccer," Beth suggested. "You never played, did you?"

I shook my head.

"So she could explain the game to you," Beth said, "and then maybe you could go watch her play. You would know the rules and what to expect then. Instant second date."

I was surprised at how much sense that actually made.

"All you have to do is figure out a couple of other things she likes," Beth said, "and then you would have dinner conversation, too."

"I'm not any good at conversation."

"You are better than you realize," Beth countered. "We are having a conversation now, and you are barely hesitating to answer. Besides, when you are out with a girl, it's important to listen more than you talk."

"It is?"

"Yes, but you also have to *really* listen. You have to stay focused on her and what she is saying."

"How do I do that?"

"Lean toward her," Bethany said. "Make sure you look at her when she's talking. Listen to her words, and ask her questions."

"I'm not sure I can do that," I said honestly. The more I thought about it, the more I didn't think I could.

"You can," Bethany said quietly. "If you really want to, Matthew, you can. Do you want to get to know her better?"

"Yes," I said.

"Do you want to have a chance at something like this? A relationship with a girl?"

I nodded.

"Then you can do it."

"I don't want to see a movie in the theatre," I reminded her.

"Then don't," Beth said. "Just dinner."

A dark, crawling feeling slid over my skin.

"I can't date her," I said quietly.

"Why not?"

"Because I would have to ask her to go out with me," I explained. "I *really* don't think I can do that."

"Do you remember when you couldn't order pizza over the phone?"

"Yes."

"Can you do that now?"

"Yes," I said, "but I have to work up to it a little."

"So we'll work on getting you ready to ask Mayra out the same way we worked on ordering pizza. I'll be Mayra, and you ask me. We'll keep doing it until you think you got it."

"But…" I hesitated.

"What is it?"

"But the pizza place never says no." I closed my eyes, and my heart started to pound. My head started getting foggy, and my vision blurred as I thought about asking Mayra out and having her say no. The next thing I knew, Beth was on her knees in front of me and talking me through some deep breathing until I relaxed. When I had calmed, I glanced at her blue eyes.

"I'm proud of you," she said softly. "You come back so much faster now."

"How long?" I asked.

"Less than a minute," she said. I thought she was probably minimizing, but I knew it hadn't been very long.

"I won't be able to do it," I said again.

"You will," Bethany told me. "We'll work on it, okay?"

I just shook my head.

"We will," she insisted. "Now come on—you've earned some cake."

As always, the cake was what I figured heaven must taste like. I didn't even mind that the cake hadn't cooled completely before Bethany frosted it. I ate the first piece in about twelve seconds and then polished off a second before I remembered it was Thursday. I needed to get the trash collected and out to the curb. Bethany waited in the kitchen while I hauled the trash outside. Once I was done, I sat across from her at the table and looked at the rest of the cake.

I swear it was calling to me.

"It's late," Bethany said. "I need to get home to Travis, but we're not done talking. You got it?"

"Yes."

"Don't eat all of that cake tonight, either," she said. "I'll be back tomorrow, and you can earn another piece."

"Can I have one more?"

"All right," she said, "but no more after that!"

Bethany smiled, and I watched her bouncy hair swing around her shoulders as she stood up and headed to the door. She had just picked up her purse and her keys and started to leave when I suddenly remembered something.

"I thought we were going to talk about sex."

"Oh, Matthew, honey," Beth said as she walked through the door and onto the front porch. She shook her head slowly and reached out to tap my nose with the end of her finger. "We have been."

She turned her back to me and sauntered down the walkway to her car. I watched her get inside, wave, and then back out of the driveway.

I was left confused, so I went back to the kitchen for more cake.

No matter what else happened, cake days were always a win.

Chapter 6—It's a Family Thing

A slight jerk whips my head forward, and I feel a sense of dread and panic come over me as I realize I've been hit. I take ten deep breaths before opening the car door and stepping around to see the damage to the car's bumper...

Shortly after five in the morning, I sat straight up in bed.

My heart was pounding, and in the wake of the dream, a variety of recent memories rushed through my head like a flash flood: the guy who rear-ended my car; the scrap of paper he shoved at my chest as he took off; the crumpled edge of the lottery ticket as I tossed it into the trash; the voice on the television saying a ticket bought in Millville was the winning ticket.

There was no way.

People were more likely to be hit by lightning twice.

The trash was at the curb, and the garbage trucks usually rolled into the neighborhood before six. I glanced at the clock and saw that it was only a quarter after five. I stared at the red numbers until they changed to twenty after, just trying to figure out what to do.

I thought about the garbage from the kitchen and how near the bottom of the bag was a folded lottery ticket, the same ticket my hit-and-run driver had shoved at me. It was now in the larger can outside, sitting at the curb and waiting for the collection truck to come around and add it to the landfill north of town. Retrieving it was ridiculous. There was no way the numbers on the lottery ticket would be the winning ones even though the license plate of the car had been registered in Butler County, which meant the guy was local.

There was just no way.

Besides, the ticket was at the bottom of the trash bag. Duck sauce and fortune cookie wrappers and greasy napkins surrounded it. Searching through the garbage would be completely disgusting, and there was no way I would ever touch it. If I did manage to find and pick up the presumably filthy ticket, the act would be pointless.

There was just no way in hell.

Disbelief continued to wash over me as I sat in the center of my bed and let the possibility unfold. I hadn't taken the time to look closely at the ticket itself, nor had I paid much attention to the news reports on the television to know what the numbers were. I had no idea if it was the winning ticket or not. The likelihood of the hit-and-run guy living in Millville was nothing more than coincidence.

I heard the distinctive rumble of the garbage truck coming down the street and bolted straight out of bed. I ran down the stairs, flung over the front door, and didn't stop until my fingers were on the handle of the large trash bin, and I was hauling it away from the curb.

The truck was parked at the house next to mine, and the driver gave me a weird look as he watched me pull the trash away, but he didn't say anything. I opened the garage door and pulled the trash can into the middle of the floor and then sat down and tried to catch my breath.

I stared at the bottom of the large, black trash bin for several minutes without the slightest idea what I should do next. I got up at one point and took the lid off, but I quickly replaced it again. I leaned against the door between the garage and the house and stared at the large bin, which seemed to grow larger as I looked at it.

The adrenaline in my system was going sour and leaving me shaky. Deciding the bin and its contents were safe for the moment, I went back inside the house to contemplate and dropped down on one of the chairs in the kitchen.

The odds against the winning lottery ticket being inside my trash were astronomical. If the ticket were in there, it would be totally covered with scum, and I wouldn't be able to touch it. There was also no way I was going to get the bag out of the bin and open it up to look.

I closed my eyes for a few minutes, and when I opened them again, my gaze fell on the small pad of paper for messages and such that sat next to the phone. I could see rather unfamiliar writing on the pad, and I remembered whose phone number had been scribbled there recently.

I stood up, still feeling like I might be dreaming, and walked to the other side of the kitchen. With shaking hands, I picked up the phone out of its cradle and looked down at the pad of paper next to it. A phone number was still on the top page.

I called Mayra.

"You want me to do what?"

Mayra stood in the center of my garage with her arms crossed over her chest. She was tapping one foot against the concrete floor and looking back and forth between me and the large, open trash can between us.

"Maybe just…dump it out?" Apparently, my suggestion that she dig through the plastic bag of kitchen garbage hadn't gone over so well. It was possibly my refusal to tell her what I was looking for—on the grounds that I would sound like an idiot—wasn't making it any easier.

Maybe I was an idiot.

I wrapped my arms around myself and wondered if it was physically possible to hold myself together.

"You want me to dump out the whole trash can full of garbage?" Mayra asked.

I nodded.

"On the floor of the garage?"

"There isn't any room to spread it out anywhere else," I said, hoping at least that much sounded reasonable.

Mayra shook her head.

"But you aren't going to tell me what we're looking for?" she asked again.

"No," I said.

"Why not?"

I didn't answer. My eyes were drawn to the top of the trash can and the bit of plastic bag that was sticking out. I tried to convince myself to take a step forward and maybe at least open the bag, but I couldn't. No one was supposed to open trash bags after they'd been tied closed.

Mayra let out a long sigh and shook her head at me. Mumbling under her breath, she turned to the can and grabbed hold of the top of the plastic bag, hoisted it out, and dropped it on the floor. That made me jump. She rolled her eyes and wrinkled her nose as she crouched down and tore it open.

Tore it.

"Couldn't you have just untied it?" I asked with a cringe.

"Heard the line about beggars can't be choosers?" Mayra said, her frustration evident. "I can't believe I'm doing this."

"I'm sorry," I whispered.

Mayra turned over the bag and let everything fall out. Seeing all of the trash on the floor was just about enough to make me nauseated, and suddenly the idea of any amount of money being sufficient to compensate for the mess seemed ridiculous.

"My God," Mayra grumbled, "I hate Chinese food."

"You do?" I asked, momentarily distracted by the idea that anyone could hate Chinese food and grateful for the diversion.

"Yes," she said. "The smell is awful."

"It is now," I agreed. "That's why I can't touch it."

"But I can?" Mayra raised an eyebrow at me as she kicked some of the trash around with the toe of her shoe, spreading it out. "You going to tell me what the fuck I'm looking for now?"

My eyes scanned the floor, but I couldn't focus on any of it. It was too disastrous, and I was thinking about what Mayra said and realizing just how fucked up it was to call her in the first place.

"Shit, shit, shit," I mumbled under my breath. I grabbed my hair and tugged hard as I dropped down to the ground on my ass and wrapped my arms around my knees. "I'm sorry!"

"Don't do that," Mayra sighed. I could hear her walking toward me and felt her presence next to me as she kneeled. "It's okay, really."

"I didn't know who else to call," I whispered. "Your number was there...by the phone. I shouldn't have called...I'm sorry, I'm sorry, I'm—"

"Stop," Mayra said, and I did. "It's okay, really. I just...I don't know what we're supposed to find."

"It doesn't matter," I said. "It was stupid. I'm sorry, Mayra. I never should have called. I won't do it again—"

"Matthew, cut it out!" Mayra said. I jumped a little when I felt her hand against my shoulder. She didn't take it away but only touched me lightly. After a minute, I relaxed into her touch, and she spoke again. "I have to admit this was not the sort of thing I was expecting when you called saying it was urgent, and I have no idea what is going on here, but it's obviously important to you. I just don't know what else I can do to help."

"Nothing," I said quietly. "I don't want you to look."

"I'm already here," she said.

"I'm sorry," I repeated.

I heard Mayra let out another quick breath, and then she pulled out her phone and pushed a button. The front of it lit up her face.

"Shit," she mumbled. "You need to get going, or we'll be late for school."

I realized at that point that I was only wearing the lounge pants Bethany bought me for Christmas—the ones with red and green M&Ms all over them. I hadn't even thought about getting dressed for school, and suddenly I was fighting a panic attack over being late. I didn't get too deep into it before Mayra told me the actual time, and I knew I could get ready without having to rush too much. Rushing put me on edge and screwed up my whole day.

I showered, dressed, and gathered up my book bag. Mayra was in the kitchen when I came downstairs, holding a napkin wrapped around two pieces of buttered toast.

"I don't know what you usually eat for breakfast," she said with a shrug. Her cheekbones turned pink. "Toast okay? We really need to get going."

"Yes," I replied as I reached out and took it from her. I looked from the toast to her face, and for a moment, our eyes locked together before I looked at the toast again. "Thanks."

"You're welcome!" Mayra beamed.

We walked out the garage to head to Mayra's car. As we walked past the mess, I cringed and shook my head. I was a total moron, no doubt about it. I was just glad Mayra didn't seem to be too pissed off at me. As I stepped carefully over the mess, I saw a small rectangle of paper, folded neatly in half.

I couldn't be late for school, so I spent the whole day wondering about it. I couldn't focus on anything in my classes, so the school day was a total loss.

~oOo~

"Have you tried Szechwan?" I asked.

There is nothing better for combating an obsession than fighting with another obsession. The only thing that kept me from freaking out over the state of my garage and the folded-up ticket in the midst of it was Mayra's apparent abhorrence of all things

Chinese. Well, at least food-wise. I had been questioning her about it all day.

"I don't know," Mayra said as she turned the corner and headed toward my street. "All of it is just nasty."

"Even eggrolls?" I reached out and poked at the little scrape mark on the inside of the passenger door of Mayra's car. It was kind of shaped like a fish.

"Ew," Mayra said as she wrinkled her nose. "Breaded, fried cabbage? Really?"

"What about fried rice? Or lo mein?"

"Matthew, you already asked me about those."

"But it's just rice or noodles with some vegetables mixed in with them."

"And that nasty, stinky sauce," Mayra added.

"But...there's this Szechwan place that does eggplant in this dark, spicy sauce—"

"Eggplant is meant to be smothered in parmesan cheese and marinara," Mayra interrupted. "It's what it was born to do."

"Italian food all tastes the same," I remarked, and Mayra glared at me.

"That's because you haven't tasted *my* eggplant parmesan," Mayra said. "Keep dissing Italian food, and I just might have to make it and force you to eat it."

I couldn't decide if it was a threat or a promise.

"What about wonton soup?" I traced the fish shape with the tip of my finger again.

"No!" Mayra screeched, which made me jump. "Now stop that! I do not like Chinese food!"

I tensed a little and brought my hand back into my lap. I was about to apologize, but then her words reminded me of something.

"Not in a box or with a fox?" I asked as I looked at her sideways. "Or on a train or in the rain?"

Mayra laughed.

"I do not like it here or there!" she said through her laughter. "I do not like it *anywhere!*"

She parked in my driveway and grinned at me as she leaned over the steering wheel.

"More project work?" she asked.

"I found an article on a website about global warming and the impact on hibernating bees," I told her. "I was going to print out a copy, but Travis has the only printer. With my car still in the shop…well, I couldn't go over there to print it out, but we can look at it on the computer."

"It's a plan!" Mayra said. She opened up her door and hauled her book bag out with her.

We spent the next couple of hours working on our project and some of the other homework we had. When we both decided we'd had enough, I pulled out two Cokes, two glasses, and eight ice cubes. I assembled the drinks and then carried them into the living room. I set mine down on the coaster and handed Mayra's drink to her.

"I'm going to…um…pick up the garage," I said as I stared at the glass on the table.

"I'll help," Mayra said.

"No," I said as I shook my head. "I still feel bad for waking you up this morning. It won't take me too long."

Mayra agreed to relax inside while I grabbed a new plastic trash bag, a small Ziploc bag, and a pair of rubber gloves to clean up the mess. I was actually quite grateful for the Chinese food because it made me think of all the conversations Mayra and I had on the way to school, between classes, and at lunch. She really didn't like Chinese food, and I still didn't understand why. I was pretty sure if she just tried the right dish, she would like it.

It was enough of a distraction that I managed to scoop everything up into a new trash bag and toss it all back into the larger can pretty quickly and without feeling like I was either going to puke or freak out. I was going to have to mop as well, but I thought I would be able to wait until Mayra went home before I did that.

The only thing left on the floor was the small, folded paper ticket.

I swallowed a couple of times as I walked around it. It felt both innocent and ominous all at the same time. For a brief moment I understood why people bought them—it wasn't because they thought they were going to win; it was the possibility of winning. How would they feel if they realized they had the winning ticket? What would they buy first? Would they donate a lot of it to charity? Give it to friends? Winning isn't the attraction; the attraction is the opportunity to dream.

I picked up the ticket and held it between my yellow-gloved fingers. It had just a bit of duck sauce on the side of it, but it didn't look like it was really messy or anything. I'd still eventually have to clean it with some Lysol wipes or something, though. I turned it around a couple of times, then slid it inside the little plastic Ziploc bag and sealed it up.

Like Schrödinger's Cat, looking at the numbers would only collapse the waveform.

Mayra was just finishing her drink when I came back into the living room.

"Dad texted me, saying he was going to be late," Mayra informed me. "So I've got some extra time. Do you want to watch TV or something?"

"Okay," I replied.

"What do you have there?" Mayra asked as she nodded toward my hands.

"Nothing." I quickly hid the plastic bag behind me, then kind of walked backwards into the kitchen and shoved it into the drawer next to the scissors.

Mayra narrowed her eyes and shook her head at me. She headed down the short set of stairs to the lower level and the family room with the television. She grabbed the remote and dropped onto the loveseat. I slowly walked over and sat down beside her on the other side of the small couch, determined to put all thoughts of dirty lottery tickets out of my head.

We found a repeat episode of *MythBusters*.

"I love this one," Mayra said. "The whole bit where they just crash the car between the semis is about as inspired as destruction gets."

I had to laugh.

We watched in silence until the commercials started. That's when the phone rang. When I answered, it was Megan's doctor on the line.

"Hello, Matthew," Dr. Harris said. "I need to talk to you about your sister."

"Is Megan okay?"

"She's fine," Dr. Harris said. "We just need to adjust her medication."

Dr. Harris went on for a while about drug interactions and how this new treatment might actually make Megan more communicative. I had heard it all before. When the doctor was done, she got to the point.

"I'll need you to sign a few forms," she said. "Basically the same forms you have signed before, just with the different dosages. Should I send them to your uncle's fax machine at work?"

"Yes," I said. "I'll look them over and get them back to you."

"Thanks, Matthew. You take care."

"Bye."

I hung up the phone and saw Mayra watching me.

"Your sister?" Mayra asked.

I nodded.

"It was her doctor," I said. "I have some forms I have to sign."

I sat back down and stared at my hands in my lap. The last time we changed Megan's medicine, she completely freaked out for about four days. She eventually settled back down, but the doctor had to adjust the medicine three times before she went back to normal. Well, normal for Megan.

"Matthew?"

"Yes?"

"Will you tell me more about your sister?"

I thought about it for a minute, finally deciding I wanted Mayra to know about Megan. I didn't want to keep anything from her, and Megan was important.

"Megan is four years older than me," I said. It seemed like as good a place as any to start. "I can't really talk about her without explaining about me, too, though."

"I'd like to know more about you," Mayra confirmed.

I nodded to her.

"I didn't understand that there was anything different about Megan until it was time for me to go to school. That's when my parents figured out I was different, too, just not in the exact same way."

I swallowed and twisted my fingers around each other.

"I guess I thought I would go to school with Megan. She went three days a week, and when she went, Dad would work from home or something while mom took her there. I kind of remember people talking about me starting school, and I just assumed I would attend the same school as Megan. I had it all worked out in my head. I was a little shocked on the first day when mom put us both in the car and then preceded to drop me off somewhere else."

I let out a humorless laugh.

"Okay, shocked isn't quite the right word," I admitted. "I went ballistic. I never really had a breakdown before then because at home, there was already a very strict routine for Megan, and I just fit into it. It was the first time something *unexpected* happened to me. I screamed and I kicked, and I tried to bite the teacher, generally freaking Mom out. Mom's freaking out made Megan freak out and…well, it was a mess."

"I can imagine," Mayra replied softly.

"Mom had to call Dad, who had to leave work to come and get me. I didn't go to the first day of school, and Dad took me home, and we talked about it a lot. He told me what was going to be there and everything. The next day, he drove me to school and walked me to the kindergarten room. I managed to last about all of ten minutes after he left, which is when I ended up in the corner screaming. That was my first real panic attack."

"Holy shit," Mayra said with a sharp breath.

"Yeah, it wasn't pretty, I guess." I took a deep breath. "I saw a bunch of doctors then, and Mom was really upset. She kept saying I wasn't like Megan at all—that she knew I was different from my sister. The problem was, she didn't have any normal kids to compare us to. I would talk for the most part, just not the same way other kids my age did."

I stopped talking for a minute and tried to figure out what I was supposed to say next.

"She thought you were okay," Mayra said. "It must have been really hard on her to hear that you weren't."

"It was," I said with a nod. "Megan didn't talk at all until she was four, and then she only talked about clocks and time. They knew there was something wrong with her early on. Mom always thought I was all right."

"Because you're on a different part of the…what is it? The autism spectrum?"

"Yeah." I remembered I was really supposed to be talking about Megan and tried to focus a bit more. "Megan gets upset when people touch her. I mean, really upset. I can tense up when I'm not expecting it, and it makes me kind of uncomfortable, but Megan screams and cries if you try to hug her or something like that. She doesn't like new people either. It takes her a long time before she'll let someone unfamiliar be in the room with her."

"What does she do?"

"She usually just curls up on a chair and won't acknowledge anyone," I told Mayra. "Sometimes she gets more noticeably upset. She'll start doing the same thing over and over again, like rocking back and forth."

I felt myself tense up a little bit, and I glanced at Mayra sitting next to me. She was just looking at me with her head tilted a little to the side.

"Animals tilt their heads to expose their necks," I said. "It's a sign of deference."

"What?" Mayra asked, obviously confused.

"Sorry." I shook my head at myself. "Sometimes I just say random shit."

We were quiet again for a minute, but Mayra didn't break the silence. She just waited for me to go on.

"When Mom got sick, and we had to move Megan to the institution in Cincinnati, she pulled out most of her hair."

"She what?" Mayra asked.

"She pulled her hair out, one strand at a time," I confirmed. "She wouldn't stop, no matter what they did. Eventually they had to keep her sedated when she went to bed."

"Oh my God," Mayra murmured.

I swallowed and waited for a minute before I heard myself say something I wasn't planning on talking about at all.

"I've done stuff like that, too."

"You pulled your hair out?" Mayra gasped.

"No...I, um..." I stopped, wondering if I really wanted to go there and decided I probably didn't. My voice dropped. "Other stuff...I don't want to say."

Mayra shifted a little closer to me, and I felt my body seize up.

"It's okay," Mayra said softly. "You don't have to tell me."

I closed my eyes and tried to fight off the instant panic. I didn't even know where it was coming from or if it was just because of my own stupid mouth. Talking brought on panic. That's why I didn't do it. I never made any sense, and I just made people think I was weird.

Right now, everything seemed so good with Mayra, and I probably just fucked it up. What if Mayra decided I was too strange to hang out with anymore?

Shit, shit, shit.

"Matthew, it's okay..." I heard her saying through the haze that had become my mind.

I jumped when I felt her hand on my arm and pulled away.

"I'm sorry," she said quietly. "I just...I don't know what to do."

I rubbed at the nail of my thumb with my other thumb three times and then switched hands. I kept my eyes closed and focused on the pressure against the nails, alternating back and forth over and over again.

"I play with my hands," I heard myself say. "I don't know why."

"It's all right," Mayra said again.

There was more silence.

"Matthew, would it be okay if..."

"If what?" I asked.

"If I gave you another hug?" she finally asked.

I was still tense, and my body didn't seem very willing to let that go. I tried to remember what it was like the last time she hugged me, and I didn't feel any worse, so I nodded.

I felt the tips of her fingers on my shoulder, and then I felt them move around the back of my neck to grip my other shoulder. With her other hand, she reached across me and held on to the top of my arm. She tugged slightly then, bringing me a little closer to her. I was too tense and didn't move much, so she shifted herself closer to me until I felt my head come into contact with her shoulder.

My eyes stayed closed as I inhaled the scent of her skin. I realized I was shaking and wanted to pull away out of embarrassment, but I didn't. I just stayed where I was, and Mayra didn't move either. After a few minutes, I reached one arm around her middle, and dug the other one between her back and the couch cushions.

"I'm sorry you've had to go through so much," Mayra told me. "I'm sorry you've had to deal with all this shit when you shouldn't have to. I wish there was something I could do…"

I tightened my grip on her a little and felt her do the same.

I don't know how long we were like that, with me wrapped up in her arms on the couch, but it felt like forever and an instant all at once. At some point, exhaustion seemed to take over, and I ended up with my head in her lap.

Another episode of *MythBusters* came on—the channel we were watching seemed to be running a marathon—and we both just started watching it. I felt Mayra's hand shift to my head, and she began to thread her fingers through my hair.

I couldn't bear the thought of changing positions, so I just stayed that way on the couch until Mayra had to go home. The conversation had been difficult, but I felt relieved when it was over, so I considered the day a win.

Chapter 7—Let's See How I Can Embarrass Myself Further

Our arrangement became routine.

Every day, Mayra picked me up and took me to school in her Porsche. We didn't usually talk very much during that time because Mayra is a self-proclaimed "non-morning person." During school, things were pretty much the same as always—I went to classes, saw Mayra during ecology, tried to ignore Justin Lords, and ate lunch with Joe. When school was over, Mayra drove me home.

Once we got to my house, we worked on our project or other homework, drank Cokes in the living room, then went downstairs and watched television. Mayra sat on the left side of the loveseat, and I would lie down with my head in her lap. She'd run her fingers through my hair while we watched either *MythBusters*, *Big Bang Theory*, or sometimes even *Top Gear*. I was pretty sure Mayra didn't like *Top Gear* too much, so we usually watched one of the others.

I should have known it couldn't last.

It was the following Thursday, and I had all but fallen asleep to the feeling of Mayra's fingers in my hair when the phone rang. When I answered it, it was the body shop telling me my car was ready for pickup.

"Cool!" Mayra said when I told her. "Now you can get yourself around again."

"Yeah." I swallowed and nodded, trying to keep the feeling of dread that was washing over me from turning into something worse.

I closed my eyes for a moment, barely hearing Mayra's offer to drive me over to the shop. If she wasn't driving me to school, would she still come over to the house? We had just finished up the last of our project—it was due the next day—so there wouldn't really be a reason for her to be there. I might start getting to sleep earlier since I had been working late to get all my website work done. I could probably pick up a couple other website jobs to take up the extra time.

I didn't *want* any other website jobs.

I wanted Mayra to come over, work on homework, and watch TV with me. I wanted to sit with her and feel her hands in my hair. I wanted to laugh at *Big Bang Theory* with her and talk about the crazy stuff that came out of Adam Savage's mouth on *MythBusters*.

The very idea of her not being here anymore after school was absolutely terrifying.

"Matthew? What's wrong?"

I couldn't answer. I couldn't think. I could barely breathe. I couldn't imagine coming home alone after school again every day with no one there anymore to talk to or just sit beside. Usually when I knew something was going to change, I could come up with something to fill the hole but not this time.

My chest felt like it was collapsing, and I realized I was on the floor though I wasn't sure how I got there. Mayra's voice was ringing through my ears, but I couldn't decipher her words. My own voice chimed into the mix, but I wasn't sure what I was saying either.

Everything grew blurry and then went dark.

The next thing I heard was a list of numbers.

"One, two, four, eight, sixteen…"

My back and shoulders were achy.

"Thirty-two, sixty-four…"

My stomach turned on me. There was a nasty taste in my mouth, and I wondered if I had thrown up.

"One twenty-eight, two…um…two fifty-four…"

"Two fifty-six," I corrected. "Five hundred twelve, one thousand twenty-four, two thousand forty-eight."

"There ya go…come back to me, dude." Travis's voice was soft but still penetrating. "Everything's okay. You're home; I'm here; Mayra's even here. Count with me, dude."

I took a deep breath and continued reciting numbers. When I opened my eyes, Travis was crouched down on the floor next to me, and Mayra was standing behind him. Her eyes were red, and she was squeezing her hands together.

"Fuck," I whispered.

Travis laughed quietly.

"There ya go," he said again. "It's all good."

"Do you want this?" I heard Mayra ask.

I glanced up to see her handing Travis a glass of water. He handed it to me, and I took a sip and gave it back to him. It was kind of hard to swallow, and I wondered why my throat was so sore.

Shit, shit, shit.

There was really only one reason—I must have been screaming.

Shit, shit, shit.

I must have had a full-fledged panic attack with Mayra here.

Closing my eyes again, I put my hands over my face, which was already feeling warm to my touch. I was pretty sure I had never been more embarrassed in my life. Mayra had obviously called Travis, who then had to drive over here and pull me out of it. I wondered how much time had passed.

Glancing through my fingers at the digital numbers on the cable box, I saw that it was already after seven o'clock. The last *Big*

Bang episode had just started before the phone rang, which meant it had been at least twenty minutes.

Shit, shit, shit.

"I'm sorry," I mumbled through my hands.

"Dude, shut up," Travis muttered back. "You don't have to apologize."

I glanced at Mayra and then quickly looked back down again.

"You should probably go," Travis said as he looked over his shoulder. "Thanks a lot for calling. I'll make sure we get his car to him."

"No!" I cried out, then immediately buried my head in my hands again.

"No what?" Travis asked.

"I don't want my car!" I told him.

"That's what he meant," Mayra said. Her eyes grew wide. "He kept saying he didn't want it back."

Travis looked at Mayra and then back at me.

"Why don't you want your car?"

I didn't answer. It would just sound ridiculous if I did. He asked again, and I just shook my head.

"You gotta go back into therapy, dude," Travis said with a big sigh. "You gotta go back on the meds."

"Too expensive," I said.

"Beth and I will pay for them."

"You can't afford it."

"We'll figure it out."

I shook my head again. We went back and forth for a while, and I eventually won though I had to promise to at least talk to my doctor if I had another bad episode. Once I seemed to be together again, Mayra gathered up her stuff and started to leave.

"I'm sorry," I said for the tenth time.

"It's okay, Matthew," Mayra said softly. "I'm just glad you are all right. You scared me."

"I didn't mean to scare you."

"I know," she said. She tilted her head to look up at me. I moved my eyes away, focusing on her shoulder. "It's too late to get your car now, isn't it?"

"Yeah."

"I'll see you in the morning, then?"

I felt my mouth turn up into a slight smile.

"Yeah, that would be good. Thanks."

"See you then."

The door closed behind her, and Travis leaned against the entryway to the kitchen and stared at me.

"This is certainly interesting," he muttered.

I couldn't really add anything to that comment, so I went and lay back down on the loveseat.

Travis tried to talk to me, but it wasn't working, so he let me just kind of lie there for a while. The TV was on, but I wasn't really watching it. I couldn't even tell you what the show was. I didn't really think about anything, either. Often when I've had a bad attack, I just feel kind of wiped out and empty afterwards.

Bethany showed up a while later and cooked dinner. I had no idea what we ate, but it was good, and I felt a little more human afterwards. I washed the dishes slowly while Travis and Bethany argued quietly in the living room. After a few minutes, Travis came back into the kitchen, all tight-lipped, and babbled something about needing to go grocery shopping. By the time I was done drying, he was gone, and it was just Bethany and me.

I had placed the final fork in the drawer and hung the little green hand towel over the handle of the oven before I looked up at my aunt. She stood and crossed her arms as she leaned against the doorway between the kitchen and the dining room.

"I thought this girl made you feel calm," Beth said suddenly. "You look like you've been through a tornado."

"It wasn't her," I said defensively.

"What was it, then?" Bethany pressed me for an answer. "Something with the car?"

"I don't want it back," I said, almost growling. I knew immediately that I made a mistake. Bethany's eyes lit up like she hit some kind of jackpot, and there was no way she was going to let go of the topic until I told her everything. She was just too perceptive.

"You hated having to put it in the shop," Bethany said. "Why the change of heart?"

I knew at that point that there was just no getting out of it. Besides, there was a grocery sack on the counter, which most likely held the ingredients to something delicious. So I told her about Mayra driving me to and from school and hanging out at the house afterwards. I told her about how we would sit on the couch, and she would touch my hair.

"You used to do that to Megan," Bethany said. "Do you remember?"

"Do what?"

"She would lie down on the floor, and you would braid her hair," Bethany said. "You were pretty young—maybe four or five— but you loved to braid her hair. You'd make a hundred of them all over her head and then take them all out again. Megan would just lie there and let you."

"I don't remember."

"It was before Travis and I were married," Bethany recalled aloud. "I'm sure of that. I don't think Megan ever tried to do the same with your hair. She wouldn't let anyone else do that to her, either."

"I remember your wedding," I said.

"I don't see how you could." Beth snorted. "You were in hiding throughout the whole ceremony!"

Flashes of Beth's white dress and the itchy collar of the tux I had to wear as the ring bearer paraded between my ears. I never made it down the aisle—as soon as I saw all of those people, I hid underneath the pastor's desk, and they couldn't make me come out. Mom ended up missing most of the wedding.

"Want to go sit down in the family room?" Beth asked.

I nodded and followed her downstairs. When she got there, she dropped down on the left side of the loveseat, which made me cringe. It didn't look right—not at all. Mayra was supposed to be sitting there or at least someone with brown hair, not blonde.

"What is it?" Beth said as she looked at me sideways. "I must be doing something wrong."

"Mayra sits there," I told her.

"And plays with your hair?"

"Yeah."

"Then sit down with me," she commanded.

I sighed and sat down next to Bethany. Flopping over sideways, I placed my head in her lap and tried not to tense up too much as her hand touched the top of my head. It didn't feel like it did when Mayra touched my hair—not at all—but it wasn't bad.

"Like this?" Beth asked.

It wasn't, but I nodded anyway.

"We never continued our conversation," she reminded me.

"I don't think you ever really started it," I told her.

Beth laughed.

"You are the one who said you didn't know anything about sex and dating," she said. "If that were the truth, how do you know if we have talked about it or not?"

Twisting my neck around to look up, I scowled at her. Bethany remained unfazed as she looked down at me with her eyebrow raised. I rolled my eyes and looked back toward the television. It was off now, but I stared at the blank screen anyway.

"Did you ever ask her to go to dinner?"

I shook my head.

"We were going to practice that."

"I don't want to," I told her.

She scratched gently against my scalp.

"Of course you don't want to," she said. "No one wants to, but if you want to ask her out, how else are you going to get ready?"

"Maybe I won't ask her out," I said.

"You changed your mind?"

I shrugged again.

"You know I have a bag full of cupcakes up there," Bethany said. "Red velvet cupcakes."

"With cream cheese icing?"

"Yep."

My gaze darted to hers briefly.

"Sprinkles?"

"The tiny dark red ones," she said. "The kind that match the color of the cake."

She didn't play fair. *At all.*

"Fine." I sighed. "It's just that…everything is just right as it is now. If I get my car back, then there isn't a reason for her to come over anymore. The same goes for asking her out. Right now, she's here with me every day after school. What if I ask her out and she says no? She might get mad and not ever come over again. What if she says yes but then has a horrible time?"

"Have you kissed her?" Bethany asked.

"What?" I replied as I gathered myself again. "No!"

"Would you like to?"

"I…I…I don't know."

"Come on, Matthew." Bethany continued to press for an answer. "Close your eyes for a minute."

I scowled at her again.

"You want those cupcakes?"

I growled under my breath but did as she said.

"Now think about kissing her," Bethany said quietly. "Just keep your eyes closed, and think about it."

Her suggestion was enough to get my mind going.

In my head, Beth's hands become Mayra's, and she is here with me on the loveseat. I turn over and actually look into her deep brown eyes—keeping my focus on them for far longer than I really would be able to do. I sit up slowly, moving closer and closer to her

118

until our lips touch. Hers are warm and soft, and I can feel my heart pounding in my chest.

My eyes fluttered open, and my tongue darted out over my lips. It was a little difficult to catch my breath.

"You want that to ever be reality?" my aunt asked, her tone still soft.

"Yes," I whispered back.

"Then you have to start by asking her out." Beth shifted in the seat, and I sat up next to her. "You have to take the first step, or you are going to be stuck where you are now with no chance of progress. This is just like when you moved from junior high to high school. Remember how much you didn't want to go? But you couldn't stay in eighth grade forever, could you?"

"No."

"And you can't just sit here day after day watching television with Mayra if you ever want a chance at something more."

"I'm scared," I admitted.

"I know you are, sweetie," Bethany said with a gentle nod. "And you know what the awesome thing is? Everyone is scared about this. It's not just you."

I peeked at her sideways before I started rubbing at my thumbnails and twisting my fingers around. As I contemplated, Beth sat quietly and waited. She was right, and I knew it. I did want the chance at something else—something I never really considered with any girl, let alone someone like Mayra. If I had to take the next step and ask her out in order to have that possibility, I was going to do it.

I couldn't bear the thought of stagnation, so I agreed to practice asking Mayra out on a date.

A half hour later, I lost it.

"This just isn't going to work!" I yelled and stomped out of the family room. I turned abruptly and headed down the stairs to the basement. The heavy bag took the brunt of my anger, frustration, and disappointment in myself.

By the time I was done, my muscles were sore, and I was still a mess. The exertion had exhausted me but didn't do much for my state of mind. On a plate for me, Bethany had a cupcake, which I ate in silence when I came back upstairs,.

"You want to try again?" she asked as I polished off a second one.

"No."

"You know that isn't going to fly with me."

"If I can't even ask you, how am I supposed to ask Mayra?" I mumbled. "Besides, there is absolutely no way she is going to say yes."

"Why the hell not?"

"Seriously, Beth? I mean, I know you weren't here earlier, but it's not like you haven't seen it before. Why would anyone agree to go out with me after watching me freak out? I'm a fucking mess!"

I pushed myself out of the chair and stalked off with no particular destination in mind. I ended up standing in the middle of the living room and staring out the window at the trees in the woods. The squirrels were back.

I hadn't meant to blow up at Bethany. I knew she was trying to help, and I knew she just wanted what was best for me, but even she had to realize there wasn't any hope. I was about as lost as a lost cause could get.

"Matthew, stop it."

"Stop what?" I snapped.

"Stop beating yourself up," she said. "I thought you had taken all that out on the punching bag."

"Well, for as big of an idiot as I am, the bag isn't nearly enough."

"Matthew…"—my aunt sighed and flopped down on the couch—"you are far from being an idiot. As a matter of fact, *very* far from it. You also have a lot to offer a girl."

I snorted.

"Yeah—instability and insanity. What a catch I am."
Set sarcasm to *kill*.

"That's enough!" Beth yelled loud enough to make me jump a little. I glanced over to her, and her face was bright red. "You are not unstable or insane, dammit! You have a mild form of an extremely common disorder that a lot of people live with day in and day out. You are smart, dedicated, sweet, and hot as hell! I can't believe there aren't dozens of girls asking *you* out!"

"Don't be ridiculous." I furrowed my brow and looked away from her.

"I'm not," she stated. "It's probably highly inappropriate or something, but Matthew, you are an extremely attractive guy. Don't you ever look in the mirror?"

"Of course," I said, still frowning. "And what you are saying is still ridiculous."

"It's not."

"Girls don't look at me like that," I said. "They don't look at me at all."

"For the love of God," Bethany moaned. She stood up and headed out of the room. "Come on!"

I followed her down to the den where the computer was. She dropped herself onto the desk chair and pulled up Facebook. I watched her log in and scroll around until she came across a photograph from Christmas. Travis was standing by the tree and hanging up ornaments, and I was sitting at the foot of it with a string of lights in my hands, smiling up at the camera.

I couldn't recall what Travis had said to make me laugh, but I did recall Bethany taking the picture when I wasn't expecting it. I didn't usually care to have my picture taken, and she had just called my name and snapped the picture before I could react. I didn't like looking into the camera, so pictures usually came out with me looking like I was constipated or something.

"I wasn't going to show you this," Bethany said, "but you obviously have no clue, do you?"

121

"No clue about what?" I asked.

"Read this," Beth said. She scooted the chair back so I could get a look at all of the comments listed under the picture.

Who is the guy on the floor?

Hot damn! That's your nephew? Makes me wish I was twenty years younger!

OMG, what a hottie!

Whoa—do you have to lock him up at night?

I bet the girls in his school fail classes just watching him!

Send him over my way, please!

There were pages and pages of similar comments.

"If you had ever given girls a chance to get to know you," Bethany said softly from behind me, "and they found out how warm and caring you are, I don't see how any of them could resist you. It's very obvious Mayra cares about you, or she wouldn't be spending all her free time over here, would she?"

"I don't know," I mumbled. I scrolled back up and looked at the picture, trying to figure out what Bethany's friends were talking about. It was just me. My hair was a mess like it always was. With the Christmas tree in the background, you could tell my eyes were green. I did look a little different from a lot of pictures of me but only because I was smiling and looking at the camera.

"Travis thought you'd be embarrassed if I showed this to you," Beth said, "but I think at this point, you need to know. You're a good-looking guy, Matthew. Any girl who says no to you would have to be blind and stupid."

"Mayra's not stupid," I said defensively. "She's really smart."

"You're making my point."

I shook my head slowly and read a few more of the comments. They all had a pretty similar tone though knowing most of Bethany's friends were thirty or so made me feel weird. I glanced over at her.

"You think she might say yes?" I asked.

"You won't know unless you manage to ask her," Bethany replied with a raised brow.

I couldn't argue anymore, so I agreed to go back to practicing. The whole activity was incredibly stressful, and I went to bed with my stomach in knots.

There's no way I'll ever manage to ask Mayra out.

Lose.

Chapter 8—Sometimes You Just Have to Go for It

"Are you all right?" Mayra asked for the twelfth time that day. She slowed the car down to take the curve into my neighborhood as I tried to keep my heart from actually jumping out of my chest.

It had been like that all day. Every time I got near her, I could hear the words in my head that I had practiced with Bethany. I couldn't say them, but they kept going through my head anyway. I took a deep breath and poked at the little scratchy fish-mark on the inside of the door, realizing at the same time that it had become a habit. Habits were dangerous for me, since once I started a pattern, I could almost never stop, but at least it was distracting me from the topic at hand.

"Matthew?" Mayra's voice dropped a little, and I glanced at her.

"Sorry," I mumbled.

"It's okay," she said. "You just seem very distracted today."

I snorted a little.

"I'm usually distracted," I said.

"More than usual," Mayra said, amending her statement.

"Just thinking," I admitted.

"About?"

SHAY SAVAGE

About asking you to go to dinner with me tomorrow.

I didn't actually say anything, just like I hadn't said anything the other eleven times she had asked today. I closed my eyes for a minute and pictured what I had practiced with Bethany the night before. My mouth ached to make the words, but I couldn't seem to do it.

With my eyes directed out the passenger side window, I decided to start a little easier.

"Tomorrow is Saturday," I said. That was a good start, wasn't it?

"Yes," Mayra replied. She looked over at me as she drew out the word.

"Are you, um…? I mean, do you…?" I trailed off, trying to figure out exactly what I wanted to say. The windows were a little steamy from the cold rain outside and the warmth coming from the car's heater. As I spoke, I watched my breath spread condensation on the window. "Are you…*doing* anything tomorrow?"

"Not really," Mayra said with a shrug. She flipped up the turn signal and sat to wait for an oncoming car to pass, then pulled into my driveway and shut off the vehicle. "Dad was supposed to go fishing with one of his friends from Hamilton, but I guess that got canceled. I'll probably get that English paper done early if I can't come up with anything else to do."

It was now or never.

With a pounding heart, shaking hands, and unsteady breaths, I spit it out.

"*Doyouwanttogotodinnerwithme?*"

I closed my eyes and tried to endure the silence that came afterwards. I could hear my own breathing and beating heart, but they were loud enough that everything else was blocked out. I was probably pretty close to exploding when I felt the edge of Mayra's finger against my hand.

126

"Matthew Rohan"—Mayra's voice contained both a tone of surprise and a hint of a fake southern accent—"I do believe you are asking me out on a date."

"Would that, um…?" I had to stop, swallow a couple of times, and then take a deep breath to go on in a voice low enough I could barely hear myself. "Would that be okay?"

"Yes, it would be," Mayra said with a soft laugh. "I'm glad you finally asked me."

"You are?" I glanced at her quickly and then looked back to my hands.

"It took you long enough," Mayra said. When I peeked at her face, she was smiling.

"I didn't know what you would say," I admitted.

Yes. She said yes. *She said yes to* me.

"After all the time we spend together?" Mayra shook her head a little. "We're going to work on that self-confidence."

"We are?"

"Yep."

She turned toward me then, first bending her knees up onto the seat and then raising herself up so she was sitting on her legs, facing me. She angled her head off to the left to look into my face. I didn't move. My insides were still all twisted up.

"You know," Mayra said softly as she tilted her head farther over to look at me, "I was just about to give up hope. I would have asked you out a long time ago, but I wasn't sure how you would take it. I'm glad you finally asked me."

"You are?" I glanced up at her for a moment then looked away again. Everything was happening so fast and so slow at the same time, which was leaving me horribly confused.

"Of course I am." In my peripheral vision, I could see her shaking her head.

"You never look at me," Mayra remarked suddenly.

I tensed and tried to understand her tone. She didn't seem angry, but memories of other times when people have made the same statement in anger were haunting me. It was often the last thing they would say before walking away from me and not coming back.

"I do," I whispered as fear began to creep in. My hands were starting to shake. "I look at you more than almost anyone else."

"It's okay." I heard her quiet voice beside me. I stared down at my lap as she moved a little closer. "Matthew, really—it's all right."

I felt the tips of her finger against my jaw.

"Just look at me," she said quietly. "I'm not going to hurt you."

I forced my eyes in her direction as she put pressure against my jaw, turning me toward her. Her eyes were so flawlessly brown, and her lashes were only slightly darker and completely devoid of any chemical compounds to make them look longer. They didn't need it.

So beautiful.

Unable to hold her gaze any longer, I lowered my eyes and looked to the right, focusing on the light green stripe that ran down the sleeve of her shirt. Every muscle was still tensed, and I knew I would have to hit the heavy bag tonight.

"Why is it so hard?" she asked.

I had no idea what to say. No one had ever asked me before. No one had ever just come right out and asked like that. How could I explain that sometimes it actually *hurt* to look people in the eye, like maybe they could see into me and see something awful? Even worse, maybe I would see something inside of their souls, and I would find out something horrible about them. What if reincarnation was real, and if I looked long enough, I would be able to see the past lives of the souls inside of people?

Maybe she'd figure out what a total freak I was for even thinking these things.

Her fingers stroked over the edge of my jaw, tickling it a little. I tried to glance at her again, but I still couldn't hold my gaze.

I looked down, and my eyes focused on her mouth as she wet her lips with her tongue.

"It just is," I finally said. It was probably the lamest answer in the world, but it was all I had.

"Close them, then," she said.

"What?" I asked. I looked at her lips again as she moved a little closer to me, so close, our faces were almost touching.

"Just close your eyes," she said softly.

Not ready, I thought to myself, but the internal battle had already gone into overdrive. I knew what she was thinking—I didn't have to be a mind reader to understand as she moved our mouths closer together. Part of me wanted to run screaming from the car, but there was another part, one deep inside the pit of my stomach, that wanted to know what it was like.

My eyelids drifted closed.

I felt the touch of her lips—warm and soft—against mine.

I couldn't believe what was happening, but there was no way I was going to stop it.

I didn't move.

I didn't even *breathe*.

When I felt the touch of Mayra's lips against mine, I just froze. I sat there on the seat of the car with my eyes closed and just felt the pressure of her mouth on mine. She pushed gently, then just a little harder. My first and second kisses combined. The pressure stopped briefly as I heard Mayra take a short breath and then resumed.

I still didn't move.

My heart was pounding in my chest, harder than it had been when I was trying to ask her out. My hands clenched a little against my legs as Mayra's hand pushed against the side of my face. Her touch was soft, and where I would have normally leaned against her palm, I still did not move at all.

The cool air around us brushed over my mouth as Mayra moved away and sat back on her heels. Parting my eyelids, I focused on her knees beside me, my body still turned away from hers. With my gaze locked on her knees, I ran my tongue over my lips. They tasted different than I was used to, but it was okay. It was better than okay.

It was good.

Really good.

Mayra's lips moved then.

"I'm sorry," she whispered. "I shouldn't have done that."

"What?" I muttered as I tried to wrap my head around what she was saying.

"I shouldn't have pushed you, Matthew—I'm so sorry!"

I blinked a few times and looked up at her eyes, which were tight and full of concern. Looking back to her lips, I wondered what I had done wrong to make her think she needed to apologize for anything, but I couldn't find any words. I licked my lips again as I remembered the pressure against my mouth.

I hadn't kissed her back.

Shit, shit, shit.

She must believe I didn't want her to or that I didn't like it because I hadn't kissed her back. I was completely and totally inexperienced, but I'd certainly seen enough television to know you are supposed to kiss back.

"Again?" I asked quietly as I turned my eyes up to meet hers.

Mayra paused and looked at me as I tried to hold her gaze. I didn't last long—I had to look away after only a few seconds—but I kept glancing back to her eyes.

"Are you sure?" she asked.

"Yes," I replied with a nod.

Her whole body seemed to relax a little as she shifted in the seat and brought her hand back up to my face. Her fingers trailed over my jaw and into the hair at the back of my neck as she leaned in again. I closed my eyes until I felt the touch of her lips on mine.

I pressed back.

Slowly.

Carefully.

Testing it all out.

For a fleeting moment, I was taken back to the first time my dad took me to the gym. There was a trainer there who led me to the back and showed me how to put on the boxing gloves and then how to hit the heavy bag. The first couple of times I hit it, it felt both strange and good all at once. Then once I got the rhythm, my trainer had to practically pull me away from it to get me to stop.

I pressed again, feeling her lips move with mine as I increased the force. Her fingers curled around my neck, encouraging me to move more, so I did. My head tilted to the side as I kissed her again, harder this time. I reached out and touched her leg, then ran up the outside of her thigh to her hip, where my fingers gripped her right at the edge of her jeans.

Mayra gasped a little as I pulled her closer to me, wrapping my other arm around her shoulders and turning my head the opposite direction at the same time. Her tongue touched my lips, and I didn't hesitate at all to meet it with my own.

Better than chocolate cake.

Her tongue felt smooth against mine, and I found myself rising up to my knees like she was—turning sideways in the car and finding myself somewhat above her to avoid the emergency brake between us. It gave me a better angle, and I used it. I kissed her again, my tongue in her mouth and my hands twisting her back down against the seat. Her legs unfolded from below her, and a moment later, I was on top of her in the driver's seat, still not removing my mouth from hers.

We just kept kissing and kissing and kissing.

My lower leg was really uncomfortable, and one of my arms was kind of trapped underneath her body so I couldn't move it, but my other hand was free. I ran it up and down her side as our mouths moved together. Mayra's fingers dug into my hair with a sensation that was definitely different from when we sat and watched

131

television but still felt really good. She used her other hand to grip my back, which sent small shivers all over my skin.

Every once in a while, we would pause to take a breath, but that was about it. Other than that, we remained the same—mouths locked, hearts pounding, and Mayra's body pinned beneath mine in her car. I never wanted it to stop, and if left to my own devices, I might very well have just starved to death rather than move away.

"Matthew," Mayra mumbled against my lips.

"Mayra," I replied, mumbling against hers. My mom had been a big fan of the daytime soaps, and I was pretty sure that was the right response.

"Matthew…stop."

I sucked in a breath as I pulled away. That single word felt like a punch to the chest, and my mind started spinning in a counterclockwise circle. I hated it when my mind went counterclockwise. As I hovered over Mayra and wondered what I had done wrong, I realized just what sort of position we were in.

I had one leg over her lap, practically holding her down in the seat of her car. The windows were all steamed up, and when I looked down at Mayra's face, her lips were all red and puffy.

"Shit, shit, shit—I'm sorry!" I cried out as I backed away from her and into the passenger seat.

Mayra immediately giggled. She shifted herself up in the seat and tried to smooth out her hair a bit with her fingers.

"For what?" she asked. "Practically kissing me to death? I didn't mind at all."

"You said 'stop.'" I narrowed my eyes and looked off to her shoulder, perplexed.

"Matthew, we've been at it for a while, and this seat is not exactly comfortable."

"Oh."

She leaned farther up in the seat and brought our lips together briefly.

"How about we take this inside?"

"We haven't kissed in there before," I told her. I couldn't even imagine it.

"We haven't kissed in here before," Mayra pointed out. She waved her hand toward the foggy windows and giggled again.

"I wasn't thinking."

"You aren't supposed to think about it," Mayra said. "You're supposed to just let it happen."

"But if we go inside, I will be thinking about it."

"Don't." Mayra shrugged her shoulders.

"I have to." I sat with my back against the seat and ran my hands through my hair. "When we go in my house, first we do our homework. Then we drink Cokes in the living room, and then we watch TV. It's what we *do*."

"Are you telling me that we can only make out in my car?" From the corner of my eye, I could see Mayra looking at me. She was shaking her head and probably deciding I really was a nutcase.

"Probably not..." My voice trailed off. "There could be other places. Just...we can't when we're supposed to be doing those other things."

Mayra let out a long sigh as she slumped against the seat.

"What about add-ons?" she asked abruptly.

"Add-ons?"

"Yeah." Mayra sat up straighter and turned toward me again. "Like, could I give you a kiss when you bring me a Coke? As a thank-you?"

I thought about that for a little bit. When I brought her the Coke I poured for her, I usually bent down a little to place it on the coaster. Our heads were close together then, and if I just turned a little, we *could* kiss.

"That *might* work," I said with a nod.

"I'm glad to hear there's some room for negotiation," Mayra said. She chuckled quietly. "Let's get inside and see what we can work out because I am *not* done with you, Matthew Rohan."

"Okay." Wondering just what she might have meant by her last statement, I opened up the door beside me and backed out of the car while I grabbed my book bag from the floor. As I climbed out, I poked the little fish shape one more time—maybe just for good luck or something—and then shut the door.

As I turned to go to the house, I was confused by the presence of my own car in the driveway, parked next to Mayra's car. While I tried to figure out just how it had managed to appear there— it was certainly not there when Mayra and I first pulled up—I heard a sound to my left.

Travis was leaning against the hood of the car with his arms folded over his chest and his eyebrows raised. There was a bit of a smirk on his face as he looked me up and down and scratched the back of his head with his fingertips.

"Having a good day?" he asked with a snicker.

I couldn't really deny it, so I took a deep breath and faced my uncle. Before I could say anything, Mayra's voice distracted me.

"Oh my God! My hair is a disaster!"

Mayra laughed as she climbed out of the car and tried to smooth the hair on the back of her head with her fingers. It really was all over the place, which made me think of my own, untamable hair. She moved around the front bumper, where both her steps and her laughter stopped abruptly as she looked up with her wide, brown eyes into my uncle's wry grin.

"Oh shit," she said softly.

"Sounds about right," Travis replied. "Must have been difficult driving with all that fog on the windows, huh? You want me to have your defroster checked out?"

"The defroster doesn't work," Mayra responded with her eyes still bugged out. She glanced sideways at me and bit down on her lip. "It's hard to find parts for that model."

"Well, you're in luck." Travis chuckled. "Matthew is great at looking up 'parts' on the internet. I'm sure he can locate just what you need eventually."

Mayra turned bright red, but I wasn't completely sure why. Travis looked back at me, and I didn't understand his expression as he shook his head and motioned us both inside. Mayra looked hesitant, as if she might bolt for the woods, but she dropped her gaze to the ground, and we all went inside. I could feel heat in the tips of my ears and tried to decide what was causing it.

"I was supposed to find out for Beth if you managed to ask Mayra out," Travis said quietly as we walked into the living room. "I guess we've already moved past that, huh?"

"Um…" I didn't really know what I was supposed to say at that point, so my next words ended up sounding like a question. "We're going to have dinner tomorrow?"

"You're supposed to do that *first.*" Travis snorted.

Mayra plopped down on the couch, her face still red but her eyes now narrowed. She crossed her arms over her chest and glared up at Travis as he kept shaking his head at her and snickering. She huffed out a breath and turned her eyes to the coffee table in front of her.

"I guess you two really are connecting." Travis laughed. I didn't think I had heard him laugh quite like that before. He didn't sound amused at all.

"You know, I've had about enough of your insinuations!" Mayra suddenly yelled loud enough for me to startle a bit. "It's none of your damn business anyway!"

"Whoa!" Travis's eyes narrowed as well, and he took a half step toward the couch. "You are the one who said you just wanted to make friends with my nephew, and I do believe I called bullshit on you then. What's your story now? This still a science project for you?"

"My story, as well as everything else, is none of your damn business!" Mayra shouted. "You were the one who was practically proud when you thought you had caught him with me before!"

"Please don't," I mumbled, but it must have been too soft for them to hear me because neither of them stopped.

"Yeah, and I asked you then just what you were planning, and you were all wanting to be *friends* and shit. Now you're doing it in the car in the driveway."

"We were not!" she yelled back at him. "And even if we were, that is none of your damn business!"

There was definitely a theme to Mayra's comments.

"He's my nephew, and that makes it my business!"

"He's eighteen, and so am I!" Mayra said. "Are you planning to treat him like a little kid forever?"

"What the fuck?" Travis growled back. "You have no idea what you are talking about. You don't know anything about us, and you have no idea all the shit we've been through as a family. Shit he couldn't talk to any *friends* about because none of you fuckers ever gave him the time of day before!"

"I didn't know before!" Mayra yelled back. "What do you want me to do, apologize for not getting to know him sooner? Really?"

"How about apologize for all the shit you people have given him his whole life?" Travis shouted. "How about for the black eye he came home with in the third grade? How about the time someone swiped all the stuff out of his locker and threw it around on the floor? How about that shit, huh?"

"I never did any of that!"

"But your friends did!"

"I have no idea who did that!" Mayra said defensively. "And if I had, I would have stopped them!"

"Oh sure you would, just like you did when that asshole Lords was harassing him the other day! You remember Lords, right? One of your friends, right? As a matter of fact, I'm pretty sure you used to go out with him, didn't you?"

"That is none of your—"

"What's your game, Trevino," Travis asked, interrupting her, "because it's gone too far!"

"You son of a..."

I turned slowly and walked out of the living room and down the stairs to the basement. I pulled off my shirt, pulled on my gloves, and stood on the mat. I took one, long breath and then beat the living shit out of the heavy bag.

By the time I stopped, my arms and shoulders ached, and I had a shooting pain through my hip. I probably went too long—I had done that before. At least I couldn't hear any more shouting coming from upstairs. I took a couple of slow breaths to calm myself before stepping off the mat and leaning over to brace my hands on my knees.

"You okay?"

I raised my head and turned to face my Aunt Bethany, who was leaning against the wall just outside the exercise room.

"No," I replied. "Where are Travis and Mayra?"

"Upstairs," Bethany said, "in time-out."

"Time-out?"

"Yes," she replied, "and they are going to stay that way until they both stop behaving like children. At least *she* has the excuse of age."

"I don't know why they were so angry," I said. "They wouldn't stop."

"Well, I can answer at least part of that," Beth said. "They both care about you. They're also both doing a crappy job of showing it right now."

"Travis brought my car back."

"Yes," my aunt said. "I came to pick him up when I walked in on the two of them going at it. You want to tell me what happened?"

"Um..." I wasn't really sure what to say.

Bethany snickered.

"I thought you were just going to ask her out."

"I did," I said with a bit of a smile. "She said yes."

"So I gathered," Beth replied. "Then what?"

I felt my face heating up and decided I didn't really want to go into a lot of detail. I finally just told her Mayra kissed me.

"When we got out of her car, Travis was there."

"And he got all protective, huh?"

"Yeah, I guess." I dropped down on a stool near the mats and started to pull at the Velcro on the gloves. "Why does he do that?"

"Because he's torn," Beth replied.

"What do you mean, 'torn'? Torn by what?"

Bethany sighed and placed one hand on her hip.

"Torn between wanting to say something extremely inappropriate about how proud he is of you based on his own thoughts and wanting to say what he thinks your dad would have said at the same time."

I peeled off my gloves and held them in my lap while I thought about that.

"He thinks Kyle would be concerned," Bethany said, continuing. "He thinks your dad would have told you to slow down and think about it, make sure this is what you want. On the other hand, Travis wants to high-five you and shout, 'Go get her!'"

I scowled a bit. I didn't like the idea of Travis talking about Mayra that way.

"He wasn't nice to her," I finally said.

"No, he wasn't."

"I don't want him to be like that to her."

Bethany cocked her head to one side, and I tried to hold her gaze for a second, hoping she would know I was serious. I didn't want him to talk like that to Mayra. I wanted him to be nice to her.

"You really like her, huh?" Beth said.

I lowered my eyes and shrugged. Then I thought about it for a minute and remembered what it felt like to be touching her lips with mine and how her body felt underneath me. I started to feel warm inside, and felt myself smile a bit as I licked my lips.

"You do," Bethany confirmed.

"Yes," I said quietly.

"Why?"

I narrowed my eyes, but I knew Bethany wasn't trying to be nasty at all—she just wanted to understand. To make her understand, I was going to have to figure it out for myself.

"She...she's patient," I told my aunt. "She doesn't make me feel stupid."

"You aren't stupid."

"I know," I said, "but sometimes I feel that way, and sometimes other kids at our school try to make me feel stupid or weird. I know I'm not 'right.'"

"There is nothing 'wrong' with you," Bethany said vehemently. "You're just different. It's not bad; it's just not the way most people are. Not everyone can deal with that."

"Mayra can."

"I could tell by the way she was ripping into your uncle." Bethany laughed.

I had to smile a bit at that. Mayra certainly hadn't backed down at all.

"You ready to go upstairs?"

"Okay," I said.

"Put a shirt on," Bethany said. "And for the love of God, I hope you're going to head up and take a shower."

"I will." I snickered as I stood up and placed the gloves back on their little holding shelf before turning to my aunt. "She makes me feel normal. She makes me feel like maybe I can have what other people have."

"You can," my aunt said. "I always knew you could."

I couldn't wait to get back upstairs to Mayra, so I followed my aunt out of the basement.

As I came up the stairs and looked into the living room, I could see Mayra sitting on the far end of the couch with her arms crossed. Travis was sitting all the way on the other side of the room on the far side of the dining room table, scowling at the tabletop.

"Matthew!" Mayra jumped up from the couch and ran over to me. I took a slight step back but didn't flinch as her arms wrapped around my neck. "I'm so sorry! I wasn't thinking...*again*."

She tucked her head against my chest, and I found my arms going around her as if they were on autopilot. I tilted my head down a little until it was resting against the top of her head. Her hair smelled good, and I closed my eyes and inhaled for a second. I didn't really know what to say, and hearing her apologize to me made my stomach feel weird.

Mayra moved her head to look up at me, which made her hair go up my nose. It tickled, and I flinched a bit. Mayra bit at her lip and looked somewhat upset. I pulled her a little closer to let her know it was okay—I didn't mean to flinch away from her. It wasn't what I wanted to do. I wanted to kiss her again, but kissing her with Travis and Bethany in the room didn't feel right at all.

"She must like you to get so close to that stench." Beth chuckled as she walked past me and over to the table where Travis was sitting.

"Sorry," I mumbled to Mayra as I took a step back. Mayra indicated that she didn't care, but she was wrinkling her nose a little bit. "I need to get in the shower."

"I need to get home and feed Dad," Mayra told me. "I wanted to make sure you were okay first, though."

"I'm all right," I said.

"I didn't mean to upset you. Really, I didn't. He just made me so..."

I glanced up at Travis as Mayra's voice trailed off.

"He didn't mean it," I said.

"I'm not so sure about that," Mayra said with a huff. She looked back up at me and gripped my arms. "Are we still going to dinner tomorrow?"

"If you still want to," I replied.

"I do," she said. "Where shall we go?"

"I thought maybe we'd go to this Italian place near Northgate," I said. "You, um...you said you liked Italian food, right?"

"I love it," Mayra said with a smile. "Are you going to pick me up?"

"Sure!" My heart started beating a little faster, and I smiled at her. My eyes focused on her left cheek but kept drifting back to her lips. "Maybe about five o'clock? That way we have plenty of time to get there."

"Great!" Mayra beamed. "I'll see you tomorrow, then."

She stood up on her toes and pressed her lips against the edge of my jaw before she looked over her shoulder at Travis. Her eyes were narrowed at him as she walked around me and headed out the door. I turned to go up the stairs for a shower, and Travis followed me.

As I pulled towels out from under the sink in the master bathroom, Travis dropped down on the chair where my mom used to sit and tie her shoes, backed up to the side of her old dresser. He leaned over and rested his elbows on his knees and sighed.

"I didn't mean to be shitty to your girlfriend," he said. "I just...I worry about you."

I didn't reply. I didn't know what to say, and I was still a bit ticked off at him.

"Your dad...he was always so great with you. He always knew what to say and how to get you motivated to do stuff. I don't know what to do with a kid, and you're not even a kid any more. Maybe that's why Beth and I haven't had any yet."

"Are you still trying?" I asked, distracted by the turn in the conversation. "I thought you were going to stop trying and just see what happens or something."

"Well, yeah—I guess we are," Travis said. "That's been a while, though. We don't talk about it much."

I squeezed the towel between my fingers and tried to determine if I was supposed to say something. I probably was. I usually had this weird little ache at the bottom of my throat when someone was talking to me, and I didn't know how to respond. It was as if there were words there that wanted to come out, but my brain didn't know what they were.

"I'm surprised Kyle and Tiffany even let me babysit you," he eventually said. "Do you remember when I would do that?"

"Usually when they had to take Megan to an appointment."

"Yeah." Travis nodded.

Megan would go to a doctor every month to be checked out. She would never complain if there was something really wrong with her—like if she felt sick or something. Once she had a bad ear infection, and Mom didn't realize it until it was in both ears.

"I don't know if you even remember this," Travis said, "but when you were about nine, and Megan had the flu, I took you out to the park for a while to give your parents a little break."

"We went to the park by the elementary school," I said, remembering the scene. "They had just put down new mulch, and it smelled weird."

"Yeah!" Travis laughed. "You wouldn't walk where the mulch was, so you sat on one of the climbing playsets where there was one of those big tic-tac-toe games."

"The ones you are supposed to hit with a bean bag." I thought it was the only real way to play tic-tac-toe, which always ended up in a tie, assuming both players knew what they were doing. With the beanbags, there was always an element of surprise.

"Right!" Travis grinned. "You didn't want the beanbags. You just wanted to make the X's show up in front, and they all had to be lined up perfectly."

"I had to keep doing it over again." I scowled, recalling that I had ended up having a meltdown on the playground because the board kept getting messed up.

"It was that Lords kid," Travis said with a growl. "Even at that age, he was an asshole. He kept coming up behind it and kicking it so you would start all over again. And Mayra dated that fucker."

"How do you even know that?" I asked. I hadn't *really* known. Suspected, yes, but I didn't pay much attention to the social interactions of my classmates.

"I asked around," Travis mumbled with a shrug of his shoulders.

"You checked up on her?" I asked with obvious shock in my voice. "Why did you do that?"

"Because you won't let me protect you!" Travis suddenly yelled as he stood up. "You wouldn't let me adopt you. You wouldn't let me take guardianship. And you wouldn't even come and *live* with us! I've got to do whatever I can to look after you, Matthew!"

My throat and chest seized up, and I found myself leaning back against the counter. I swallowed a couple of times just to make sure I could. The tone in Travis's voice was not a tone I heard from him often. In fact, the last time was at Dad's funeral.

"You don't have to," I whispered. "You don't have to protect me."

"I do!" he bellowed. He covered his face with his hands for a moment and then sat back down heavily in the chair. "I owe him that much. He was my only brother."

"I know that," I told him. "That doesn't mean you owe me anything."

"Yes, it does," Travis said. He leaned his head back until it touched the side of the dresser behind him. "Even if it didn't, you are still my nephew. I want to be there for you."

"You are," I said to him. "When I need you, you're always there."

Travis glanced over at me.

"Not always," he said as he gestured down the hallway and presumably toward the driveway.

"I didn't need you then," I said. My face felt hot again. I twisted the edge of the towel back and forth between my fingers, trying to give them something to do before I headed back to the basement.

"I'm not so sure," Travis mumbled. "If she ends up…"

"Ends up *what*?" I snapped.

"Hurting you," he finally replied.

"Then what?" I asked. I rubbed my fingers against my eyes. "How would it be any different from any other kids that date? If it doesn't work…well, it doesn't. But you can't just walk in and go at her because you think I need saving."

Travis chuckled low.

"That's what Bethany said."

"Well, she's right!"

"I know," he admitted, "but that doesn't mean I have to like it."

I turned my eyes to my uncle and held his gaze as long as I could.

"I don't want you to talk to her like that again," I told him. "Not ever."

My gaze dropped though I wasn't trying to look away. It was almost a reflexive action. I tried to move my eyes back to his face—to focus on his eyes a little longer—but I couldn't do it.

"I gotcha," Travis said with a sigh. "I'll try to play nice."

Beth yelled for Travis to come back down before she left him here, and Travis got up from the chair and walked toward the master bedroom door. Before he walked into the hall, he turned back to look at me.

"You really like her, huh?"

"Yes," I said. I fiddled with the edge of the towel some more.

"And she likes you?"

"I think so," I replied.

"I hope you are right," Travis said. "I want you to have this. You know that, don't you? I know I overreact, but it's just because I get worried."

"I know," I told him. "I know you are just trying to look out for me, but Mayra…she makes me feel good."

Travis chuckled.

"Yeah, I'll bet." He smiled and winked at me before he walked out.

Tossing the towels over the edge of the shower wall and my clothes into a hamper, I stepped onto the mat by the door to the shower. Twisting the knob, I got the temperature just right before climbing in. The shower was nice and steamy, which was just how I liked it, by the time I closed the door.

I couldn't stop images of Mayra from going through my head, so I thought about kissing her again.

Turning my face up toward the showerhead, I closed my eyes and let the warm spray cover me. The heat from the water pushed away all the tension I had been feeling along with the soreness in my muscles from the workout. Tilting my head down, I took a long breath before I stepped out from under the direct spray and wiped my face with the towel hanging over the shower door.

I filled my palm with shampoo, rubbed my hands together, and then started scrubbing my hair. Usually I would count the seconds as I washed my hair, but I couldn't concentrate. I kept thinking about Mayra.

How her lips felt against mine.

How she tasted when my tongue was in her mouth.

How it felt to have her body underneath mine, practically pinned below me as her hands gripped my back and shoulders.

I swallowed hard and tilted my head back into the spray, keeping my eyes closed as the suds cascaded over my face, neck, and shoulders. I wiped my face off again. I hated the thought of getting water or—God forbid—shampoo in my eyes. I added conditioner to my hair because Mom always insisted on it and then dumped a handful of body wash in my hands to work on the rest of me while the conditioner did its thing.

When I washed my arms, I thought about Mayra gripping them as she rose up on her toes to kiss me goodbye. When I washed my legs, I felt the slight ache in my thighs from holding myself over her. When I washed my face and neck, I wondered how kissing her neck would differ from kissing her lips.

The tempo of my breathing increased, and my eyes closed again. I could feel the rapid thump of my heart inside my chest and wondered how I could tell if I was sweating in the shower. I knew the temperature of the water seemed a little warmer all of a sudden.

I also had a full-on erection.

As an eighteen-year-old guy, I had experienced many erections before. I remembered my dad telling me about wet dreams and the like when I was a kid, and I had woken up a few times to such things though I never remembered the associated dream. I hadn't forgotten the first time I took myself in my hand and masturbated, either, though the act was never a frequent pastime. Those times I had indulged, the woman in my thoughts was always nameless and faceless.

Not this time.

My hand seemed to find itself wrapped around my cock without me really even thinking about it. With images of Mayra underneath me in the car fresh in my mind, I heard myself hiss as I stroked myself from base to tip. I ran my tongue over my lips from left to right, and I could almost still taste her there.

I angled my head back into the water for a moment, quickly rinsing my hair of conditioner before I took a step back and leaned against the cold tile wall. My body shivered as I gripped my erection again with my right hand and my left palm flattened on the wall behind me.

In my head, I see Mayra and myself exiting the car after our make-out session and heading into the house. She takes my hand and leads me upstairs to my bedroom. She turns and walks backwards through the doorway, holding both of my hands in hers as she moves toward my bed. She sits down and pulls her shirt over her head.

My breathing increased to the point where I was practically panting. Base to tip, tip to base.

I reach behind her and deftly unhook her bra, but the details of her exposed flesh are unclear. My hands still find her soft, warm skin, and my mouth finds her waiting lips.

The moisture from my tongue joined the moisture from the shower as I licked at my lips, swallowed, and stroked again—base to tip, tip to base. With my back bracing me against the wall, I moved my free hand to the opposite arm—shoulder to wrist, wrist to shoulder.

Our clothing is gone, and she is beneath me on the bed. She reaches up and takes my head in her hands, stroking my cheeks, down to my jaw and neck.

My fingers danced over my skin, imagining her light touch on my face and shoulder. My hand and fingers mimic what hers do in my mind as I feel a tightening in the bottom of my stomach.

Her hands slide over the skin of my chest and down to my stomach. She traces the outlines of my abdominal muscles before her hand moves lower. Her fingers circle my cock as she spreads her legs out before me. She guides me between her thighs.

I ended up surprised by the sudden intensity of sensations running through my body. I moved my hand faster over my cock, gripping it a little as I moved back and forth from tip to base, base to tip. My back arched away from the cool tile wall, and my other hand gripped the top of my thigh. Tip to base, base to tip.

I'm inside of her, and it's warm and soft, and I feel...

An audible grunt escaped as my legs quivered and my balls tightened up against my body. A quick and intense vibration echoed through my skin until it focused between my legs. With one last shudder, I came on the shower floor with far more force than I recalled ever feeling before.

I nearly fell.

"Holy shit," I murmured. My hands continued to shake a bit as I tried to catch my breath and maintain my footing. I felt dizzy— like all the blood was gone from my brain. Maybe it was. I stepped back into the stream of water and washed off again, still in a daze.

I quickly got out of the shower and dressed in an older pair of lounge pants that were really too short for me now. They had pictures of Sponge Bob on them, for goodness' sake, but I wouldn't get rid of them because my mom had bought them for me when I was fourteen or so, and I still liked them. I towel dried my hair and then just climbed into bed, still somewhat afraid my legs were going to give out.

Masturbation hadn't felt quite like that before.

My heart started to pound again just thinking about it. A couple minutes later, I was hard as a rock and my hand had already found its way into my pants.

Nope—definitely hadn't felt like this before.

And ending the day with thoughts of Mayra? A definite win.

Chapter 9—Almost the First Date

There were several times in my life when I had thought God hated me. I remembered talking to my mom about it a couple of times, asking her why He made me the way He did. She always insisted I was special for a reason and that God never made us go through anything in life we couldn't handle. The next day was one of those days when I thought all of that was a crock of shit.

Next to the day my parents died, it was the worst day of my life.

It started out pretty good. I didn't have any homework, so I managed to get all my website updates done before noon. It was also payday, so I transferred from my PayPal account to my bank account all the money I collected from the website owners, which gave me plenty of money to take Mayra out for dinner in Cincinnati.

Everything started to go downhill right after I got back from the bank, starting with Mayra's phone call.

"Hey!" she sang out. "Are you ready for tonight?"

"Not really," I admitted. "I don't know what I should wear."

Mayra laughed.

"It's just Olive Garden," she told me. "I don't think they require a jacket and tie."

"I know," I said, "I just wanted to…I don't know…"

149

My voice trailed off. I realized I probably should have been having this conversation with my aunt, not my actual date.

"If it helps, I'm just wearing some decent jeans and a blouse."

"Yeah," I said with a pointless nod toward the phone, "that does help."

"There's just one thing," Mayra said. Something about her tone of voice had me tensing before the words even came out of her mouth. "My dad says he has to meet you before we go out. I know. It's goofy, but he's just like that."

"Your dad"—I swallowed hard to keep from choking—"wants to meet me?"

"Yeah, he's kind of insisting on it."

I started to hyperventilate, and I could barely hear Mayra asking if that was going to be all right and me saying it was just fine so I could get off the phone and sit down with my head between my legs before I passed out.

It didn't help much, and my head continued to swim.

I tried not to harp on it inside my mind—I really did. I tried to get myself all worked up over what shirt to wear with my black jeans and what shoes would be best with the whole thing. I even picked up the phone ten times to call Bethany for help, but I didn't dial. If I did, she would definitely hear the panic I was feeling right through the phone, and then she'd be over here five minutes later. I didn't want her to come. I wanted to do this by myself. I told Travis I didn't need help, and I was determined to do it all on my own even if that meant going up to Mayra's house to meet her father.

Mayra's father was a salesman of some sort. I wasn't sure exactly what he did for a living, but I knew what his hobby was—hunting. He even went to the mountains and hunted bears. He was often pictured in the local newspaper with a kill of some kind, and he was very well known and respected around town.

He had to have a lot of guns in the house.

Shit, shit, shit.

Okay, so I knew he wasn't going to shoot me, but what if he hated me? What if he thought I was weird and told Mayra she couldn't go out with me? He would probably want me to shake his hand and look him in the eye as well. If I *didn't* do that, he was bound to think something was wrong with me.

What had Mayra already told him? Did he know I had panic attacks, that I freaked out in school on a semi-regular basis or that I hit a heavy bag when it got to be too much? Would he be worried I would get mad and hit Mayra?

I would never, ever do something like that, but what if he thought I would? What if he asked me about it, and I hesitated? I would certainly hesitate because just *thinking* about the potential question was enough to start me freaking out again.

I tossed on one of the shirts in my hand and shoved my feet into my black and white Converse. I couldn't think about what I should be wearing right now. Then again, clothing probably counts as far as first impressions go, and he would notice what I was wearing. I tossed the blue shirt back into the drawer and grabbed the green one.

Hunters liked green, right? I didn't own anything with a camouflage pattern on it.

By the time I was out in my driveway, sitting in my car, I couldn't even turn the key in the ignition. My palms were sweating. My head was throbbing, and my eyes were starting to tear up.

"Don't do this; don't do this," I whispered to myself. I tried taking a few deep breaths, but they ended up sounding like gasps instead. I placed my left hand on my chest and pushed against my sternum. I wasn't sure if I was trying to help myself breathe normally or just keep my insides from escaping. I tried to get my right hand to turn the key, but it just wouldn't listen.

I glanced at the clock in the car. I would have to leave pretty much immediately to get to Mayra's house on time.

"No, no, no," I muttered. I tried the key again, but my hand was shaking too much to get it to turn.

Change the scene, I remembered my therapist telling me. If things get to be too much, do something differently.

I got out of the car and started pacing back and forth in the driveway. I ran my hands over my face, trying to calm myself. I just had to go over there and meet him—that was it. Sixty seconds of *How do you do?* and Mayra and I could be off on our date.

Date.

I had only managed to keep myself together regarding the date itself because the idea of meeting her father was so completely overwhelming. Before Mayra's call, I had sufficient distractions, and I did like the idea of seeing her even if the setting was different. Besides, Bethany had given me a lot of ideas about things to talk about during the drive. I had never asked Mayra anything about the soccer team just so I could save the conversation for tonight.

Maybe she could just come over to my house instead.

No, I made reservations at the restaurant.

Shit, shit, shit.

I pressed my fingertips into my eyes as I leaned against the car and tried to convince myself that it was normal to be nervous meeting your girlfriend's dad, and I didn't have to worry about it.

Girlfriend?

I spent a couple of minutes wondering if that was the right word or not. I thought it was. I mean, she came over almost every day, and she kissed me. I was pretty sure that made her my girlfriend, but I probably ought to confirm it with her.

That is, if I could even get to her house.

"You're being stupid." I growled at myself as I got back in the car. I gritted my teeth and turned the key. The car roared to life, and I managed to put it in reverse, but I couldn't take my foot off the brake.

One step at a time.

I closed my eyes and tried breathing slowly again. All I had to do was drive over there. It wasn't even that far, and I drove most of the way there when I went to school. Of course, I hadn't been driving myself to school lately since Mayra had been picking me up.

Tightening my grip on the steering wheel, I eased my foot off the brake and backed out of the driveway. I continued to concentrate on the act of driving to Mayra's house rather than what would happen once I got there. The drive over was difficult, but I had done it before, and I focused on using my turn signals properly and staying exactly at the speed limit. Of course, as soon as I got to her house, I just drove past it.

The mere idea of stopping was mind-numbing.

I went about a half mile past the Trevino house and pulled over onto a side road. I slowly put the car in park and turned off the engine. For a moment, I just stared out the front windshield, but after a minute of that, I adjusted the seat so it was lying nearly flat. I curled up on my side and just started to shake.

I couldn't have what other people had, so I just gave up.

Time stopped, started again, and then became irrelevant as I lay on my side in the driver's seat of my car, staring at nothing. My heart thumped rapidly in my chest, and my breaths came in short, labored gasps. For a while, my body shook though that gradually wore off as exhaustion took over.

At some point, it got dark and started to rain.

My breathing had slowed a bit, but my heart was still racing. More than anything, I felt stiff and numb. I was as pathetic as I could possibly be. It was ridiculous to think that I could actually try to have a normal relationship with a girl. Of course her father would want to meet me. I mean, he'd be letting me take his daughter out of town for several hours. What father wouldn't want to meet the guy she was going to be with?

I couldn't even go up to the front door.

I couldn't even park in the driveway.

I couldn't even stop the car.

Mayra was definitely a very special person, and she deserved the absolute best. That wasn't me. She deserved to be with someone who wouldn't freak out on her just because she had an argument in front of him or because she wanted to watch television before doing homework.

I shuddered a little at the thought.

She was worthy of someone who could give her anything and everything, and I couldn't even offer her a normal date where I go up to the door, shake her father's hand, call him "sir," and promise to have his daughter back by midnight, all with a smile on my face. I couldn't have done any of that.

I reached out haphazardly to flip open the little plastic compartment designed to hold change. Inside was a small blue cap from a water bottle. My dad used to drink bottled water constantly when Mom wasn't looking. She said it was too expensive, but he claimed it tasted better, so he'd buy bottled water from the vending machine at work and drink it on the way home.

I remembered how he would deftly untwist the cap with one hand and steer with the other. It always scared me when he took one hand off the wheel, but he could do it so fast, I would barely notice. He'd drink the whole thing down and smack his lips when he was done with it. Then he'd forget and leave the little cap inside the car when he took the bottle to the recycling bin at the service station near the house and panic all evening, thinking Mom would find it.

I pulled the cap out with my fingers and gripped it in my fist, thinking of the way my dad would blush and look all guilty when my mom walked by. She knew he was up to something and would purposely do things to make him agitated until he confessed. He'd still do it again the next day.

They always ended up smiling, laughing, and holding each other.

Mayra deserved that, too, and she wasn't going to get anything like that with me. I wouldn't be able to joke with her about that sort of stuff, and if she gave me a hard time—even in jest—I'd probably just fall apart like the idiot I was.

I mean, really—what did I have to offer Mayra?

You have a lot to offer...

My father's voice rang in my head as I remembered a conversation we had when I was about fifteen. We were in the car on our way back from Cincinnati where I had been meeting with a new specialty therapist. I was supposed to be trying out new ways of making conversation with people, and she had told me to pick a topic that was different from the week before and tell someone about it.

"There's a new girl in my class," I told my father.

"Oh yeah? What's her name?" Dad asked me.

"Traci," I replied.

"Is she pretty?" Dad looked over at me sideways with a half grin. I shrugged my shoulders in response, but he didn't let it go. "Well, is she?"

"How should I know?"

"It's a matter of opinion, son," he said. "Do you find her physically attractive?"

"I don't see the point."

"Human nature," Dad replied as he turned off the freeway and onto a smaller highway. "We are attracted to those we think might be suitable mates."

I snorted.

"Is that funny?"

"Mates," I repeated and snickered a little.

"Girlfriends, then," he amended. "Future wife—whatever you want to call it."

"I still don't see the point."

"Why not?"

"I'll never get married."

"Why in the world not?" Dad asked, sounding shocked.

"Seriously?" I replied with heavy disbelief in my voice. I could tell by the way he was gripping the steering wheel that he wasn't happy with my response. "I can barely function in our family, Dad. What could I offer a prospective wife?"

"A lot." He grumbled under his breath. It was one of the few times he had really gotten angry with me. *"You have a lot to offer, Matthew—that's what. You're very smart. You are considerate, and you help out around the house and with your sister. You know how to figure things out, and you are organized and detailed. You are thoughtful, loving, and you have your dad's good looks."*

His tone lightened as he chucked a bit.

"You never forget anything," he added, *"so you wouldn't be in the kind of trouble I was in last month when I forgot our anniversary, and your mother just about had me castrated."*

We both laughed then but quickly fell into silence again. Just before we got to Talawanda High School, Dad looked over at me.

"You'd be a fine catch, Matthew," he said. *"Don't let anyone, yourself included, try to tell you otherwise. You have a lot to offer, and any girl who is smart and kind enough to realize that is going to be very lucky indeed."*

I squeezed the bottle cap a little tighter.

Did I have something to offer Mayra? I did get straight A's. I had a house that was paid for, and I had budgeted all of Dad's death benefits from the military to keep up with the bills while going to school. I would need to have a scholarship to pay for advanced schooling, but both Miami and Ohio State University already indicated they would accept me. If I went to Miami, I would be able to live at home. OSU was farther, but I would still be close enough for Megan.

Was I considerate? I thought about the thank-you card I gave to Mayra, but I only had to do that because I had forgotten to say it in the first place, so it didn't seem all that considerate. Thoughtful, maybe. The memory brought me back to that first day she was at my house and how she had given me a haircut, and I felt myself smile a little.

Mayra didn't run away from me that day and even continued to come over again and again. She fit into my routine almost without me noticing, and I liked having her there.

She was definitely smart and kind.

If she was willing to accept me and like me the way I was, maybe her father would be able to accept me as well. If I told him all the things my dad said about me—all the ways I might actually be okay for Mayra—there was a chance he would listen and not just see me as a freak. If he didn't believe me, I could even show him my report card or something.

I had proof, at least.

The bottle cap was cutting into my palm a little because I was holding it so tightly, but I didn't want to let it go. It was probably from the last bottle of water Dad drank before he died. It had been in the center console of his car, sitting in its parking spot at the base while he had been out with his unit.

The rain got a little louder, and my back started to get wet. Wind whipped around the inside of the car, and the sounds from a radio found their way into my ears. My throat was sore and hurting as the cold night breeze covered me.

"I got him," a deep voice said. "Go ahead and send an ambulance to Kehr Road just south of town, right before the road splits. The lights are on, so you'll be able to see my truck easily enough."

I didn't hear a response, but I did feel a hand on my shoulder. As I was rolled over, I looked up at a large, burly man in a thick, camouflage hunting coat. As I stared into the mustached face of Mayra's father, Henry Trevino, I tried to remember what I wanted to say, but his mustache was hanging below his nose like a dark, foreboding caterpillar, and my heart started to pound loudly.

"I get straight A's," I said.

I couldn't think of what else I had wanted to tell him, so I passed out.

Lose.

~oOo~

I woke up in an ambulance.

It probably hadn't been that long since I had lost consciousness because the ambulance was still moving, and McCullough-Hyde hospital wasn't all that far from where I had been parked. I opened my eyes and looked around, and one of the two EMTs noticed me.

"Hey there," he said with a smile. "Just hang on—we'll be there soon."

"You have to let me out," I muttered.

"Not just yet," he responded.

"We're just going to have you checked out," the other one said.

"My insurance doesn't cover ambulance rides," I told them. "I can't go to the hospital."

"Don't worry about that right now," the first one said. "Let's just make sure you're okay first. Your blood pressure is pretty high, and you just might be in shock."

"I'm okay," I said. I tried to get up, but I was strapped onto one of those rolling tables. "Just a panic attack—I have them all the time."

The second guy put his hand on my shoulder, and I pulled back from the touch.

"Just lie still," he said in a commanding tone.

I continued arguing for the last couple of minutes of the ride and then also when they pulled me out and started rolling me into the ER.

"I can't afford it," I told them again and again. "It's not in the budget, and ER stays are expensive. I don't have good insurance!"

"We'll just worry about that later, all right?" another voice said. I tilted my head up so I could see who was walking in front of the gurney. It was Henry Trevino.

"I don't want to be in the hospital," I told him. "I'm okay now, really."

"Considering my daughter has been just about crazy, worrying about you," Mr. Trevino said, "I'm going to make sure you get checked out before you are released. If I didn't, she'd have my head."

I let out a big sigh and gave up the argument—for the moment, at least. Once they saw there wasn't anything they could really do for me, they would release me anyway because hospitals liked getting paid. This was one fact I knew well.

Within about five minutes, I was in one of those rooms created by hanging a giant shower curtain from the ceiling. Thankfully, Mr. Trevino was outside of the curtain, talking to one of the nurses. My head was still far too swimmy to try to face him. I was already a little concerned I might have said something ridiculously stupid to him—I really couldn't remember. Another nurse came in and insisted on taking my vitals, which were back to normal. About two minutes later, Bethany and Travis arrived. Travis immediately started arguing with the nurse while Bethany fussed over me and asked me over and over again why in the world I had parked in the middle of nowhere.

I had no idea what to tell her, so I said nothing. I just sat there on the edge of the hospital bed and let them go on and on while I remained silent.

Travis was now talking to a doctor about my insufficient insurance and how much it was going to cost to have me here. Before I could throw out that I wasn't conscious and didn't agree to be brought to the ER in the first place, there was more noise from just outside.

"Where is he? Is he okay?"

I could hear Mayra's frantic voice from out in the hallway just before she grabbed the curtain and yanked it back. Before I could say anything, she threw her arms around my neck and buried her face in my shoulder.

"Oh my God," she cried into my ear, "I was so worried about you!"

For a long moment, I remained stiff. I was too surprised by everything going on around me to react and desperately trying not to freak out again. I heard Beth gasp and Travis clear his throat, but I couldn't move a muscle or respond in any way.

Mayra leaned back and looked into my face. Her eyes were red and swollen, and her cheeks were stained with tears. I could see the relief and sadness combined in her eyes slowly melt into something that fell only just short of fury.

"Don't you ever do anything like that again!" she snapped at me. "Don't you ever run off like that! I had no idea where you were, and I was worried sick! If you need to fall apart, you at least fall apart somewhere where I can find you!"

"Sorry," I gasped. My throat burned a little as the word came out. Mayra's shoulders dropped with her anger, and her hand traced over my face.

"You said it would be all right," she reminded me. "Maybe I should have known it wasn't, but when I asked you, you said you didn't mind meeting him, but you did, didn't you?"

"I guess," I muttered back and looked away from her and down to the floor. She cupped my chin and tried to turn my face up to hers. I let her reposition my head, but my eyes remained over her shoulder.

"You have to tell me the truth," she said. "I know that can be hard, but you can't just tell me what you think I want to hear, Matthew. You just can't."

"You know, maybe if you didn't push him into shit he's not ready for, he wouldn't be here!" Travis said.

"Travis!" Bethany said, his name sounding like a hiss, and then grabbed Travis by his arm and started hauling him out into the hallway. "You and I are going to have a little talk—*again*!"

Mayra watched their retreating forms, and I took the opportunity to look more closely at her face. Her hair hung in slight curls, which rolled around her head and framed her pale face. There were smudged, dark marks underneath her eyes, and I realized she had put on eye makeup, which I didn't think I had seen her wear before, but it had smeared a little around her eyes. It was dark blue, the same color as the shirt she was wearing. As I looked at her, a tear slipped over her lashes and fell down her cheek.

"Why are you crying?" I asked, confused.

Mayra turned back to me, and I looked off to one side.

"I was worried about you," she said again. "Also, Travis is probably right. I am pushing you too hard, aren't I?"

She slid her fingers up and down my jaw.

"Please tell me," she whispered. "Please tell me if this is too much for you."

"If what is too much?" I found myself whispering as well.

"Me...you...*us*..."

I swallowed and tried to gather my thoughts, but they weren't interested in revealing themselves to me. I was still numb, and my muscles ached from the exertion of the attack. It was difficult to focus after I had a major attack, and I still wasn't quite myself. Even if I had been, I wasn't sure I would fare much better.

"It is, isn't it?" Mayra said, her voice still hushed. In my peripheral vision, I could see her head and shoulders droop. "You don't...want to do this, do you?"

I knew I needed to say something. I wanted to say something. I just didn't know what. I didn't want to lie to her, and a lot of this *was* too much for me. At the same time, it was worth the discomfort of being pushed to my limits to be with her. When it came right down to it, if I was told I could be with Mayra, but it would cost me a high-level panic attack a day, I would agree without hesitation. The problem was, I had no idea how to tell her that.

Taking a deep breath, I forced my arms from their locked position at my sides and wrapped them around Mayra's waist, pulling her body close to mine. I tucked my head against her shoulder and pressed my lips to the skin at the top of her collar.

I couldn't say what I wanted to say, so I tried to show her instead.

I felt like I could have just fallen asleep sitting there on the edge of the hospital bed with Mayra's hands in my hair and my nose tucked into the crook of her neck. She smelled good, and she was soft and comfortable and warm. I almost felt like nothing had happened at all and that we had just spent the evening sitting on the loveseat in my family room, watching TV.

"Don't do that to me again," Mayra whispered against the top of my head, which broke the façade that all had been just fine. "I mean it. Whatever is going on in your head, we'll deal with it together, okay? Don't run off on me again."

"I'm sorry," I whispered back. "I just…couldn't stop. I couldn't stop the car."

"I'm getting you a damn cell phone," Mayra growled. "At least then I could have found you."

Before I could argue, the sound of someone clearing his throat interrupted us. I didn't have to look up to know it was her father standing at the opening in the curtain and looking in on me touching his daughter after he had to haul me out of my car in the middle of the night.

My composure had to have been the result of Mayra being there, totally calm about the whole thing, because I managed to not freeze up too much. Either it was her, or maybe I was just too wiped out from my earlier breakdown. I did tense up to the point where I couldn't let go of her right away. My fingers dug into her sides a bit as I clutched her to me. Then I realized how much worse that was going to make this look, so I let go and leaned back. Mayra took a half step away from me, and I looked down at the tile floor.

"Hey, I just wanted to let you know the hospital bill isn't an issue," Mr. Trevino said. "Since I brought you in here, and it sounds like they're going to release you in a few, there's no charge, okay?"

"Um, okay. Thanks," I managed to mumble. It might have even been loud enough for him to hear. I knew it wasn't right—it wasn't *enough* of a response—but I wasn't sure what else I was supposed to say.

"No problem," Mr. Trevino responded. For a long moment, he didn't say anything else. I didn't know what to say, and Mayra seemed content just running her fingers up and down the top of my thigh. She scratched lightly at the denim, which was extremely distracting. I couldn't seem to focus on much else.

"Your aunt and uncle said they were going to retrieve your car," Mr. Trevino said. "Mayra, I assume you're going to be taking Matthew home when he's released?"

"Yeah, I will," Mayra replied.

"Don't stay long," he told her. "It's late. I want you coming right home afterwards. I'll wait up."

"I will," Mayra said without hesitation. I tried not to show my disappointment at the idea. I wanted to get the hell out of the hospital, but as long as I was here, Mayra was with me.

"What time is it?" I asked. Visions of Megan and how she could tell you what time it was in any city at any given moment came into my head.

"Almost four a.m.," Mayra told me.

I looked up at her, and the shock must have been easily read in my eyes.

"Yes," she said, "that long. You see why I was so worried?"

"I'm sorry," I said again.

"Stop apologizing," Mayra sighed. "Just don't do that again."

I nodded, knowing full well that I couldn't guarantee anything like that but not wanting to really talk about it in front of her father. I couldn't believe I was in the same room with him and not having another episode. Maybe it was because I still felt numb.

"So...Matthew," Mr. Trevino suddenly said, "you like sports?"

"Um...sure," I said. I tried to make eye contact with him, but the mustache was in the way. I just kept looking at that until I realized that I was looking at *that*, not him. I quickly looked back to the ground. "I hope to see Mayra play soccer when the season starts up, and my dad used to take me to a Reds game every summer."

"Baseball, huh?" he remarked. I could see him nodding in my peripheral vision. "I usually watch them at home. Got a flat screen just for that."

I nodded back, not sure what else I was supposed to say.

"What do you think about fishing?"

I glanced over at him, trying to understand his questions, but looking at his mustache definitely didn't help.

"I *like* fishing," I finally said.

Mayra chuckled, and I peeked up at her. There was a huge grin on her face.

"Did you coach him?" Mr. Trevino asked as he winked at her.

"Not a bit," she replied.

"Why do you like fishing?" he asked.

I thought about it for a minute before answering. I had the feeling my answer was going to be important, but I didn't know how. I decided to go with the truth.

"It's quiet," I said. "Peaceful."

"Yeah," Mr. Trevino said. "It is. We'll go sometime."

I froze again and wondered if he was serious.

"So—what you said in the car," he added before I could even fathom a response, "was that true? You get straight A's?"

"Um, yes," I replied, and then I realized what I hadn't been saying that I should have been saying the whole time. "I mean, yes, *sir*."

He nodded again as he turned to leave.

"Well, Mayra," he said, "this one's definitely got that Lords kid beat."

With that, he tossed the curtain aside and left.

Mayra laughed, and I just shook my head. I didn't understand the joke, so I just pulled Mayra back close to me.

Without a doubt, this day belonged in the lose column, but I couldn't help but feel like a winner in Mayra's arms.

Chapter 10—Follow the Cake

Mr. Trevino wasn't kidding when he said the hospital bill wasn't going to be an issue. Something about him being the one to call the police who then called the ambulance meant I couldn't be charged for the ER visit or something. I was still a little too dazed to comprehend it all. The doctor came in and checked me out thoroughly, then said I was free to go but not before he slipped me a half dozen sample packs of Valium.

I must have dozed off in Mayra's car on the way home because I didn't remember the ride at all, just Mayra shaking my arm a little bit and opening my eyes to see the door to the garage in front of me.

"Come on, baby," Mayra said softly.

"Baby?" I mumbled back. I poked the fish spot on the passenger side door before opening it and climbing out unsteadily. Mayra chuckled as she slipped an arm around me and helped me inside.

"You don't want me to call you that?" she asked.

"I don't know," I answered honestly. I considered it as she took my keys and opened the door. There was a part of me that definitely didn't like to be referred to as an infant, but there was also a part of me that kind of liked having Mayra give me a pet name or whatever you were supposed to call it. Girlfriends did that sometimes, I was pretty certain.

That reminded me of something I wanted to ask.

"Mayra?"

"Yes?"

I had to stifle a yawn as we stopped in the foyer, and Mayra lifted her arms up around my neck. I placed my hands on her hips and my head on top of hers. Her hair always smelled good.

"Are you my girlfriend?"

She chuckled again.

"Well, what do you think?" she asked as her nose drew a line up my neck. I felt her lips press against my skin.

"I think so," I told her, "but I wanted to make sure you thought so, too."

"I think so, too," she confirmed. "And that makes you my boyfriend in case that wasn't clear."

She tilted her head up, and I was just thinking about kissing her when the door opened, and Bethany and Travis came in. Beth looked over her shoulder as she headed into the kitchen.

"Travis!" she said. "No delaying!"

"Hi, Mayra," Travis said as he walked in the door. "I'm a total ass and I need to mind my own business."

Mayra busted out laughing.

"That was sincere." She snorted.

"I might have been coached a bit."

Mayra laughed again, and Travis narrowed his eyes at her. I looked back and forth between them, not really understanding what was transpiring in front of me.

"Regardless," Travis added, "I was an ass. Matthew is my nephew, and I worry about him, okay?"

"He's my boyfriend," Mayra said. "I worry about him, too."

Travis glanced up and met my eyes. I looked down to Mayra's shoulder and stared at a little curled strand of hair lying across her pale skin.

"Just so there is no confusion," Bethany said as she came back to the entrance of the kitchen and held up a little grocery sack, "there is no cake in here, and you aren't getting any for a long time!"

"Cake?" Mayra looked up at me, confused.

I just shrugged, but Travis laughed out loud.

"Betty makes awesome cakes."

"Don't call me Betty!" my aunt yelled from the kitchen, which made Travis cringe a bit.

"It makes her think of Betty Rubble," Travis told Mayra. "Anyway, Bethany has used cake as an incentive to get Matthew to do shit because he will do anything for a piece of her chocolate cake."

"He will, huh?" Mayra said. She had an odd look in her eye when I glanced at her.

"Her cakes are the best," I said quietly.

"Hmm," Mayra responded with her lips smashed together. "Are they now?"

Bethany started making me something to eat, telling me I was taking one of the Valium the doctor gave me, and prohibiting me from doing that on an empty stomach. Mayra said she had to go, reminding me that it was almost daybreak, and her dad was waiting up for her.

"I'll call you later today," Mayra said.

I nodded and gave her a small smile. She stood up on her toes and briefly touched her lips to mine. Before I could react and remember to kiss her back, she was gone.

Bethany made me a sandwich with a side of potato salad. Though I thought it would have been more appropriate for breakfast food at the given hour, I didn't notice after I took the first bite. I was ravenous, and the whole plateful was gone within a couple of minutes.

Bethany created a list of things I would need to do before I went to bed. She knew how Valium could affect me, and I'd worry if I didn't have a list. There wasn't much to be done, which was good. My aunt then placed a glass of milk and one of the Valium in front of me, made sure I took it, and then she and Travis left as well.

I checked the list, washed the dishes, and cleaned up the kitchen. I put the pen away in the junk drawer and noticed a Ziploc bag with a piece of paper inside—the lottery ticket.

I swallowed hard as my head began to swim. I knew I should check the numbers, but I was in no condition to think about doing something like that right now. Besides, it wasn't on my list of things to do.

I closed the drawer and went upstairs, beginning to feel the effects of the Valium, and forgetting the ticket entirely. I managed to get myself into pajamas and bed before the drug really took hold. I might have liked to think about Mayra a little longer or maybe do a little more than just *think* about her. My head got all fuzzy, though, and as the sun started peeking through my bedroom window, I let go of consciousness and slept.

It was afternoon when I finally crawled out of bed. My head was throbbing a bit, so I ate some breakfast and took some generic pain pills I found in the medicine cabinet. I still felt like I was in a bit of a fog. I didn't like the way tranquilizers affected me, and I ended up just sitting on the couch and watching television until the phone rang.

It was Mayra, and she was going to come over to see how I was doing. I would have been tempted to tell anyone else that I was fine, and there was no need to check on me, but I wanted to see her. About twenty minutes later, Mayra was walking up my front walkway with a large, round Tupperware container in her hands. I opened the door, and she smiled as she took the big round container into the kitchen and placed it on the table.

I tilted my head and watched as Mayra put enough pressure on the bottom of the container to break the seal, and she then lifted the dome off the top of the plastic plate below. Once it was out of the way, a tall, round cake with butter-colored frosting was revealed.

For a long moment, I just stared at the thing in silence.

Mayra finally spoke up.

"I made you a cake," she said quietly. Her voice sounded strange—not her normal tone at all. I looked at her and saw her neck and cheeks were tinged with red.

"What kind?" I asked.

"Chocolate," she replied.

I swallowed hard and closed my eyes for a moment, fighting the urge to drop to my knees and confess my undying love for her and asking her to bear my children and bake me cakes forever. I was fairly certain it wasn't the right time for that, and such an act would certainly fall into the "inappropriate behavior" category.

"The frosting is butter-cream," Mayra said. "Homemade."

"Can I have some?" I whispered. My mouth was watering, and I was incredibly relieved when Mayra nodded. She found a knife to cut a wedge and a plate to put it on. A moment later, I was sitting in front of a slice of a three-tiered chocolate cake with butter-cream frosting and what looked like chocolate pudding between the layers. I scooped a bite of it onto my fork and placed it slowly and carefully in my mouth.

It was the most wonderful thing I had ever had in my life.

I got hard just from the taste.

Aunt Bethany's cakes *never* made me hard.

I swallowed and looked up at Mayra in awe, my eyes wide and, for once, unable to look away from her. I was glad I was across the table from her and sitting down as well, because the only way to stop the erection growing in my pants was to stop eating this cake, and there was no fucking way I was going to do that. I took another bite, still watching Mayra as I did, then another bite and another quickly thereafter.

"This is incredible," I told her between additional, rapid bites.

Mayra's smile grew wide, and her eyes sparkled as I devoured the rest of the piece.

"I'm glad you like it," she said quietly before biting her lower lip. "Would you like more?"

"Yes, please."

Mayra smiled again, but the look in her eyes was strange. I looked on in confusion as Mayra took the plastic dome, covered up the cake, and sealed the container again. Then she picked it up and headed toward the front door.

"The next piece will be waiting for you in my driveway," she said. She kissed me lightly and headed out the door to her car and down the street, taking the cake with her.

Shit, shit, shit.

I couldn't just let that cake get away, so I jumped into my car and followed her.

Do it for the cake, I told myself.

It would probably have been better overall if I could have convinced myself to do it for Mayra or even just to do it for myself, but I wasn't there yet. I wasn't sure if I would ever be. Doing it for the cake was getting me as close as possible, at least.

As close as possible seemed to be driving around in circles about two blocks away from Mayra's house.

The good news was, I didn't seem to be panicking. I didn't seem to be getting any closer, either, but at least I was still able to signal right turn after right turn and burn up gas as I went around and around the neighborhood in the vicinity of my girlfriend's house.

My girlfriend.

I smiled and tried turning left. Somehow, the turn indicator ended up pointing me right again, so I followed it. The next couple of attempts had similar results.

I sighed.

The biggest problem wasn't Mayra's house or her driveway but the possibility that her father's truck with the shotgun rack in the back would be there as well. That was the main thing keeping me at a distance. I tried to ease my mind by replaying the short conversation from very early this morning when her dad said I had Lords beat.

That made me frown, though, not because of what he had said but because of the reminder that Mayra had once dated Justin Lords, and it wasn't even that long ago. I knew they had been together, of course, but I had never really given it much thought before. Now that she was my girlfriend, I didn't like the idea at all.

She kissed me because I was her boyfriend. I could only assume she had kissed Justin Lords as well. The thought of kissing Mayra made me think of my alone time in the shower and how that activity had a tendency to lead to *another* specific activity—one that definitely featured Mayra—and took place in my head as much as in my hand. While the thought usually made me feel pretty good, now I couldn't help but wonder what Mayra and Justin had done in addition to kissing.

It was none of my business, really.

I wanted to know.

I didn't want to know.

I felt like I should be pulling petals off a daisy.

Taking a deep breath, I made another right.

The thought of Mr. Trevino's hunting truck parked in the driveway didn't seem nearly as bad as the conversation I felt compelled to have with Mayra over the second slice of cake. Actually, if Mr. Trevino were there, it would be easier because there was no way I would broach the subject in his presence.

Did he know?

Would he tell me?

I put all thoughts of asking Mayra's father about her previous relationship out of my head. That was just too much. It was another one that I was quite sure fell into the "inappropriate conversations" category.

I turned left without thinking about it because that was the only way the conversation was going to happen. I tried to decide if it would be better to see Mr. Trevino's vehicle in the driveway or not. I slowed down as I approached, and even through the thick trees around the neighborhood, I could see the driveway quite clearly. Mayra's car was parked to one side, and the other side was empty.

I could see Mayra, too. With a small plate in her lap and a bent-over book in her hand, she was sitting on the steps leading to the front door. I wondered how long she had been sitting there waiting for me and figured I had probably been driving around for at least forty minutes.

With a deep, shuddering breath, I pulled into the driveway at about a quarter of a mile an hour.

I was not going to ask her anything about Justin Lords. I was not. Not at all. Her former relationship wasn't going to drive me crazy because the cake was going to be all I would care about.

Just to prove the point, an imaginary bell rang in my head, and my mouth started to water.

I turned off the car and sat there, looking at my hands gripping the steering wheel hard enough to make my knuckles white. Out of the corner of my eye, I could see that Mayra had not moved, other than to place her book onto the cement step next to her feet.

I glanced up, and I could see Mayra's smiling face as she waited patiently on the porch steps. My hands refused to let go of the steering wheel, but at least my mind was relatively calm. I kept breathing. It was about all I could do, other than salivate, at the thought of another slice of that cake.

"Let go," I whispered to my fingers. Remarkably they listened, at least temporarily. As I tried to wipe the clamminess off my palms, my fingers gripped my thighs instead. I sighed at myself, forced my fingers to uncurl, and gripped the handle to the door.

It opened, and I managed to get my legs turned sideways so my feet were on the ground. I stood up and stared down at my feet.

"I was starting to wonder if you really liked my baking or if you were just being polite."

"I'm not very good at 'just being polite,'" I admitted. "I usually say whatever is in my head, if anything."

"What's in your head now?"

"Justin Lords," I replied instantly.

Shit, shit, shit.

I didn't mean to say that.

Mayra narrowed her eyes and her brows smashed together right above the bridge of her nose.

"Justin Lords?" she repeated. "Why would you be thinking about him?"

I shrugged, wishing I could get back in the car and speed away, but my feet were pretty much frozen to the ground. There was also the visual of a piece of delectable chocolate cake not fifteen feet away from me. Mayra set the plateful of cake next to her book and stood up, coming around the still-open car door and taking my hand in hers.

"Did that little shit say something to you?" she asked. I was surprised by the amount of venom in her tone. "Because if he's still harassing you, I'm going to—"

"He hasn't said anything," I said quickly. "Really, he hasn't. Not since that day when you were there at school."

Mayra's expression turned quizzical.

"Well, why are you thinking about him, then?"

"Because he used to be your boyfriend," I said quietly.

Mayra just stared at me for a moment while I kept my eyes trained on her shoulder.

"May I have the cake now?" I asked her.

Mayra pursed her lips and closed one eye as she looked at me.

"All right," she said. "You do seem to have earned it."

I couldn't wait any longer, so I darted around Mayra and grabbed the plate. I was usually a stickler for silverware when eating, but cake was a definite exception. I ate the first piece standing up and then sat on the porch steps for the second piece.

By the time I made it to Mayra's kitchen table, I had eaten half the cake and was a little sick to my stomach. It was all worth it though. As I polished off the last piece I could manage to stuff into my face, Mayra handed me a glass of cold milk to wash it down.

"I don't think I have ever seen anyone eat that much cake in one afternoon," she said with a laugh.

"It was good," I replied. I wiped my mouth with the back of my hand.

Mayra took my hand and led me to the living room. The focal point for practically the whole house was Mr. Trevino's flat screen television. It dominated the room with both the couch and reclining chair angled toward it. Mayra and I sat on the couch, which was a little worn but still quite comfortable, and I looked around the room.

The living room was the majority of the house, really. A modest place that seemed quite suited for just Mayra and her father. It was comfortable…*lived in*.

I liked it.

"You okay?" Mayra asked.

"Yes," I said.

"Do you want to watch TV?"

"Okay." It was about the same time in the afternoon when Mayra and I would usually be watching television at my house after homework. Watching at her house instead wasn't too far off. I glanced at her and smiled, and she flipped through channels. "I like the TV."

"It's Dad's pride and joy," Mayra snickered. "He talks about the TV like it's my little brother or something. He and Brad will spend hours and hours watching baseball on it."

"Brad?"

"My uncle," Mayra said. "Brad Conner, my mother's brother. He's my dad's best friend. They got close after my mom ran off, and they both tried to hunt her down, for whatever good it did. Brad's the chief of police in Oxford."

"Oh, yeah." I didn't think I had ever met the man, but I had heard his name before. "What happened to your mom?"

"She got fed up with being an adult and left." Mayra shrugged. "I was just a baby, and I don't really remember her at all. They found her in Mexico or something. Dad's convinced she's involved with some drug cartel, but he doesn't know I heard him talking about it."

"I'm sorry." I was pretty sure that was the appropriate response. It was all I could think of to say.

"Not a big deal." She shrugged again. "You can't really miss someone you don't remember, and my dad is awesome."

I looked around the room a bit more. There was a Cincinnati Reds pennant on the wall and another one for the Kansas City Royals. There was a signed baseball under glass on the mantle of an inoperable fireplace, but it was too far to see the signature.

"Your dad likes baseball," I said, a statement more than a question.

"Almost as much as fishing," Mayra confirmed. "I can't believe you like both of those things, too."

"Baseball is okay," I said. "I have a hard time watching it on television, but I liked going to the games with my father. There was a lot to watch. I think the game doesn't really move fast enough to hold my attention when it's not live, but when we were at the stadium, there was a lot of other stuff to focus on as well."

"Well, you impressed Dad, that's for sure."

"I did?"

"Oh yeah," she said. "I don't think I ever dated anyone who wasn't dragged on a fishing trip with him. They all hated it."

"Oh," I said, and I frowned. I was reminded of Justin Lords and didn't want to be. Thankfully, Mayra found one of our favorite shows, and I settled down with my head in her lap.

She wound her fingers in my hair, and though I felt myself immediately relax in a way I couldn't recall feeling outside of either my own or Travis's house, I couldn't stop my mind from thinking about everyone Mayra had ever dated.

"How many boyfriends have you had?" I heard myself ask. I cringed at the same time, and Mayra's hand stopped moving across my scalp.

"Three, I guess," Mayra answered, her voice low.

"Who were they?" Sometimes my mouth just kind of went off on its own without actually consulting my head to see if I wanted to know the answer to my question.

"I went out with Sean Michaels freshman year," she told me. Her voice had a bit of a sharp tone to it. "We went out maybe two months—nothing serious at all. Then I went out with Ian Pennington for a little bit at the beginning of last year and then Justin, which you already know."

For a while, I didn't ask anything else, and Mayra went on playing with my hair while I thought about the three guys she had dated before me. I didn't really know much about Pennington—he was kind of quiet and played trombone in the marching band. Sean Michaels and Justin Lords though—they both fell into the category of people to count on to be generally nasty when given the chance.

It occurred to me that Mayra had lousy taste in guys.

What exactly did that say about me?

I probably would have asked the question if Mayra's father hadn't come home right about that time, completely scaring the shit out of me.

"Oh, hey there," he said as he walked into the room.

I quickly sat up and scooted to the other side of the couch, wondering what he would think of me having my head in Mayra's lap. Mayra gave me a weird look and just shook her head at me a bit.

"Who ate half the cake?" Mr. Trevino asked, and I quickly looked to the floor.

"I made it for Matthew," Mayra said simply. I could hear her snickering under her breath. "I bet he would share if you asked him nicely."

"Well, Matthew?" Mr. Trevino asked. "Do you think you can spare a piece?"

"Oh, um…sure," I muttered. "I mean, of course, sir."

Mr. Trevino snickered as well, his laugh bearing a close resemblance to Mayra's.

"Well, it's a good thing," he added, "because otherwise I'd have to start charging you cake as couch and TV rental."

I glanced at Mr. Trevino and then at Mayra. They were both holding in laughter, but I wasn't completely sure what the joke was. Humor didn't always come easily to me, and often what I thought was funny wasn't what others seemed to find humorous. Regardless, Mayra and her father didn't seem to be laughing *at* me or anything, so I smiled a little and tried not to think too much about being caught in Mayra's house by her father.

Really, he didn't seem to mind.

Several hours and most of a Reds game later, I headed out with the last two pieces of chocolate cake in a small Tupperware container. I got into my car, placed the container on the passenger seat carefully so it wouldn't fall when I turned corners, and drove myself home with a smile on my face.

What made me the happiest was just how normal it all seemed.

I couldn't think about anything else, so I went to bed and dreamed of Mayra's house.

Win.

SHAY SAVAGE

Chapter 11—Conflict Isn't My Thing

"Do you want to go over it again?" Mayra asked as she looked over her shoulder and backed out of my driveway.

I had to wonder if she was the most patient person on Earth or if she was just being accommodating to me for some other reason. I poked the little fish shape on the passenger side door of her Porsche and answered in the affirmative.

"We're not holding anything back," she told me. "It's going to be very obvious to everyone in our school who sees us that we're together. After I park the car, we'll walk into school together, and I'm going to be holding your hand. We'll go to your locker. I'm going to give you a kiss on the cheek, and then we'll go about our day as we usually do. We eat lunch together, go to ecology, and then back to your place for homework, television, and making out on the couch."

I laughed. She hadn't thrown in that last part before, but it definitely gave me something to look forward to later because the next few minutes were going to be hard.

"And," Mayra said with authority, "you are going to be just fine with all of it."

"Are you sure?" I asked.

"Positive," she replied.

"And after we get back to my house but before homework?"

"Cake."

I smiled broadly. It was my favorite part of the whole plan.

"But only if you keep it together today."

"I know." I took a deep breath and nodded to myself.

I was going to do this.

For cake.

Mayra sighed and turned onto the street where our school was located. She was quiet for a minute, and I ran over what the first part of the day might be like. I knew people were going to look at us, and I knew they were going to talk and stare and wonder why in the world a girl like Mayra would be with a guy like me. I knew that, and it made me about as nervous as I could be.

"I want to be with you," Mayra said quietly, and I glanced up at her, wondering if she could read my mind. "Anyone who gives you a chance would know why I'm with you."

I looked out the passenger window and contemplated a moment.

"A lot of people don't," I finally said. "I mean, some have tried, but I can be pretty trying."

Mayra snickered.

"Yes, you can," she agreed. "Ultimately you are pretty wonderful, though. You just need to be given the opportunity to show people that. Besides, you don't realize how the girls in our school talk about you."

"What?" I narrowed my eyes and looked at her sideways.

"Matthew…how can I put this?" Mayra took in a long breath and breathed it out again slowly. "You are gorgeous. Every girl in our school thinks so, and I am going to be the envy of half the population of Talawanda High School."

I was reminded of what Bethany had shown me on her Facebook page, but we pulled into the school parking lot before we could really talk about it anymore. I felt my heart start to beat a little faster as we pulled into a parking spot and Mayra turned off the ignition.

"Are you ready?" she asked.

"No," I said bluntly.

"Are you as ready as you will ever be?" she pressed.

"Probably."

"Okay, then!" Mayra took off her seatbelt while I remained still, trying to take a lot of calming breaths. I could see her gathering up her book bag to hoist it over her shoulder, but I still didn't move.

I felt her touch against my arm as she began to speak softly.

"We don't have to hold hands," she said quietly. "We can just walk in like we usually do if you aren't ready. I don't want to push you too hard. You know that, right?"

"I know," I responded. I thought about it for a moment, and Mayra waited patiently for me to continue. "I want to walk in with you. I want everyone to know we're together. I just…I don't like people looking at me, and they're going to look at me."

"We can wait until tomorrow."

I glanced over at her and then looked out the window.

"Would it be any different then?"

"Probably not."

"I guess we should just do it today, then."

Mayra opened her door, walked around to my side of the car, and waited for me to get out. I poked the fish shape twice—it had definitely become a habit, and I couldn't even say why—before I climbed out and tentatively wrapped her fingers with mine. With a quick look to her eyes and a big sigh, we started toward the front entrance, hand in hand.

Mayra leaned a little closer to me as a few of the kids in the swarm of students actually stopped and stared. I kept my eyes to the ground, but I could still feel their gazes as they lingered on our clasped hands. Mayra held her head high with a smile on her face, but I just kept my head down and tried to move quickly.

Once we got to my locker, I felt like I could let go of the breath I was holding. At this point, most of the kids were either whispering in little groups or trying to look nonchalant as they walked close enough to overhear us talking to each other.

"How are you doing?" Mayra asked in a hushed tone.

"Okay, I guess," I replied. I didn't sound very convincing. "They're all talking about us."

"Not everyone," Mayra said with a nod over my shoulder. I glanced back to see one guy banging at his combination lock as he tried to get it open. While I was looking, he turned his eyes to us, and his mouth dropped open.

"Well, he'll probably start now," Mayra said with a sigh.

I turned my attention to my locker's contents, made sure everything was in its proper place, and straightened things up a bit just to be doubly sure. The act relaxed me a little, and when I straightened back up with the folders and books I needed for my first two classes, I saw Mayra's smiling face.

"You are doing wonderfully," she said through her smile. "I'm proud of you."

I couldn't help but smile back, and though I couldn't find any words to tell her how much her encouragement meant to me, I tried to hold her gaze a little longer to show her how I felt. She seemed to notice, and her hands squeezed mine briefly before she stood up on her tiptoes and touched my cheek with her lips.

"Every girl here is so jealous of me right now," she whispered into my ear. "I can practically hear it in their footsteps. In time, you are going to show everyone how awesome you really are."

"I'm not convinced of that," I replied, glancing into her brown eyes again. I looked back to the folders I was holding and let go of her hand long enough to run my fingers through my hair. "I'm not sure you realize how big a pain in the ass I can be."

Mayra laughed as she placed her hand on my arm.

"Oh, don't be so certain," she said with wide grin, which I returned. She gave me another quick kiss before releasing my arm and heading down the hall to her first class.

People were still looking at me—some with expressions of surprise, some with awe, and some with confusion. I didn't look at any of them as I turned in the opposite direction and walked quickly to my first class. If they were still looking at me, they would have seen me smiling.

Later in the day, I stopped at my locker to exchange books and found Joe leaning against the locker next to mine.

"So, is it true?" he asked.

"Is what true?" I looked down at my lock as I twisted the combination but couldn't stop the corners of my mouth from turning up, which they had been doing on their own all morning.

"'Is what true?'" Joe said in a mocking tone. He rolled his eyes and crossed his arms over his chest. "Matthew Rohan, are you trying to be subtle or coy or whatever? Because you are a total fail."

I tried to hide my growing smile behind the locker door.

"It is true," Joe said with a nod. "Damn, I didn't realize you were so impressive talking about bees."

He laughed, and I just shrugged and continued to grin like an idiot. There were a lot of murmured voices and pointed looks toward me as Joe and I headed off to our English class. I was doing my best to ignore them.

"She's hot," Joe suddenly said.

"What?" I glanced sideways at him.

"Mayra Trevino—she's hot," Joe said again.

My cheeks felt warm as I continued to look down at my feet and tried to make some sense out of the mixed feelings Joe's words had brought forth. At first, all I could think about was the people in the school, watching me walk in with her, someone who was considered "hot." I wondered what they were thinking about me and about Mayra, which was rather odd for me. I didn't tend to consider what other people might think because most of the time, I already figured they thought I was crazy or something. Now everyone was talking about me being with Mayra Trevino—a girl who's "hot"—

and I also remembered what Mayra had said about me just before we got to school. *She* thought *I* was gorgeous.

I liked that.

I wasn't entirely sure I believed her, but everyone was entitled to an opinion. My dad had loved pineapples and mushrooms on his pizza, which was just about the nastiest thing I had ever tasted, but it was his favorite. People liked different things, so maybe Mayra really did think that about me. I definitely agreed with Joe about Mayra though I didn't necessarily mean just about how she looked. Mayra was beautiful, but there was a lot more to her than just that. There was a lot more behind her stunning face.

My thoughts continued along this line as we moved into the classroom and took our seats.

Joe was only thinking about Mayra's physical appearance, but I didn't think he really knew her. He was referring to her looks alone when he said Mayra was hot. Saying someone was hot was just another way of saying they looked good to you, and Mayra looked good to Joe. That meant he thought she was attractive. That meant he was attracted to her.

And I didn't like that.

I also had no idea how to respond to the tightening in my stomach and the almost sick feeling that came up my throat and tasted like bile in the back of my mouth. The heat that had been on my cheeks seemed to move to my hands, and even as we sat down in our chairs, I had the strangest desire to punch Joe right in the face.

I shook my head back and forth, and my hair flopped down over my forehead. It was distracting enough to pull me from such thoughts, and as I pushed my hair back off my face, Joe turned around in the seat in front of me and looked at me quizzically.

"Lords is going to be pissed, you know," Joe reminded me.

I honestly hadn't thought about it. Justin Lords had been in my thoughts a few times as I wondered why Mayra dated him for as long as she did, but I hadn't thought about the conversation we had at lunch a couple of weeks ago. He said he was going to try to get Mayra back in time for prom. I had completely forgotten about that.

"He still wants to take Mayra to prom," I said quietly. All thoughts of being pissed off at Joe's comment in the hall disappeared as I considered Lords asking Mayra to go to prom and Mayra saying yes to him.

Not yes to me, like she had for our date, but yes to Justin Lords.

I definitely, definitely did not like that.

"I should ask her to prom," I said aloud.

Joe tilted his head to one side.

"You haven't already?"

"No."

"Well, where have you taken her out?"

"Um, nowhere," I admitted. "Not yet, anyway."

"Dude!" Joe let out a low whistle. "You better fix that shit before she gets tired of waiting on you."

Joe was definitely right. Without question, I still owed Mayra one date, and as her boyfriend, I needed to plan more outings for the future. I hadn't considered prom, but it was only a few weeks away, and I should probably ask her about that as well. I glanced at the back of Joe's head, simultaneously grateful he brought it up and still a little pissed off he thought Mayra was hot.

I was going to have to get all of this worked into my budget, too.

Later on, I felt my heart rate increase a little as I took my lunch out of my locker and headed toward the cafeteria. I hadn't seen Mayra since this morning, and I knew we were supposed to eat lunch together. I hadn't eaten lunch with anyone but Joe all year, and I tried to keep it together when I realized that Mayra and I had not discussed where we would sit. Would she come to the table where I usually sat, or was I supposed to go to her table?

I decided to hang out by the line of people buying school lunch and wait for Mayra. I fully intended to tell her I'd rather she came to sit with me and Joe, but I wasn't sure how she would feel about that. Mayra always ate at a table full of other girls—mostly on the soccer team—and a few boys as well.

I shuffled my feet back and forth a bit as people began to crowd into the cafeteria. I hadn't seen Mayra yet, but her locker was in the hallway farthest from the lunchroom, so it wasn't surprising that it would take her a while to get here. Joe was already seated at the table where we always sat, and I figured I ought to at least tell him that I was going to eat with Mayra.

As I started toward the table, I felt a sharp pain in my ankle and the floor was suddenly very close to my face. I managed to get my hands out in front of me before I hit the ground, but my lunch was smashed under me and my knees hit the floor hard. I could hear a laugh from behind me, and I knew it was Justin Lords before I ever looked up.

"You need to watch where you're going," he said as I rolled over and sat up. "You get into the wrong man's territory, and you just might get yourself hurt."

I started to pull myself back up when he shoved me back to the floor with a hand to my shoulder.

"I'm the wrong man, you fucking freak."

There is some kind of high school law of physics about rules being broken when teachers have their backs turned. At that point, there wasn't a single adult in the area except for those scooping ladles full of goulash onto plastic trays. I also knew the second law that went along with the first: If I were to retaliate, that's when a teacher would walk into the room.

As much as I might have wanted to hit Lords right then, I knew I couldn't. It was against the school rules, and I was eighteen, which meant it could potentially be an assault charge. Of course he had started it, but I wasn't going to be able to prove he had tripped me intentionally.

I couldn't hit him, so I just moved away and sat with Joe.

I really hadn't had any intention of telling Mayra about my encounter with Justin Lords, not because I didn't want her to know, but I tended to leave those kinds of things in the past and not dwell on them much. Thinking about such things or acting on them didn't bring anyone anything other than additional misery. Talking to Mayra about it would just have brought it back into the present again, and I avoided such conflicts.

Joe didn't have any similar tendencies, apparently.

"So what are you two going to do about Lords?" he asked as Mayra sat down at our table. I had just begun pulling out my slightly squished sandwich and setting it up with my carrots. I was pretty sure there was a bruise on my chest from where I fell on my apple, but the apple itself seemed okay.

"What do you mean?" Mayra asked.

Joe continued before I could stop him.

"Well, he just tripped Matthew and shoved him," he blurted out. "I kinda doubt he'll be done with that. He told Matthew to stay away from you, and that was before you were out of the closet."

He snickered, and Mayra's eyes turned to me. I poked around at my squished bread, refusing to meet her gaze. I could feel her staring at me, and it seemed like there was heat radiating from her body to mine.

"That son of a bitch," she muttered. She was off the bench and stomping across the room in about the same amount of time it took me to open the zipper on my bag of carrots.

"Shit," Joe muttered. "She's pissed."

I looked up and saw Mayra marching right over to the table where Justin was sitting with some of his football buddies. I had no idea what she was planning, but I felt compelled to follow her and try to stop her from…well, whatever she was thinking about doing. I placed my carrots next to the sandwich and slowly followed her.

"What the fuck is wrong with you?" Mayra was leaning over in front of Justin with her palms flat on the table. He leaned so his chair was balanced on its back two legs and grinned up at her.

"No idea what you mean, babe," he responded with a wide grin. "As far as I can tell, I'm perfect."

His buddies laughed, and Mayra continued her tirade.

"You leave Matthew *and* me alone!" she ordered. She lifted her hands up off the table and shook one finger at him. "I don't want anything to do with you anymore, and you know that! I thought we were going to try to at least be friends, but I see you are going to make that impossible!"

The sharp sound of the front legs of Justin's chair hitting the floor as he leaned forward filled the cafeteria and made me cringe. A lot of conversations around us ended right about then, and the room grew quiet. When I looked up at him, there was a look in Justin's eyes I didn't like at all. It was beyond the normal look of someone who just wanted to show his friends how awesome he was by picking on others. I looked back at the floor, unable to keep my eyes on his. His expression was full of malice, and I suddenly didn't want Mayra near him at all. I reached out and gripped the lower part of her arm, trying to coax her away.

"Oh, we were never going to be *friends*." Justin sneered as he leaned close to her. I kept my grip on her arm, but Mayra refused to move. "Never just *friends*."

That's when they started screaming at each other.

"You piece of shit—"

"Frigid little cunt—"

"Fucking bastard!"

I pulled on Mayra's arm with some force, deciding it was best to just get her away before the attention of the school faculty was captured, if it wasn't already. Besides, I still didn't like Justin's look at all, and I wanted to get her away from him as quickly as possible. She took a step toward me but still glared at Lords.

"You can drag her away all you like!" Justin called after us as I wrapped one arm around Mayra and yanked her out of the lunchroom. She wasn't really fighting me, but she wasn't exactly cooperating either. "It's the only way she'll ever put out, you know!"

~oOo~

"You shouldn't have pulled me away," Mayra said later as she drove us back to my house. "I was *not* done talking with him!"

"You didn't need to…confront him," I told her. "Not on my account. It was no big deal."

"No big deal?" Mayra repeated with a harsh laugh. "He practically attacked you. Aimee told me all about it in last period, and you weren't even going to say anything, were you?"

"No," I admitted. "It was over. There wasn't really anything to say."

"Matthew!" Mayra turned and gaped at me. I cringed a little, looking forward toward the street and back to her, hoping she would get her eyes back on the road. She seemed to notice and turned her head to face forward again as she let out a big sigh. "You don't have to put up with that shit. Not from people like him."

"You dated him," I said. I immediately regretted the reminder. I reached out and touched the fish shape on the door.

"Yes, I did," Mayra said quietly. "But he wasn't always like that. Not with me, at least. When he…he…"

She paused for a moment and then reached over and gripped my hand. I returned the hold as she seemed to gather herself back together. Another sharp breath exited her lungs before she spoke again.

"When he showed his true colors, that's when I ended it. He never really accepted that though. I guess now he finally realizes I'm serious, and all his attempts at trying to talk me into going out with him again are pointless."

"Because you moved on," I said softly. I wasn't comfortable with this conversation at all. I was pretty sure I was supposed to console someone when they talked about a breakup, but my stomach felt tight, and I didn't know what to say.

"Oh, he's moved on, too," Mayra said, her voice harsh. "A couple of times, at least."

I wasn't one to keep up with high school relationships and gossip, so I really wasn't sure what she meant. I assumed he had dated some other girls since they broke up, but I had no idea who they might have been, and Mayra didn't offer any further explanation.

We didn't speak much the rest of the way back to my house, and once we were there, the atmosphere was different—uncomfortable. I didn't like it at all. Mayra was obviously still upset, and I wasn't sure what I was supposed to do about it. She pulled out math homework and scribbled down a few answers, but she obviously wasn't concentrating on it at all. I wanted to do or say something to make everything normal again, but I didn't know what I should do or say. I finally decided homework definitely wasn't working, and Mayra didn't seem to be accomplishing much anyway, so I poured two Cokes with four pieces of ice each, and we sat on the couch to drink them.

After a few minutes of silence, Mayra finally spoke.

"He was really great when we first started dating," she told me. "He said all the right things, kissed up to Dad, and took me out every weekend. He was a perfect gentleman the whole time, too. I thought everything was going along just fine until he made it clear he was expecting more than I was interested in giving."

I tensed, not really wanting to think of what the details of "more" might have meant.

"He got a little...demanding," Mayra continued. "That's when I broke up with him. It was kind of an ugly scene. I'll spare you the details."

I nodded, quietly relieved. At some point the lack of information was probably going to bother me, and I would ask her, but I didn't want to know just then. Mayra leaned back against the couch and ran her hand through her hair. She turned to look at me, and I felt her fingers wrapping around my arm.

"I'm sorry he did that to you," she said. "I can't help but feel responsible. It was my idea to make sure everyone knew about us. I should have realized he was going to be a jerk about it and at least warned you."

"It's not your fault," I said. "He's been a jerk to me before."

"I guess what people say is true. Once you date someone, you can never really be friends again."

"I don't know," I said with a shrug.

"Because I'm your first girlfriend," Mayra said with a nod.

I felt myself tense up again, and it didn't go without Mayra noticing.

"What?" she asked.

"Um...well, I did have another girlfriend once."

"You did?" Mayra sounded shocked, but I couldn't really blame her for that. "Who?"

"Um...Carmen Klug."

"Carmen Klug!" Mayra released my arm and sat straight up. She moved away from me a little on the couch. "You dated Carmen Klug?"

"Well, um, sort of."

"Sort of?" Mayra's eyes narrowed as she looked at me. "Out with it, Rohan."

I felt heat on the back of my neck, and I lifted my hand to cover the area I figured was turning red. I glanced at her, feeling more embarrassed for even bringing it up. I wasn't something I had thought about for a long time.

"It wasn't for very long," I said, "and it was a while ago. I was never really sure what to think about it. We weren't really friends before we were boyfriend and girlfriend, so nothing really changed after it was over."

Mayra continued to look at me, waiting for details I wasn't sure how to provide. It then occurred to me that I was leaving out something that could be considered rather important.

"We were six at the time."

"Six?" Mayra repeated. "You mean six years old?"

"Yes."

Mayra giggled and reached for my hand.

"All right, Matthew Rohan. Tell me all about your sordid love affair with Carmen in the first grade."

She giggled again.

"Beginning of second grade, actually," I admitted. Mayra waved her hand around, urging me to continue. "Well, she came over to me at recess and told me I was her boyfriend, and she was my girlfriend."

Mayra's eyes widened.

"Oh, really?"

"Yes."

"And how did she figure that?"

"Apparently, Aimee had a boyfriend, so Carmen thought she needed one, too. I had to carry her backpack on and off the bus for her—she lived just down the street from here when we were little. I think it lasted about two weeks before she told me her mother said she wasn't allowed to have a boyfriend, and that's when we broke up."

I felt Mayra's hand on the side of my face, and I turned my head to meet her eyes briefly.

"You are adorable. Do you know that?" she asked.

I just shook my head and smiled a little.

"Well, you are," she insisted.

I couldn't really argue with her, so I moved closer and pressed my lips against hers. We spent an hour on the couch, and I spent the time worrying about our date.

Overall, today was a win.

Chapter 12—Maybe Dating is a Bad Idea

I had at least an hour before I had to pick up Mayra, but I was already in the car and traveling in the same circle I had traversed when trying to get to her house for a piece of cake. Tonight was going to be our first real date. Instead of taking the drive to Cincinnati or Hamilton, we decide to stick with Uptown Oxford. We were going to get bagels from the Bagel and Deli and eat them in the park.

If I could get to her house, that is.

I figured if I left early enough, I would eventually be able to get there on time, maybe even a little early. I had the feeling Mr. Trevino was going to play the proper father-figure when I came to pick her up even though Mayra said she had made him promise to be nice when I came to get her. At least I had already met him officially, so there was a little less pressure.

I checked the gauges on my car and decided it would be a good idea to top off the tank and maybe check my oil and tire pressure, too. There was still plenty of time before I was supposed to be at Mayra's house, so I drove to the nearest gas station and filled up. While I was checking the tire pressure, I saw Justin Lords and three other guys coming out of the convenience store attached to the gas station. Justin looked over at me and smirked as he leaned over and said something quietly into the ear of one of the guys with

195

him. They both laughed but didn't come near me or anything. I found myself breathing easier after the group drove off, though.

After cleaning the windshield and wipers for the second time, I wiped down the rear view mirror and decided I could probably head over to Mayra's house now. I reminded myself that I had been over there twice this week, and everything had been fine, even when I had to park next to Mr. Trevino's truck. I drove around the block four times again but managed to get myself into Mayra's driveway with about five minutes to spare.

I sat in my car for a while, considering the phrase "fashionably late" and wondering if it applied to picking up your girlfriend for a night out. Glancing up at the kitchen window, I saw Mayra standing inside with her arms crossed and smiling at me. She shook her head a little before beckoning me with a finger. I peeked at myself in the mirror, tried to smooth out my hair a little, got out of the car, and walked up to the front door.

Mr. Trevino answered, and I had to swallow a big lump in my throat before I could speak. I wanted to say something like, "Good evening, Mr. Trevino. I'm here to pick up Mayra." However, that's not quite what came out.

"Um…hi." I turned my head a little and closed my eyes tightly as I tried to get a grip on myself. I cleared my throat and thought I would try again, but no sound came out at all.

Mr. Trevino chuckled low, then stepped aside and opened the door wide.

"Come on in, Matthew. Mayra's been ready since noon or something."

"Dad!" Mayra glared at him as she came out from around the kitchen entryway. She was dressed in a dark blue blouse and a black skirt, which flowed out around her thighs. She had done something to her hair to make it all wavy instead of straight, and she had on a bit of eye makeup, which she didn't usually wear.

She was stunning, and I realized I was staring at her with my mouth open, so I quickly closed it. Her father continued to snicker

196

softly while I tried to come up with some words to say about how nice she looked. Apparently, I had been rendered speechless.

"Come on," Mayra said. "Let's go before Dad decides to be funny again."

Bethany was definitely right about one thing: not bringing up the subject of soccer until we were on our date was a brilliant idea. Mayra talked and talked about the teams she had played on and the tournaments her teams had won and lost. She also gave me answers to the questions I occasionally asked. The conversation continued even after we finished our bagels on the park bench and watched the university students stumble from bar to bar. I was actually getting kind of excited about the soccer season starting up soon even though it would mean a fairly drastic change to our current routine as Mayra would need to make time for practices and games.

"You can work on your homework when I'm at practice," Mayra said. "There are a lot of people who sit in the stands and watch while they do their homework."

"When are the games?" I asked. We crumpled up the foil that had held the warm bagels and tossed it in a nearby trash can. Mayra grabbed my hand, and we walked up and down the sidewalks that lined the old, brick street of Uptown. It was a beautiful night with no clouds in sight. The moon and stars shone down on us as we held hands and walked aimlessly.

"Usually on the weekends," she said, "but there are some during the week as well—mostly on Wednesdays or Thursdays."

I nodded and tried to mentally prepare myself for games being on different days of the week. I thought I could cope with that, especially since Mayra said she would have a complete schedule of games sometime next week.

We continued walking and talking, not really paying much attention to where we were going. We came to the end of High Street and turned to walk past the old library and around the corner. The side street held a lot of student housing, and every house seemed to be having a party of some sort. There were a lot of obviously drunk people laughing and passing cups of beer around.

I was all for turning around and going back the way we came, but Mayra was concerned it was starting to get late, and we had both promised her father we would be back before midnight. There was a dark alleyway that made a good shortcut back to the car, so I didn't protest.

There weren't any streetlights in that area, only the light outside of Mac and Joe's, the dive bar popular with students and townies alike. Mayra let go of my hand and moved closer so she could wrap her arm around my waist, and I placed mine over her shoulders. My face was actually starting to ache from smiling so much, and I wondered what I had done to be so lucky.

Turning my head a little, I leaned my cheek on the top of her head, inhaled the sweet scent of her hair, and placed a light kiss on her temple.

"Well, isn't that sweet." A voice came from behind us, followed by laughter both from the darkened alley entrance in front of us as well as behind us. "A couple of little lovebirds out for a stroll."

Two figures stepped out of the alleyway right in front of us, and when I glanced over my shoulder I could see the silhouettes of two more approach from the way we had just come. The ones in front blocked our forward progression, and I felt Mayra tense next to me as her arm tightened around my torso.

I couldn't take Mayra safely forward or backward, so we stopped in the middle of the dark street as the figures in front of us stepped out of the shadows. I heard Mayra's sharp intake of air.

"I told you we weren't done," a voice said as the figures walked toward us.

"Justin, what the hell are you doing here?" Mayra yelled as Lords' face became visible in the moonlight. I pulled her a little closer and whispered her name in caution, hoping maybe she'd just consider being quiet for a minute. Bullies usually backed off and got bored if you were quiet and didn't respond to them. The more she talked, the more it would egg him on.

"Just taking a little stroll, same as you," he retorted. The guy next to him cackled, and I recognized him as someone who had graduated a year or two ago. I was pretty sure his name was Mark, and he had also been on the Talawanda football team.

"I've had enough of your shit," Mayra told him. "Come on, Matthew."

Mayra started moving forward, but before I could even take a step with her, Justin nodded toward his buddies behind us, and I felt my arms being grabbed from behind. Mayra cried out and turned toward me as I was pulled backward, but as soon as she did, Mark moved forward and grabbed her arms, too.

My arms were wrenched behind my back, and I immediately noticed the two guys grabbing onto me smelled of stale beer and cigarettes. As I felt an arm move around my neck, effectively holding me in a headlock, I had a strange, surreal feeling I had only encountered once before. It had been in the hospital when my mom was dying. I recalled the doctors telling Travis it could be any time now, and his reddened eyes had turned to mine as he walked over and pulled me close to him.

"Come here, Travis," Mom had said, and he released me to sit on the chair beside her bed. In a raspy voice, she told him to make sure he took care of me, and he promised her he would. Then she called me over, and I sat beside her and held her hand to the side of my face because she couldn't quite hold her arm up without help.

"My beautiful boy," she whispered. "So much we were still supposed to do."

Even with the warm feeling of her palm pressed to my cheek, it felt like I wasn't there—like I wasn't even in the room at all but watching all of this happen to someone else. She didn't look like she was supposed to, and I didn't feel like myself. In my head, I wondered if it was just a dream and what I was going to have to do to wake up from it. Deep inside of me, there was a tiny ember of anger over what was happening to her—to me—but there had been nothing I could do to stop it. The burning feeling just sat there in my gut with nowhere to go.

But it hadn't been a dream, and neither was this.

"Get your fucking hands off of me!" Mayra screeched as she twisted and turned in Mark's grip.

"Oh, I don't think so," Lords said as he walked up to her. "It's time to get what was always supposed to be mine."

I wondered what it was like to float in the air the way birds of prey soar on the wind and if it felt similar to the way I was feeling now. I also knew my mind was getting far too distracted, and I was having trouble focusing on what was going on around me. I could hear Mayra cursing and see her writhing around to try to escape the hands holding her, but her actual words were somewhat lost as well as the meaning of what was happening before me. The fire in her eyes was strangely beautiful, though. That detail didn't escape me.

Everything seemed to speed up as Justin and Mark grabbed Mayra and shoved her into a darker part of the alley behind the bar.

I heard the tear of cloth as Justin's hands met at the top of Mayra's blouse and tore it open, buttons flying around and making little clicking sounds on the asphalt. His low laugh echoed around the deserted street as he pawed at her again, tearing the dark blue bra off of her with an audible snap. As Mayra's eyes widened in terror, Justin moved one of his legs in back of hers and tripped her at the same time Mark started pushing her to the ground.

Mayra's head snapped back, and she started to let out a scream before Mark's hand covered her mouth and muffled her cries. There was hot breath on the side of my face as one of the two holding me back leaned a little closer. The smell of his beer breath crawled over my face as he spoke.

"Don't worry, bud," he said. "When we've all had our turn, we'll let you have some fun with her, too."

I felt my body turn cold as the implication of what he was saying poured over me like a bucket of ice water. My head was immobilized, but my gaze found the dark corner where Justin now had Mayra on her back and was pushing her skirt up over her hips. I could see a sliver of deep blue—the same color of her torn blouse and bra—right at the top of her thigh. Justin's fingers wrapped around the delicate blue lace and started to pull. Mayra tried to kick him, but she was pinned beneath him, and Mark had her wrists captured in the hand that wasn't covering her mouth.

The numbness of the detachment I had been feeling seemed to fall to my feet as the iciness in my body was rapidly replaced by the burning heat of a rage I had never felt in all my life. Even when Mom's hand had slipped from my face as I watched her eyes close and her chest rise and fall for the last time, I had felt only the emptiness of helplessness.

But I was not helpless this time.

I couldn't do anything to stop what had happened to my mother, so I turned the rage I was feeling toward Mayra's attackers. I closed my eyes in an attempt to assess my situation in more detail.

There was an arm around my neck, holding firmly but not overly tight. I could breathe just fine. The bigger problem was my hands, which were locked behind my back. One arm was behind me, held by the same guy with his elbow holding my neck, and the other arm was immobilized by the second guy to the right of me though his grip was not as tight.

Justin's laughter fueled my anger and reminded me that I didn't have much time before he hurt her—before he *really* hurt Mayra. I could still hear her muffled cries from the ground a few feet away from me, and I knew I had to incapacitate the two guys holding onto me before I could help her. I didn't have a whole lot of time to ponder my actions, so I went with instinct.

Turning my head as far as I could to my right, I made the loudest retching sound I possibly could. The guy holding my right arm took a half step back to avoid what he surely thought would be puke in his face and loosened the grip on my arm just enough.

With a quick pull, his fingers slipped from my forearm. A moment later, my elbow connected with the underside of his jaw, and he flew backwards. My right arm was now free, and I didn't hesitate to swing it around and connect my fist with the nose of the one holding me by the neck.

My mind screamed about the lack of gloves, but Mayra's muted cries were louder in my head.

The dark-haired guy with a serious acne problem was not someone I recognized even before his nose exploded. He was decently strong, though, and didn't lose his grip around my throat. Instead, he tightened his hold, which gave me just the leverage I needed to bring my knee up with a twist of my hips and pound it into his gut once, twice, three times in quick succession.

With the air gone from his lungs, his hold on me relaxed enough for me to duck down and escape the grip on my neck and left arm. I brought my hands together in a double fist and slammed them down on the back of his neck as he doubled over to try to catch his breath.

I felt the impact of a fist to my temple before the acne-faced guy dropped to the ground. I winced as the skin across my temple was torn open by a ring on the other guy's third finger. He was short and stocky and had a buzz cut of dirty blond hair. He swung at me again as I ducked and spun around to my left, bringing my leg up and smashing into his side with my foot. With another spin to my right, I landed a roundhouse kick to the side of his head, and he dropped beside his companion.

With both of my captors on the ground, I turned my attention to Lords and Mark.

Justin was still above Mayra, up on his knees between her legs. His hands gripped her thighs tightly, holding her against the cold ground. He was apparently oblivious to what had just transpired between me and his two friends, but Mark was looking up at me with a shocked expression. A filmy red haze covered my eyes as I looked at Justin holding Mayra on the ground, and I lost all ability to think.

"Shit!" Mark cried out, but not in time. I tackled Justin with my head crashing into his side, and we both went rolling away.

I bounced back up and turned to face Lords as Mayra started to really scream. A quick glance to the side showed me Mark's retreating form as he ran down the alley and out of sight. Justin was still on the ground, looking up with a dazed expression. The buckle of his belt and his fly were undone, and the current of rage washed over me again.

I cried out as I jumped on top of him, landing my knee and all my weight into his groin before shifting upwards and slamming my forehead into his face. He pulled his arms up to cover his head, but my blows found their marks anyway. Face, head, chest, shoulders—I just continued to hit him. Every few strokes, I kidney punched him before going back to his face. A couple of times, I raised myself up only to bring my knees into his stomach.

He struggled beneath me but was getting slower in his movements. I was pretty sure he was screaming at me to stop, but I wasn't listening to anything he had to say. The cliché red haze over my eyes seemed to be impacting my hearing as well.

I have no idea how long I kept hitting him. I only know that when I finally snapped out of it, he was unconscious, and Mayra was curled up on her side, sobbing. She had the remnants of her torn blouse gathered up in her hands, and she held it tightly against her skin.

I crawled off of him and over to her, reaching out tentatively.

"Mayra, are you okay?" Stupid question. My hand touched her shoulder, and she flinched. It reminded me of all the times I had flinched from people when they tried to touch me and how I had even done that to her a few times in the beginning.

Moving up behind her, I reached around and stroked her hair away from her face the same way she usually did to me when we were on the couch watching TV. As the adrenaline in my system soured, my arms and legs began to ache, and I was increasingly aware of the pain in my head and the dried blood on my face and in my hair.

"Mayra? I need your phone."

I watched her chest rise and fall twice with deep breaths before she pointed with her finger to her purse on the ground. I reached over her and pulled the cell phone out of the bag and dialed 911.

"My name is Matthew Rohan," I said quietly. "My girlfriend and I were attacked in the alley. I'm pretty sure we need an ambulance here."

After giving the operator all the pertinent information, I placed the phone back in Mayra's purse and looked over my shoulder. Justin was still sprawled out on the ground where I had left him and so was the dark-haired guy who had me in a headlock. Both Mark and the boy with the buzz cut were gone.

Mayra shifted a little and pulled her knees up closer to her chest. She sniffed audibly, and her shoulders began to shake as she continued to clutch the scrap of fabric against her chest. I quickly unbuttoned my shirt and got her to sit up long enough to get her arms in the sleeves and the buttons at least partially closed in the front. As soon as my shirt was on her, she started to lie back down on the asphalt, but I stopped her.

I couldn't let her lie on the ground. Instead, I gathered her up in my arms and held her until blue, red, and white lights started to flicker around us. Before the first cop could even get out of the car, there was another coming from the other direction. Mayra seemed to snap out of her stupor a little at that point as she looked up at me.

"You're hurt," she said. She reached up to my forehead, but she didn't quite touch it. "You're bleeding."

"I'm okay."

Mayra turned her head to look toward the light and then buried her face back against my shoulder.

"Is he dead?"

"Who?"

"Justin."

"No," I said. I looked over and saw his chest rise and fall again. "He's out of it, though."

"I wish he was dead."

"Don't tempt me," I mumbled.

The first police officer walked quickly to Lords, placed his fingers against his neck for a moment, and then went and checked the other guy. He said something into the radio at his neck and then came over to where Mayra and I were on the ground.

"Looks like you've had a rough night," he said. He looked at me as I stared at a little piece of Mayra's hair lying across her shoulder. "There's an ambulance about three minutes away. Are you up for telling me what happened?"

Mayra kept her head tucked against my chest, so I gave a quick overview of what had transpired in the alley. The cop wrote down a bunch of stuff on his pad of paper and then handed it over to another cop. Just as the ambulance was coming around the corner, he reached out and placed his hand on Mayra's shoulder.

"I'm sorry, ma'am," he said quietly, "but I need to ask you something before we head to the hospital."

Mayra's eyes looked up at mine and then over to the officer. She nodded once.

"Did he penetrate you?"

I felt her go stiff in my arms for a moment before she shook her head.

"Matthew stopped him before he could."

"She was fighting him the whole time," I added.

"Good for you," he said. "I'll be right back, okay?"

I nodded, and Mayra leaned her head back against my body. Two EMTs showed up then and lifted a groaning Justin Lords onto a rolling bed. I had to admit to a little sense of satisfaction when I saw one officer handcuff him to the edge of it. Lords and the acne guy were both cuffed and loaded into the back of the ambulance, and then the officer walked back over to us. I gave him descriptions of the other two guys as well as the name Mark, though I didn't know what his last name was. The cop wrote all that down, too, and then one of the police cars drove away.

"What time is it?" Mayra asked.

"Eleven thirty," the officer responded.

"I need to call my dad," she said. "We're not going to be home on time."

Mayra finally sat up next to me and started rooting through her purse for her phone. Once she called, she told him we had a little problem, and we were going to be late. I could hear his voice getting louder on the phone, but when she said we had been attacked, he went quiet.

"He wants to talk to you," Mayra said as she held the phone out to the officer.

"Ma'am, I really can't discuss…"

"It's Henry Trevino," Mayra said quickly. "He says you probably know him."

The officer's eyes widened a little.

"Henry Trevino is your dad?"

"Yes."

The officer took the phone and placed it up to his ear.

"Mr. Trevino," he said into the phone, "Peter Gregory here…She looks just fine, but we're going to be taking her to the hospital for a quick check just as a precaution…No, sir…I don't believe so. I get the idea the boyfriend here managed to stop that…Yes, sir…He's definitely making the trip—he's going to need some stitches…Yes, sir…Oh…yeah, of course. I can take care of that. I'll meet you in the ER when you arrive."

~oOo~

I winced as a nurse injected my skin with some kind of local anesthetic before she started stitching up my temple. I had already

206

recapped the whole ordeal twice with two different police officers, and I was pretty sure they were doing the same thing with Mayra. I supposed they just wanted to make sure they were getting the same story from both of us though they didn't seem to doubt what happened.

I had heard one of the officers talking to a doctor, and not only was Lords way up on the intoxication scale, but they found cocaine in his system as well. The other guy they brought in—the one with the acne problem—apparently had cocaine in his pocket and was known to the police. They were hoping for more information when Lords regained consciousness.

When I thought back to just a couple of hours ago when my fists were connecting over and over again with Justin's head like they usually did with the heavy bag, I just felt numb. I remembered every moment of it though it didn't really feel like me at the time. Everything in my head just screamed that he was going to hurt Mayra, and I had to make sure he would never, ever try to do that again.

The nurse finished with my head and then fussed over the cuts all across my knuckles and fingers. She also had me lie down on my side and applied some sort of cream and a bandage on my leg, which had been badly scraped on the asphalt when I tackled Lords.

Mr. Trevino walked in just as the nurse finished. She nodded to him as she walked out, glancing at me briefly before disappearing. Mayra's father stood for a minute by the curtain separating me from the open hallway before he came over and sat on the rolling chair by the bed.

"Matthew," he started to say, but his voice cracked, and he closed his mouth. He paused to take a couple of breaths and run his hand over his face before he continued. "You saved my daughter from something about as horrific as it gets. I don't even know where to begin to express how grateful I am that you were with her tonight."

He stood up and took a couple of steps away and then turned around.

"I'm paying your hospital bill. Not going to listen to any argument about that, so save your breath."

He walked over to the curtain and pulled it back.

"Mr. Trevino?" I called out.

"Yeah?" He turned around again to look at me.

I fiddled with one of the bandages on my finger, took a moment to collect my thoughts, and then spoke.

"I'd never let anyone hurt her," I told him. "No one. Ever."

I continued to look down at my hands, but I could see him standing motionless off to my left. After a minute, he ran his hand over his face again.

"Matthew?" Mr. Trevino said with another long breath.

"Yeah?"

"Call me Henry."

I nodded slowly without looking up from my hands. I wasn't completely sure how this changed our relationship, but I sensed the shift. He walked out without saying anything else.

Hours later, I finally got to see Mayra just as we were both being discharged.

She looked tired and still shaken, but she smiled when she saw me and wrapped her arms tightly around my neck. We stood there just outside the ER for a few moments as Henry talked to the lady at the front desk. Mayra was still wearing my button-down shirt, and I was still in just the T-shirt I had been wearing underneath.

"Mayra?" I said into her ear.

"Yeah?"

"I was going to ask you if you wanted to go to prom with me," I said, "but I'm kind of thinking maybe we could just stay in? Maybe rent a movie or something?"

"I'll pay for the movie *and* pizza," Henry piped up as he walked by us.

Mayra laughed quietly against my shoulder.

"It just seems when we plan a date, it doesn't go so well," I said with a shrug.

"I can't dance anyway." Mayra giggled. "Pizza instead of prom is the plan!"

It was four in the morning before we managed to actually leave the hospital. The doctor had given me a bunch of painkillers, which made me dizzy, so I wasn't allowed to drive myself back home. Travis and Beth came to get both me and my car and drove me back home, and Mayra ended up going home with her dad.

Unfortunately, it was a bit too much like the end of our last failed date night.

Travis drove in silence though he kept looking at me with a strange expression on his face. I didn't think much about it since I was asleep before we were halfway back to the house. When we got home, Travis helped me inside. It was kind of hard to walk because the medicine really wiped me out. I wasn't completely sure, but I thought he said something about being proud of me when he dropped me on my bed.

I woke to the phone ringing and stumbled my way out of bed to answer it. It was raining and pretty dark outside, so I couldn't tell what time it was.

"Hello?"

"Matthew?"

"Yes."

"It's Henry."

"Oh...um...hi..." I blathered. I rubbed at my eyes with my free hand and stood up a little straighter for no particular reason.

"Look, I was wondering if you could come over."

"Is Mayra okay?"

"Well...that's just it." I heard him take a deep breath. "She hasn't slept much at all—she keeps having nightmares and waking herself up. She's kind of a mess, and she's asking for you."

"I'll be right there."

I pulled on a pair of jeans and didn't even think about anything but Mayra needing me as I got in my car and drove to her house. The clock in the car read nine twenty in the morning though it didn't really feel like I had slept more than an hour. My head was pounding, so I figured the pain pills must have worn off. My back and shoulders were stiff, too.

As soon as I turned into Mayra's driveway, I was out of the car and heading up the steps to her door. Henry was there, waiting for me, so I didn't even have to knock.

"She's up in her room," he said. "I think she might be asleep again, but it doesn't seem to last long."

I glanced up the stairs where Henry was pointing. I had never gone upstairs in Mayra's house before and certainly hadn't been in her room. I felt the tingle of panic wash over my skin but then reminded myself that not only had her dad asked me to come over, but he was pointing the way, so it must be okay for me to go in there.

"Matthew, I should tell you something."

I turned my head to look at him, but I had to drop my eyes to his shoulder. The mustache waving around in the middle of his face was just too distracting.

"I got a call a while ago—from Officer Gregory. They caught one of the other guys—Mark Johnson. He must have been pretty freaked out and ended up giving them a full confession. Apparently there was some sort of bet between Lords and the coke dealer. Mayra heard me talking on the phone about it."

"Bet?" I was pretty sure I didn't want to know, but I asked anyway.

Henry growled under his breath as he turned his head to one side. His right hand balled up into a fist.

"Lords bet his buddies he could...have sex with Mayra. When they broke up, he stood to lose a lot of money to the coke dealer. This was his way of winning the bet."

My hands started to shake as I processed what he was saying. I had to close my eyes and breathe slowly for a few minutes before I could even speak again.

"They followed us," I said.

"Yeah," Henry confirmed. "I don't think they were counting on you to offer much resistance and figured they could threaten you both into silence. I'd say you gave them a bit of a shock."

"What about the fourth guy?" I asked.

"The police have a name," Henry said, "Steven Blake. They haven't found him yet. At least they hadn't as of a couple of hours ago. They have a warrant out for the assault charges, especially considering he was the one who busted you up the most. His brother is the dealer—the other guy you knocked out."

"I'd never even seen them before."

"I think Mayra has," Henry said, his voice low. "Mayra's mentioned their names before. I think Justin was hanging around them when she was still dating that...that..."

He growled again.

"Henry?" I said quietly, trying out his name for the first time.

"Yeah?"

"I kind of wish...wish I hadn't stopped hitting him, you know?"

"Yeah, kid," Henry said with a sigh. "I do know."

Henry reached out and clapped my shoulder with his hand. I tried not to flinch, but I really couldn't help it. I knew he was trying to be nice, and I knew he was grateful, but that didn't stop me from cringing anyway. He pulled his hand back and dropped it at his side.

"Sorry," I muttered.

Henry shook his head and waved his hand dismissively. He looked toward the stairs, scratched at his mustache, and tapped his foot a few times.

"She's in her room," Henry finally said. "Go on up if you want."

Taking a deep breath, I walked up the stairs slowly and then peeked into the partially opened door. Mayra was lying on a twin bed with her legs hanging partway off the side. There was a blue and white comforter lying most of the way on the floor, which Mayra had apparently recently kicked off.

Her eyes were closed, but she was restless.

I approached her slowly, walking softly across the floor before kneeling next to her bed. I reached out and touched her arm gently, and she jumped. A second later, she sat straight up and screamed.

"Mayra! Mayra! It's just me!"

"Matthew!" she cried as she grabbed hold of my shoulders. I hugged her to me, her body shaking under my fingers.

"It's okay," I said quietly. "It's just me."

She tugged at me until I was lying down next to her. As soon as we were side by side, she nestled her forehead against my chest and closed her eyes.

I glanced at the doorway to see Henry standing there with a scowl on his face. Tensing up a bit, I wondered what he thought of me lying down with her, but as she drifted off again, his mustache twitched into a bit of a smile. He nodded at me once and then turned to go back down the stairs, leaving the door wide open.

Without his eyes on us, I settled down and pulled Mayra closer to me. My head was right above hers on the pillow, and the sweet scent of her hair filled my nose. Her fingers clutched at my shoulders, and I realized she wasn't quite asleep.

"I'm here," I said quietly. Her fingers tightened on me again.

"I'm glad," she whispered back. "I can't sleep."

"You can now," I told her.

Mayra just shook her head.

"I can't stop thinking about it." Her hand slid down my arm until it came to rest on my bandaged knuckles.

I wished I knew what to say to her, but as usual, I didn't. I didn't know what to say, so I didn't say anything. I just lay there next to her and let her fiddle with the edge of my bandage. My mom would have had all the right words to say—she always did—but that was not a trait she passed on to me.

"I was a *bet*." Mayra suddenly snarled, startling me from my thoughts. "He *bet* he could talk me into giving him my virginity. It was the only reason we were even going out at all, because he made a *bet* on me. When I wouldn't give it to him, he thought he would just take it!"

My grip on her tightened.

"I won't let him hurt you." I made the same promise to her that I had to her father.

She placed a hand on my chest and pushed back until she was looking up into my face.

"He's not going to get another chance!" Mayra exclaimed. "No one will *ever* get that chance again! You can't be there all the time, Matthew. I've got to fix this."

"Fix this?" I asked, confused.

"Yes, fix it," she said again.

Her hand came up to the side of my face, and she pressed her lips desperately to mine. She broke away quickly and looked into my eyes.

"I want it to be you, Matthew," she told me. "I want you to be my first. Then no one else can ever threaten to take that from me again. I'm going to give it to you."

I couldn't even fathom a way to respond to that, so I just freaked out.

Lose.

Chapter 13—From Freak to Hero

The sheer number of emotions that passed through my head probably equaled the average spending budget of a congressional member for the month of July, fireworks included.

The first set of thoughts focused on exactly what Mayra was saying and whether she meant right here and right now with her father downstairs, watching a baseball game on the flat screen. The notion of being unprepared didn't even come marginally close. It wasn't just a matter of not having a condom in my wallet, like Joe always did. He claimed he never wanted to have the opportunity and have to bail because of something like that though I was pretty sure he had never had the opportunity anyway. No, I was unprepared in five hundred different ways. Well, maybe not five hundred, but plenty.

Or at least three.

First, Mayra was scared. Second, her dad was right downstairs and definitely within earshot. And third, I didn't have the slightest idea how to have sex with any level of understanding past "Tab A goes into Slot B."

Cognitively, I knew this was a reaction to what had happened to Mayra and not something she would be considering if the events of the previous night had not occurred. She was scared and reacting without thinking. She didn't really want this at all.

215

The last wave of emotion that covered my skin was nothing short of sheer, raw desire.

I wanted to do it. I wanted to do *it*. I wanted to *do it* with Mayra.

In my fantasies I had known just what to do, and sweat had glistened on her forehead as her neck arched back, and she called out my name. I moved in and out of her effortlessly, and every touch of my skilled fingers brought shivers from her heated skin. We went on for hours though the fantasy itself would only last a few minutes. Still, there was little more I could have asked for than having her want this from me.

It didn't matter.

Regardless of desire, I was not going to have sex with her when that mustache was waving around on the ground floor just below us.

The very thought of Henry and my own unpreparedness would have been enough to send me over the edge, but combine that with the understanding that Mayra only said this because she was frightened was far, far too much.

Her fingers against my jaw became electric, and I felt as if I was shocked right off the bed. I fell onto the floor and conked my head on the wood slats. Prying open my eyes, I was met with a vision of a pair of dirty blue socks just beneath the bed's dust ruffle.

"No...no...can't...wouldn't be...don't know...no...no..."

My limbs acted on their own, quickly propelling me across the room until my back hit the door to her closet. My body began to shake, and my rapid heartbeat threatened to move right out of my chest and into one of the residence halls on campus. Finding my way into the corner between the back wall of the room and the closet, I huddled. I didn't even fight it as my mind started to close in around me, shielding me from everything outside. I knew I couldn't deal with this, so I let the panic take me.

Part of retreating inside of myself was extraordinarily comforting. Everything around me would just disappear as my mind would shut down to keep at bay all the thoughts that threatened to overwhelm me. If only I could also keep out the physical reactions at the same time—the pounding of my heart and the difficulty getting enough air into my lungs—then it wouldn't really be bad at all.

Of course, were that the case, I might not bother to come out of it.

Through my choked breaths, I vaguely registered Mayra's voice. I couldn't make out the words, but I knew she was talking to me. There was something she was trying to tell me—something she wanted me to do—but I had pushed it away from my conscious mind.

A distinct ache in my shoulders crept up my neck, and I wondered how long I had been punching the bag. Something wasn't quite right, though, because I was sitting in an uncomfortable position and was not sprawled out on my bed or the couch like I usually was after a long workout. I realized my head was against my knees, and my legs were drawn up tightly against my chest.

Shit, shit, shit.

The moments leading up to my attack came back to me, a little slower than the first time but almost as strong. Mayra curled her hand into the hair right above my ear, and she stroked my jaw.

"I'm sorry, I'm sorry," she whispered again and again.

"I...I...I *can't*, Mayra!" I stammered. "You're just scared! I don't...I don't want to just because you're scared!"

She moved her arms around my head and pulled me against her shoulder. My body resisted at first, but I was calmed enough by her scent to let my forehead drop against her. With her hands in my hair, she just whispered "Shh" over and over for a few minutes.

Eventually my breathing slowed, and my heartbeat returned to its more natural rhythm. Once my own body calmed, I realized how agitated Mayra was and looked up to her tear-streaked face and cringed, knowing I was responsible.

"You're scared," I whispered.

"I want to do it," Mayra insisted.

"Not because you're scared." I shook my head, running my cheek on the top of her arm. "I don't want it to be like that."

"That's not the reason," Mayra said.

My gaze met hers briefly, and I narrowed my eyes. Mayra sighed.

"It's not the only reason."

"Your dad is right downstairs…"

"I didn't mean right *now*," Mayra said with another sigh. "I guess I should know better by now than to spring things on you like that. I just never know what will upset you. When we were…in the alley…I couldn't even think past trying to scream, but you took on all four of them. You looked so…I don't know."

"What do you mean?"

"You were so angry," she said quietly, "but calm at the same time. As soon as you...as soon as you pulled him off me, and Mark let go…I just looked at you and knew everything was going to be okay again. You were completely in control. That's when I just fell apart, I guess. I knew it was safe to do so."

She reached under my chin and tilted my head up a little. I didn't quite meet her eyes, but I came close.

"How could you be so calm with all of that happening?"

"I don't know," I said with a shrug. "It's all kind of a blur. I couldn't let them hurt you."

At some point, we left the floor by Mayra's closet and crawled back onto her bed, completely exhausted. I wrapped my arms around her shoulders and pulled her close to me, wondering how we managed to switch roles so quickly again, I now the caregiver and she the recipient. Mayra let out a long, slow breath before curling into my chest and closing her eyes. The grey light from the overcast morning penetrated the thin curtains hanging over her window, casting soft shadows around her shoulders.

"Have you ever thought about it?" Mayra's quiet voice floated over the blankets.

"About what?" I asked, somewhat lost, watching the little floating pieces of dust above the bed.

"About you and me…" Her voice went very quiet. "You know…*together*."

I swallowed hard and willed my heart to stay right where it was and not jump into my throat. Before I could process exactly what she was saying, my mouth opened.

"Yes."

I couldn't take the words back, so I stuck my head underneath Mayra's pillow. She tried to pull it off, but I gripped it tightly and held it against my cheek.

"Are you going to come out of there?" she asked after a few minutes.

"No." Frankly, it was kind of nice under her pillow. It was soft, warm, and smelled like Mayra. It was also dark, and my face was hidden so Mayra couldn't see me after my admission of thinking about having sex with her.

I could hear her deep sigh and feel her fingers rubbing the spot between my shoulder and my neck. I was still sore there, and it felt good.

"You're being silly."

I shrugged, causing the blanket to fall off my shoulder. Mayra pulled it back up.

"It's not like I don't know where you are!" she said with a bit of a giggle. I shrugged again, but she kept the blanket in place. She trailed her finger down over my shoulder and upper arm. It felt a little like it did when she ran her fingers through my hair, and I felt myself relax.

"I have too, you know," Mayra said quietly.

"You have what?" I asked.

"Thought about you," she said. Her voice dropped lower. "While I was here…in bed."

I swallowed hard and closed my eyes even though I couldn't see anything from where I was anyway. I understood what she was saying, and I definitely remembered what I had done while in bed, thinking about her.

She traced farther down my arm with her finger, and my hand gripped her side reflexively. She slipped her hand off my arm and onto my hip. With her palm placed firmly against my thigh, she rubbed against the material of my jeans. I had to swallow again, trying to decide if I was hoping she would move her hand around to the front or hoping she would just send me home.

"Mayra," I said as I finally pulled my head out from under the pillow and glanced at her face, "I want to, I do…but you *are* scared." I took in a long breath, still not knowing if I really agreed with what I was about to say. "On top of that…well, I…I…Mayra, *I'm* not ready."

She stilled her hand and let it lie on my leg for a moment before she brought it up to my face again. She cupped my cheek and tried to get me to turn to face her, but I was more likely to dive back under the pillow than meet her eyes at this point.

"Why do I feel like we've reversed roles here?" Mayra said with a soft laugh. "Isn't the guy supposed to be trying to talk the girl into it?"

I shrugged again.

"I don't know," I answered. "But Mayra…I'm still trying to get used to the idea that I *have* a girlfriend, especially one as beautiful as you are. I don't want…"

My voice trailed off, and I tilted my face back toward the pillow. Mayra's hand stroked my hair.

"Don't want what?" she asked quietly.

"I don't want"—I gritted my teeth and made myself say it—"I don't want to disappoint you."

This time, when I wouldn't turn my head toward her, she ducked down and pushed her face into the pillow beside me, pushing down the fluff and exposing my face. She moved forward until our noses touched.

"I don't know what to do either," she told me. "But I'm pretty sure you wouldn't disappoint me."

Our lips brushed softly together before Mayra settled back and closed her eyes. I wrapped my arms tightly around her, pulling her close against my chest. A few minutes later, she was asleep.

~oOo~

Mayra and I ended up sleeping away most of Sunday, not realizing the story of our attack had gotten to the local news. Henry knew, but he must not have thought to tell either of us. Maybe he just didn't want Mayra to think about it so she could sleep that night. Regardless, when we got out of Mayra's car on Monday morning and started walking toward the front doors of the school, everyone stopped and looked at us.

"Oh shit," Mayra muttered under her breath.

"What?" I asked.

"Half the football team is over there," she said. "Look at them. They all have to know what happened."

When I took a quick look toward the school, I could see they were all watching our approach. Mayra turned into me and started to try to push me backwards.

"What are you doing?" I asked. "It's almost time for first bell. We have to be at my locker before first bell, or I'll never get to class on time."

"Matthew, they know!" she cried out a little louder. "Those are all Justin's friends! His teammates! I have no idea what they might be planning!"

I grabbed her arms and pulled her in front of me. I met her eyes and stared into them as hard as I could.

"I will never let anyone hurt you."

"What if they want you?" she whispered.

I glanced over my shoulder, and six big guys stood near the entrance—all football players. There were at least three dozen other

221

kids standing around as well, and I really didn't think they'd try anything with that big of an audience.

"We'll be fine," I told her. "They aren't going to do anything right in front of the school. They'd get expelled."

I turned her around, put my arm across her shoulders to keep her near me, ducked my head down, and started for the doors. As we neared the entrance, they all stood up a little straighter, and some of them took a slight step forward.

My body tensed. Despite what I said, I wasn't sure what I would do with six of them. I could handle two at a time, assuming they weren't more skilled than me, but I couldn't really take on more than that. If my assessment was wrong—if they were going to try something—I didn't really stand a chance.

I tightened my arm around Mayra's shoulders and considered turning and running with her. When I glanced up, I saw Scott O'Malley, who was also on the team. He was looking right at me as he brought up his hands.

That's when the applause began.

Every football player, every student, and even a couple of teachers just stood there in the common area outside the school and applauded as we walked toward the doors, slowing in bewilderment. Mayra looked from me to the clapping students and back again and then smiled.

I couldn't figure out what that was all about, so I just kept Mayra close to me as we walked through the crowd.

After that day, school just got weird.

All these people who never even acknowledged my existence before started coming up and trying to talk to me. Everyone wanted a detailed, eyewitness account of what happened. The thing was, neither Mayra nor I really cared to go over it again. She was pretty good about just saying we got jumped, and I beat them off, but everyone wanted more. I would tense up, not wanting to say anything to the people who never said anything to me before but also wanting to protect Mayra so she wasn't being harassed about it. By the end of the first day, Mayra had broken down and cried twice when people were asking questions, and Aimee Schultz—contrary to her usual, compassionate demeanor—completely went off on Carmen Klug and told her to leave Mayra alone.

I was quite grateful.

I actually did pretty well, all things considered. I only freaked out a couple of times when a bunch of people came up to me at once, and Mayra wasn't there.

At the end of English, a couple of the football players kept asking me how I managed to beat up four guys. They seemed somewhat skeptical, and I could barely even get much more than an "um" out of my mouth when Joe stepped up.

"Matthew's been kickboxing for years," he told them. "I saw him in a tournament once when my older brother was competing. Matthew kicked ass, won every trophy, and he was competing with guys older than him, too. He does kickboxing, Tae Kwon Do, Aikido, and warshoes. "

"Wushu," I said, correcting him quietly.

"Yeah, that. Anyway, he kicks ass and always has. Sent two of them to the hospital, and you can read that in the fucking paper."

They left after that, and Joe just kept looking at me sideways as we made our way to the next classroom. Eventually, I couldn't take it anymore.

"What?" I finally asked.

Joe laughed and shook his head.

"I always knew you *could*," he said, "but I really never would have guessed you had it in you."

The weirdest bit was when I was doing some research in the library, and I overheard some of the girls on the soccer team talking. I was at one of the desks with the high sides on them, so they must not have seen me from where they were standing between shelves full of biographies.

"I don't see why it changes anything," Carmen was saying. "He's still just weird."

"He's just quiet," said another voice. I was pretty sure the remark came from Samantha. "Besides, he's *fuckhawt*."

There was a bunch of giggling then.

"You're crazy," Carmen said. "You're just as nutty as Mayra for dating that weirdo. She could have anybody. Now that Justin has completely fucked himself and got expelled, she'll be totally out of options when she comes to her senses."

"She's not about to give him up," Samantha said. "Did you hear her talking after Spanish? She said if you ever saw him with his shirt off, you'd all be biting and scratching to get a closer look."

"I just can't believe she'd give it up to someone so weird. Come on, girls—we are talking about *Matthew Rohan* here. He can't even talk half the time!"

"He's always been cute," another voice said. I wasn't sure who it belonged to.

"Beyond cute. He's dead sexy." That was Aimee. I didn't even realize she was with the group. "He was cute even when he was younger. From what Mayra has told me, he is seriously all man under that shy exterior."

"He can have a piece of me." It was Samantha's voice again.

"Everyone's had a piece of you!" Carmen snapped back.

They moved down the aisle of books and out of earshot. My ears and neck were burning, and I realized I had been squeezing my eyes shut the whole time. Even though I heard what they said, I couldn't really process enough to make any sense out of all of it. Mostly I wondered what else Mayra might have told other people about me.

The more I thought about it, the more I didn't like the idea. I knew I would see her later, but I didn't know if I would be able to confront her on the ride home.

"You all right?" Mayra asked as we pulled into my driveway.

I just shrugged.

"You're quiet even for you," she said with a smile.

I knew she was trying to lighten things up, but I was still feeling odd. I just shrugged again, poked at the fish shape on the door, and got out of the car. I knew I felt pissed off; I just wasn't sure what I was supposed to do about it or why I still wanted to kiss her at the same time.

"Matthew? What is it?" She stopped in front of me, blocking my way down the sidewalk to the front door. "Did someone say something to you today?"

"Not exactly," I mumbled.

"What, then?"

I glanced up at her, my eyes narrowed, then looked away and walked around her to the front door. I could hear her footsteps behind me as I turned the key in the lock, and we walked inside.

"Matthew!" Mayra finally yelled. She grabbed onto my elbow and stopped me from going any farther. "What the hell happened?"

I pulled my arm out of her grasp and stomped over to the couch. I dropped down hard on my ass and leaned forward with my elbows on my knees and my head in my hands. Mayra walked over slowly and sat down beside me while I tried to keep my breathing slow. I couldn't even figure out what was going on in my head. I was *angry*. I was angry with Mayra for talking about me to her girlfriends. I was also embarrassed because of what they were saying about me, and I was blaming Mayra for that, too.

She didn't try to touch me or push me to talk; she just waited for me to be ready. By the time I was, I had already figured out that I wasn't being fair—Mayra hadn't been there with those girls. I really had no idea what she might have said or not said.

"What did you tell the girls on your team about me?" I finally asked.

"What did I…? Matthew, I have no idea what you mean."

I took in a long breath and then let it out slowly.

"I heard some girls talking—Aimee, Carmen, and Samantha—I'm not sure who else. They were talking about me and about...things you said about me."

"What *things*?" Mayra said. Her tone was dark.

"About...what I look like..."

"What you *look like*?" Mayra sighed loudly. "Matthew, I'm sorry, but I have no idea what you are saying."

"About what I look like with my shirt off!" I finally yelled.

Mayra's eyes were wide when I looked at her, and her mouth was hanging open slightly.

"Matthew..."

"What else did you tell people about me?" I asked quietly. At this point, I just wanted it all out in the open.

"Nothing," she said. "Nothing at all, really. Even that was...well, nothing."

"Nothing?" I repeated as I glanced at her sideways.

Mayra huffed out another breath and then spoke in one long sentence.

"Carmen was being a bitch, like she does, and said there was no way you could have saved me from a whole group of guys, and she said she doubted any of it happened at all. I said she was a fucking moron, and if any of them had seen you with your shirt off, they'd know how fucking built you were and how well you can handle yourself."

She grumbled inaudibly and ran her fingers through her hair.

"That's all I said," she told me. "Nothing else at all, I swear."

Mayra leaned back against the couch cushions, and my head spun around like the girl's in *The Exorcist*. Once Mayra explained what had happened, I knew she had just been ticked off, and all of that had just come out of her mouth—probably in a fashion similar to how she repeated it to me. If that was all she had actually said, then I really didn't have anything to be mad about, and I had no reason to doubt her.

"That was it?" I asked softly.

"That was it."

"Oh," I said. I realized I probably needed to say something else now because I had been mad, and we had probably just had our first fight. The problem was, I had no idea what I was supposed to do or say when it was over. Was it over? How did I know? I wasn't mad anymore, but I was still a little embarrassed by what those girls had said. That wasn't Mayra's fault, though. I couldn't blame that on her.

"What is going on in that head?" Mayra whispered as she reached out and pushed my hair off my forehead. I met her eyes for a moment and smiled.

"Your guess is as good as mine," I said with a snicker. "It's okay, I think. I just…don't know what I'm supposed to say now. What am I supposed to do now?"

"Now?"

"I mean now that we're not fighting."

Mayra's lips smashed together, and her eyes sparkled with humor.

"Well, I believe 'kiss and make up' is tradition."

"It is?" I asked. I thought that was reserved for movies.

"It is," Mayra confirmed. She touched my cheek as her mouth covered mine. I found her waist with my hands and pulled her a little closer to me. As the warmth of her mouth left me, I heard her soft voice.

"You're really not mad?" she asked with trepidation.

"I'm not mad," I said. Mayra leaned in and brushed her lips over mine. I could feel her smile against my mouth before she trailed kisses over my jaw. My heart began to beat faster, and my skin got warm and tingly.

"You really are damn hot shirtless," Mayra whispered against my cheek.

My skin tingled with her words. When the other girls were saying things about me, I felt incredibly uncomfortable, but hearing

Mayra say the words was completely different. I was nervous, but not in the same way.

Without thinking, I pulled my shirt up over my head.

We had never been like this before. The time when Mayra was at my house and I had been hitting the bag wasn't the same even though we were on the same couch and similarly dressed, or rather *undressed*.

Without moving, I kept my eyes on her hands as Mayra reached out and lay her fingertips against my shoulders, then slowly moved down over my chest and down to my abs. There was a slight smile on her face, and I saw her tongue dart out to lick her lips.

Once she reached my stomach, she slid her hand around to my back and pulled me close to her. My heart was beating fast enough that I was sure she could hear it right through my chest. The feeling of her lips against mine, though familiar, seemed completely different this way. It felt like an electrical current running from her fingers on my skin down to my groin and an unexpected feeling of uncertainly in my gut at the same time.

Our lips moved together, and her hands ran up and down from my shoulder blades to my lower back. I placed my hands on either side of her face, deepening the kiss and making sure she still had room to move her hands over me at the same time. I could feel and hear her breaths increase in tempo as she turned her head slightly and ran her tongue over mine, which called attention to the fact that I had been holding my own breath, and I had to break away for a moment.

Mayra's eyes were wide, and her gaze seemed to be dancing around my chest and stomach. In a flash, she let go of me and grabbed the hem of her shirt.

"Mayra…" I whispered, not really sure what it was I wanted to communicate to her.

"It's only fair," she replied softly before she pulled her T-shirt over her head and tossed it on the couch behind her.

Awe was the only word that came to mind.

My mouth was hanging open as I stared unabashedly at the lacy, off-white bra that was now the only thing covering her breasts from my eyes. They weren't even totally covered because the tops of them weren't completely hidden from view by the fabric but seemed to sort of spill out the top.

My hands moved before I could even think about what they were doing.

My fingers trailed up from her wrists to her shoulders and then slowly traversed the thin straps that held the scrap of fabric covering her. There was a small birthmark just to the side of the strap on her right, which was, oddly enough, slightly fish-shaped—just like the little mark in the door of her car. Without thinking, I poked it softly with the tip of my index finger.

Mayra giggled, and the sound made my heart beat faster.

Following the line of the strap, my finger traced over her skin, moving down slowly until it was right over where her flesh curved and rose up. I glanced at her face and saw her lips slightly parted with the corners still turned up. Dropping my gaze back to my hand, I continued down to the smooth, soft skin over the top of her breast.

My hands were shaking a little, and I couldn't believe how soft her skin felt. I stopped right at the little dip between her breasts and took a long, shaky breath. Then I repeated the action with my other hand, again stopping at the dip between.

I let out a long breath and glanced at Mayra, wondering what I was supposed to do next. I would have been perfectly happy just looking at her for the rest of the afternoon, but I was pretty sure she was expecting more, which also made me wonder just how much more she might want.

"I'm...I'm not ready to...to..." I stammered.

"Shh..." Mayra put a finger over my mouth. "Just kiss me—we don't have to do anything else."

That suited me just fine, and as our bodies came together along with our lips, I pressed against the soft warmth of her skin and wondered if there was such a thing as karma and if I was finally on the right side of it. Mayra's hands roamed over my back and arms, and I just wrapped my arms around her and concentrated on the feeling of her breasts pressed against my bare chest like that. It sweetened the kisses, and I felt like everything was finally just…*right*.

I might not have been ready to have sex, but making out with a half-naked Mayra was a win all the way.

Chapter 14—A Watch is a Bad Substitute for a Ring

"No Mayra?" Travis walked into the kitchen with Chinese carryout in a large bag and started pulling cardboard containers out of it. I couldn't tell from his tone if he was happy about her lack of presence or just curious.

"Her team has practice late today," I told him.

"I thought you usually watched," Travis said.

"I do," I replied, "but I knew you were bringing dinner, so I only watched the first part. If they get done in time, she'll be over later, but she said not to get her anything. She really doesn't like Chinese food."

"She ain't right," Travis said with a snicker. "Did you get to second base yet?"

"I don't even know what that means," I said with a shake of my head. Travis had completely gotten over any reservations he had about Mayra and I being physical and had turned it into conversations I didn't really want to have with him. Still, even though he'd ask me questions, he wasn't too good at answering any of mine. He left that to Bethany.

"Have you touched her tits yet?"

"Travis!" I wasn't about to answer that even though I really hadn't, not any more than the very tops of them. I did manage to touch Mayra's birthmark almost every time we made out, at least. It always made her laugh, but she didn't seem to mind. Sometimes when we were at school, I'd think about it and want to touch it. I knew I couldn't, and I'd usually end up with the teacher calling on me about that time, and I wouldn't know what question had been asked.

Travis laughed and dug into a pile of Lo Mein. Just as I started dishing out rice, the phone rang, and I grabbed the receiver off the hook, expecting it to be Mayra. It wasn't her, though—it was Megan's doctor.

"The new medication seems to be having a little bit of an effect," Dr. Harris said. "I'm really looking forward to seeing how she reacts to you tomorrow. I have some forms and such for you to sign as well."

I looked up at the calendar and couldn't believe I had forgotten tomorrow was my visit with Megan. With everything else that had been going on, I had completely lost track of time. As soon as I hung up, I had a serious load of guilt churning around in my stomach.

"What's wrong?" Travis asked.

"That was Megan's doctor," I told him. Travis's eyes went wide, and he stood halfway up before I shook my head. "She's okay. I just forgot tomorrow was our day to go up there. I didn't even say anything to Mayra about it."

"Is she going with us?" Travis asked. His brow furrowed a bit.

"I don't know," I said. "I haven't asked her. I want her to meet Megan, though. Well, I sort of do."

"You and Mayra getting pretty serious?" It was more of a statement than a question.

"Yeah, I guess so."

Travis sighed.

"I want to talk to her first," he stated.

"What? No! Why?" I didn't know what Travis was thinking about saying to her, and though they were definitely getting along better now than they were initially, it wasn't exactly what you would call a friendship.

"Matthew…you know you and Megan together are…well…"

"Are what?" I asked.

"Different," Travis said. "I think Mayra needs a little prep, and I think I need to give it to her."

"I don't know what you mean," I told him.

"I know," he said. "That's why I'm the one that needs to talk to her."

"As long as I'm there, too."

"If you want."

Mayra came over later that evening with her hair tied up on the top of her head—still wet from her post-practice shower—and wearing a white tank top. It was a little bit low-cut, and I could see the strap of her bra when she moved a certain way. We had been doing a lot of making out shirtless this week, and I was pretty sure I hadn't seen that particular bra on her before. I wondered if it was one of those with a tiny pink flower in the center.

She didn't seem overly thrilled about Travis still being there and was definitely skeptical when he said he wanted to talk to her. I thought I'd better fill her in before he got started.

"I forgot, but tomorrow is the day I go visit Megan in Cincinnati." I ran my hand through my hair. I was just about due for another haircut, and I wondered if Mayra would do it for me again. I tugged at the ends and glanced up at her. "Do you want to go meet her?"

"I'd love to," Mayra said with a smile.

"That's why we have to talk," Travis said. "There are some things you need to know."

"O…kay…" Mayra eyed him warily. "Let's talk."

I made our customary Cokes, and we all sat down in the living room. I sat next to Mayra on the couch, and she reached over to take my hand. I really didn't know what Travis wanted to tell Mayra, but I was definitely nervous. Sometimes I didn't remember much about my visits with Megan, and Travis would often ask me about things I didn't recall.

"I know Matthew's told you a bit about Megan," Travis started.

"I know she's autistic but more severe than Matthew," Mayra said. "I've done a little research online about it since Matthew and I started going out."

"Good," Travis said. "Then maybe you'll be a bit more prepared."

"Prepared?" she questioned.

"Matthew and Megan are very close," Travis said. "Closer than you might expect, considering the severity of Megan's autism. She's never really talked to anyone and has never called any of us by our names—"

"She said 'mom' once," I said, reminding him.

"True," Travis agreed. "Just that once, as far as I know. But for the most part, she doesn't communicate with anyone, but when Megan and Matthew are together, Matthew is…well, different."

"What are you talking about?" I asked.

"You two get in your own little world with each other," Travis said with a wave of his hand. "Sometimes you stop responding to everyone around you and just focus on her. I don't want Mayra to be unprepared. It's not the same as when he's having an attack, but it kind of looks like it in a way. It's hard to explain. I used to think they were both telepathic and talking through each other's heads or something."

"We're not." I scowled. I did remember various conversations throughout the years about Megan and me together, but I didn't really think much of it. I just liked to give her my attention when I was there, like we did when we were kids.

Travis continued to talk, but I wasn't paying close attention to what he was saying. I had just noticed that Mayra's tank top had shifted again, and I could almost see the birthmark next to the strap of her bra. *Almost.*

"So, no need for me to be worried about him?" Mayra inquired. "Is that what you mean?"

"Pretty much," Travis answered. He scratched the back of his head and glanced around the room nervously. "I just wanted you to know since...well, since you're with Matthew and...and, well...part of the family, I guess."

"Travis Rohan!" Mayra placed her hand over her heart and used the other one to fan her face. "I do declare! You are warming up to me!"

They both laughed, but the humor was lost on me. I was glad they were getting along better, but I was mostly wondering if I could see the fish-mark on Mayra's skin if I just shifted my position. I leaned in close to Mayra and tilted my head a little in an attempt to see under her shirt a little better. Mayra suddenly shoved me with her shoulder, snapping me out of it.

Travis's laughter turned to howls, and he quickly excused himself to go to the bathroom. Mayra covered her mouth, and I knew I had been caught. I shrugged and wrapped my arm around Mayra's shoulders. I pulled her a little closer, which made the tank top sleeve and her bra strap bunch up, revealing the birthmark.

I couldn't resist the opportunity, so I reached over and poked the fish.

~oOo~

Mayra and I sat in the back seat of Bethany's car while she and Travis rode in the front. Beth drove slowly even though she liked going faster. She knew it made me nervous. Travis played with the controls for the radio as we went in and out of the reach of various stations' signals between Oxford and Cincinnati.

Mayra had come over early to try to help me get myself together for the trip, but I wasn't having the best of days. Nothing I tried to say came out right, and she was starting to give me strange looks. At this point, she was leaning her head against my shoulder and staying pretty quiet. I had the feeling she figured out I didn't feel much like talking.

My head was filled with memories of Megan.

I remembered the day I realized she was different from me. I had received a pile of Mighty Beanz for my birthday, and Megan and I were sitting on the kitchen floor and spinning them around in circles. While we were playing, Megan suddenly stood up and started spinning around in circles herself. That wasn't so odd, but she wouldn't stop even after she hit the refrigerator door with her head, and her head started to bleed.

I had asked Mom why she did that, and that's when she told me Megan was different from other people, and that was why she liked clocks so much. I knew about that, of course—Megan would take any kind of clock or watch and hide it under her bed. Sometimes she would even crawl under there with them and listen to them tick. I went under there with her once, and we both stayed there listening to the ticking until Mom made us stop.

"Oh yeah," I muttered, startling Mayra. "Here."

I handed Mayra a small wristwatch.

"What's this?"

"It was…um…it was my mom's," I told her. "Megan likes clocks and watches. If she sees you wearing one…well, she might like you, too."

I held up my own arm and showed her I was also wearing one. Mayra slipped the watch around her wrist, and I helped her get the tiny little pin through the hole in the strap so it would stay on.

"Thank you," Mayra said quietly. She kissed the edge of my jaw, which made me shiver a little.

The building where Megan lived was tall, white, and surrounded by gardens. It was a warm and clear day, and after I got all the paperwork signed, one of the aides helped us find Megan. She was sitting in the grass outside, and a group of young kids was nearby. A woman was blowing bubbles for them. Some of the kids watched and tried to touch the bubbles, but others just stared into space or played with their fingers.

Megan was sitting behind a wooden bench and away from the rest of the group. Her dark hair was hanging in her eyes as she looked down at a line of ants carrying little crumbs through the grass. Dr. Harris was sitting on the bench and writing in a notebook.

"Hello, Matthew," she said. She reached out to shake my hand, and after a few seconds, I remembered I was supposed to do the same. Our hands touched briefly before she moved to Travis and Bethany. "And who is this?"

Taking my eyes off Megan for a moment, I looked in the direction of the doctor's gaze.

"That's Mayra," I told her.

"It's good to meet you, Mayra," Dr. Harris said with a smile.

"Good to meet you, too," Mayra replied. "I'm Matthew's girlfriend."

"Are you now?" Dr. Harris's smile widened, but I wasn't really paying attention. I took a step toward my sister.

"She's not having a great day," I heard the doctor say to Travis. "I think most of her breakfast ended up on the floor. She hasn't talked for a while, either. The new medication she's been on was helping for a while, and I thought we were making some progress with communication, but she hasn't said a word since yesterday."

I moved away from the rest of them and went up to Megan. My skin felt like it was vibrating as I approached my sister. It was like all the hairs on my arm were standing up and pointing toward her, drawing me closer. She didn't move or say anything, just continued to watch the ants.

Slowly, I sat down beside her on the ground and leaned close to her but not quite touching. I raised my hand and held my wrist near her ear. The ants continued their journey—half of them empty-handed and heading in one direction, the other half heading the opposite way with tiny white crumbs in their mandibles.

After a few minutes, Megan moved.

She reached out and grabbed my wrist, bringing it around to her face so she could see the dial of the watch I wore. At the same time, she leaned closer to me.

"This clock has Roman numerals," Megan said quietly.

"How do ants tell time?" I asked her.

"They don't have any watches their size," Megan replied.

"So how do they know when to go home?"

"There are four clocks in my room." Megan used her finger to trace over the smooth face of the watch on my wrist. "Four clocks."

"Four clocks," I repeated. "One is green."

"My brother has green eyes."

I froze and my muscles tensed. I felt heat on my neck and pressure behind my eyes. I could count the times she said the word *brother* on one hand.

"I'm right here," I whispered. She didn't say anything else, but we leaned against each other a bit more. The ants continued their tasks, regardless of timepieces. As the sky darkened, they disappeared into their holes, and I felt pressure against my shoulder.

"It's time to go, Matthew."

I looked up to see Travis. Behind him was Mayra with a strange expression on her face. I pulled my hand away from Megan slowly, and Megan's hands fell away from my wrist.

"Megan has to meet Mayra," I said.

Mayra took a step toward me but hesitated. I reached out and took her hand to guide her closer to my sister, then pulled her down so we were both sitting beside Megan.

"Megan, this is Mayra." I took Megan's hand with my right and Mayra's hand in my left to bring them closer together. Megan noticed the watch on Mayra's wrist immediately and latched onto it. "Mayra, this is my sister, Megan."

"Hi, Megan," Mayra said, her voice barely above a whisper.

Megan didn't respond but focused intently on the watch around Mayra's wrist. Her eyes narrowed, and her mouth turned into a scowl.

"Not right," she growled, and I felt Mayra tense up a little beside me. "Not right, not right…"

"*Shit, shit, shit*," I muttered.

"What is it?" Travis asked.

"I think she recognizes Mom's watch," I said.

Megan was clearly getting upset and began to rock herself back and forth, crashing her head against the bench at the same time and still repeating the same words over and over. Dr. Harris came over, and we brought Megan back to her room.

"Are you going to have to sedate her?" I heard Bethany ask.

"Hope not to," Dr. Harris replied. "Maybe Matthew can calm her down."

The aide moved away from Megan, where she was sitting on the edge of her bed. Her arms were wrapped around herself, and she continued to rock.

"Megan," I said softly as I held my wrist back up to her ear. She turned and grabbed at it, holding it to her stomach and pulling me onto the bed beside her.

"Not right," she said again. For a brief moment, she looked up to my face. Her focus was on my mouth or chin, not my eyes, but it was pretty close for her. She spoke very, very softly, so no one else could hear her. "You're supposed to give her a *ring*, not a *watch*."

I couldn't believe my ears, so I just laughed.

Spending time with Megan was always a win day, but it was also over too soon. I said goodbye without Megan even acknowledging me and started to head out.

"Matthew, do you have a minute?"

I turned around and saw Dr. Harris standing in the doorway to her office. We were almost to the lobby and the doors that headed to the parking lot. I glanced over at Travis, and he nodded.

"We're not going to get back until late anyway," he said with a shrug.

I followed the doctor into her office and sat down in the chair on the other side of her desk. Something about Dr. Harris's office always put me on edge. Maybe it was because we always talked about Megan here, and it wasn't always good news, or maybe it was because I knew I could have ended up in the same place—locked away from the rest of the world the same way Megan was.

Warm guilt slid over my skin at the thought, and I wished there had been some way for me to keep Megan at home with me. There wasn't. Even if I didn't have my own issues, I couldn't take care of Megan and go to school at the same time. The only other option we had briefly considered was having Bethany or Travis quit their jobs to care for Megan, but there was just no way to do that and get the bills paid.

With these thoughts in my head, I rubbed the pad of my right thumb over each fingernail on my left hand—swooping over them from cuticle to edge. Once I had gone over each one, I switched to my left thumb and right-handed fingernails. I went back and forth until the doctor spoke.

"How are you, Matthew?" Dr. Harris asked.

"Fine," I replied.

Dr. Harris had never been my actual doctor, but over the years of treating Megan—first as an outpatient and then here at the center—she knew as much about me as my other doctors did. I hadn't seen any other doctors since Mom had died, and Dr. Harris knew that. When I came to visit Megan, she always wanted to know how I was doing as well.

"Just *fine*?"

I glanced up at her briefly and saw her smile. I went back to rubbing my fingernails.

"Mayra seems nice," Dr. Harris prompted.

I nodded.

"Will you tell me a little about her?"

A thousand different things went through my head about Mayra. I thought about how patient she was and how she would wait for me to be ready whether it was to say something, to go inside a new place, or to take our relationship further. I thought about how good it felt to have someone who would listen to me without being obligated to do so and without getting tired of waiting for me to get to the point. I thought about how she didn't seem to mind some of the weird shit I did, even when we both knew it was weird, and how it felt when she ran her fingers through my hair and laughed at the same television shows.

"She plays soccer," was what came out of my mouth.

"She's athletic, then."

"Yes," I replied with a nod. "I watch her team practice."

"That's a new activity," she said. "What was it like to do that for the first time?"

I thought about it for a while, the memory of pacing back and forth at the back doors of the school, looking out the window at the girls on the field, and not knowing for sure if I could go out there. Then I had seen Mayra run by in a tight T-shirt and a *very* short pair of shorts, and I managed to convince myself that I would have a better view from the stands.

"Mayra makes new things...a little easier."

"You seem very close," she said, and I nodded. "She seems very attentive and protective of you, as well."

I nodded again.

"You're also protective of her," the doctor said. "You made the papers here in Cincinnati, you know."

I felt my neck heat up and dropped my gaze to the floor. There was a little piece of paper—the wrapper from a piece of candy, maybe—on the floor under the doctor's desk. I tilted my head a little to see if I could read what was printed on the cellophane.

"Matthew…" The doctor reached over and placed her palm flat on the desk right in front of my face. "What you did was incredibly brave and selfless. Do you understand what that means?"

I shook my head.

"For the first time in your life, you are thinking about someone outside of your own family before yourself. You've done enough research to know how difficult it can be for you to connect with someone outside those you have known all your life. Think about how long it took you to warm up to Bethany."

"Mayra bakes cakes," I said quietly, and Dr. Harris laughed.

"Your consistency remains," she said with a kind smile. After a moment of silence, she spoke again. "What did Megan say to you in her room? What did she say that made you laugh?"

"Um…" I chuckled again. "She said I got Mayra the wrong thing. I was supposed to give her a ring, not a watch."

The doctor's eyes went wide.

"That's what she said to you?"

"Yes."

"Matthew, that is…remarkable. Do you realize how significant that is for Megan?"

I frowned and shook my head.

"She not only recognized the connection between you and Mayra, but she took the next step, realizing your relationship could lead to a more permanent situation. Beyond that, she showed concern for you—concern that you might have misunderstood some of the traditions behind that next step—and tried to make sure you knew what you were supposed to give a prospective bride."

I shrugged, not really getting why it was so important.

"Matthew, Megan was *correcting* you," Dr. Harris said. "She was acting like a big sister to you."

I let the thought swim around in my head for a bit and realized Megan really hadn't ever done or said anything like that before. Even when we were young, I usually did things to help her, not the other way around. Sometimes she would say things that indicated a lot more awareness than what normally came out of her mouth, but those occasions were very few and far between. What she had said to me earlier didn't just indicate awareness; it was unlike anything she had ever said to me before.

"Does that mean the medicine is working for her?" I asked.

"It's too early to say," she told me. "I would consider it a good sign, though."

I nodded and stared underneath the desk again, wondering what similar medication might do for me if I could afford it. Dr. Harris asked me a few more questions about Mayra and me, but I wasn't really paying attention any longer. The wrapper lying under the desk was making my fingers twitch.

I couldn't take it anymore, so I reached down underneath the desk and grabbed the little piece of plastic. It was from one of those peppermints that usually came from restaurants. I flattened it out against my leg and then puffed it up so it looked like it still had a mint in it. Mints were sweet, and I liked the kind with chocolate around them, which made me think of chocolate cake.

"Dr. Harris?" I asked nervously.

"Yes, Matthew?"

"Don't tell Bethany," I begged, "but I like Mayra's cakes better."

Dr. Harris's smile widened, and she nodded twice.

"I am sworn to secrecy," she vowed.

I couldn't argue with a doctor's vow, so I accepted her promise.

It was dark by the time we got to the car, and I was exhausted. After we slid into the back seat, Mayra reached over and took my hand in hers. Even though I knew Bethany and Travis could see us, I adjusted my seatbelt and lay down with my head in her lap. As soon as I felt her fingers in my hair, I closed my eyes and drifted.

I could hear soft voices that seemed to come from all around me and nowhere in particular.

"Thanks for the warning, Travis. That was a little…freaky."

"They get in their own little world, that's for sure."

"It scared the hell out of me the first time I saw them like that." Bethany's voice was soft. "It was like everyone else around them disappeared. Were they talking to each other?"

Gentle fingers stroked through my hair, and I sighed.

"Your guess is as good as mine." Travis chuckled quietly. "Tiffany always said they had their own language inside their heads, but Kyle thought they just enjoyed not having to interact with anyone."

"Matthew doesn't really talk about his parents very much," Mayra said. "He doesn't say much about Megan, either."

"It's still hard for him," Bethany said. "He feels so needlessly guilty about where Megan is now, and his father was the only one who could ever really convince him otherwise once he got something in his head."

"My brother was great at that. He always knew what to say to the kid to get him to rethink something. I've tried, but he just doesn't trust me as much."

"You have been amazing for him." I could hear Beth shifting in her seat. "I don't know what you're doing—"

A short laugh came from Travis, and Mayra's fingers paused for a moment before resuming their trek around my scalp.

"Well…whatever it is, I'm not going to argue. It's working."

"He means a lot to me." The soft, whispered words were combined with a stroke of warm fingers over my cheek. It was enough to send me into further, quieter darkness.

Win.

Chapter 15—Dive Straight In

"Will you consider it? You have three weeks to prepare, and I'll help any way I can."

I squeezed my palms together to try to stop the shaking. The movement seemed to transfer to my leg, which started bouncing up and down instead. My head filled up with all kinds of imagery I wasn't prepared to handle, so I jumped up and ran downstairs.

The gloves felt good on my hands as my fists connected with the heavy bag repeatedly.

Mayra wanted to go to a graduation party at Hueston Woods, right by the lake. It was over three weeks away, and almost everyone in our graduating class was going to be there, sans one Justin Lords, who had pled guilty to assault and possession charges and would be attending his sentencing hearing instead of wearing a weird, square cap.

Mayra wanted me to go with her.

I had already decided there was no way I was going to attend the graduation ceremony and sit there in the middle of a bunch of other kids, waiting to walk across a stage that probably couldn't hold the people who were standing on it. There was no way I was going to do that while everyone looked at me and waited for me to trip on the stairs or just freak out when it was my turn to shake the principal's hand. There was just no way. My grades would already be in, and my diploma would already be secured. I didn't have to attend the ceremony, and I wasn't going to put myself through all that.

All of Mayra's friends from the soccer team were going to be at this party.

It was going to be her last time to really hang out with them, which she hadn't done much of since she started dating me.

I didn't want to be the one to hold her back.

I didn't want to go.

People weren't treating me quite like they were after that fateful night Uptown, which I considered a blessing, but a lot of them still tried to strike up conversations, and I just didn't know what to do or say. They would ask about my fighting experience or just questions about various homework assignments—it didn't matter. It still came down to the same thing: I couldn't cope with all the attention.

But Mayra was different.

She was popular, accepted, and liked by almost everyone.

I was holding her back.

My fist slammed low on the heavy bag. Then I spun around and landed blow after blow with my feet.

There was something incredibly selfish inside of me that just wanted her all to myself. I wanted to take her away and hide her with me, and me alone, so I wouldn't have to share her with anyone. I had absolutely no desire to go out for both the first and last time with a bunch of people I would likely never see again. I'd never been to a party, and I didn't know what to expect. I didn't even *want* to know what to expect.

It wasn't right to make Mayra stay with me when she should be having fun with her friends, but I knew she wouldn't go without me. What about when we went to college, and she wanted to go out and meet people, and I didn't? Was I going to hold her back then, too? What about after college graduation? Would I keep her from getting a great job because I didn't want to move to wherever she got an offer?

I couldn't do that to her.

My arms ached, but I kept punching.

Mayra was one of the most important people in my life. I never thought I would have the kind of relationship I had with her, and if I did anything to fuck it up, it was unlikely I would ever find something like this again. Even if I did find someone as patient and willing as Mayra, it wouldn't be her. No one else would ever touch me the way she had.

With panting breaths, I stepped off the mat and made my way back upstairs. Mayra was in the kitchen, stirring something that smelled like vegetables and spices in a big pot.

I silently watched her for a long moment. I didn't think she realized I was back upstairs as she continued to cook and rock her shoulders a little to a song in her head. Knowing how much I didn't like to be startled by people behind me, I moved slowly into her field of vision and leaned against the counter.

Mayra looked up at my face and then down to my bare chest. She raised her eyebrows slightly before she looked back to the pot.

"I used up all the potatoes you had in the pantry," she said.

"I'll put them on my shopping list." I pulled open the junk drawer and grabbed a pen.

For a second, my gaze caught the Ziploc bag with the lottery ticket in it. I'd done a pretty good job of forgetting about it, but now I couldn't stop thoughts of it from swirling around in my head.

No one had claimed the winning ticket yet. I didn't know what the winning numbers were, and I didn't know what numbers were on the ticket. If I looked at one set of numbers, I'd have to compare it to the other. If they matched, I'd be forced to act on it.

If the ticket was the winner, I'd have more money than I would ever know what to do with. I could buy a bigger house for Travis and Bethany. I could get Megan private care. I'd have to hire an accountant and a lawyer. People would constantly ask if they could have some of the money. They'd come up with good reasons, and I wouldn't know if I could believe them or not. If I said no, they might be angry with me. I might even need a bodyguard.

The skin on the back of my neck warmed and my stomach cramped up. I squeezed my eyes shut and tried to force the thoughts from my head. This was why I couldn't even look at the ticket. The idea of making such crucial decisions was just too overwhelming. I couldn't even make a decision about attending a get-together with people from my graduating class.

"Matthew? Are you okay?"

I swallowed hard and quickly closed the drawer.

"I'll go to the party," I said quietly.

"Are you sure?" she asked. "You've gone a little pale."

"I'm sure." I watched as her smile took over Mayra's face. She dropped the spoon in the pot and wrapped her arms around my neck.

"Thank you," she whispered. "Thank you so much."

~oOo~

For the next three weeks, I tried not to think about the party.

Normally, I would do the opposite. I would try to imagine what something new would be like, how it would look, or what it would feel like to be in a new place, but this was different. Every time I even tried to think about going to a party, I'd start to panic, and I didn't want Mayra to realize I was getting upset and call it off.

So I just tried to forget about it.

Mayra was really excited and kept talking on the phone to various people on her soccer team and in our class about what time to be there, what everyone was wearing, and who had decided to go to Aimee Schultz's parent-chaperoned party instead.

The best way to not think about it was to make out with Mayra on the couch, which we did a lot, usually shirtless, though

Mayra always left her bra on. Still, it was warm skin-on-skin and added a lot to the experience.

The second best way was to read a set of books that mysteriously appeared on my desk about two weeks before school let out. Bethany had been over earlier to make me dinner, and when she left, they were there next to my computer—books about women and sex.

It wasn't the same shit they taught you in health class—that was for sure.

With a week left before we graduated, Mayra was on her back, and I was on top of her with my shirt off. Mayra was wearing a white, short-sleeved, button-down blouse with most of the buttons undone.

"Should I take this off?" Mayra groaned against my mouth. I felt her hand move to her collar.

"Mmm...I got it," I replied. I pushed at the sleeve over her right shoulder while I trailed kisses over her jaw and down her neck. As I reached her throat, I opened my eyes to find and poke her birthmark. That's when I realized I had pushed not only her shirtsleeve down but her bra strap as well.

I froze for a minute, looking at her completely bare shoulder where there was usually a little thin strap of white or blue or beige. Without thinking, my fingers traced over her skin and down the imaginary line where her strap was normally located. I watched my index finger as I tapped the fish-shaped birthmark then moved a little farther down to the top of her breast.

Swallowing involuntarily, I peeked back up at her bare shoulder and then her face, my eyes questioning. Mayra licked her lips quickly then raised herself up a little and reached around her back. A moment later, her bra went slack—revealing just a little more of her breasts to me.

My gaze moved from her eyes to her nearly-showing nipples about six times before Mayra nodded at me.

"Go ahead," she said quietly.

I quickly moistened my lips and tried not to think too much about excerpts from those books. I couldn't help it though—there were phrases about how nipples were a direct line to a woman's clitoris. I couldn't stop thinking about it, so I froze up again.

"Do you want me to take it off," Mayra asked, "or do you want to stop?"

"I don't want to stop," I whispered.

"Shall I?" She grasped her shirtsleeve and bra strap, bringing them further down. I could only nod in response.

A moment later, she was topless. I was still on top of her, and I was about to combust.

My breathing was too quick, and I was starting to get a little lightheaded. Well, it might have been from breathing too fast. It also might have been just the reaction to seeing her like that—breasts exposed, lying on her back underneath me—and what it did to my body.

Jeans kind of sucked, really.

A warm shiver covered my skin as I looked down at her. It was a strange, almost animalistic feeling and completely foreign to me. I wanted my hands all over her—pressed up against her skin and feeling her heat on me. There was a need deep inside my stomach to see more—to get more. It was raw and desperate and needy.

I wanted her.

Now.

"Mayra?" I had no idea why I was whispering—it's not like there was anyone else in the house. "Do you, um…maybe want to go upstairs…I mean…to my room?"

"Your room?"

"Yeah." I tried to shrug it off like it wasn't a big deal, but I wasn't the least bit convincing, and she wasn't going to buy it anyway. Mayra had never been inside my room, and other than in her car, all our make-out sessions had been on the couch. "It might be more comfortable than the couch."

"Let's go," Mayra said. She raised her eyebrow at me, and I moved off her to let her up. She picked up her clothes, took my hand, and we walked up the stairs to my room.

Mayra tossed her shirt and bra off to the side as she sat on my bed. She reached out, took my hands, and then pulled me to the bed with her as she lay down on her back. I tried to steady myself with my hands but couldn't touch her if I did that. I ended up balancing on one as I tentatively ran my other hand up her side.

I wanted to kiss her, and I wanted to cup both of her breasts in my hands. I wanted my fingers and hands and palms all over her bare skin. I also wanted to kiss her breasts, tongue them, suck on her nipples, and maybe even refer to them as "tits."

I didn't know what to do first.

Thankfully, I had Mayra, who grabbed both my hands and just put them over her chest. I lost my balance and fell to the side, but I really couldn't have cared less at that point.

"Fuck," I muttered. My eyes stayed on my hands, which were now totally concealing her breasts from my view. I was completely torn—I wanted to keep touching them, but I also wanted to see them at the same time.

They were just so *soft*!

I ran my thumbs over the tops of them and then moved my hands lower so I could see and touch and squeeze them at the same time. Her nipples constricted and seemed to stand up, *just like the book said they would!*

My thumbs circled the darker spots in the middle of her breasts, and they puckered under my touch. I glanced up at Mayra to find her smiling.

"Do you like that?" I asked.

She nodded emphatically.

"Can I...kiss them?"

She nodded again, and I quickly ran my tongue over my lips before repositioning myself a little lower on the bed to get a better angle. I could definitely see and reach them better that way. I tilted my head a bit and quickly kissed each nipple.

My eyes darted to Mayra's, and I found her gaze dark and wanting. Her chest rose with her breaths, and I kept my eyes on her for a moment before ducking back down and taking one of her nipples all the way into my mouth.

I ran my tongue over it and heard her groan. Looking up quickly, I saw her head tilted back, her eyes closed, and her mouth slightly open. Her fingers gripped my shoulders—encouraging me further.

I moved to the other side, first kissing and then sucking gently on her flesh. The taste was a lot like the taste of her tongue with just a touch of salt. I gripped her nipple with my lips and teased the end with the tip of my tongue.

"Holy shit!" Mayra cried out.

I raised my head in alarm but knew immediately she wasn't at all upset. She grabbed my face in her hands and pulled my mouth to hers. My breathing had become rather ragged, and it almost seemed like a struggle to kiss her, breathe, fondle, and actually keep my autonomic nervous system regulating my heartbeat all at the same time. It was all too much—and it was all fucking fantastic.

I kissed down her chin and her neck, smiling to myself as she arched her back when I moved farther down. I kissed the top of each mound and then took one of her nipples in my mouth again. I sucked a little harder and heard her moan my name.

"Oh…*God*…Matthew…"

She moved her hands from my shoulders to the back of my head, gripping my hair in her fingers and holding me to her. I took the hint and sucked hard again. She shuddered, and I moved quickly to the other nipple. I didn't want it to get lonely.

I kissed all around it and then used my tongue to circle it. I kissed in larger, concentric circles until I was licking and sucking all around the outside. I kissed between her breasts before sliding down a little farther to kiss her stomach, which made her giggle.

I looked up at her face, not even bothering to withhold my grin. She echoed my expression as she pulled me back up to her lips, which were warm and wet. As my tongue tangled with hers, I felt her hands on my back again, sliding down to my waist and then around to my stomach. Her fingers traced a line from my navel up to the center of my chest, and I rolled more to my side to give her better access.

All of this was a *lot* more comfortable on my bed.

With one hand on the back of her neck, I brought her mouth back to mine. I kissed her softly as she fingered the slight grouping of hairs in the center of my chest and ran her hand farther down. She outlined my stomach muscles and then ran her finger down the thin line of hair above the button of my jeans, stopping right at the hem.

"Can I touch you?" Mayra's lips moved to my jaw and kissed up the side. I turned my head to give her better access while I tried to figure out what she was asking.

"You are touching me," I told her, snickering.

Mayra's breath puffed out against my neck.

"I mean...lower," she said. She pressed her fingertips against the skin at the base of my stomach for emphasis.

I squeezed my eyes shut and tried to keep myself from hyperventilating. My hips kind of rose up on their own, and I wasn't even going to try to hide how excited my body was at the very thought. How many times had I imagined it? Mayra's hands on me...her mouth. I'd lost count.

"Please," I gasped, keeping my eyes screwed shut.

My hand tensed on her neck as I felt her fingers leave the bare skin of my stomach and slowly move over the top of my erection. I held my breath and tensed the muscles in my thighs as Mayra gripped me through my jeans.

A moment later, some of the pressure was relieved as she opened the top button and tugged at the zipper.

"Mayra..." I moaned.

"Too much?" she asked.

I could only shake my head.

"I want…I want you to…" I couldn't have formed a coherent sentence if someone had told me my life depended on it. My head was swimming in a big bowl of stew, and I still couldn't bring myself to open my eyes. I was quite sure if I actually watched her with her hand on my dick, I would just come all over the place.

She started touching me through my boxers but couldn't really get her hand inside. She pushed the fly of my jeans open and shoved both them and my boxers slightly down my hips as my cock sprang out from the cloth. She was quick about it, and I didn't have time to think, react, or protest.

I was far beyond protesting at that point anyway.

With the tip of one finger, she circled the head and then followed the path of a vein down to the base.

"Your skin is so soft," she said with a whisper that almost sounded reverent.

My skin burned under her touch, and I could feel sweat gathering at the base of my neck and the small of my back. I still couldn't bring myself to open my eyes, but the feeling of her fingers on me was really quite enough as it was. Her fingers slipped around me, and she slowly stroked upwards.

"Like this?" she said softly.

I couldn't move or respond at all. I was sure if I did, I wouldn't be able to stop myself, and I was also pretty sure I was supposed to be able to last longer than twelve seconds.

But it felt *so…fucking…good.*

Warmth from her hand moved from the base of my cock to the tip and back down again. I couldn't stop my hips from rising off the bed and pushing against her fingers as she moved up and down. The tension in my legs and back was incredible, and the tingling sensation from deep in my stomach dropped abruptly to my balls.

I grunted, gasped, and tried to form a sound that resembled *Mayra* but totally failed. Her hand gripped me a little harder as I bucked against it and felt the rush of sensations cascade over my body in a shudder.

My eyes flew open as I realized what the hell had just happened and that I had come all over Mayra's stomach. Before I had a chance to panic over it, Mayra giggled and shoved herself up and over me. She dashed off to the hall bathroom and came back rubbing a hand towel over her belly. She crawled back over me and quickly wiped me down with the damp cloth, her cheeks turning pink in the process.

I might have been embarrassed if I hadn't suddenly realized my mistake.

"*Shit, shit, shit*," I muttered.

"What's wrong?" Mayra asked.

I could hear the alarm in her voice, and I cringed.

"What is it?" she asked again.

"I fucked up," I whispered.

"What do you mean? Matthew, it's fine. Just needed a towel; that's it."

"No," I said with a shake of my head, "it was all out of order."

"What's out of order?"

"I was supposed to make *you* come first."

"What?" Mayra's eyebrows knitted together. "What are you talking about?"

"The book," I said quietly.

"What book?"

"The book that…um…that said I'm supposed to make you come first."

Mayra's eyes stayed narrowed.

"What is the name of this book?" she demanded.

"Oh…um…" I stammered. "It's…um…called *She Comes First*."

I couldn't believe I actually told her what I had been reading, so I shoved my head under my pillow to hide.

"Stop that!" Mayra laughed and tried to pull the pillow away from me, but I held tight. "Now you are just being silly!"

She dug her fingers into my sides, which made me break out into a fit of laughter. Being ticklish is not something I had really thought about. Tickling me wasn't the sort of thing anyone had ever tried to do before. My mom had tried when I was little, but it never produced much of a reaction. But like everything else, it was different with Mayra.

I twisted around and grabbed for her hand, which is when she grabbed my pillow and tossed it across the room. I reached up to catch it, but I missed. Instead of catching the pillow, I got tangled up in my pants, which were still half way off my hips, and nearly fell off the bed. Mayra held tight to my forearm to keep me off the floor and continued to laugh her ass off.

Once I had righted myself again, I yanked up my pants so I was at least mostly covered and grabbed Mayra around the waist. I pulled her over the top of me and began to tickle her sides. Mayra started to shriek and try to get away, but I held tight to her and attempted to not be totally obvious about watching her boobs bounce around as she struggled.

Everything inside of me felt energized and tight. It wasn't unlike the feeling I sometimes got right before going into a panic attack, but at the same time, I couldn't stop smiling. Mayra continued to laugh; her boobs continued to bounce, and I felt incredibly, incredibly…

Happy.

Pulling her against my chest, I tucked my head into the space between her shoulder and her neck and pressed my lips to her throat—a silent announcement to the end of tickles. Her arms draped around my shoulders, and she pressed her lips against my forehead. With a deep inhale, I snuggled against her skin and just held her—still and quiet.

With my eyes closed and the scent of her skin in my nose, I felt calm and warm. Different things Mayra had done for me—

everything from the first ride in her car and the haircut to cakes and hand-jobs—flowed through my head and added to the warmth I felt just under my skin. It wasn't just that she had enough patience to wait for me to get my shit together when she was ready for anything and everything now, and it wasn't just that she did things for me without really wanting anything back or expecting me to figure out the right words to express my gratitude. It wasn't just her apparent desire to see and touch me or her willingness to reciprocate.

The warmth came from somewhere else.

As I sat on my bed and held her close to me, I knew what it was. It was different than what I felt for my parents or Megan, Travis or Bethany—more intense, tangible, and undeniable.

"I love you," I said aloud as the realization came into my head.

Mayra went completely still, and for a moment, I was sure I had fucked up in some kind of major way, but I wasn't sure how. Expressing anything was often uncomfortable and strange, but expressing emotion was more difficult than talking about anything else. It was too abstract, too conceptual. What if someone asked me why? Or wanted further explanation or description, and I couldn't supply one?

I was starting to wish I hadn't said anything and was even thinking about how I could take it back or make it sound like I had said something else or even how quickly I could retrieve my pillow and hide when Mayra spoke.

"Do you mean that?" she asked. "You're not just saying that because I got you off?"

I knew I had screwed something up. Something in one of the books said declaring love right after orgasm was rarely seen as sincere. I took a deep breath and raised my head to look into her eyes for a moment.

"I mean it," I said emphatically. "You...what you've done for me...you...you're...you're everything to me. Everything good in my life is about you. You make me want to try harder and do things I never would have considered before, and I know even if I fail, you'll still be there to help me get back up afterwards."

I had to look away, and it was very difficult not to go back to staring at her breasts again.

"I will," Mayra promised. "I'll always be there to help you. I love you, too."

"You do?" I looked at her and tried to figure out if she meant it or if it was the kind of thing you just said because someone else said it first. As soon as our eyes met, I knew she was serious. Hers were too dark, too intense for anything other than the absolute truth, and the nod of her head was just redundant.

"You're my hero," she said quietly as she looked into my eyes. I had to look away—the intensity of her eyes and everything boiling around inside of me was too much.

"You're my heroine." I nestled once more against her throat.

Within minutes, we were kissing and touching again. Mouths on mouths, skin against skin. For a while she was on top of me, straddling my waist and kissing down my chest. It was intense and wonderful. We rolled, enjoying the freedom of movement the bed allowed, and I gave her breasts more attention before moving down her stomach.

My mouth brushed slowly and lightly over her skin as I kissed across the edge of her jeans. I had to stop and inhale frequently because the scent of her was different here—deep, musky, and raw. It was addictive, and every time I inhaled, my cock responded.

Mayra reached down and unbuttoned her jeans. She nodded to me, and I slowly pulled them over her legs, leaving her pink panties in place. I couldn't look back at her face, so I stared at her bare legs and swallowed a few times to try to get myself together.

I wasn't sure where this was going. I wasn't sure where I *wanted* it to go.

Actually, that wasn't true. I knew what I wanted to do, but it scared the shit out of me.

With my jeans still unbuttoned and unzipped, it wasn't as uncomfortable as it often was when I was with Mayra or thought about her a little too much. My dick bulged out between the teeth of the zipper but at least stayed inside my boxers. When I moved back up Mayra's body to catch her mouth with mine, my erection rubbed deliciously against her thigh.

Mayra moaned, so I rubbed against her thigh again.

She placed her fingers under my jaw and tilted my head to hers. She met me with parted lips and searching tongue. As she kissed me, she shifted her hips underneath me, which caused my cock to move from the top of her thigh to between her legs.

Her panties were still on, but I felt the heat from her center. It kind of felt like it does when you walk up to a bonfire on a cool night, when the front part of you is suddenly very hot, but your back stays cool. While my dick felt like it could catch fire at any moment, the rest of me went cold.

There was nothing keeping us from having sex except Mayra's thin satin panties. If I pushed those down, I could be inside of her in a matter of seconds. Was I ready to do this? Was she? I knew she thought she was, but I still had my doubts for both of us. I fought against impending panic.

Then I realized we really couldn't.

"Mayra...I don't...I mean, I don't have any condoms or anything like that."

"I'm on the pill," she said softly, and I had to look up at her eyes to see if she was still teasing me. She nodded. "I just started taking them after...um...after my last period. It's been long enough that I should be protected."

"Should?" I really didn't like that word all of a sudden.

She shrugged.

"It's never a hundred percent," she said, "but it's about as good as it gets."

"You have to remember to take them every day," I said, recalling the section about birth control in one of the books my aunt left for me, "and at about the same time."

"I set an alarm on my phone."

The one thing Travis had told me about sex was to always use a condom, no matter what. Yeah, she could be on birth control, but condoms were still supposed to be used. Always.

I wasn't ready for this. I didn't have everything I needed, and if we did it now, I was going to screw it all up. After I screwed it up, I was going to be in panic mode until she had her next period. For me to get out of panic mode, I would have to ask her about her periods, and there was no way in hell those words were every going to come out of my mouth.

"I...I don't...I mean..."

"Shh..." Mayra took her fingers and placed them over my lips. "Not now. Not today."

"I'm sorry," I whispered.

"Don't be," Mayra replied. With her fingers under my chin, she brought my lips to hers. "I know it will be you. I don't care if we wait a few days or a few weeks—I know it will be with you, and I know it will be exactly how it is supposed to be."

I closed my eyes and pressed my lips against the top of her breast. I could feel her heart beating beneath my touch. My arms wrapped around her, and I felt her grip my hair with one hand and my back with the other. I didn't know what I was supposed to say to her, and she didn't seem to mind that I said nothing. As long as I could find a way to show her how much she meant to me, I didn't have to worry about finding the right words.

Win. So much win!

Chapter 16—Poke the Fish

I woke to Mayra's kisses along my jaw and neck.

"I have to leave in about a half hour," she said quietly as I stirred. I glanced over at the window and saw it was dark outside. The clock read eleven-fifteen.

"I fell asleep," I said. It was a totally pointless statement, and I felt my ears heat up.

Mayra didn't say anything; she just kept kissing my throat.

"Gotta get up," I said. Mayra moved over and I scrambled out of the bed. Ever since I was a kid, I always had to pee as soon as I woke up. My jeans slid down as I stood up, since they were still undone at the top, and I had to yank them up at the sides to race off to the bathroom. After I flushed the toilet, I looked at my face in the mirror as I lathered up my hands.

Did I look any different?

I didn't think so. I wondered if I would look different when we really had sex. I ran my tongue over my teeth and decided I needed to brush them before going back to my room. I did so quickly and then retraced my steps.

I intended to make good use of the half hour we had left, so I jumped into the middle of the bed and covered Mayra with my body. I crushed my mouth to hers, and she gripped my shoulders to pull me close. Her still bare breasts pushed up against my chest.

"Mmm...minty!" Mayra exclaimed with a laugh as she pulled away.

"I brushed my teeth," I told her. It was another stupid, obvious thing to say. I shook my head, trying to rid myself of pointless sentences. "So...um...do you want to stay here until you have to leave?"

"I don't know where else I would go," Mayra responded. She narrowed her eyes a bit. "Unless you're sending me home early."

"No!" I cried out. I wrapped my arms around her and pressed her down against the mattress with my body. She laughed and wrapped her legs around my waist.

That was all it took.

Mayra glided her fingers over my cheek and jaw, down my throat, and over my chest. I rose up a little to give her more room to move, but she tightened her grip with her legs, effectively pushing my erection right up against her.

I closed my eyes tightly and tried to figure out if I wanted to let myself enjoy the combination of her fingers on my abdomen and my cock pushed up against her. If I didn't...well, it was kind of painful not to pay attention to it, really. Then again, if I did pay attention, I was likely to make another mess.

I was *not* going to do that—not without making her come first. I wasn't sure if it was a rule or not, but I wanted to at least try.

"Mayra?"

"Hmm...?" She pushed her hips up against me, and I nearly lost it. I shook my head to gain some clarity.

"Can I...?" I realized I had no idea what I was supposed to say or how I was supposed to say it. *Can I touch you? Can I finger you? Can I make you come?*

I was clueless.

Mayra reached up to cup my face and tilted my head to look at her. I could only focus on her eyes for a second, but I saw her smile. She took my hand in hers and brought it up to her face. She held it there for a second and then slowly moved it down.

Past her neck.

Over her breast.

Paused at her stomach.

I felt the edge of her panties on my fingers, and closed my eyes.

"Watch," she said. Her voice was soft but still commanding. I opened my eyes and looked down between our bodies as she tucked my fingertips underneath the hem and pushed my whole hand down into her underwear.

I felt soft curls of hair, then warm, wet flesh.

"Fuck," I muttered involuntarily. Mayra only smiled as she brought two of my fingers together and pushed them between her legs. I could feel *everything*.

The sound she made was nothing short of divine. A grunting, moaning utterance that should not have sounded as sexy as it did, but the sound went straight to my cock. I desperately tried to collect myself and remembered something from some television show or book somewhere that said to think about basketball. I tried, but all I saw in my head were Mayra's boobs bouncing when I tickled her.

"What do I do?" I whispered, realizing that despite the book's graphic pictures and explanations, I was at a total loss now that I was touching her.

Mayra didn't miss a beat but shadowed my fingers with two of her own, pressing them in a slow circle right at the top, where I knew her clitoris was. She moved my fingers down for a second, where they got wet, then moved them back up to circle. I could feel a small, tight little nub there, and when I pushed just a little harder against it during one circle, she made that sound again.

"Matthewww..." She moaned as she pressed her lips against my temple. I turned my head and kissed her hard, my tongue finding its way into her mouth and circling the same way my fingers did.

She released my hand, and I continued on my own. Moving down only for a brief moment before going back to the place right at the top, I kept it up until her hips started to rise against my hand.

She grabbed my wrist then, holding my fingers in place as she bucked up against my hand. I looked at her face and saw her eyes closed and her mouth slightly open. Her breaths came in gasps as she quickened the pace and then let out a completely different sound. It was higher pitched, almost a scream, and was accompanied by her body tensing. I could feel the shaking of her thigh muscles as she cried out again.

Mayra went slack against the mattress, and I would have thought she had passed out if she didn't look up at me with a dreamy sort of half-awake gaze.

"God, that was awesome!" she exclaimed.

"It was?"

"Oh yeah." Her eyes almost seemed to roll into the back of her head. "Fucking awesome."

My face hurt from how much I was smiling, the tightness in my pants completely forgotten as I looked into her face and just watched her, my heart pounding at the sight.

I couldn't even dream of a more wonderful thing to see, so I planned to do it again as soon as possible.

~oOo~

Mayra opened the passenger door of the Porsche.

"Are you going to get out?" she asked.

I stared down at the floor of the car and wondered how I should answer that question. I had managed to not think about the whole after-graduation beach party for pretty much the entire time since I agreed to go, and now that I was here, I wasn't so sure that had been a good idea. My stomach was all tied up.

"Matthew?"

I sighed and turned my legs toward the door, poking at the fish shape on the way out and wishing we were back in my room doing other things. Mayra wrapped her fingers around my hand and pulled me toward her before placing her lips right next to my mouth.

"It will be okay," she said. "And if it gets to be too much, we'll take a little walk down the beach away from everyone and calm you down. If that doesn't work, we'll leave, okay?"

"Okay," I mumbled, not sure if it was or not. I didn't want to ruin the whole night for her.

Graduation was over. I had skipped the whole ceremony and gone out to dinner with Travis and Bethany instead. I would receive my diploma in the mail sometime next week. Mayra and I had both been accepted to Ohio State University in Columbus—she was going to major in education, and I chose information technology. I had ended up with nearly a full scholarship and then had been contacted by Brad Conner about the remainder. The Oxford Police Department apparently had their own grant for citizens who helped reduce crime, and since my actions had brought down a fairly significant drug ring—for the area, at least—I had won the grant money. It would only last my first year, but it was a good start. Mayra received a loan for what her scholarships and financial aid wouldn't cover, so we were both set for the fall.

My eyes stayed on the ground as Mayra led me over to a large group of kids already occupying a decent chunk of sandy, man-made beach at the edge of Acton Lake. When I glanced up, I could tell most of our class was already here. Someone had a few Bluetooth speakers set up on the nearby picnic tables to play music from their phones. I could smell the grilled burgers and hotdogs, and bags of chips and other snacks covered the tables. A large popcorn machine was plugged into a power outlet sticking out of the ground, and a decent-sized bonfire burned in a fire pit not far from the edge of the water.

Mayra had a huge smile on her face as she moved closer to the other graduates, waving and greeting them like it was perfectly normal for me to be there with her. A few people said hello to me as well, but in the chaos of the people and the stuff all over the beach, I couldn't manage to respond to any of them.

"Hey, everyone!" Scott O'Malley stood up on one of the picnic tables and waved his hands in the air. "Now that Mayra is *finally* here, I have a little announcement."

Aimee glared up at him from her spot on the sand.

"What, baby?" He leaned his head down and she whispered into his ear. "Oh, shit—sorry. Now that Mayra *and Matthew* are here, I have an announcement. Or rather, Aimee and I have one."

He pulled on Aimee's hand until she was on top of the table with him and wrapped his arm around her waist. He had a huge grin on his face, and Aimee appeared to be blushing.

"Now that graduation is over, we want to let you all know"— he paused then and looked over at her with a smile—"Aimee and I are getting married this summer!"

A whole bunch of people started talking at once—lots of squeals and screeches from the girls, snorts and chuckles from the guys, and one voice resounded above all the rest.

"Oh my God!" Carmen yelled out. "You're pregnant?"

The whole group went so silent, the only sounds that could be heard were the surf behind us and the crackling of the wood as it burned. My body went tense as I tried to figure out just what was going on. When I looked at Mayra, her mouth was hanging open, and her head was shaking slowly back and forth.

"You promised!" Aimee screamed as she reached back and ripped Scott's hand from around her waist. "You said no one would know!"

She gasped then and covered her mouth with her hand. Scott's eyes were wide, and he began shaking his head slowly, the same way Mayra was. Then Aimee burst into tears and ran off down the beach.

I felt like I was watching a movie.

"Shit," Scott muttered.

"What the fuck is wrong with you?" Samantha yelled at Carmen.

"What?" Carmen asked with innocence that was obviously disingenuous, even to me. "Why else would you get married at eighteen?"

Everyone exploded at that point—Carmen defending herself, Scott standing in shock with one of his friends trying to get him to confirm the news, Sean and Ian restraining Samantha from attacking Carmen, and everyone else in a tsunami of gossipy talk, shock, bemusement, and horror.

"Matthew"—I felt Mayra tighten her grip on my hand for a moment—"I have to go after her."

Our eyes met for a moment, and I felt myself nod right as she released my fingers and raced through the sand after her friend. I was at the very edge of the group, wondering if I should be eating popcorn or not. My feet danced back and forth a little bit, and I considered heading over to the Porsche, but I wasn't sure how Mayra would feel about it, and she had the keys.

I really had no idea what to do but figured it was especially weird to just kind of stand there. Besides, my feet were getting tired and my shoes were going to get covered in sand if I stayed where I was. I meandered slowly over to one of the picnic tables and sat down.

There was still an exceptional amount of chaos at the edge of the water. Mayra and Aimee hadn't come back, but a couple of people were trying to get Scott to relax. I wondered what he must have felt like, not just because of how everything came out but also because of the whole idea of impending fatherhood. It certainly would have scared the shit out of me.

"Dude." Joe dropped down on the bench next to me. "Some way to start a party, huh?"

He laughed, and I knew he wasn't expecting me to reply, so I didn't.

"It kinda completes high school," Joe said. "I never would have thought I'd see you at a party at all, but here you are!"

He took a large swig out of the red plastic cup in his hands and laughed again.

"Come on, Scott, just sit down a minute."

I moved over on the bench as Ian and Sean brought Scott over and sat him down on the other side of me. He looked pale and was kind of mumbling to himself.

"Should have gone after her," he said. "Probably never should have suggested the engagement thing at all…"

"It's all good, dude," Sean told him. "It would have come out soon enough anyway."

"At least her dad doesn't have a rack of guns in the back of his truck, right, Matthew?" Joe's laughter seemed to be completely out of control, and I kind of looked at him sideways as I processed what he was saying. Then I realized Scott and Aimee must have had to tell her parents at some point, and I understood what Joe meant. Henry just might shoot me if something similar happened.

I shuddered a little.

"Here ya go," Ian said. He handed Scott a red plastic cup like the one Joe had, and he tilted it back to take a long swallow and then wiped his mouth with his sleeve.

"Mayra went after Aimee?" Scott said as he turned to me.

I wasn't expecting him to talk to me and was definitely taken off guard. I felt my mouth open as if I might say something, but nothing actually came out. I ended up looking away as Carmen answered for me.

"Mayra will bring her back," she said. "Don't you worry."

"Mayra's a damn fine girl," Scott said.

His hand clapped me on my shoulder, and I tensed up. My chest felt heavy, and I couldn't breathe or swallow past the lump that had formed at the base of my throat. He continued to pound on my shoulder as he talked.

"She's a damn good friend to Aimee, and I know Aimee was going to tell her tonight anyway," he announced to everyone around us but kept looking at me. "She'll get her all calmed down and bring her back so we can have some fun for a while. I didn't mean to put a damn damper...damned-per...I mean, I didn't want to ruin everyone's..."

His voice trailed off, and I started tuning him out. He wasn't making any sense anyway.

"I thought Aimee was having a party at her house." Ian suddenly piped up.

"That's what everyone whose parents wouldn't let them come out here tonight think." Scott nodded vigorously. "'Cept Aimee's parents. They think the party is at Carmen's."

"Don't drag me into this." Carmen grumbled as she picked up an empty red cup from a stack of them and filled it from a large cooler with a spout at the bottom. The liquid coming out of it was red and smelled sweet.

"I gotta go find her." Scott abruptly stood, stumbling a bit. He shoved his cup at me, and I grabbed it before the liquid inside ended up all over my pants.

"You're not going after her," Carmen said. "Mayra's got her, and they'll be fine."

"But she needs me!"

Scott shoved away and started down the beach with Ian and Carmen running after him and grabbing him by the arms. I took a deep breath, glad the area had cleared out a little. I looked around and noticed a large basket of potato chips near me on the table and took a handful of them.

They weren't exactly popcorn, but the whole night still had a movie theater quality to it.

The chips were salty, and I was getting pretty thirsty. I still had Scott's red cup in my hands, so I tipped the liquid into my mouth, glad germaphobia wasn't on my list of issues. It was some kind of fruity punch, but it had a nasty aftertaste. I drank a bit more and then ate another handful of chips as I watched kids move back and forth. Some of them were still talking about Aimee and Scott, but most seemed to have moved on to the graduation ceremony or their plans for the summer.

I finished the cup of punch, but I was still hungry and thirsty, so I kept eating chips and then refilled the cup from the big cooler. Joe left and then came back a few minutes later with a cigarette in his hand. I never knew him to smoke, but once I saw him, I checked around and saw a few other kids smoking as well. The smell was nasty, and I turned my face away when he sat down next to me again.

"Never thought I'd see the day," Joe muttered. He belched loudly and refilled his cup, too.

"Never thought you'd see what?" I asked. I wasn't sure why I was suddenly curious about Joe and his random remark, but I felt compelled to ask.

"You with Mayra Trevino," he said. He flicked the butt into the sand. "I mean…Matthew, you know I love ya like you're my own brother, right?"

"You do?" I said. My eyebrows went up in surprise. I didn't recall asking them to, but they went up anyway.

"Of course I do!" he said. For some reason, all the words ran together in my head, which was hilariously funny, so I laughed out loud.

Joe laughed as well.

"You're my brudder from anudder mudder," he informed me.

"A mudder?" I asked. My eyebrows crunched down now in confusion. They weren't the only things confused though. I was baffled about how my eyebrows had suddenly come up with their own ability to move around without me asking them to. "What the fuck's a mudder?"

"Did you say *fuck*?" Samantha plopped down on the bench next to me, and the whole table shook.

We all seemed to think that was funny.

"Why is hearing you say *fuck* so hot?" she asked.

"Um…I dunno?" It ended up sounding like a question, but I didn't mean it to.

Great, now my inflections also had a mind of their own.

"Mayra said you're really, really hot, you know," Samantha said. She leaned over close to me and spoke in a very loud hushed tone. "She said you have the chest of a Greek god."

"She did?"

"Mm-hmm…" Samantha's lips squeezed together into a thin little line. I had a weird desire to poke at it, but I didn't. "She said you work out a *lot*, and you look fabulous naked."

"She said that?" Now I was genuinely surprised because I didn't really think Mayra would talk quite that freely.

"Well, she actually said with your shirt off," Samantha said, correcting herself. She was starting to slur her words a bit, or maybe the waves from the lake lapping against the rocks were affecting my ears.

I took another drink and finished off what was in that cup.

"Want more?" Samantha asked. She grabbed the plastic cup out of my hands before I had the chance to say yay or nay.

Horses say neigh.

I giggled and took another drink from the full cup Samantha handed me. It was kind of cold and wet, so I held it up to my face, which made my face cold and wet.

Damn!

I laughed again, and Joe did, too, so it must have been funny.

"You should take off your shirt," Samantha said.

"Huh?"

"See? Some of the other guys have." She pointed toward the water.

She was right. A few of the guys were running around without shirts. I was pretty sure they had been swimming though. They were all wet, at least.

"I don't like swimming much," I said. "Not in the lake, anyway."

"You afraid of drowning?"

"No," I said. "Catfish. They're very common here. They have spines near their gills that can sting, just like a jellyfish in the ocean. They're quite dangerous."

Joe spurted his drink out in front of him as he laughed again.

"Jellyfish!" he screamed. Samantha started laughing as well. A couple other kids whose names I wasn't sure of joined us, and we all started yelling "jellyfish" at each other. Joe got up on the table and yelled it out at everyone. Pretty soon, all the kids were yelling it out over and over again.

"Jellyfish! Jellyfish! Jellyfish!"

Something about Joe being way up on that table was quite intriguing, and I decided I should join him. When I stood up, my legs were all wobbly, and I figured I had been sitting there way too long. I saw the basket of chips and grabbed a handful of them on my way as I clambered onto the bench and then stood on the table.

"Portuguese man o' war!" I yelled at the top of my voice.

Joe stopped and looked over at me. His eyebrows and mine must have been in cahoots, because they were dancing all over his face.

"What the fuck did you say?" he asked.

"Portuguese man o' war," I repeated. "It kind of looks like a jellyfish, but…"

I glanced around, making sure no one else could hear us.

"But, I'll tell ya a secret."

"What's that?" Joe asked.

"It *looks* like a jellyfish, but it's *not*." I looked at him and nodded seriously. I had the feeling my eyebrows were trying to escape into my hair. Actually, my whole face kind of felt like it was crawling around.

Joe's bulging eyes suddenly crinkled as he started laughing again along with almost everyone else in the vicinity. I wondered if they had heard the secret, too. Joe raised his cup, and I looked down at my hand, pleasantly surprised to see my own red plastic cup was still there. I brought mine up, too. We tapped the plastic cups together and drained them.

Samantha took them both from us, refilled them, and handed them back.

"Now dance!" she said with a laugh.

"Dance?" I repeated.

"Yeah," she said. "You're on a table. You must be doing a table dance. You definitely need your shirt off for that."

"I do?"

"Yep." Samantha nodded seriously.

I looked over at Joe.

"I think she's gotcha there, dude," Joe said, nodding in agreement.

"Are you going to take your shirt off?" I asked him.

"Sure," he said. He placed his cup down on the table between his feet and yanked his shirt off over his head. Then he swung it around in the air before hooting and throwing it off into the shrubs by the beach.

Well, hell. I guess I was going to have to do it, too.

I had a little trouble—both with putting the cup down and with getting my shirt off, but Samantha was quite helpful with both. I stood up with my cup in one hand and my shirt in the other. I looked at them both and then threw them behind me with a shout. Punch went everywhere. Joe held his stomach as he laughed, and I joined him.

Then I noticed just how high up I was on the table.

"Damn," I mumbled as I looked around. The bonfire was a lot lower now, but I saw a couple of guys hauling more wood from the nearby forest to rebuild it. There were kids everywhere, and from where I was, I could see the tops of all their heads. When I looked past them, I could see two feminine figures walking up the beach, arm in arm.

"Mayra!" I called out, waving my hands frantically. "I'm over heeeeere!"

Mayra approached with a tear-stained Aimee on her arm. She looked up at me with her forehead all furrowed into a bunch of cute little tiny lines as she handed Aimee over to Scott, and they hugged.

I wanted to poke at the little forehead lines, so I headed over in her direction.

I kind of forgot I was on top of the table though.

I landed face first in the sand but didn't have any trouble rolling myself over and staring into the night sky. Nothing hurt, either, which was kind of odd. I could see Joe high above me, still laughing his ass off.

"What the hell is going on here?" Mayra said as she stood over me.

I turned my head toward her, and the expression on her face was just incredibly funny. I couldn't stop laughing, and the stars above her head starting spinning around her hair, which was also pretty funny.

"Matthew, where's your shirt?"

"I dunno." I raised my arms over my head to shrug but then realized they weren't really up in the air since I was on my back on the ground. I flailed my arms around in the air a bit, but I didn't think it had the same effect.

"Matthew!" Mayra gasped. "What the hell is wrong with you?"

"There's nothing, nothing wrong here." Joe hopped off the table much more skillfully than I had managed. "Nothing at all wrong with my main man, Mister M, here. No, ma'am."

"Joe, are you—"

"Nope, nothing wrong with him that can't be fixed by a jellyfish."

"Can I poke it?" I blurted out.

Mayra glared down at me, and I started laughing again. She really did look kind of mad, though, so I figured I'd get up and try to figure out why. The thing was, I couldn't seem to stand.

It was probably my damn eyebrows holding me down.

I couldn't manage to get up, so I just stayed there in the sand, laughing.

"Matthew, have you been *drinking*?" Mayra's eyes bugged out, and her neck seemed to stretch forward and toward me. I was still on my back in the sand, which was a little itchy but nice and cool at the same time.

I thought the question was kind of strange. Yes, I had been drinking. I was thirsty, especially after eating all those chips.

"The chips are salty," I told her.

Joe and Samantha both laughed, and Mayra turned toward them with her hands on her hips.

"Did you two give him that punch?"

"Don't look at me!" Samantha said with her hands moving up toward her chest, palms out. "He was all giggly before I even came over here! I just gave him a refill."

"More like three." Joe chuckled and gestured toward me with his arm, which had a nice collection of other arms trailing after it. "He's fine!"

"So, you're responsible!" Mayra growled.

"Nope," Joe told her. "He had his own cup before I sat down, I think. I mean, *I* didn't give it to him."

He started laughing again, so I joined him. I mean, if he was my other brother something-or-another, I should laugh with him, right?

"Joe's my nudder brudder," I told Mayra.

"Your *what*?"

"It's like a brother," Joe explained, "except without the geriatrics…er…*genetics*."

"For the love of all that's holy," Mayra muttered. "Help me get him up."

Joe grabbed one of my arms, and Mayra got the other one. They both yanked at the same time, but Joe's pull was quite a bit more forceful than Mayra's, and I ended up falling into him.

"We're not that kind of brothers!" he cried out with another laugh. He pushed me, and I stumbled against Mayra instead.

Falling into her was a lot nicer anyway—softer, too. I leaned on her a bit just to steady myself. I seemed to have a bit of a head rush from getting up so quickly. I felt her hands come up over my back to steady me, and I grabbed her hips. My head was a little floppy, and when it landed on her shoulder, I inhaled with my nose against her skin. She smelled so good, and it made me want to taste her.

Pushing my body against hers, I captured her mouth and kissed her deeply. She moaned into my mouth—or maybe she was trying to say something—as my tongue touched hers. She grasped my bare shoulders, and her fingers felt warm against my skin. I heard a low whistle and a few snickers as Mayra pushed against me.

I broke the kiss but still held her hips. I was fairly certain my head rush was keeping me off balance because everything was still spinning. I moved my nose over her shoulder—right next to the strap of her tank top. That made me think of the little fish shape just beside the strap, and my hand started moving up from her hip. My fingers touched the smooth, rounded underside of her breast, and Mayra grabbed my hand.

"Matthew!" she yelled. "Don't!"

"I wanna poke the fish," I whined.

"Oh my God!" Samantha cried out. She turned away with her head in her hands as Joe spewed punch all over the sand.

I ignored them and tried to move my fingers up and over her breast again—wanting to move up high enough to shift the strap a little to the side and find her birthmark, but her breast was in the way, and my hand couldn't seem to figure out how to get around it. Mayra tightened her grip on my hand and pushed it back down.

"Matthew! Stop it!"

"But I wanna poke the fish!" I said again.

"TMI!" Samantha called out as she walked away from us quickly.

"Not *here!*" Mayra's voice sounded a lot like a dog snarling.

I really, really wanted to poke the fish, but she had a good enough grip on my hand. I decided to kiss the fish instead. My lips pressed against her shoulder and then started downwards.

"Ugh!" Mayra grabbed both of my hands and held them down to my sides as she pushed me away from her a bit. Her touch made my skin tingle, but when I looked down to where we were connected, everything was still blurry. I was also getting really dizzy all of a sudden. I looked up at her face, and her eyes were shifting around and around.

My stomach lurched a bit, and my head really began to swim.

"Mayra," I whispered, "I don't feel so good."

"Joe, Sean!" Mayra called out. "Help me get Matthew back to my car."

Arms went around my waist, and I was yanked forward by the two guys. They dragged me across the sand, following Mayra's footsteps until we reached the Porsche. I kept telling them I was fine to walk, but the words came out all garbled.

"Walking is not that hard," I told Joe as he propped me up against the hood.

"You're a fucking mess." Sean chuckled. "And your shirt smells like a fucking frat house. I cut Scott off, but I didn't even think to watch out for Matthew."

"Just get him in the car." Mayra sighed. "I need to get him home."

I struggled to poke at the fish shape as they piled me in and buckled the seatbelt. Joe tossed my used-to-be-gray shirt, now covered in red splotches, onto my lap. I ended up falling a little to the side with my head on the window, which at least let me touch the fish-shaped mark in the car's interior.

Mayra got in the driver's side and started up the engine. It was a lot louder than I remembered, and I jumped a little as it roared to life. Shaking my head, I tried to sit up a little straighter, but everything I looked at was still spinning around in circles.

I wasn't too bad off until we started moving.

As a kid, I remembered my mom telling me to look out the window toward the horizon if I was feeling carsick, but that didn't help in the slightest now. It actually made the queasy feeling in my stomach worse. It didn't get any better when I tried to focus on something inside the car, either. It felt like there was something bubbling around in my gut, and I knew I wasn't going to make it home.

"Mayra, pull over!"

"Ah, shit!" she cried out. She pulled off to the side while I undid my seatbelt and yanked open the door. I dropped to the ground just before I heaved onto the edge of the road.

Even though I was shivering, I felt hot and was pretty sure I must have a fever or something. Could I have caught a bug from someone at the party? Mayra was next to me as I threw up once more.

"I think I'm sick," I said softly.

"No kidding." Mayra's voice was deadpan.

"Do I feel hot?" I asked. "I think I might have a fever."

"You don't have a fever," Mayra said. "You're drunk."

"Drunk?" I asked with incredulity. "I don't drink."

"Well, you did tonight," she said with a sigh. "What did you think was in that punch?"

"Um...punch?" I said. My head was still spinning, and I couldn't make it stop. "Hawaiians?"

I wanted to laugh, but my gut hurt too much.

"And then some," Mayra replied. "It had an entire bottle of Everclear in it."

"What's that?"

"I'll tell you tomorrow," she promised. "Do you think you can make it back home now?"

"I think so." I did feel a little better after throwing up. We both got back in the car, and I ended up falling against her, which is where I stayed until I got home. I made it to the bathroom just in time to start vomiting again. I'd had food poisoning once after eating clams at the Red Lobster near the mall. All in all, I think I might have preferred to go through that again.

Not only did I feel awful, but my head seemed to just flop around on top of my neck, and the dizziness wouldn't stop. I felt like I had gone on a merry-go-round at top speed for ten minutes, only the dizziness didn't seem to be getting any better. If anything, it was getting worse.

Mayra knelt beside me and pushed my hair off my forehead. I couldn't stop throwing up long enough to thank her. Once I completely purged everything out of my body, I tried to collapse on the floor beside the toilet. Mayra wouldn't let me though. She hauled me back up by one arm and dragged me to my bed.

Lying down made the spinning worse, but at least it was more comfortable. I also didn't think I had anything left to vomit. Mayra crawled in beside me, and I nudged my face against her shoulder and brought my finger up to—finally—poke the fish.

"I don't feel good," I told her for the twentieth time.

"I know, baby."

"I don't want to feel like this anymore."

"I know."

"Why do people drink that stuff if it makes you feel like this?"

"I don't know, Matthew," Mayra said. "Just close your eyes and try to go to sleep."

"I don't like this."

"I know. Hush."

"Everything is spinning around," I told her. "It won't stop. Will it ever stop?"

"It will stop," she promised. "Just go to sleep, and when you wake up, you'll feel like shit in a whole new way."

I couldn't really fathom that it could get worse, so I closed my eyes and passed out.

Lose.

Chapter 17—Cookies Aren't the Only Things That Start with "C"

Even before I opened my eyes and saw the dark of night outside my window, I knew I hadn't slept long. For one, my head was still spinning about as much as it had been, and my tongue felt gross. From the hallway just outside my room, I could hear Mayra's soft voice.

"...he had no idea," she was saying. "No one is confessing to giving it to him, anyway... I couldn't leave him by himself...he was such a mess...yes—the whole gamut...no, I did not...not a drop, I swear..."

I didn't hear any other voices and figured Mayra was talking on the phone. I wanted to get up and brush my teeth, but I was afraid if I moved my head at all, it just might fall off and roll across the floor. It occurred to me that it might pop off even if I didn't move, and I had a random thought about dying with unbrushed teeth. I tried to roll over and groaned.

"Oh, I think he's awake. I should go...oh, yeah—good idea..."

Through blurred vision, I saw her standing in the doorway to my room with her cell phone in her hand.

"I didn't want you to worry...in the morning, but don't expect it to be early...you too, Dad...bye."

I closed my eyes again, not daring to keep them open in case it made my head worse. I felt Mayra sit down on the bed next to me, and I reached out to her.

"I'm sorry," I whispered.

"You don't have to be sorry."

"Are you in trouble with Henry?" I asked.

"No," Mayra sighed. "He's probably calling the cops to head out to break up any party that is left over, but he didn't sound like he was mad at either of us. He won't be too happy if he finds out who gave you spiked punch, but I don't think he's going to blame you."

"I was thirsty," I said. "I didn't know what was in it. I thought it was just—"

"Shh…" Mayra's fingers drifted through my hair and stroked it backwards, away from my face. "It's okay. I'm going to go get you some water. I'll be right back."

"My teeth are furry," I said.

"I'll help you." I heard Mayra's soft snicker.

Mayra maneuvered me to the bathroom and helped me get toothpaste on the brush. I tried to figure out just where my teeth were while she brought me a large glass of water and two ibuprofen tablets.

"Drink it all," Mayra commanded.

"That's a big glass," I told her. "I don't need that much to take pills."

"You need that to get yourself rehydrated," she said. "You'll feel a lot better tomorrow if you drink it all."

I argued a bit, but it hurt to argue, and I really needed to lie back down. I stumbled into bed after drinking the full glass, and Mayra followed me. She wrapped her arms around me, and I snuggled into the place between her shoulder and neck, which was really quite a nice spot to be.

Just having her here this way in my bed at night was quite a nice thing, too.

"You should live here," I told her.

"Don't be ridiculous," Mayra laughed.

"I mean it," I said. I tried to move a bit so I could look up at her, but as soon as I did, my head got all swooshy again. I swallowed hard and tried to steady myself. "I like you being here."

"I like being here, too," she said. "But Matthew, we graduated from high school a few hours ago. Let's take things a little slower, for the sake of Henry's heart if nothing else."

I had to think about that for a minute, imagining how Henry might react if Mayra said she was going to move out of his house and into mine. It would be quite a shock to him, that was for sure. Would he still like me if he thought I was taking Mayra away from him too fast? But she was planning to move to campus at the end of summer anyway.

"Will college be hard for him?" I asked. "I mean, when you go away?"

"Yes," she said. "I think he's already kind of freaking out a little. He worries a lot. Staying in town helps since he can keep an eye on me. I think you going to the same school actually makes him a lot happier about it."

"It does?"

"He knows I'm safe with you," Mayra said quietly.

"I love you," I told her.

"I love you, too," Mayra responded. "And I think Henry does in a way as well."

"Henry?" My eyebrows lowered and scrunched at the top of my eyes. I reached up with my fingers to try to get them to stay in place.

"I think he sees you like he would a son, you know?"

"I think so," I said, but I wasn't entirely sure I did. Love was weird and confusing. Outside of my parents, Megan, Travis, and Beth, I had never really thought about loving anyone else besides Mayra. Now that she was in my life, I couldn't imagine it being any other way.

I didn't sleep well. My head went from spinning to pounding, and I kept waking up every hour or so. There was the slightest tickle against my neck where Mayra's fingers rested as she cradled my head to her shoulder. I sighed against her skin and wrapped my arms around her. I still felt crappy, but having her close made it bearable. The only problem was, the huge glass of water had gone straight through me.

I wriggled around a bit, but it didn't help. I was still dizzy and really, really didn't want to leave either the comfort of the bed or the comfort of Mayra's arms. The pressure on my bladder soon became too much, and I had to get up.

As I washed my hands, I glanced at myself in the mirror. I looked really rough. My head still hurt, so I headed down to the kitchen for another large glass of water.

Throughout the day, I slowly recovered physically, but I was still quite embarrassed. When Mayra woke up, she made me fried eggs and toast, which settled my stomach. I vowed to never touch alcohol again, and Mayra laughed.

I didn't understand the joke.

With school out, we spent most of our time over the next week planning for the move to Columbus to begin college at Ohio State University. I was worried about moving even though it really wasn't very far. Knowing Mayra would be there with me made the idea a little more palatable.

When we weren't talking about college, we were making plans for the weekend. When Saturday finally rolled around, I couldn't help but worry about it.

Today was *the* day.

Well, more precisely—tonight was *the* night.

I wasn't sure actually planning it out was the very best of ideas. All in all, the whole party fiasco wasn't completely bad, and I had managed to avoid thinking about that for the better part of a week. Granted, I learned all about how much puking and hangovers suck, and Aimee and Scott were still trying to get things worked out between themselves and their parents, but it wasn't all bad.

Now that high school was officially over, Mayra was mostly happy she didn't have to face any of our classmates. Apparently, I said a few things at the party that weren't taken the way they were intended. She wasn't inclined to tell me exactly what I had said, and I admitted I didn't remember it all very clearly.

Regardless, Mayra thought events at the party would have gone better if we had talked about them and planned everything out, which led to planning out tonight. We had talked about it and talked about it until she was blue in the face, and I was blue in the balls.

We were going to have sex tonight.

Dinner would be first. I was to pick Mayra up at six o'clock and bring her back to my house to cook. She was making pad Thai from scratch, and I was really looking forward to it. She had also hinted at chocolate cake, and I was definitely hoping she wasn't joking about it because that would just about kill me.

After dinner, we would relax, watch television, and make out. We were just going to be casual and keep it at about the same level we usually did. Then I was going to go punch the heavy bag for a while to release whatever pent-up energy I was bound to have, take a shower, and then meet her in my room.

I swallowed hard as I dropped my head back down to my pillow and took my dick in my hand.

For the last week, I had thought in enough detail about having sex with Mayra that it often required some attention before I could go back out in public. I thought about what she would look like when I walked into my room. Would she already be naked and on my bed? Or would she be wearing one of those sexy lingerie items I had seen in catalogs? Would she light a bunch of candles and sprinkle rose petals all over the place?

Should I do that?

My hand slid up and down—base to tip, tip to base. I ran my tongue across my lips, and imagined Mayra straddling me. In my mind, she leaned over and placed her lips against mine as she lowered herself over me.

Moisture covered my palm as I ran it over the head of my cock, and then I dragged it back down to my balls. I could practically feel her body against me—the sweat from her skin mixing with mine as we moved slowly together.

"Ahh!" I cried out. For a moment, I just lay there and tried to regain my breath and my senses. I glanced at the clock, which read seven forty-five in the morning, and let out a long sigh.

There was no way I was going to make it through till tonight.

I pushed myself out of bed, showered, dressed, and sat down to make a list for the store.

A loaf of bread, a container of milk, and a stick of butter.

I shook my head, pushing *Sesame Street* memories from my thoughts as much as I could. That same phrase always came into my head when I made a list for the grocery store, and it would randomly repeat itself until I was through the checkout lane.

I started writing what I really wanted to get.

Mac and cheese
Bread
Carrots
Coke
Doritos
Cereal
Milk
Bagels
Cream cheese
Apples
Bananas
Flowers
Cond

I couldn't even write the whole word at first but also didn't want to chance actually forgetting them either. That was at least part of the reason for planning this all out, right? I didn't want to forget anything, so I wrote "oms" at the end of "cond" and folded up the paper. Once it was shoved into my pocket, I headed out the door and drove to the store.

Partway there, I pulled over and took out the list. I scratched out everything but the letter "C" since that should be a big enough clue for me, and anyone reading my list over my shoulder wouldn't know what it meant. It could stand for carrots, chicken, or cookies.

Cookie, cookie, cookie starts with C!

Mayra said it was superfluous since she was on the pill. One quick reminder about Aimee and Scott had her seeing things my way. The last thing I wanted to do was to miss planning *that* particular aspect of the evening.

The store was crowded for a Saturday morning, and I tried to move silently between people and not meet anyone's eyes as I gathered up the items on my list. Most of it was stuff I bought every week, but once I got to the flowers, I just stood in the floral department of the store and stared at all the different types and colors. I had no idea what to get for her or even what kind of flowers she liked.

What if she didn't like flowers?

What if she was allergic?

"May I help you?"

I nearly jumped right over the cart as the woman who worked at the floral counter sneaked up behind me. I closed my eyes tightly and hoped she would go away.

"Are you looking for an arrangement?" she asked. "Who is it for?"

"For whom," I whispered.

"Excuse me?" the lady said.

I couldn't answer her. I'd already corrected the grammar of a total stranger who was just trying to be helpful, and I could feel the panic rising in my chest. Keeping my eyes closed, I shifted the cart away from her a little. She huffed and walked away.

Maybe flowers weren't necessary.

Next to the floral department, there was a big selection of balloons, and I tried to find an appropriate one for the occasion, but it just didn't exist. *Congratulations* seemed the most fitting, but that still seemed wrong. There were, however, boxes containing a small tank of helium and an assortment of balloons sitting nearby. I smiled to myself and put one of them in my cart. It was twenty-five dollars, and I hadn't budgeted for it, but I was pretty sure I could make up for it without too much trouble. I ran my hand through my hair and started toward the pharmacy area.

Mayra had already saved me thirty dollars in haircuts, I thought to myself. That covered the balloons.

I pushed the cart up and down the aisle full of vitamins and then the one full of cold-relief products. I checked over all the different hairbrushes and combs and even looked at the various types of makeup in a large display. I wondered what kind Mayra used and if she would be wearing any tonight.

Maneuvering the cart closer to the actual pharmacy counter, I saw someone who I thought might be related to someone else I had seen acting as a substitute teacher at school a couple of years ago, so I quickly pushed the cart back to the produce section on the other side of the store.

About an hour later, I had made it back.

I stood with my body angled toward a display of ankle and wrist braces, but my eyes kept moving right beneath the drop-off counter for prescriptions to the assortment of boxes labeled Trojans. My heart was pounding in my chest, and I had to work hard to keep myself from hyperventilating.

Trojans was a ridiculous name for a brand of condoms. It conjured up images of war and horses, and I didn't want to think about either of those things.

I had to get out of there.

But I couldn't leave without one of those boxes.

I was going to have to get through checkout with it, and I had more than ten items. I couldn't even use the express lane!

I had to get ahold of myself, grab a box, and get the fuck out of there.

Taking a deep breath, I looked around to quickly ascertain that there was no one else nearby, and then I darted out and grabbed a large, gold-colored box. I didn't look at it or read the label; I just shoved it in the cart underneath a box of Cheerios.

Moving back to my original position, I nonchalantly began to peruse the ankle braces again.

After another five minutes, I decided it was safe to make my way toward the cashiers. The line for the self-checkout was really long, and after all my dawdling around the pharmacy, I didn't have the time to spare.

My hands were shaking as I approached the checkout lane. There were two people ahead of me, which was fine, but when another person came up behind me, I had to change lanes. I did that two more times before I managed to get to the front without anyone coming up and watching what I put on the conveyor belt.

I saved the Cheerios and the hidden box beneath them for last, stacking them together on the belt and shoving the bananas and apples around them to hide the words on the box. Of course, the checkout person had to pick everything up separately to scan it so I could pay, but at least it was a guy.

"Hey there, Matthew!"

My body went completely stiff and not in any good kind of way.

Samantha stepped up behind me with a bottle of Diet Coke in one hand and a large bag of powdered donuts in the other. For a moment, the sheer incongruousness of it distracted me enough that I didn't consider what she might see on the conveyor belt. Diet Coke and a huge bag of donuts? Really?

"So, looks like you're playing a little 'poke the fish' tonight." Samantha giggled and pointed toward the bagger, who was carefully examining the large box of forty Trojan Ultra Ribbed condoms.

I couldn't figure out what she meant, and there was no way I was going to form words to express a response, so I just handed the cashier my debit card and ran the hell out of there without uttering a sound.

I made it out alive and with condoms, which counted as a win.

Chapter 18—Sex is Better than Cake

Three hours.

Three hours before I was supposed to pick up Mayra and bring her back to my house so we could have dinner and end the night up in my bedroom, giving our virginity to each other.

I was a fucking mess.

Even though I had actually made it out of the grocery store with all my purchases, I was still on high alert. I had to make sure none of the neighbors could see what I had bought, so I closed the garage door after pulling inside. After I checked the side windows to guarantee the neighbor who was mowing his lawn couldn't see inside, I opened up the trunk and pulled out the bags of food and…and…and…

Condoms.

I should have asked Travis to get them for me, except then I would have been barraged with questions for hours afterwards. The whole experience, even without Samantha's strange interruption, was horrifying. Now that I had a chance to think about our classmate's remark, I had no idea how she knew about Mayra's birthmark, my obsession over it, or why she was bringing that up in the first place. My hazy memories of the beach party weren't any help in this regard, either.

I recalled something about jellyfish, but the memory was unclear.

I carefully unpacked all the food, avoiding *that* bag until the very last second. Once everything else was put away, I pulled the large gold box out of the plastic sack and looked at it. It didn't seem quite as frightening as it did at the store, but it was still definitely intimidating as hell. I had no idea where to put the damn things but figured somewhere in my room made sense.

What if Mayra didn't want to be in my room? What if she'd rather do it on the couch? Or a chair? Or the kitchen table? People did that, didn't they?

Hell if I knew.

I opened up the box and pulled out a long string of little square packets, all attached to each other. Taking a deep breath, I tore them off in groups of four—so I knew they would come out even—and placed some in every room of the house, even the bathroom. Maybe Mayra would want to do it in the shower—the same shower where I touched myself and thought about her, the very idea of which would likely send me into a panic attack if she were there.

I ran to the basement to punch the heavy bag.

It didn't help.

Neither did television, working on my websites, or reading. All I could think about was how many different ways I could single-handedly screw it all up.

Fall asleep after dinner.

Not be able to make her come.

Not be able to get hard.

Not be able to get the condom on right.

Come too soon.

Come too late.

Just generally suck at the whole lovemaking thing.

Squeezing my eyes shut, I curled up in a ball on the couch. I pulled my legs up to my chest and just held on, trying to keep the insane panic that was washing over me from taking too tight a hold. I could hear my panting breaths in my ears, and my heart felt like it was going to rip right through my ribcage. I could hear the clock ticking, bringing me closer and closer to the time I would have to make a move.

The phone rang.

I wanted to just keep myself in the fetal position and ignore it, but I was not good at ignoring the phone. Once it rang, I always felt compelled to answer it. It was one of the things Mayra found amusing about me. Even though I knew it was usually telemarketers calling, I couldn't *not* answer the phone.

"Hello?"

"I love you." Mayra soft voice flowed out of the phone's speaker and into my heart.

My legs gave out, and I dropped to the kitchen floor. I used my free hand to tug my hair, and I let out a long breath. The phone felt cold against my cheek, and I pressed against it as if I were closer to Mayra that way.

"I'm scared," I whispered.

"I know," she replied easily. "I am a little, too. It's all right. We're all right. I love you, and I'll still love you tomorrow, no matter what happens tonight."

Her words covered my skin and relaxed my muscles. I rubbed my fingers against my closed eyes as I leaned back against the wall.

"I want it to be good for you," I said quietly. "I don't want to mess it up."

"Matthew, I don't know what I'm doing either, you know. But this is also about the most natural thing two people can do together. Remember the first time you kissed me?"

"Yes." I would remember it forever.

"You remember how you just let go—let your instincts take over?"

"Yes."

"Do that again."

"I don't know," I said. I shook my head back and forth, rolling it against the wall behind me. I considered what my "natural instincts" might be and envisioned myself pounding into Mayra as hard and fast as possible. "If I did that, I might hurt you."

"I don't think you could ever hurt me," Mayra replied.

"I love you so much," I told her. "I want everything to be perfect, and I don't even know what perfect looks like."

"Perfect looks like you and me together," she said. "Everything else is icing. Oh! Speaking of icing…I made it from scratch."

"You're bringing cake?"

"Yep."

"Chocolate?"

"Yep."

"Is it six o'clock yet?"

Mayra laughed.

"Almost," she replied. "I still have a few things to do around here, and Henry doesn't leave for another hour. Don't come too soon, or he'll still be here."

"Does he know you are coming over?"

"Yes," she said with a sigh. "I have the feeling he knows I'm spending the night there, but he would rather pretend not to know, you know?"

"I guess," I said. "You didn't tell him?"

"Hell, no!" Mayra cried. "Why? Did you tell Travis and Bethany?"

"No," I said, realizing her point. "I guess that would be weird, wouldn't it?"

"Yes, it would," Mayra agreed. "Okay—I need to get back to it. Stay calm. I love you."

"I love you, too." It was strange how easily that phrase slipped from my tongue.

The phone went silent, but I just sat there and held it for a few minutes. I realized I was smiling and wondered how she knew right when to call. Maybe women's intuition was real.

~oOo~

"Here—carry this," Mayra said as she thrust a paper grocery sack into my hands. She leaned into the trunk of my car to pull out something else, and I could see a thin sliver of skin between the hem of her shirt and her shorts.

I sighed and refocused on the bag in my hands. I was pretty sure it had a cake in it. I tried to peer into the top of it, but Mayra straightened back up and shook her finger at me.

"No peeking!"

"I can already smell it, you know," I told her. The scent of chocolate and sugar and warm, moist cake filled my nose.

"Well, you still can't *see* it, and that's the important bit."

"Why?"

"No questions!" Mayra laughed and headed into the house with another bag, which was filled with rice noodles, vegetables, and various bottles of Asian sauces.

I glanced over my shoulder, half expecting Henry to suddenly arrive and announce he was skipping the fishing trip and joining us for dinner. If not Mayra's father, maybe Bethany or Travis would show up to check on me. I hadn't seen either of them since Wednesday, and it wouldn't be unusual for Travis to show up with dinner while Beth was getting ready for a business trip.

"Stop it," Mayra said in a soft, singsong voice.

"Stop what?"

"Thinking about all the worst case scenarios."

"Oh."

Mayra pulled all the items out of the sacks and lined them up on the counter. I helped chop up green onions while she made the sauce and cooked the noodles. I watched intently as she expertly fried up the tofu and vegetables in the sauce, then added noodles, egg, and peanuts into the mix. She dished out heaping portions onto our plates, and we dug in.

It was delicious.

"How can you like Thai and not Chinese food?" I asked.

"Totally different," Mayra said. "Thai sauce is curry based, and there are no water chestnuts. Water chestnuts are nasty."

"But…they just taste like…water."

"Exactly."

"That doesn't make any sense."

"Water shouldn't be crunchy."

I shook my head.

"I'm not completely sure chocolate cake is appropriate with Thai food," Mayra said.

"Cake goes with anything," I said with a shrug. Mayra smiled and glanced up at me through her lashes. I looked away quickly, feeling heat in my neck and cheeks. "I mean, cake is so good, it doesn't matter what else you have with it."

We finished dinner, cleaned up, and then Mayra let me have a piece of the chocolate cake she had made, which was elaborately decorated with all kinds of frosting and read *Congratulations, Graduate* on it.

"I felt bad you didn't get your diploma with the rest of us," Mayra told me, "and the party was kind of a disaster. I thought we could finally celebrate our graduation a little."

In all honesty, it hadn't been important to me in the slightest. I didn't care about walking across a stage with everyone else or even that I got my diploma in the mail instead of having it handed to me by Principal Monroe. I almost told her this, but then I realized she had gone to a lot of trouble to decorate the cake to celebrate with me. When I looked up at her face, I could see the smallest amount of worry there.

Celebrating is important to Mayra.

This realization, and the subsequent realization that Mayra wanted to celebrate *my* graduation, not just her own, shocked me and nearly made me have to sit down on the couch for a few minutes. It was as if something inside my head suddenly switched to the on position, and it sent a shiver of electricity down my backbone.

Even when my mother and father were alive and would do things for me, I never grasped the concept of wanting something on behalf of another person. I didn't have the kinds of thoughts where you forgot about what was important to you and only focused on what was important to someone else. My doctors in the past had talked about it, but I never really understood what they meant. How could I feel like that about someone else?

But I did now. Now I understood. With wide eyes, I reached out and pulled Mayra against me, my mouth covering hers and molding against her lips softly.

"Thank you," I whispered. "Thank you so much, Mayra…you have no idea what this means."

"Matthew"—Mayra snickered and wound her fingers into my hair—"it's just a cake."

The sparkle in her eyes told me differently.

"No," I said with a shake of my head, "it's not. It's not the cake. It's you. It's all you. You are everything to me and more. That doesn't even make sense, but it's true."

The cascade of emotions that poured over me all at once wasn't overwhelming like I might have expected. It was invigorating. Revitalizing. Exciting. Captivating.

Erotic.

They were the purest feelings I had ever experienced.

I reached down and lifted Mayra up into my arms, cradling her against my chest. I looked into her eyes and watched her look back at me. For once, there was no anxiety—no strangeness as our souls connected through our gaze. When she reached up and trailed her hand over my cheek, I didn't move, tense, or flinch. I just stared into her eyes, wanting to figure out how I could possibly express to her what she meant to me.

"I love you," I told her.

"I love you, too," she replied.

Words weren't enough. They weren't even close. I shook my head slowly, still keeping my eyes on hers.

"I want to show you."

"Show me?"

My mouth pressed to hers, and I used the tip of my tongue to reach out and touch her lip.

"I want to show you," I said again. "I want to show you how much I love you."

I couldn't wait another second, so I carried her up to my room.

Mayra, lying down on her back in my bed, was the most beautiful sight I had ever seen. Her eyes were bright, and they never left mine as I leaned back long enough to pull my shirt over my head. Mayra reached up and ran the tips of her fingers over my chest and stomach before quickly unbuttoning her blouse and pulling it from her shoulders.

I knelt, straddling her with each of my knees lined up with her waist as Mayra reached behind her back and released the clasp of her bra. Before she could remove it completely, I touched the shoulder straps with my fingers. I trailed down her shoulders and brushed my fingertip over her fish-shaped birthmark and then leaned down to place my lips over it.

"Why do you do that?" Mayra asked quietly.

I looked at her and saw nothing but curiosity in her eyes. I blinked a couple of times as I tried to figure it out myself.

"It's part of you," I said, "a mark of your birth, which makes it important."

Mayra raised an eyebrow.

"Also," I said as I smiled sheepishly, "it is very, very distracting until I touch it."

"And it looks like a fish." Mayra snickered.

I nodded.

Mayra's hands cupped the side of my face, and she brought our lips together for a moment.

"You're adorable."

I shrugged, felt my face heat up a little, but was then distracted by the exposure of the tops of her breasts and forgot to be embarrassed by any of it. Instead, I kissed them both as I pulled her bra away.

The feelings I experienced in the kitchen hadn't dissipated. If anything, the emotions increased as Mayra's clothing began to disappear. I knelt above her again as she shifted under me to unbutton and unzip her shorts. I watched her thumbs hook into the sides as she pushed them down over her hips and felt my cock respond to the sight.

Would she also get excited from watching me?

Again, I knelt over her. I watched her eyes follow my hand as I moved it over my stomach and to the buttons of my jeans. I popped the first one open, then the second, and immediately saw Mayra's eyes widen as she ran her tongue across her lips.

"Do you like that?" I asked her. My voice had taken on a strange, husky tone. I swallowed once, and then opened another button. "Do you like watching me?"

"Shit, Matthew…"

Her chest rose and fell, and she didn't have to say any more. I pulled the final button through the loop and pushed my jeans slightly off my hips—just enough to reach in and pull my cock out of my boxers. Mayra let out a long breath as she reached for me. I took her hand in mine and wrapped her fingers around my shaft.

She stroked me as I pushed my jeans and boxers off, only letting go so I could shift them the rest of the way down my legs. We finished by removing her panties together and then spent a moment just looking at each other.

"You're so beautiful," I told her as I reached out and ran my fingers over her neck and chest and then down to her stomach. My hand dropped lower, cupping her and using my thumb to stroke over her clit, just like she had taught me.

"And you are incredible," she replied. "Everything about you just…surprises me."

"Is that good?"

"Definitely."

"Are you, uh…"—I had to stop and swallow hard to keep speaking—"…are you ready?"

"Yes," she said, her voice dropping in tone as her cheeks darkened. "Please."

I reached over and opened the top nightstand drawer, pulling out the string of condoms and wondering why I hadn't detached them all beforehand.

"Prepared for a long night?" Mayra chuckled.

"Most definitely," I replied. I pulled one of the little squares away from the rest and held it up for Mayra to see the wording on the package.

"I hope these are okay," I said softly. Mayra just nodded.

"Do you know how to put one on?" she asked.

"I think so," I said. "I did a little…um…internet research on it this afternoon."

I decided *not* to tell her about practicing on the bananas.

Holding the tipped end of the condom, I placed it over the head and then rolled it down. It got kind of caught up at one point but otherwise seemed to go on without much trouble. It felt a little strange and kind of confining, but I was a little too preoccupied with what was coming next to care too much.

"Are you ready?" I asked. "I mean…really ready?"

"I'm ready," Mayra responded. "Are you?"

"Yes." I meant it, too. I didn't have the slightest doubt.

Mayra nodded, and I saw her bottom lip disappear beneath her teeth as I positioned myself between her legs, took a deep breath, and shifted my hips forward.

Not much happened.

"Here…" Mayra reached down and repositioned me a bit, and I moved forward again with about the same amount of luck.

I closed my eyes, trying to stop my mind from spinning into the terrifying circles of self-fulfilling prophecy.

Mayra moved around a little under me, pulling her legs up and bending her knees so they were right up against my hips.

"Try again," she said. Her fingers were still wrapped around me, and I moved with her guidance. Once the head was pressed against her opening, Mayra released me and reached up to grip my shoulders. This time when I moved forward, I felt her body spread and give in to the pressure.

For the briefest moment, it felt like there wasn't enough room for me to get inside of her, but when I pushed just a little harder, that pressure was gone, and my cock sank into her partway as Mayra gasped and dug her fingernails into my skin.

"Are you okay?" I asked through panting breaths. My mind warred between the feeling of her tight body gripping half my dick and the pain of her nails in my flesh.

"Yes." She was panting, and her eyes squeezed shut for a minute.

"Are you sure?"

"Just…give me a second."

I held completely still, watching Mayra's face as she moved slowly under me, adjusting her position for a moment before lying back against the bed and sighing.

"I hurt you," I said softly.

"No," she said, "you didn't. It feels…*strange*…but it doesn't hurt now. Just for a second."

"You're okay?"

"Yes," she said. Her hips shifted, which sent some pretty interesting feelings up my cock, into my balls, and then right up my spine. I groaned, arching my back a little, as she moved again.

"You like that?" she asked. Her expression was one of awe and amusement combined.

"Yes," I answered. "It's different…I like it. I like it a lot."

"Are you"—she paused a minute, her face tingeing red again—"all the way in?"

I looked down and shook my head.

"Not yet."

"Keep going."

"Okay."

I pulled out a short way and then pushed forward again. She tightened her fingers on my shoulders but didn't dig in. Another nod from her, and I pushed a little harder, feeling myself become flush with her, all the way in.

All the way.

Much like when her hand was around me the first time, I couldn't think of anything else but the sensation, no matter how hard I tried. I wanted to think about website design, past school projects, the weather—anything but this feeling of her warm, tight, wet flesh encompassing the most sensitive part of my body. I couldn't, and I had to pull out.

"What's wrong?" Mayra asked.

"Too much," I said. "Feels too good. I don't want to…not too soon. Just give me a sec."

Mayra stayed still, patiently waiting for me, which was one of the best things about her. It only took a minute before I could breathe easily again and was ready for another try. I didn't need help lining up this time, and when I pushed inside of her, my cock slid in easily.

"Oh, wow." Mayra sighed.

"Okay?"

"More than," she replied. "Really good. I think that little break was good for us both...oh wow..."

I moved again, pulling a little less than halfway out before pushing back in. Mayra's legs gripped my hips and she pushed up to meet me.

"Is that good?" I asked.

"Perfect," she whispered. She closed her eyes and tilted her head back as I pulled back and thrust forward again. She wrapped her feet around my legs and steadied me. One of my hands went to her head, stroking through her hair as I stroked into her body lower down.

We moved together, slowly and rhythmically, with the tempo set by nothing more than the beating of our hearts. I gasped each time I drove down inside of her—feeling the warmth and tightness of her body surrounding, enveloping, and holding me closely...safely. Her arms were wrapped around my shoulders, and her fingers dug into my skin. My hand gripped her hip.

In my fingers, I could feel the gentle push of her hips off the mattress, and I used my hand to pull her against me at the same speed. It perfected our motions, and I could feel the slight quivering in her thighs as she panted against my neck.

"Matthew...I'm...I'm..."

I could *feel* it.

Her heels dug into the back of my thighs, and it probably should have been painful but wasn't. I felt her body shudder from the inside out, and it was the most incredible sensation I had ever experienced. My hand cupped the back of her neck as I held her up to me to kiss her jaw, her mouth, her cheek.

There was wetness there just below her eye, and when I looked at her, I didn't have to wonder or ask why she had tears—I knew. They were mirrored on my own cheeks.

I didn't look away when our eyes met, and I didn't turn from her when her hand brushed the moisture away from my cheekbone. Our gaze remained connected. I should have felt uncomfortable, but

I couldn't bring myself to look away at all. My heart beat faster, and I moved inside of her quickly and with more urgency than before. I could feel every part of her muscles constricting around me as I thrust deeper, listening to her muted grunts each time I was completely buried inside.

The buildup was more gradual than it had been when her hand was wrapped around me but a thousand times more intense, too. I dropped my cheek to Mayra's neck, and her arms coiled around my head. My body seemed to be on autopilot as the pace increased along with the beat of my heart and the breath from my lungs. I was fully aware of the tingling shudder that came up from my thighs and down from my stomach, reaching a point in the center before exploding outwards.

I cried out against the skin of her throat, my final thrust held tightly against her until my body stopped quaking inside of her. Twice more I move inside her flesh, my sanctuary, before reaching down and gripping the edge of the condom and pulling out of her. I discarded it in the basket beside the nightstand and then wrapped her up in my arms. With the scent and warmth of her surrounding me again, I closed my eyes and held her against my chest.

"I love you," Mayra whispered into my ear. I moved my mouth to her lips though I didn't open my eyes. I just kissed her, murmuring the words back into her mouth as she did the same into mine. I pressed every inch of my body against hers, both hungry for more and completely sated at the same time.

"I love you…I love you…" we repeated in unison between kisses.

I couldn't imagine anything else could be closer to bliss, so I gave in to the warmth of her love.

Best win ever.

Chapter 19—You Have What in Your Kitchen Drawer?

Still warm and dazed from sleep, I opened my eyes to the dim light coming through my bedroom window. There were no thoughts of having dreamed the experiences of the night before— they were far too extraordinary to be passed off as nothing more than a dream.

Mayra was in my arms, and I was in hers.

When I turned my head slightly, I could see her closed eyes and peaceful look. I was immediately reminded of the first time we fell asleep in each other's arms, right after I had told her everything about what was wrong with me and about my parents' deaths. Even then, when I barely knew her, I knew how right it felt to be lying with her, our bodies twined together like the cover of some cheesy romance novel. I didn't understand it then, but I did now.

Shifting a little, I realized the arm tucked underneath Mayra's torso was pretty much numb. I tightened my fingers into a fist a couple of times to get the tingling sensation to go away but didn't bother letting go of her. I'd take the pins and needles. They weren't all that bad as long as I could stay like this and look at her.

I watched her sleep, completely fascinated by the slight flutter of her eyelids, her slow, rhythmic breathing, and the tiny murmured words I couldn't quite make out. The sun brightened the room, and when her eyes opened, they met mine. She smiled immediately, and I felt my heart begin to pound.

"Hi," Mayra said, and then she giggled and blushed.

I glanced away, feeling my own cheeks heat up. Flashes from the previous night scurried through my head—the feeling of being inside of her, the look on her face during orgasm, and the glory of falling asleep afterwards with her in my bed.

"Hi," I finally repeated. I couldn't bring myself to look back into her eyes again. Even when I tried, I had to look away pretty quickly. Apparently, whatever had happened last night didn't actually fix me.

Maybe it was a lovemaking thing.

Mayra's fingers traced over my jaw and up into my hair. Her touch was light and warm, and it reminded me of other ways she had touched me only a few hours ago. Closing my eyes for a moment, I could almost feel her hand on my chest…my stomach…my…

"What are you thinking?"

"Huh?" I sputtered, brought out of my fantasy. "Um…nothing?"

"Oh, really?" Mayra smirked.

"No." I blushed at the confession.

She shook her head a little and pulled my head against her chest. I felt her lips press into my hair.

"I want you again," I told her.

"Well, maybe you should do something about that."

I felt my face heat up, and my cock began to make its own way toward her thigh. I licked my lips and cringed a bit.

"I need to…um…not yet," I said.

"What's wrong?" she asked.

"I need to brush my teeth."

"Me, too." Mayra laughed again.

We shared the sink, both of us still completely naked and standing in front of the mirror, ready to brush. It was weird, and I didn't like it too much. For some reason, brushing my teeth in front of her made me feel far more naked than just lacking clothing. Thankfully, her toothbrushing made her boobs shake up and down a little, which I could watch stealthily in the mirror.

Back in my room, Mayra pushed me onto the bed and crawled over the top of me. Her hand slid down my side, over my hip, and then she gripped my thigh for a second before wrapping her fingers around my already erect cock.

"Shit," I mumbled. I closed my eyes and pushed the back of my head into the pillow.

Mayra leaned over and covered my mouth with hers, and the sharp taste of mint flowed between us as we kissed. She pulled back long enough to grab another condom from the nightstand, insisting that she wanted to try putting it on herself. It didn't work out very well and ended up kind of twisted at first. Eventually she got it on right and rolled it over me.

Mayra got up on her knees, straddling my hips. I swallowed hard as I realized her intent and then gripped the sheets on the bed as I watched her position me at her entrance before lowering herself. She hissed; I groaned, and we slowly became one again.

At first, Mayra just lay her head on my chest as we both reveled in the feeling of connectedness. I cupped her face in my hands and kissed her slowly, trying to keep my focus on the feeling and taste of her mouth and not the subtle movements of her hips and how those movements encouraged me to move with them until I burst.

She sat up and leaned back, and it felt like electricity flowing through my cock and up my spine. I groaned again, arching my back and thrusting up into her. Mayra began to move with me, sliding up and down over my cock as her breasts bounced in rhythm with the strokes. I reached up and gathered them both in my hands, pulling slightly at the nipples as Mayra moaned.

"That feels incredible," she breathed.

"What about this?" I asked as I dropped my hand down her belly and started massaging her right above where we joined.

"Oh, God! Oh, Matthew!"

I kept my fingers against her clit and moved my hand with her. My other hand went to her hip, giving me a bit of leverage to push up. Mayra's hands were braced against my chest as she leaned over me, and her hair fell over her shoulders to tickle my skin as she moved. She dug her fingers into my skin as she began to pant out my name like a chant. She shuddered, and I followed a moment after.

"Ahhh!" My fingers dug into her hips, and I pulled her down against me, shoving as deep inside of her as I could go. As soon as my grip loosened, Mayra dropped her head to my chest and wrapped her arms around my shoulders.

I couldn't decide if I liked it better on top or bottom, so I thought we should try for the best two out of three.

~oOo~

Whereas normal, daily tasks are difficult to master, undertaking activities considered only problematic for most people is nearly impossible for me. If it hadn't been for Mayra's constant reassurance, I might not have been able to face the transition from high school life to college.

With my eyes squeezed shut, I tried to keep myself grounded. I didn't need to get upset. I didn't need to freak out and panic. I could get through this. Mayra was just in the other room. Everything was all right.

It didn't work.

My hands started shaking until the photo album I had been looking through dropped from my grip with a thud. I tried to lower myself carefully but ended up stumbling a little and knocking a small candy dish off the coffee table before landing on my ass.

"Matthew?"

I couldn't answer her. Even when I felt her arms around my shoulders and felt my face pressed against her skin, my vocal cords just wouldn't work. I kept my eyes closed and tried to focus on breathing slowly, which was made easier by the sweet smell of Mayra's skin and hair.

How long anxiety attacks lasted was always a mystery to me. They seemed to simultaneously last both forever and a fraction of a second. I only knew that when I could focus again on where I was and what I was doing, I was still wrapped up in Mayra on the floor of the living room, and a photo album from my childhood was lying open on the floor.

A picture of my parents holding me as a newborn was on the displayed page.

"I miss them," I said quietly. "It's been so long. Why do I still miss them?"

"It's only been a year," Mayra said. "That isn't very long at all. Besides, you're getting all uprooted right now. It makes sense you are going to be thinking about how things were before. Isn't that what Dr. Harris told you?"

"Yes." I tucked my head back against her and sighed. I listened intently to the slow beat of her heart beneath her chest and the gentle sound of her breaths. "Can we make love yet?"

Mayra snickered.

"You don't get out of it that easily," she said. "I told you a minimum of three boxes packed first. You've been in here for an hour and only have half of one filled."

"I don't like doing this."

"I know, baby."

"Can't we just commute?"

"It's more than a two-hour drive, Matthew," she reminded me. "You know that isn't going to work. We'll be able to visit on the weekends. Maybe we can have Henry, Travis, and Bethany all join us for dinner here once a month or something."

"Which day of the month?"

"Um…how about the second Saturday?" Mayra suggested.

"Every month?" I asked.

"I can't promise every month," Mayra said, "but we'll try."

Mayra had gotten very good at not allowing me to manipulate her words—that's what Dr. Harris called it—to serve the facilitation of my own issues. Sometimes it pissed me off, but most of the time, it reminded me that she was trying to make everything smoother for me. I needed a lot of that this week.

On Sunday, we would move to Columbus to attend Ohio State University.

Not surprisingly, I had been a basket case as the day grew near and had all but refused to pack anything to take with us. After about the tenth time I had managed to convince Mayra to do something else—anything else—she started bribing me with cake. When the cake stopped working, she started bribing me with sex.

Cake had the potential to make me full, but I never seemed to get enough sex.

I pressed my lips against her collarbone and then nuzzled the fish-shape with my nose. That wasn't quite enough, so I brought my hand over to poke it with my index finger, then my middle finger, then my ring finger…

"That's enough!" Mayra giggled. "Pack."

"I can't right now," I said. My arms tensed and my back straightened. I was prepared for her to push me to get more done, and I needed her to, but that didn't make it any easier. What she suggested surprised me.

"How about a quick break?"

"In my room?"

"No," she said, "that never ends up being quick."

"I could try."

"Not falling for it." Mayra twisted a little on the floor to get me to look toward her. "TV for a bit?"

"Okay."

Mayra sat on the couch and I put my head in her lap. I could feel my muscles relaxing as soon as her fingers wound around my hair.

"You need a haircut," Mayra told me.

"That's how all this got started," I said, reminding her.

"Oh really?"

"I think I loved you then," I told her.

"Because I cut your hair just right?"

"Uh huh." I nodded and looked over at the screen to focus on a rerun of *House*, which Mayra just loved. I thought most of it was kind of cheesy. This episode was about a guy who had a whole lot of money, but his son was dying. He convinced himself he couldn't have both money and happiness, so he dissolved his company, gave away the assets, and his son survived.

Cheesy.

It still served its purpose, though, because throughout the episode, I pretty much forgot about packing and moving and going to college. As soon as it was over and the news started, I knew I would have to actually get something accomplished if I didn't want to sleep alone tonight.

The problem was, Mayra's fingers in my hair felt really good, and I didn't want to get up. I closed my eyes and listened to the hum of the newscaster's voice.

"...but authorities aren't sure if he is a viable suspect.

"In Butler County, time is running out for the person who possesses the winning lottery ticket purchased back in February. The six-month timeframe to claim the jackpot expires tomorrow."

"How can you buy a lottery ticket and then never check the numbers?" Mayra asked.

My stomach kind of twisted up, and the recollection of the smell of kitchen trash hit my nose. I had no idea why—the trash can in the kitchen was empty. It seemed more like a memory than a real smell, though.

"I mean, the whole idea of it is the excitement of watching the little balls pop out," she went on. "You have to watch those and watch your ticket and get excited. That's the beauty of the game."

"I never thought about it like that," I said. "The odds against winning are so astronomical, I never really gave it any kind of consideration."

"It's a game like anything else," Mayra explained. "It isn't about winning. It's about the feeling you get when you have that ticket in your hand, and you are wondering if you might have the winning one. Right then, it's still possible. It's thinking about the possibility that is fun."

"I've never bought one," I said. The gnawing feeling came back to me, and a flash of an image of paper in a plastic bag along with a memory-smell of duck sauce invaded my head. "I do have one, though."

Shit, shit, shit. I hadn't meant to say it out loud.

"One what?"

"A lottery ticket."

"You do? Why?"

"Um…when that guy hit my car, he gave me a lottery ticket and told me that we were even," I told her. "He just didn't want to pay for the damage. Travis looked him up, but he moved away without any forwarding address and didn't have any insurance anyway. It wasn't worth trying to track him down."

"When did this happen?"

"Right before we started working on that honey bees project."

"In February?"

"Yes."

"And this guy was from around here?"

"Yes."

"Matthew?" Mayra sat up straighter and moved to one side of the couch, making me have to sit up, too.

"What?"

"What did you do with that ticket?"

"I threw it away," I told her.

"Threw it away?"

"Yes." I nodded, and then my ears heated up as I looked away. I had never told Mayra why I had her dump out the trash with me in the garage and hadn't really thought about it since then anyway.

"What are you so nervous about?" Mayra demanded.

I sighed. I could see in her expression that this wasn't a topic she was going to let drop. I would have better luck trying to convince her we didn't need to pack anything.

"That day...um...that day I called you in the morning and asked you to come over, and we were in the garage...do you remember that?"

"You wanted me to dump the trash all over the place with you," she said dryly. "I almost bailed on you then, you know."

"I'm sorry," I said.

"Go on," Mayra prompted.

"I was looking for that ticket," I told her. "I threw it in the trash, and it was trash day, and I heard people at school talking about how no one had brought in the winning ticket yet."

Mayra's eyes got wide, and her mouth dropped open. For a moment, she just stared at me while I rubbed at my thumbnails over and over again. It occurred to me that I had intentionally not allowed myself to think about the ticket in the kitchen drawer or the implications of having a winning ticket in my possession. There were too many unknowns. Too many possibilities. Too many considerations for my mind to be comfortable with the possibility of such a major, life-altering event.

I would never have considered the lottery ticket game Mayra had described as *fun*.

I couldn't bring myself to think about it, so I started to shut down again.

Mayra sat on the couch looking at me while I fiddled with my hands and pretended nothing was happening. It was the only way I was going to get through this.

"Is it?" she finally whispered.

Of course, she wasn't going to let me just ignore it.

"Is *what* what?" I asked. Maybe if I pretended not to know what she was talking about, I would get off the hook. I wondered if I got the remote off the side table and started flipping channels if I would get lucky enough to find that *True Blood* vampire guy she likes so much. Then she'd stop thinking about it.

No such luck.

"Is it the winning ticket?" Mayra snatched the remote before I could get a good hold of it.

"I don't know," I replied. "I never checked."

"You had me dig through piles of trash for a lottery ticket that you never checked?"

"Um…yeah, I guess so."

"Why didn't you check it?"

"I forgot about it," I admitted. "It's in that little drawer in the kitchen, which is full of stuff I don't know where else to put. It's disorganized and I don't like looking in there, but Mom always kept that kind of stuff in there, so I never straightened it."

Mayra sat up and grabbed my hand.

"Matthew, it could be the winning ticket!"

"The odds are—"

"Fuck the odds!" she yelled as she stood up, startling me. "We have to find out!"

I glanced at the television, remembered the *House* episode, and started thinking about the guy with all the money who was about to lose his son.

"What about the show?" I asked. "What if you can only have a certain amount of good luck?"

"What does that mean?" Mayra asked.

"What if I can't have both?"

"Both of what?" Mayra demanded. I could tell she was getting frustrated, but I didn't really know how to answer.

Still staring at the television, I didn't think the episode seemed cheesy anymore.

"I'm going to find it," Mayra exclaimed, and she started to walk out of the room and up the stairs.

"No, Mayra! Please!" I ran after her and latched on to her arm just as she reached the kitchen.

"Why not?" she asked.

Mayra slowly turned back to face me, and I let go of her arm. My hands went into my hair and tugged a bit. I had no idea how to figure this stuff out in my own head, let alone explain it to her. I decided to start with the basics.

"That drawer is a mess," I told her, knowing as soon as the words were out of my mouth that such tactics weren't going to work. Mayra raised a brow at me and tapped her toe a couple of times. I decided to just come out with it. "Because it might be the winning ticket."

"That's the whole point, Matthew!" Mayra tossed her hands up in the air. "It might be worth over a hundred million dollars. Do you realize that?"

"Yes," I said.

Mayra stood still and just looked at me for a minute, her hands now placed firmly on her hips. My mind wandered to the previous evening when my hands were on those hips as I pulled her against me.

"Matthew…" Mayra's voice dropped down a bit, and she turned her head to look up at me. Her eyes held warnings about getting distracted.

I sighed.

"In the show we were just watching," I said, "you remember how the dad thought if he kept all that money, he would lose his son?"

"Yeah?" Mayra's brow furrowed as she looked at me quizzically.

"I can't take that chance," I told her. "No amount of money in the world would be worth losing you."

"It's just a TV show," Mayra said, pointing out the obvious. "Even in the show, there was no real proof that getting rid of the money was what made his son better."

"But what if it's true?" I asked. "Even if there is any chance—even a chance as small as actually winning the lottery—that I could lose you…"

I shuddered.

"Mayra, it just isn't worth it."

"You aren't going to lose me," Mayra insisted. She took a step toward me and wrapped her arms up around my neck. "Why would you think that?"

"It would change everything," I whispered. "Nothing would be the same—not ever. So many things could happen."

My mind flashed through the possibilities as quickly as my mouth sputtered them out.

"If it's the right one, and I claimed it, people would know. Even if you would do it anonymously, people would still find out. They'd want to ask me about it, or they would bug you or Travis or Beth about it. They would find out where we live, and they might even find Megan. Everyone would think you only put up with me because I was rich, and they'd say you knew about it or something way back in February. People would be asking for money all the time, and I'd want to give it to them. Then it would be all out, and other people would ask. They would need it just as bad as someone else, and it would be too late then. I'd have to figure out who needed it the most, and then I might screw it up, and…and—"

"Shh, Matthew, shh…" Mayra dragged me over to the couch and pulled me down beside her. "Relax, baby—it's okay."

I hadn't realized how panicked I had sounded or that my hands had started to shake again.

"It could change everything," I told her. "It could change me. It could change you. It could change *us*. I can't take that chance, Mayra—I can't. I can't be without you…I can't…I can't…"

"Shh," Mayra said again. She held me against her shoulder, and I tried to keep the rising panic spurred by all the possibilities from consuming me.

For the second time in an hour, I flipped out while Mayra comforted me. It only solidified my opinion that there was nothing worth risking my relationship with her, and I was, by no means, going to find out if that ticket was the winning ticket with the intent of cashing it in before midnight tomorrow.

No way.

Eventually I calmed though I had to admit a lot of it had to do with my own refusal to discuss it anymore. I made Mayra swear she wouldn't go digging for it herself, and then I untangled myself from her arms and placed the old photo album in the cardboard box next to the couch.

I couldn't even consider looking at the ticket, so I went back to packing, feeling like a loser.

Chapter 20—If It's Ignored Long Enough, It's Still There

"Are you really going to let me sit here, knowing that ticket is in the next room and that it might be the winning ticket and that it's going to expire tomorrow? Are you really, really going to do that?"

"Yes."

"You are so stubborn."

It was at least the fifteenth time in the last hour Mayra had brought up the ticket. I really, really wished I hadn't said anything about it, and I was considering sneaking down to the kitchen in the middle of the night to throw the damn thing back in the trash where it belonged.

On the plus side, my avoidance of the ticket and all things related to discussing it had led to getting a lot of packing done. My third box was almost filled, and as soon as it was finished, I was going to make sure I ended up with cake *and* sex. Maybe both at the same time.

I thought about what that would be like, and a smile crept over my face as the images and tastes flashed through my mind.

"Matthew, I've been thinking about the ticket," Mayra said.

Fantasy destroyed.

"No," I said automatically. I shoved a calculator and stapler into the box, figuring those were always needed at school, and wondered where my staple remover might be.

"Listen to me for a minute," she said.

I shook my head vigorously.

"You're avoiding this," she claimed.

"Yep," I answered.

"Matthew—that's not good for you."

I ignored her and continued to take various office supplies out of the desk drawer and put them into the box. A notebook, a pair of scissors, seven different pens, all different colors—one for each day of week—and a three-hole punch joined the stapler and calculator.

"Dr. Harris told you avoiding things that upset you is not the same as coping," she said.

I sighed and crossed my arms over the top of the desk. I dropped my forehead to rest on top of them. I felt Mayra's fingers on top of my head, and I let out another long breath.

"Why don't you want to know if the ticket is the winner?" Mayra asked quietly.

"Because if it is, I have to do something about it," I said. "As long as I don't know, I don't have to make the decision."

"But if you wait, it definitely doesn't win," she told me. "It will expire, and then it doesn't do you any good."

"It wouldn't do me any good anyway," I insisted.

"You don't want the money?"

"No, I don't."

"What bothers you the most—not wanting the money or having to make a decision about it?" Mayra asked.

"The decision." I knew as soon as the words were out of my mouth that they were both true and a mistake.

"You can't avoid decisions," Mayra said. She kept running her fingers through my hair, which was keeping me relatively stable as she talked. "Making choices is important in all aspects of your life, and avoiding the hard ones isn't going to help you in the long run. You can't just wait for things to go away. What if you couldn't decide on what to have for dinner? Eventually, you'd starve."

"I haven't done that in a long time," I told her.

"But you have, haven't you?"

"I haven't starved," I pointed out.

"Went to bed hungry?"

"Yeah."

"If you don't want the money, Matthew..." Mayra paused and let out a long breath. "Well, I guess I'll support that. I won't like it, and I won't pretend to understand it, but I will support it. But refusing to make a decision? I can't let you do that."

Lifting my head, I looked up into her eyes for a brief moment before looking down again. Her expression told me everything. She was right, and she knew it. She wasn't going to let it go. I also knew she was right. Refusing to look at the numbers wasn't about the ticket or the money. I just didn't want to have to decide. There was too much to consider, too much to worry about, too much riding on such a choice. I didn't want to face it.

I couldn't deny the truth in Mayra's words. What if I continued to ignore everything I didn't want to have to face as I went through life? What would that be like for Mayra? If I wanted her to stay with me, and I definitely did, I couldn't just avoid major decisions in our lives. I couldn't put all of that on her and expect her to make decisions for me. It wouldn't be fair, and it wouldn't be a partnership, which was what we were supposed to have.

"Okay," I heard myself whisper.

"Okay?" Mayra repeated, turning the single word into a question.

"I'll look," I said. "I'll look to see if it's the winning ticket."

Both my arms and legs felt cold, numb, and hot all at once. My hands were shaking so badly, I couldn't see the numbers on the slightly duck-sauce stained and stinky piece of paper.

"I found it," Mayra announced. She turned my laptop around and displayed the Ohio lotto website. "Do they match?"

I tried to focus on the trembling paper, but I couldn't really see it. I ended up dropping it on the table next to the computer and trying to read it that way.

The screen showed 8, 19, 28, 29, 32, and 38.

Just like the ticket.

"Oh my God," Mayra muttered.

My hands stopped shaking, and a cold feeling of dread washed over me. In a moment's time, images of my life as a ridiculously rich man flooded through my brain. At first, everything seemed great. I could afford the best health insurance and medication. Megan's care was solidified with private specialists and in-home care. Mayra's and my tuitions were not a problem. Then things in my head began to change. Arguments over what to do with the money, what charitable organizations were the most deserving, and which relatives to avoid this month became the focal point of my imaginary conversations with Mayra.

"I don't want it," I whispered. My gaze moved to her face. Mayra looked like she was suffering from shock, much as I was. "I don't know what to do with it. I can't take that chance, Mayra. I can't."

For several minutes, we both just alternated between staring at the ticket and staring at the computer screen. The weird feeling was still permeating my limbs because I knew this wasn't really over yet. It wouldn't be over until I burned the damn ticket in the fireplace or maybe just flushed it down the toilet.

Of course, it was Mayra who broke out of the trance first with all the answers on the tip of her tongue.

"I know what to do with it," Mayra said suddenly. When I looked up at her face, her eyes were sparkling. "I know exactly what to do."

I gripped the edge of the computer desk with my fingers. My hands were shaking, and I couldn't look Mayra in the eye. I had the feeling she wasn't going to suggest flushing the ticket, and I wasn't sure I could cope with any other options.

"It will be okay," Mayra said softly as she placed her hand over mine. "I'll be there with you every step of the way."

"What are we going to do?" I could barely hear my own voice.

"We're going to give it away."

~oOo~

It was entirely possible I should have made Mayra drive.

Of course, that never would have worked because I wouldn't have been able to get out of the car and move with any sort of stealth, and this was a stealth mission. I turned down the proper street and slowed the car down as we approached a simple brick house near the end of the cul-de-sac.

Two weeks ago, we had quietly and anonymously claimed the prize money. With a little help from the attorney Dr. Harris recommended to me, I got a financial advisor, opened a money market account, and chose the lump sum payment. Even after taxes, the number on my bank statement made me queasy.

Mayra had a stack of one-hundred-dollar bills tucked neatly into a card, which was stuffed into an envelope. There was also a check, written by the attorney I hired so it couldn't be traced back to me, for half of the winnings. On the envelope, there were three simple words: *For the Baby*

"What if they don't believe it's real?" I asked for the hundredth time. "What if they just assume it's fake and throw it away? What if—"

"Stop the 'what-iffing,'" Mayra said. She craned her neck out the car window to look down the street. "I don't see Scott's car. I think we're good."

"I don't want them to know where it came from," I said, knowing I was repeating the same fears over and over. "What if Dr. Harris—"

"Hush," Mayra said. "I know, baby. Don't worry. She said she wouldn't tell, right?"

"I guess so."

"Then we'll be fine."

With my foot planted on the brake, we came to a stop near the driveway of the brick house. Mayra jumped out, ran up to the door, and slipped the envelope into the mail slot. She turned quickly and raced back to the car, threw herself into the passenger seat, and whipped the seatbelt around her.

"Let's go!" she shouted. "Down the street and out of sight!"

We parked at the top of the next street over and waited. Mayra was breathing hard though I knew the brief run hadn't exerted her. I really didn't know how to feel, so I just sat and stared at my hands on the wheel as Mayra got out her iPhone.

"We're all set," she said into the phone. "The envelope is through the mail slot, and Aimee should be getting off work right now. Do you still have the number I gave you? Good!"

I glanced over at Mayra as she turned to face me. Her eyes were bright with excitement and held no concern at all. They served to calm me a bit though I couldn't look her in the face for very long.

"Perfect!" Mayra said. "Thank you so much for agreeing to do this, Dr. Harris. I think you are the only one Matthew would trust to keep this anonymous. Talk to you soon!"

Mayra reached over and grabbed my hand in hers.

"Let's go," she said. "I've got to hear this!"

I shook my head, not at all convinced this part of the plan was a good one, but I got out of the car and followed Mayra between the houses, through a couple of back yards, and to a large clump of lilac bushes just to the side of the driveway of the Schultz's house. We crouched down and out of sight just before Scott's light blue Civic pulled into the driveway.

"I still think it's a bunch of crap," Scott was saying. "I mean seriously, Aimee—who would do such a thing?"

"I don't know," Aimee said as she maneuvered out of the car. "It can't hurt to find out though, right?"

They walked around the corner to the front door, which was out sight but within hearing range. It was only a minute later they were coming back, envelope in hand.

"If it's all fake, what would be the point?" Aimee said as they came back outside. "No one would go through that kind of trouble for a joke."

"It's not funny," Scott grumbled.

"Well, it not like we'll be any worse off if it is fake."

"It's going to cost me in gas money just to get to the bank," Scott stated.

"It's worth a shot…"

The doors to the car shut, and the pending parents backed out of the driveway and continued down the street. Mayra turned toward me and grasped both of my hands. Her eyes still sparkled with excitement, and she squealed slightly as she gripped my fingertips before we both ran back through the yards to my parked car.

My hands were shaking a bit, which made it hard to turn the key. My heart pounded, and I could even see my pulse thumping on the insides of my wrists. I tried a calming breath, but I knew there was nothing panicky about how I was feeling—I was just as excited as Mayra was.

"Let's do the rest!" Mayra beamed at me as she held up a pile of envelopes full of cash.

We stopped at the local animal shelter, the community center, the homeless shelter, and the VA. At each stop, we left the envelopes quickly and quietly before rushing out again. Once we'd hit all the charities in Oxford, we placed envelopes of cash in the mailboxes of all our friends and teachers.

We found ourselves smiling a lot when we glanced at each other on the way back to my house. As soon as I parked the car in the driveway, we both leapt out and ran for the house. I fumbled with my key while my heart pounded, and Mayra shoved past me as soon as the door was opened. She ran straight into the living room and threw herself on the couch, laughing.

"Oh my God, that was awesome!" she cried out.

Caught up in her enthusiasm, I flung myself through the air and landed on top of her. She continued to laugh as I kissed her neck and her shoulder and then quickly moved her shirt up so I could kiss and poke the birthmark next to the strap of her bra. She coiled her hands into the hair on the sides of my head and brought my face to hers for a long, deep kiss.

"I love you," she said.

"I love you *and* your ideas," I told her. "I never would have thought to give half of it to Aimee and Scott for the baby. They were both so worried."

"And now they don't have to be."

"Aimee is almost as lucky to have you in her life as I am," I said, and I leaned back down to kiss her again.

"Feels good to do something like that, doesn't it?" Mayra said with a nod. "And they'll never know where it came from, thanks to Dr. Harris."

"That works for me," I replied with a smile.

I couldn't deny how happy the day of altruism made me feel, so I pulled the feelings close to me, turned them around inside of myself, and gave them back to Mayra a thousand times over.

~oOo~

I was deliriously happy.

Still psyched from sneaking around Aimee's house and running off without getting caught, I finally got to use two of the three condoms tucked into the little drawer of the end table in the living room. When Mayra saw I had them stashed there, it led her to ask where else I had them hidden, which led to a weeklong "Where shall we have sex now?" marathon.

Today, we were in the overstuffed blue chair in the living room—the last piece of furniture in the living room we hadn't christened. Mayra was on top of me with her hands pressed against the arm of the chair above my head, while I had my legs dangling over the opposite arm. It gave me great leverage, and I met every movement as she bounced on top of me.

In the background, I could just barely hear the television. It was tuned to the local news, which was continuing its story about the anonymous donations that had been showing up all over town, speculating about the donor's ties to the lottery ticket winner, and hypothesizing where money was going to show up next.

"Do you know how much I love that?" I asked as I pulled her by her shoulders until her ear was near my mouth. "How it drives me nuts when your tits bounce around?"

Once I figured out how much she liked it when I talked like that, the words just kind of started to flow naturally.

Mayra smiled slyly and leaned back a little, giving me a better view. Moving my hands down to grip her hips, I started increasing the pace as she rode me.

"Oh, fuck! Matthew!"

"You like that, dontcha?" I growled as I pushed against her. She buried her face in my shoulder and moaned. "Dirty…little…ugh!"

She collapsed on me as I collapsed in the chair. I reached my hand around her head and entwined my fingers in her hair, pulling her head back enough to kiss her softly.

That's when the doorbell rang.

"Shit, shit, shit!" I scrambled around in the chair, almost dumping Mayra on the floor in the process. She moved a lot more gracefully, jumping up and off of me and grabbing her jeans in one fluid motion while I struggled with the condom. My sweats were on the floor nearby, and I hauled them up over my hips while Mayra pulled my T-shirt on over her head.

"What am *I* going to wear?"

"You can go shirtless!" she hissed. "It'll take forever to button up mine!"

She rolled my boxers and her shirt up in a ball and then tossed them, along with the condom, back behind the chair, which made me cringe. She quickly tried to straighten her hair with her fingers as she motioned for me to answer the door. I rubbed my hands over my face a couple of times and then walked to the foyer as calmly as I could. I opened the door slowly and peered around the edge. Who I saw there had me so flabbergasted, I couldn't move or talk.

"Aimee!" Mayra said as she came out of the living room. She reached around me and pushed the door back a little wider. My shirt was tied up in a little knot at her side to keep it from falling off of her, and her hair was still a disaster. I fought with the desire to fix it, but it would only bring attention to the fact, and Aimee might not notice otherwise. "What are you doing here?"

Aimee looked back and forth between Mayra and me for a moment and then focused on me.

"I know it was you," she said quietly. "I know you left me the money."

~oOo~

I fixed drinks for the three of us—Coke for Mayra and me and a Sprite for Aimee since she didn't want to drink anything with caffeine in it. Aimee's drink went on the side table next to the chair where, a few minutes ago, Mayra and I had been naked. It was really, really hard not to think about that, but I focused on setting the other two drinks in their usual spots on the coffee table before I sat on the couch. Mayra and Aimee were already talking.

Apparently, using Dr. Harris in order to remain anonymous was a pretty bad idea. As soon as Scott looked up the number and saw where it came from, Aimee remembered a conversation with Mayra about my sister.

"I checked," Aimee said, "and I found a girl with the last name of Rohan at the same hospital. I knew it had to be your sister."

Mayra had her head in her hands, and she kept looking up at me. I knew what she was doing. She was waiting for me to freak out, but I couldn't blame her. I was kind of waiting for it myself.

"You said no one would know," I reminded Mayra. Aimee's words felt like they were crashing down over my head, and I could feel the tension flowing over me from my scalp to my toes. "You said Dr. Harris would keep anyone from knowing."

"I wasn't expecting them to go all NCIS on me," Mayra said. She glanced at Aimee out of the corner of her eye.

"You're the ones who have been giving money away all over town," Aimee said. "Why?"

"I don't want it," I said emphatically. My fingers twisted around each other, untwisted, and then twisted up again. I tapped my index fingertips together and then moved on to the other fingers, tapping each one in turn.

"I knew how worried you were," Mayra said. "With the baby coming and money being so tight, it just made sense to give most of it to you. We donated to the autism center for Megan's—"

"Mayra!" I whispered under my breath. I didn't want to give away any more than we had to.

"She's going to figure it out anyway," Mayra said with a roll of her eyes. "Matthew didn't want to deal with it all, and he didn't want the attention."

"But it would help you and your family, too," Aimee insisted. "I'm sure they have needs as well."

I shook my head.

"It's so much," Aimee said. "We can all share it."

"Not me," I replied. "I don't want it."

"You have to!" Aimee shook her head rapidly. "I can't take this from you, knowing you aren't even saving any for yourself."

"I don't want it!" I yelled. As I pulled my feet up off the floor and brought my knees to my chest, I wrapped my arms around them. Mayra reached over and rested her hand on my shoulder, but I shook it off. This was exactly what I didn't want—I didn't want to have to think about the money ever again, and here we all were talking about it some more. "Just take it and don't say anything else!"

"But, Matthew, your own family—"

"No!" I moaned as I hid my head between my knees and started to shake. Giving it to anyone in my family was the same as keeping it for myself. I would always have to be involved in the decision-making and planning, which is exactly what I did not want.

"Matthew…it's okay," Mayra said. She had moved closer to me on the couch but wasn't trying to touch me.

"I don't understand," Aimee whispered, and I could hear the stress in her voice.

"It just won't work for him, Aimee," Mayra said quietly. "That's why giving it away was the perfect answer. I didn't think you would figure out where it came from, and I knew you would be responsible with it—use it for the baby and school for you and Scott. I knew you would have your dad help you figure it out and not do anything stupid. We're saving some to pay for school, but we won't be spending any of it on us. If we did, people would figure it out. Giving half of it to you means you wouldn't have to put your whole life on hold, and Matthew and I could just move on the way we had already planned."

There was a long silence, which I used to try to keep myself from totally falling apart. None of this was working like it was supposed to, and what I thought was over and done with had suddenly made itself a huge part of my life again in a matter of minutes. I was shaking so badly, I could hardly even hear anything around me anymore.

"Is it really that hard for you?" Aimee asked. When I glanced at her, her eyes were wide and sympathetic.

I could only nod in response.

"All right," she whispered and then spoke a little louder. "We'll keep it."

"You will?" I asked, peering up at her.

"Yes," she replied.

"Please," I begged softly, "I don't want anyone to know where you got it."

"I won't tell anyone," Aimee said.

I let out a long breath.

"But my silence is conditional," Aimee added.

Mayra stiffened and sat up in her seat, and I echoed her posture.

"What condition?" she asked.

"If you are giving this to me, I get to spend it the way I want without any argument from either of you," Aimee said.

My eyes narrowed. There was something about the way she was presenting her conditions that made me feel wary.

"It's for the baby," Mayra reminded her friend.

"Yes, it is," Aimee said. "And as the baby's mother, I get to decide what's good for the baby, right?"

"I suppose so," Mayra said.

"Matthew?" Aimee turned to me, and I quickly looked away from her eyes. "Would you agree I get to choose what is right for my child?"

"Yes," I said. I couldn't argue with that.

"And if I want my child to learn about generosity, I expect the two of you to support that."

"I guess so," I responded. I had no idea where she was going with this, and I was still on edge.

"Good," she said, "because I'm going to make some arrangements. For starters, I'm setting up a scholarship at OSU for a student with autism—in the baby's name, of course. I expect you to apply for it."

I couldn't believe what I was hearing, so I sat there with my mouth wide open.

Did I just win or lose?

Epilogue—The Biggest Win of All

"Yes! Yes! Yes!" Mayra squealed, and I had to smile.

"I take it you got the *A*?" I said with a smile.

"One-hundred-fucking-percent!" Mayra screeched and danced around the apartment we shared just outside of the university grounds.

"Can we go home now?" I asked. As happy as I was for her, I really just wanted to get back home and relax for the holidays, and we still had to pick up Megan along the way.

The first semester of college at Ohio State University had been extremely trying. I was starting to get used to everything, but the students and teachers weren't exactly understanding when it came to me. It actually made me miss high school. If it hadn't been for Mayra and our little sanctuary off campus, I probably wouldn't have made it.

"Yes, we can go," Mayra said. She came over and planted a quick kiss on my lips. "Let's go pick up your sister and get back to Oxford."

The donation for Megan's care hadn't exactly changed her life or anything, but it certain did make a lot of things better. Her medication was the best she could get, and there was, apparently, a stipulation in the donation for my treatment as well. I didn't have any major breakthroughs, but the panic attacks were less severe and a lot less frequent. Megan was also able to have more specialized care, and it allowed us to bring her home for the holidays, provided Mayra was also there.

Megan really liked Mayra.

She was also still mad at me for not buying a ring to replace the watch. She didn't exactly say it, but I could tell.

Maybe someday.

Aimee had turned herself into our fairy godmother though she would deny it most of the time. All sorts of things just seemed to fall into place for us, including anonymous scholarships popping up for Mayra and a major refund for me on my housing costs.

Travis and Bethany were suddenly accepted by an adoption clinic around the same time and had a baby that was due to come home with them in the middle of January. I wasn't sure how Aimee could have arranged for something like that, but it was definitely suspicious. Bethany also had a major windfall drop into her lap, which she used to get a baby's room together. They've already decided to name the baby Kyle when he's born.

I gave up trying to tell Aimee to stop. For one, it didn't work. For another, she always had the perfect justification for how little Maggie would benefit from whatever she'd done with her lotto winnings. Besides, Scott had managed to start his own business—a used sports equipment shop in Hamilton, and it was doing really well for them all.

They were happy.

I didn't know what to think of it all, but I was content with not knowing what to think.

I picked up our suitcases and checked everything in the apartment fifteen times before leaving it. Even though there was a security system in the building, leaving the place for two weeks made me nervous. I kept thinking of all the things that could go wrong while we were gone.

Mayra opened the trunk of my car, and I laid the suitcases side by side.

"Did I turn off the light in the bedroom?"

"You turned off all the lights," Mayra assured me. "Actually, you unplugged the one in the bedroom."

"Well, it turns on when anything touches it," I said. "If something fell on it and it turned on, it might start a fire."

"It's all going to be fine, Matthew," Mayra said with a sigh. She took my hands in hers and tilted her head to look into my eyes. I held the gaze for a moment before looking away. "Stop thinking about it, and think about getting back home."

"Henry said he's expecting you to cook Christmas dinner," I told her. "I don't think there's any food at my house."

"Shopping will be done tomorrow," Mayra said.

"What about Megan?"

"It will be a great opportunity for you and Megan to spend time with Travis and Bethany. They're already planning on coming over after lunch. I'll do the shopping."

I sat in the driver's seat and checked all the gauges and dials before backing out of the parking garage and heading along the route that would take us to the institute. Mayra was still excited about her grade on her final. She picked up the phone to call Aimee as I drove. I didn't really pay much heed to their conversation until Mayra said something that caught my attention.

"Oh, Aimee...he's going to freak...I know, but...all right...no, I'm going to tell him before we get there...yeah, but you don't have to deal with it!"

She glanced at me out of the corner of her eye as she said her goodbyes and hung up.

"Do not freak out," she commanded immediately.

"What did she do?"

"Well, we only have two days until Christmas," Mayra said. "She just wanted to help, you know?"

"What did she do?" I asked again, my tone a little louder.

"She...um...got us a tree."

"A Christmas tree?" My brow furrowed.

335

"It's all decorated and everything," Mayra added. "She called Travis, and he let her in to put it up."

My fingers gripped the steering wheel. The whole idea of a tree being put up in my house when I wasn't there was a little disconcerting, but I knew there had to be more to it than that.

"And?" I pressed Mayra for more information.

"Well, she kind of went with a certain…'theme' in the decorations."

"What 'theme'?" I demanded. I was getting a little tired of the whole game.

"Well…she called it 'time is money.'"

I glanced at Mayra then back to the car in front of me as I contemplated what kind of Christmas tree decorations would go with a theme like that. There was really only one answer.

"She covered it with dollar bills or something, didn't she?" I growled.

It was one thing when Aimee just magically made shit happen, but I didn't like being handed cash. For one, I never knew what to do with it, and making money decisions was just not something I liked to do at all. I liked being short of money and having to budget everything—it was what I knew. I was used to it, and I was comfortable with it.

"Well, yes, partially. Knowing her, it's probably not singles, though."

I shook my head sharply.

"Why does she do that?" I asked with a sigh.

"Because she's grateful and wants to help us." Mayra's fingers touched my thigh. "It's Christmas—don't be angry about it."

"I'm not angry," I said. "I'm…frustrated."

"You are expressing yourself well," Mayra said with a smile. "You've been doing really great with that lately."

"You're trying to change the subject," I said. "I'm not falling for it. What else is on the tree?"

"Um…clocks."

"Clocks?"

"Yes, for Megan."

"She's going to go nuts," I said with a laugh.

"It will probably keep her entertained the whole weekend."

"She won't get bored. That should help her time at home go smoothly."

"You are taking this much better than I thought you would," Mayra said.

"I think I have given up on trying to change Aimee's ways."

"Smart boy."

"Well, I know one thing," I told her. I reached down and wrapped my fingers around her hand. "I have great taste in women."

"That you do," Mayra said with a smile. She leaned close and pressed her lips to my cheek.

I couldn't have asked for more, but I seemed to keep getting it anyway.

We picked up Megan and brought her back to the house. As soon as she saw the tree Aimee had provided, she sat in front of it, stared open-mouthed, and counted the clocks on the branches.

She couldn't have been happier.

"I've got the shopping list done," Mayra said.

I glanced over at her and swallowed. I'd never hosted a family gathering before, and I wasn't sure I could cope with so many people being in the house. The last time a family dinner was held here, Mom and Dad were still around.

"You sure you want to do this?" Mayra asked as she tilted her head to look at me.

"No," I said. I shrugged and scrunched up my face at the thought of what all of this meant.

Though there was that logical part of me that knew it was perfectly normal to host a dinner party, it didn't stop my hands from shaking at the thought.

"I'm pretty sure I don't want to," I told her, "but someone a few years back taught me that even though change is really hard, I can't go through life just avoiding difficult situations."

"You don't have to like it," Mayra reminded me. "Lots of people don't like making adjustments. You accept change now, though, which is a big change in and of itself."

"I guess so," I said with a shrug.

Mayra rested her hands on my shoulders and turned me toward her.

"Don't you sell yourself short now, Matthew Rohan," she said. "You have made so much progress in the past year, it's amazing. You don't only accept change, but you make decisions without debating and worrying about them for weeks beforehand. I don't think we'd be standing here even having this conversation if it were last summer. You haven't freaked out during any of this, not even when Dad said he was bringing Officer Gregory with him."

I met her eyes for a moment before looking over her shoulder and out the window again. Mayra dropped her hands to her sides and turned to look through the glass with me.

"There were times when decisions were almost impossible to make," I agreed. "It's still hard, but I know this is the right thing to do. I think I've probably made the wrong choices in the past just because I refused to make a decision one way or the other."

"You could be a millionaire," Mayra teased.

I shrugged again and turned away from the window. In my mind, I was at birthday parties when I was a child—both for me and for Megan, though she would never open her gifts. I remembered the first time Travis brought Bethany into the room and how much Megan had hated her. There were also thoughts of a darker sort, though—like when the unit's commanding officer came to the door with the chaplain to tell us that Dad wouldn't be coming home.

I walked across the living room and remembered all the times Mayra and I had spent there. I recalled our project on honey bees that just might have been responsible for bringing us together. I remembered sitting on the couch and drinking Cokes with four ice cubes in each glass. Most distinctly, I remembered waking up on the couch and having her beside me, wrapped up in my arms and making me feel safe and loved.

"Yeah, but I wouldn't be happier," I said. "That's not a decision I regret."

"What do you regret?"

"Well, going back a ways, there are a lot of things," I told her. "I wish I would have kissed you the first time you brought me cake. I wanted to."

Mayra laughed.

"Is that all?"

"Not quite," I said. "I wanted to kiss you at least a dozen times before it ever really happened."

"Well, if it makes you feel any better, I wish I had kissed you sooner, too."

I gave her a crooked smile, which she claimed went straight into her panties, and considered making love to her right there on the floor. She was still looking out the window, and I probably could have surprised her from behind, but there was something else—something more important—that I had to do.

"There is something else I wish I had done sooner."

"What's that?"

"Well," I said quietly, "there's only one thing that could make me any happier than I am now."

"Oh really?" Mayra said. "What's that?"

With shaking hands, I reached down into my coat pocket.

"Mayra Trevino," I said softly. I bit down on my lip. I'd practiced this speech one hundred and forty-seven times, and I was sure I was still going to screw it up.

Mayra turned from the window as I walked closer to her and slowly lowered myself onto one knee. I heard her gasp and saw her hands clench and twist together. My body and mind tensed, and I knew how much parts of me wanted to panic over this. I also knew this was the only way to move forward with our lives—for real and for good.

"I know living with me is hard," I said quietly. "I need everything done in certain ways, and I can lose my control over the smallest of things, but you're still patient with me. You still stay beside me even though I know there are times when it's hard on you. I'll never find someone more loving and kind and wonderful than you are, and I'll never love anyone like I love you. Will you…"

My voice cracked and failed me. I had to pause and squeeze my eyes shut, swallow hard, and force my hands to hold up the small, black box with the simple half karat diamond solitaire in it.

"Will you marry me?"

I moved my eyes slowly from the satin box in my hand up to her face. I focused on the bridge of her nose and tried to keep myself from looking away. She made it a little easier by staring at the box in my hand instead of at me. Her eyes were bright and glistened with unshed tears.

I watched her mouth open and close a couple of times, and her hesitation was almost long enough to make me get up and run from the room, but I wouldn't do that. I wouldn't back down from this, and I wouldn't second-guess or hesitate.

This was a decision I wanted to make.

It was the most important decision of my life.

"Yes," she said softly and simply.

"Oh, good." I breathed in relief.

I stood up, and Mayra threw her arms around my neck, openly crying against my shoulder. My arms wrapped around her middle, and I held her tightly against my chest.

"That's better."

Mayra and I both turned at the sound of Megan's voice. She wasn't quite looking at us, but her head was turned in the right direction.

"Much better than a watch."

I laughed, Mayra grinned, and Megan went back to counting the clocks on the tree.

"I love you," I whispered in Mayra's ear. "I will always love you."

"I love you, too, Matthew."

Like my dad always said—you win at some things in life, and you lose at others. Before Mayra, I'd been satisfied just trying to keep a balance. Now I felt like there was no way I could lose as long as she was with me.

Had I lost anything of value when I gave away almost all of that money? No, not really. I had Mayra. I had love and peace. As far as I was concerned, I had won.

~*The End*~

WIN SOME, LOSE SOME

Author's Notes

Hey there! Thanks so much for joining me on this journey of young love and acceptance. I hope you have enjoyed it! So many of my friends have been touched by children on the autism spectrum, and I hope the character of Matthew has done the disorder some justice.

If you want to understand more about autism, I highly recommend a book called *The Reason I Jump* by Naoki Higashida. The book is non-fiction and written by a teenager with autism. I found it quite enlightening!

Until next time!

Much love,

Shay Savage

More Books by Shay Savage

Surviving the Storm Series:

Surviving Raine

Bastian's Storm

Evan Arden Series:

Otherwise Alone

Otherwise Occupied

Uncockblockable (a Nick Wolfe story)

Otherwise Unharmed

Isolated

Irrevocable

Unexpected Circumstances Series

The Handmaid

The Seduction

The Consummation

The Shortcoming

The Concubine

The Apprehension

The Devastation

Stand Alone Novels:

Transcendence

Offside

Worth

Alarm

Novella Collection:

Savaged

Caged Trilogy:

Caged: Takedown Teague

Trapped

Released

About the Author

Shay Savage is an independent author from Cincinnati, Ohio, where she lives with her family and a variety of household pets. She is an accomplished public speaker and holds the rank of Distinguished Toastmaster from Toastmasters International. Her hobbies include off-roading in her big, yellow Jeep, science fiction in all forms, and soccer. Savage holds a degree in psychology, and she brings a lot of that knowledge into the characters within her stories.

From the author: "It's my job to make you FEEL. That doesn't always mean you'll feel good, but I want my readers to be connected enough to my characters to care."

Savage's books many books span a wide variety of topics and sub-genres with deeply flawed characters. From cavemen to addicts to hitmen, you'll find yourself falling for these seemingly irredeemable characters!

Made in the USA
Middletown, DE
21 October 2016